Pr

"A classic story fueled by hip-hop sensibilities about strivers . . . about what it takes to make it, and that some prices are too high no matter how many ducats are dangled."

—Gary Phillips, author of *bangers*

"And the Sun Gods sent down a powerful ray of light toward earth and named her Black Artemis. The streets, yearning for a serving of realness and truth, in a language that speaks to all of us, celebrate the arrival of *Explicit Content*, eating up the pages as if it were the Last Supper."

—Toni Blackman, hip-hop artist, and author of *Inner-Course*

EXPLICIT CONTENT

BLACK ARTEMIS

NEW AMERICAN LIBRARY

New American Library
Published by New American Library, a division of
Penguin Group (USA) Inc., 375 Hudson Street, New York, New York 10014, U.S.A.
Penguin Books Ltd, 80 Strand, London WC2R 0RL, England
Penguin Books Australia Ltd, 250 Camberwell Road,
Camberwell, Victoria 3124, Australia
Penguin Books Canada Ltd, 10 Alcorn Avenue,
Toronto, Ontario, Canada M4V 3B2
Penguin Books (NZ), cnr Airborne and Rosedale Roads,
Albany, Auckland 1310, New Zealand

Penguin Books Ltd, Registered Offices:
80 Strand, London WC2R 0RL, England

First published by New American Library,
a division of Penguin Group (USA) Inc.

First Printing, August 2004
10 9 8 7 6 5 4 3 2 1

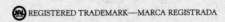 REGISTERED TRADEMARK—MARCA REGISTRADA

LIBRARY OF CONGRESS CATALOGING-IN-PUBLICATION DATA:

Black, Artemis.
Explicit content / Black Artemis.
p. cm.
ISBN 0-451-21275-4 (trade pbk.)
1. Puerto Rican women—Fiction.   2. African American women—Fiction.   3. Female friendship—
Fiction.   4. New York (N.Y.)—Fiction.   5. Women singers—Fiction.   6. Young women—
Fiction.   7. Music trade—Fiction.   8. Hip-hop—Fiction   I. Title.
PS3602.L24E97   2004
813'.6—dc22   2004005815

Set in Horley OS
Designed by Ginger Legato

Printed in the United States of America

PUBLISHER'S NOTE
This is a work of fiction. Names, characters, places, and incidents either are the product of the
author's imagination or are used fictitiously, and any resemblance to actual persons, living or
dead, business establishments, events, or locales is entirely coincidental.

BOOKS ARE AVAILABLE AT QUANTITY DISCOUNTS WHEN USED TO PROMOTE PRODUCTS OR SERV-
ICES. FOR INFORMATION PLEASE WRITE TO PREMIUM MARKETING DIVISION, PENGUIN GROUP
(USA) INC., 375 HUDSON STREET, NEW YORK, NEW YORK 10014.

For all the women who continue to love hip-hop even when hip-hop fails to love them in return.

ACKNOWLEDGMENTS

It's such a daunting task to remember and acknowledge all those who made this book possible but my deep appreciation won't allow me to not try.

My family José, Providencia, Beatríz, and Anthony who love and support me no matter what I do.

My cousins Carmen M. Sinclair for everything she did throughout the years, small and large, to enable me to become a writer and Pafnushus whose endless knowledge of hip hop kept me on point.

Chica Luna Productions and Chica Sol Films who gave me a holistic space to learn, grow and heal. I especially want to thank Elisha María Miranda who always gave me what I needed to persevere even when I didn't know for what to ask and Alexander Ramirerz who supported silently yet immensely.

Johanna Castillo who gambled high, worked hard and dreamed big. Your neverending confidence and tireless advocacy took this to a level much higher than I ever imagined.

Boricua Lumpen, E-Fierce, Jaymes Jam, Myteeafrodytee, and R-Cool, the illest readers a sista could have.

Frederick Douglass Creative Arts Center where after a long search I finally found a creative home.

The myriad of social justice organizations and their dedicated staffs and volunteers whose daily work in the community afford me the ability to make art that matters.

The team at Penguin who worked so diliently to make this novel the best it could be especially Kara Cesare, Rose Hilliard, and Anthony Ramondo.

Kim Violet Davis, David Sheingold, and Julie Barer—the degrees of connection that made all this happen.

For all of the hip hop revolutionaries—past and present—working to prove that another world is possible from the artists provided the vision to the organizers making it a reality. And most of all the everyday gods and goddesses in the hip hop nation whose support and inspiration make this all possible. I remain hopeful and active because you exist.

CHAPTER 1

CUANDO LAS GALLINAS MEAN

Bitches diss the way I dress
'Cause the lyrics I kick be causin' stress.
Kiss the ring of a true goddess
'Cause Fatal's the hottest
And I don't front modest.

"Almost but not quite." I made a correction, then handed Leila's notebook back to her. "Try it again, but don't clip your words. Just let it flow like one long phrase."

Leila sucked her teeth like she'd trademarked the expression. "How many times you gonna have me do this, Cassie? This is like the fifth time and shit."

"Just do it."

She kicked the verse again, and while it sounded better, it was still a bit off. But before I could ask her to do it again, she snapped at me. "It ain't my flow: it's the rhyme, which is your specialty. Like you always be reminding me."

Leila was right about the rhyme, but she never understood how hard it was for me to write for her. I've never been into the Queen Bee shtick, rhyming about whose name is on my ass, how I get down, or any of that. Sistas claim they want the dudes in the game to respect them, only to rap about the same bullshit guys do or say whatever they think guys wanna hear. But that's how Leila rolled as Fatal Beauty, and like it or not, heads be feelin' it. Plus, I guess it was no easier for her to coach me on my flow with my *SAT vocabulary* as she calls it.

If you got it, flaunt it, they be telling us, but truth is, it depends on what *it* is. *It* only pertains to tits and ass. Which I got. But so does every other female. What I got that every female has but doesn't flaunt is a brain. They don't really want a sister flossin' that, but that never stopped me. Might as well stop breathing.

Not that Leila never tried to step up her lyrical game. Once Leila bought a thesaurus and a rhyming dictionary and sat in the kitchen trying to compose something. Looking for an alternative for the word *skills*, she fell in love with the word *sleight*. Plenty of good words that rhyme with *sleight*, but Leila obsessed over leaving no doubt what she meant. Pointing at the definition in the dictionary, she explained, "It's gotta be clear that I mean 'skill or dexterity' and not 'cunning or craft used in deceiving.' " Then she flipped ahead to a dog-eared page where she'd highlighted the word *slight*. "Or worse, that I mean 'having little weight, strength, substance, or significance' and shit. Can't have that."

Leila started at four in the afternoon and was still scribbling in her notebook when I went to bed at midnight. I woke up at eight the next morning to get ready for work to find her sleeping on the couch and the notebook on the floor. I picked it up and found that after pages of failed attempts to use *sleight* to her satisfaction, Leila had written a three-page rhyme blasting our high-school English teacher Mr. Burke, who spent more time trying to fuck her than teach her.

So now the occasional rhyme written by Leila has a catchy tempo and simple words like a nursery rhyme, but that's what the crowds love the most. Although I penned the bulk of our rhymes, Leila recently cultivated the knack of writing hooks. When we ripped our last performance for Da Corridor—an underground showcase for aspiring MCs that changed venue each month like the legendary Lyricist Lounge—at its Valentine's Day Special at SOB's, the audience quickly picked up Leila's refrain and rapped along. Leila has always been the ticket onstage, grabbing the audience's attention with her low-cut halters and stiletto heels and keeping it with those contagious chants. It was all good, because after the show while young girls were rushing Leila for her autograph and asking where she bought her gear, I was the one the other MCs stepped to saying, "Yo, your rhyme got me mad open" or "You got a tape I can cop?" She caught their interest onstage, I kept them thinking after the show, so I didn't hate on Fatal 'cause it was our differences that made us such a tight duo. But that's exactly why I didn't appreciate her coming at me like she did.

"Fine," I said. I lifted myself off the sage Natuzzi sofa. "You don't want to work anymore, just say so. Don't be bitin' my head off."

"Whatever." Leila flicked her hand at me, flashing her latest silk wrap with a Puerto Rican flag painted on each nail and the middle finger of each hand topped with a genuine half-karat diamond as the star. The manicurist had flipped when she busted out with real gems and said, "I don't wear fake shit." Sitting next to her getting my French manicure touched up, I reminded Leila of the dye jobs, hair extensions, padded bras, and the wrap itself. She wagged an undone finger at me and said, "¡Callate! How you gonna put shout me out when I'm treating you? ¡Maldita morena!"

That was two weeks ago and the last time we laughed together. That night we performed at SOB's and brought the house down, but she had been ornery ever since, and I was sick of it. Leila's always been moody, but she should have been fiending to iron out this rhyme so we could schedule a session with Darnell, record the track, and get out the album instead of hating on my writing.

"Don't *whatever* me." I grabbed my own notebook and took off to my room. "You need to quit snappin' at me. . . ."

"I don't need to do nothin'," Leila called after me. "You need to remember who pays the rent on this muthafucka."

I walked into my room, whirled around to yell, "You mean your pimp?" and slammed the door as hard as I could.

At the moment, I·didn't think anything of it. Leila and me, we might as well be sisters. We love and fight each other equally hard. She's my living diary and I'm hers, and we say shit to each other that if some other heifer said would get her tenderized. In fact, Fatal and I became tight because we fought.

Back at Raphael Hernandez Middle School in the Hunts Point section of the South Bronx, Leila rolled like the villain in an old Western. The badass whose name rippled spines. Then you'd see this tiny Puerto Rican girl dressed in royal blue leather from head to toe, parting the crowd in the hallway between classes. You'd wonder, "*This* is the infamous Leila Aponte?" as she was all of four-eleven, maybe a good eighty-five pounds if she got caught in a thunderstorm. But that stone-cold look with those icy eyes would freeze you in place.

Leila seemed even smaller when flanked by her crew. She ran with three of the biggest-boned Black girls you did not want to fuck with. Tasha the LL Cool J fanatic with buttons of him all over her knapsack, Mean Monique (because there was another sweet Monique in our class who looked just like Aaliyah, may she rest in peace), and Vaseline whose real name I can't remember. We called her Vaseline because her face was always greased up, ready and looking for a fight she usually found.

Leila had sent Vaseline to pick the fight with me. She admitted that only a few years ago, when we heard that some woman stabbed Vaseline at a street festival in broad daylight. Now Leila claimed to forget why she'd sicced Vaseline on me, but I remember like it was yesterday: this kid she liked named Craig.

Craig sat next to me in math class, and all I did was lend the scrub a pencil. You ask to borrow a pencil, most people give you the most busted one they find at the bottom of their bag. All chewed up, eraser so flat that if you make a mistake you might as well crumple it up and start over on fresh looseleaf because using the eraser is just going to jack up your page anyway. But my mother, Genevieve, always said, "Cassandra, if you're going to do someone a good deed, then do the deed good." So I handed Craig a new, freshly sharpened pencil and told him he could keep it. Next thing you know, Leila got it in her head that I was after her man, even though everyone knew Craig was messing with some chick at I.S. 98.

So Vaseline stepped to me in the locker room, claiming I'd made some wisecrack about the way she ran the bases in gym class. Leila entered followed by Mean Monique and Tasha, and I immediately knew what time it was. I won't front seven years later like I wasn't scared. Vaseline and Leila were notorious for catching whomever they wanted no matter how long it took, and the longer it took, the worse it would be. I figured it would cost me less time and pain to face the inevitable than to run around scared trying to avoid it.

So when Vaseline accused me, I found it in me somewhere to push past her, step to Leila, and say, "Leila tell you that lie?" Until this day Leila insists that I did not know she was behind the whole confrontation, that I singled her out because I assumed that because she was little I could take her. I tell her I chose her because she was the ringleader and therefore the toughest and not just to make her feel good. It was true.

Vaseline tried to rush me from behind, but Leila signaled her as if to say *I got this*. She got into my face—or more like my chest, because when I was thirteen I was already about five-six and a 36C—and said, "What if I did say something?"

I looked down and said, "Then you need to stop starting trouble with bitches you don't know and concentrate on getting your sixteen-year-old ass out the seventh grade."

I never thought Leila would hit me first, but I should have known better. Most girls would talk mad shit and even get in your face but would never throw the first punch. Leila was not one of those sisters, and she rang my head with a solid cross to my jaw.

So it was on with Leila and me rolling around on the floor, scratching, pulling, and cursing, you name it. Although she caught me by surprise, I quickly got the upper hand. Her girls tried to jump in, but Leila started cussing and swinging at them as if they were *my* crew. "Mind your fuckin' business!" she yelled. "I can kick her ass by my damn self." Then she flung herself at me like a wrestler off the ropes. Her screaming got the attention of the gym teacher, who ran in, busted it up, and sent us to the principal's office.

Once there, Miss Olivera took one look at Leila and said, "I don't want to hear a word from you." Since I had never gotten into a fight before, she gave me detention for the rest of the week. But without asking a single question, the bitch assumed Leila had started the fight and suspended her for two weeks. I guess when you get a reputation for looking for trouble, sometimes trouble saves you the time and energy and comes looking for you. But how the hell was Miss Olivera so sure that I hadn't started the fight just to prove I wasn't the Moesha everyone made me out to be? Leila was pissed and even then I couldn't blame her. I spent my detention filing in Ms. Olivera's office. The real punishment though was hearing her boring lectures about how smart I was, how much potential I had, why I didn't need or want to turn out like Leila Aponte, who was going to wind up dead or in jail before she turned twenty-one.

While filing, I peeped at Leila's records and found out that she had a mad high IQ but some learning disability, too, that was likely caused by her mother's druggin' while she was pregnant. She lived in the projects with a foster family, the fourth in the last two years, after her mother died of a heroine overdose. I started wondering why no one was looking out for her. When a guy's getting into trouble, they usually run tests, expecting—maybe even hoping—to find an excuse to stick him in special ed. But if they realize he's restless 'cause he's mad smart, if he's lucky, they stick a ball or an instrument in his hand. I mean I was busting out nineties and higher in all my classes, but the only time I got any recognition was the once in a blue moon when I fucked up. Then it was, "Cassandra, you're too smart for this foolishness."

So on the last day of my detention, I headed over to the Adams Houses, where Leila lived. You know that saying about running toward what you fear? Once I overheard Genevieve joke to my aunt Treece that she often wondered when I was a toddler if she should kill me for my own good like a plantation mother. She said I despised being afraid, so too often I failed to heed my fear even when it was for my own damn good. Not that I shoved my fingers in an open flame or followed strangers. But instead of steering clear of the fire or the stranger altogether, I was the kinda child that climbed the stove and twisted all its knobs trying to turn off the flame or got in the stranger's face to shout him out about his nasty self. And even though she seemed the complete opposite of me in every way, I recognized a similar fearlessness in Leila. And after I peeped at her records, I stopped hating being afraid of her and started wanting to earn her respect, if nothing else.

When I got to Leila's building in the projects, she was standing out front with some guy who was screaming on her—too young to be her father, too old to be her boyfriend. When she spotted me, Leila shoved the guy aside and walked toward me. "You come here looking for another ass kicking?"

I expected her to say something like that if I found her, so I was ready. "I came all the way over here to thank you and you throw me shade?"

That took her off guard like I'd hoped it would. "Thank me? For what?"

"For fighting fair. Not letting Mean Monique and them jump me. You got heart. For a Puerto Rican girl."

Leila looked so bugged I was convinced she was gonna start swinging. Not up to another fight, I backed up and bounced. Dude took that as his cue to resume screaming.

"Yo, Leila, get your ass back here!"

"Shut the fuck up already, Jay. I promised my friend I'd help her study for her test tomorrow. You should try it some time, ignorant ass. . . ."

"When you gonna be back?" Jay Dude yelled.

"*¡Cuando las gallinas mean!*"

We must have walked a whole block in silence when I got over the shock that I was walking arm in arm with Leila Aponte. And I was leading the way, too. I was sure the moment we turned the corner, she would yank her arm away, shove me, and warn me to stay the hell away from her if I knew what was good for me, but she didn't. Although she was strolling down Tinton Avenue, I know her mind was back where I found her with whatever situation had her eating from Jay what she would never take from anyone at school. I finally asked her, "What's that you said?"

"I didn't say anything."

"I mean, he asked you when you'd be back and you answered in Spanish."

"Oh. I said I'd be back when chickens piss."

"Don't they?"

She laughed. "No, *estupida*. Don't you know that?"

I never like being called names, not even in fun. Especially stupid, since I knew that was the last thing I was. But Leila had the coolest laugh. She giggled like a little girl, teasing me like a friend and not like an older girl bullying me. So I laughed, too. "Why should I know some shit like that?"

" 'Cause you supposed be Ms. Honor Roll and shit."

"Yo, teach me how to say that."

Leila snickered. "I ain't no teacher. Ask Mr. Fuckin' Diaz."

"Mr. Diaz's not gonna teach us anything cool like that. He

teaches that bougie Spanish that y'all Hispanics don't even speak."

"Word. He be teaching Thpanish."

"C'mon, Leila, teach me that line so I can tell the ol' Dominican guy on my block who keeps asking me when I'm gonna go out with him."

That's when Leila really cracked up. She walked me all the way home to my tenement building on Longfellow Avenue and said she would see me in school. I hoped she would at least nod in my direction at lunchtime but actually expected her to ice me in front of her girls.

During math class the next day, Craig poked me in the side with the pencil I had given him. When I looked over to cuss him out, he pointed toward the door. Leila had her face pressed against the window of the classroom door, waving me to come into the hallway. I got a bathroom pass.

"What are you doing here? I thought you were on suspension?"

Leila smirked and rolled her eyes. "Flaco let me in."

"Flaco?"

"I mean Anthony." I still must have looked confused because she added, "The security guard. Yo, what you doing Saturday?"

"Nothing. Why?"

"I want you to go with me to a hip-hop concert."

I got mad hyped. My notebooks held more rhymes than schoolwork, but I had never showed them to anyone let alone gone to see a show. But in a flash my excitement quickly turned to disappointment. Genevieve would never give me the money or permission to go, never hesitating to point out every news article about a kid getting hurt or killed at a hip-hop concert. It was just my luck that they often turned out to be honor students bound for college.

"I can't go," I told Leila. "Even if I had the money, my moms won't let me."

Leila said, "That's the thing, Cassie. The concert's free."

"Free?" No one at school ever called me Cassie, and only a week before this girl had tried to kick my ass in the locker room.

"Yeah, and your moms don't have to know 'cause the concert's right over there at Crotona Park at three o'clock."

"For real?" The excitement returned like a flood. "I thought you meant at night downtown somewhere."

"It's gonna be da bomb, Cassie. All the ol' school heads from the Bronx are supposed to be there." Leila's eyes sparkled as she counted names off her inch-long nails. "Afrika Bambaataa, Kool Herc . . ." She didn't know or care if I recognized let alone appreciated those cats. Leila was on a mission and intent on getting me to join her. Not that she had to try that hard. The few girlfriends I had liked hip-hop, but the depth of their interest stopped at mourning B.I.G. and swooning over Mase. They changed the subject when I mentioned anyone before Bad Boy, let alone any founding fathers of the music they claimed to love so much. The only thing that amped me more than the chance to see these hip-hop legends was the discovery that I had found someone who shared my passion for hip-hop. Although I never cut school, even on a snow day, had Leila asked me to roll with her right then and there, I would have said "Later" for Ms. Olivera and her warnings and bounced.

So that Saturday at two thirty I told Genevieve I was headed to the library to do research for a school project, and I met Leila at the token booth of the Simpson Street subway station. We decided to walk, and I quickly learned that Leila and I had different tastes in hip-hop when we got into a big debate over whether Lil' Kim helped or hurt other female rappers. Still, Leila's knowledge and passion for hip-hop matched mine and I *liked* fighting with her about it.

The concert took place on the handball courts before two hundred heads of all kinds, from toddlers in diapers to seniors on canes. I rarely saw white folks in this 'hood, but that day quite a few represented, and no one gave them any beef. Afrika Bambaataa rolled solo, but the crowd convinced him to perform "Planet Rock." He left immediately after that, but that alone made the walk there worth it. It only got better when Herc mixed and scratched for an hour-long medley that included old-school cuts from "Rapper's Delight" to "The Message."

The highlight for me came when I learned about a group called the Cold Crush Brothers, but Leila knew all about them. As they rocked this song called "It's Us," Leila taught me everything about them. How they were from Sedgwick Avenue. That they never recorded a studio album. How the leader Grandmaster Caz was the same lyricist who wrote the funny Superman dis on "Rapper's Delight" and probably was the first MC to tell stories in his rhymes instead of just flossing about what he had. She promised to get me a classic rap mix tape from that dude Jay who was teaching her about the early hip-hop. "That's the only reason why I bother with his ass," she said.

During the concert, not a soul lit a blunt or brought a forty. No gray heads complained about noise, and no new jacks called the music soft. The positive vibe was so powerful, I found myself patting my chest and crying. Overcome with euphoria so painful, I forgot that Leila was with me until I felt a tug at my sleeve. I rushed to wipe my face and turned to look at her only to see that she was crying, too.

Leila grazed away a tear with a single nail and forced a smile. "What you crying for, silly?" she asked.

It took me a few seconds to understand why myself, and it never crossed my mind to play tough and front like I caught something in the eye. "This is the way it's supposed to be," I said.

"Damn, Cassie, you such an old soul and shit," said Leila, "but I feel you."

"Is that why you're crying?"

"Nah." And she tried to leave it at that.

But I wouldn't let her. "So . . ."

"Nothing. It's just that I wish there was somebody up there, you know . . . who kinda looked like me." And I didn't have to ask what she meant. Before I could say anything at all, Leila said. "Don't tell nobody or I'ma have to kick your ass again."

I felt for Leila. Her peeps had been part of hip-hop from day one but had less to show for it than mine, especially the females. Not that I was all that crazy about where my folks were taking it. So I just shoved her and said, "Whatever."

After the concert, we moved to the playground. We must have looked silly on the seesaw, a skinny sixteen-year-old with her tiny feet dangling in the air on one end and a thick thirteen-year-old squatting like a cricket on the rubber mat at the other. But we were too busy taking turns throwing old-school verses at each other to care. Then I spit out one of my own.

"Yo, that's dope, Cassie," Leila said. And she tossed out one of *her* rhymes. I pretended to fall off the seesaw from lyrical devastation, and poor Leila came crashing to the mat. Then we both got up, laughing, and moved to the swings.

I got home after eight o'clock and found Genevieve fuming next to my cold dinner on the stove. I admitted to her where I was and with whom, and she grounded me for a week. Leila had her own drama on account of me, too, although with her crew. The first day after Leila's suspension she called me over to her table during lunch. She handed me the mix tape she promised me, and just as I was about to walk back to my table, Leila invited me to sit with them. Vaseline asked her why the hell she inviting me to stay, and Leila told her she could have lunch with whoever the fuck she felt like. Vaseline said this, Leila said that, and the next thing I knew, Vaseline was wearing Leila's leftovers. On the verge of getting expelled herself, Vaseline held back then but waited for Leila after school. Leila must have made a telephone call that kicked off a phone tree, because at three o'clock a posse of older project girls stood in front of the school. I went to the front of the pack to have Leila's back, but Tasha and Mean Monique left Vaseline hanging by cutting out a period early. We stared Vaseline down as she hurried down the block and onto her bus, and as much as I disliked her, I was happy that we didn't chase her.

Ever since, Leila and I had been two sides of the same coin. I drifted from my in-school friends whom I never saw otherwise because their moms were as strict as Genevieve, and Leila obviously dropped Tasha and them and her project crew quickly aged out of the foster-care system.

And no matter how bad our occasional fights were, I never dreamed that some Irv Gotti wanna-be would have us going at each other like Foxy Brown and Lil' Kim.

CHAPTER 2

LEILA TURNS

When I graduated from high school, Leila hounded me to move in with her. She had dropped out two years earlier and had a phat two-bedroom apartment on Riverside Drive overlooking the Hudson River. Rent paid by the married and whipped Diego, rooms furnished by the funny but undependable Junior, art and fixtures selected by the sophisticated yet arrogant Vance.

I liked Junior for Leila if he weren't such a flake. She said I favor him because he's Black like me, but that wasn't true at all. Junior treated her well. That is, whenever he rolled through. As far as I'm concerned, Diego and Vance are two sides of the same coin with their uppity selves. Whatever points I might have given Vance over Diego for being single and reliable, he lost when he proved to be one of those liberals who runs from their white guilt by surrounding themselves with so-called minorities. Like Genevieve always says, "Never trust anyone who can't stand to be around his own kind."

Diego's not only married to some Spanish woman with money

in her own right—and when I say Spanish I do mean from Mr. Burke's beloved Spain—he was a Vance wanna-be. That automatically put him on the bottom of my list, and just my luck, he would be Leila's favorite. Must have been the cultural connection or something. Leila met Diego at Chanel in Saks. She was pining over a watch when he confused her for a sales associate—or so he claimed—and asked her to help choose one as a birthday present for his wife. Instead of getting offended, Leila used the opportunity to convince him to buy one for her.

With Leila's pair-and-a-spare approach to dating though, I never took Diego or any of her boyfriends seriously. Still, knowing I would feel like a voyeur with Leila's boyfriends coming in and out at all times, I resisted the temptation to move in with her.

But after a mind-numbing semester of accounting at Baruch College, I told Genevieve I was quitting to focus on my music. It didn't matter that I intended to get a full-time job, pay rent, and help with the bills. According to Genevieve, if I was not going to college, I was not going to live under her roof. As committed as I was to my music, I bounced on principle really. After being the model daughter for eighteen years, I felt that I had more than earned my mother's respect, trust, and support. Leila took me in, and I never thought about finding my own place.

Especially when Leila did everything to make me feel like the place was mine, too. She even tried to make Diego return his key. Since his name was on the lease and he paid the rent, Diego insisted on crashing in Manhattan whenever he wanted to stay close to his Wall Street office or avoid his Chappaqua wife. But Leila told him, "I ain't gonna be responsible when you come creepin' up the hallway and Cassie mistakes you for a rapist and busts a cap in your ass." Leila knew damn well I don't mess with guns, but Diego didn't, so they compromised. He kept the keys but promised never to come unannounced.

As I was unpacking, Leila asked me how I planned to decorate my room. I told her I'd just bring whatever linens Genevieve

would let me have in addition to my own stuff like my Queen Latifah and Lauryn Hill posters. For the next week, while I was at my
job as a salesclerk at Tower Records, Leila and Junior would bring
in new pieces of furniture. She got Junior to use his connections to
hook me up with a brass bed straight out of a fairy tale. Remembering that I had always wanted a vanity table, Leila moved hers
into my room. She even framed my posters and hung a new one
from the movie *Jason's Lyric* behind the door because she knew I
loved me some Allen Payne.

At first I felt guilty about all the money she was spending on
me, but Leila just laughed, reminding me that it wasn't her
money. Then she grew serious and said, "The way these dudes be
flippin' on me, Cass, I'ma live it up on their dime while I can. And
if I don't have to do the starving-artist bullshit, neither do you."

The best thing to happen, though, was when Leila finally agreed
to produce our album independently. Before, she'd insisted that we
cut only three or four tracks for a demo and submit it to record execs
at major labels. But after reading Moses Avalon's *Confessions of a
Record Producer,* I was convinced that we needed to produce our
own debut even if it required more work, time, and cash. (I'm surprised the industry hasn't gone after that cat the way they did Nap-
ster. You'd think he'd be more of a threat to their bottom line than
any software program. But then again, in their infinite ignorance,
record company honchos probably sleep well thinking, "Niggers
don't read." Or worse. As time goes on, record company honchos
themselves *are* niggas who don't read, especially when it comes to
hip-hop, where so-called brothers start their own labels and adopt
Massah's tricks.) The only way to retain control over everything—
our lyrics, our image and, most important, our money—was to produce ourselves. But while I dreamed of doing the Wu and releasing
an independent hit underground that would position us to negotiate
a respectable deal with a major label, Leila fantasized about being
the female Big Pun and being the first Latina MC to go platinum on
the drop of dime, preferably someone else's.

We had finished the third track in Darnell's studio when Leila pulled off the headphones and said, "We've got a demo now, y'all." I must've had on what she calls my *Stubborn Look*, because she picked up Darnell's phone. "So we need copies, postage . . . Darnell, how much would we need for that?"

Darnell shrugged. "At minimum a G, if you keep it simple."

I knew what she was up to. "Don't, Leila."

Leila dialed a number. "Hello, may I speak to Mr. Mirabal?" she said in the best businesslike voice she could hustle past her Bronx accent. "This is Ms. Aponte calling with an urgent matter." Then Leila switched to that syrupy voice she reserved just for romancing Diego. "Hey, *papi*, how're things at the office? OK, I understand. Lemme get straight to it. I need you to give me a thousand dollars." Her eyes clouded and she took a deep breath. "So that Cassie and I can finish this demo."

Then Leila turned her back to us, but I could see her shoulders tense. When she first hooked up with Diego, she had asked him to finance us. Homeboy was excited until Leila played him our first track and he realized we were rapping and not singing. The man would have nothing to do with it. Even though we sing like muppets, Diego said if we wanted to cut an R&B, pop, or even a dance music demo, he would back us all the way. Maybe even manage us—not that I would've been down with that even if Leila convinced him to bankroll a rap demo. It didn't matter, because Diego said that if we insisted on recording *pelea de perros*—which Leila said means dogfight—we would have to find our capital elsewhere.

That was bad enough, but then Diego went too far. Leila asked me to excuse them and led Diego into the bedroom. I sat seething on the couch, tempted to blast the track. But knowing that would ruin Leila's seduction attempts, I just turned the television on to MTV. Halfway into the premiere of Mary J. Blige's new video, I heard Diego say, "Why the hell do you want to make that noise anyway, Leila? Aren't you proud of who you are?"

"Of course I'm proud of who I am!" she yelled. "What kind of bullshit question is that?"

That's when Diego ranted about hip-hop not being a part of Puerto Rican musical heritage, which was so rich with the talents of Hector Lavoe and Willie Colón and Tito Puente. And why was Leila trying so hard to be *una negra*? And rap music was another hustle Blacks used to avoid real jobs. I took mad offense, but it was nothing compared to the way Leila did. Maybe it was because I was used to hearing that from Genevieve. Maybe because Diego often made Leila feel gutter without trying. Whatever the reason, Leila tore into Diego bad enough for every head in the entire hip-hop nation regardless of race, sex, or creed.

"If you don't know who Crazy Legs, Daisy D, Hurricane G, and Big Pun are," she screamed, "then you don't know the first fuckin' thing about your Puerto Rican heritage." She said he'd better ask Harvard for a refund if after six years there Diego still believed his great-great-grandfather was some conquistador and did not know that *bomba y plena* came from Africa. And wasn't it just like him to mention Hector Lavoe and all those men as if Ruth Fernandez and Lucecita Benitez never existed. Leila finally told Diego to shove his Riverside apartment and Wall Street expense account up his ass. "I'd rather go back to living on the streets and picking leftover McDonald's from garbage cans than take your money." Even I hadn't known that she had done that, assuming that she crashed with another girl who'd grown out of foster care or lived with a boyfriend.

For three weeks that whipped fool called night and day trying to get her back. Diego became so desperate, he broke their compromise and began showing up at the apartment at all hours, hoping for a chance to grovel in person. Leila had just hooked up with Vance—a recent acquisition and shit—and was staying at his place. She eventually did take Diego back, and they promised to never discuss the demo again. Leila was cool with that because she had already gotten Vance to give her a couple of hundred, although we argued about whether to record another song or price print shops for the demo cover.

So for Leila to admit to Diego she wanted the money for our demo was a big deal. She could've told him it was for a new leather jacket or a gold necklace, and he'd jump into a company Town Car to fork over the cash. Maybe even go with Leila to buy it and then back to the apartment so she could *model* it for him. But looking back I understand that she told him the truth for my sake. To prove she wanted to break through as much as I did.

Leila listened to Diego holler. Sitting across the room, Darnell and I couldn't have heard him better if he were actually in the damn studio with us. She let him carry on a while and then said with the nonchalance of a token clerk, "Fine, Diego. Don't give me the money to finish my demo. Give it to me so I don't tell your fuckin' wife were you really were when you told her you were on a business trip to Washington."

"Oh, shit!" Darnell yelled out laughing. I hit him in the arm to shut him up. Sure enough Diego asked Leila who the hell was that guy with her.

"That's my spouse, *cabrón*." Leila said. "I figured you got one so good you can't leave her, I decided to go get one of my own." Nobody can heap on the sarcasm like Leila when she's too through. I can't count how many times she made me wonder if she wasn't bullshitting. "Except our thing is real honest," she contin-ues. "Darnell knows all about you and me."

That's when Darnell stopped laughing. "Don't be telling 'im my name! You crazy? What if he comes after me and shit?"

Leila ignored him. "So if Diana's so wonderful, why can't you tell her you want me, too? What's the big deal if I give her a call, invite her to tea at high noon and shit, and let her get to know me so we can be one whole happy family? What you think about that, Diego?"

That night Leila went out for a long time and came back home with twenty-five hundred dollars. Her mascara was smeared across her cheeks and she didn't want to talk about what happened between her and Diego. She just handed me the cash and told me to deposit it in our joint account.

I tried to give the money back to her. "We don't need his help," I said. "And you don't need his ass at all."

But Leila forced the cash back into my hand. "Look, I already got it from him, so let's put it to good use."

"You OK?"

Instead of flipping me off a halfhearted answer, she actually gave my question some thought. "No," Leila said. "But I'm gonna be, 'cause I've been thinking, Cassie, and you're right," she said. "I'm tired of men thinking that they own me. I'm tired of *feeling* like they own me. Let's do this album ourselves." Then Leila hugged me and went to her room. But I couldn't fall asleep until I heard her stop crying.

CHAPTER 3

BETRAYAL

Sitting in my room remembering this, it hit me. I'd been so psyched after our performance at SOB's, I'd totally forgotten that Leila had invited Diego. Although things had been tense between them, she never doubted he would show. After all, he had yet to see her perform live, and it was Valentine's Day. Leila had said that she didn't want any more money from him, and I didn't doubt that, and not just because she could easily get it from somewhere else. Leila also claimed she didn't want him back, but that I didn't believe. I also knew that she could get over him, too, if she put her mind to it, so it wasn't really about that, either. What Leila needed was for Diego to know she was good at something besides being his damn mistress.

Only after our fight did I remember that she had disappeared for a spell after we got offstage. She tried her best at first to focus on the girls who crowded around us requesting autographs and tips, but eventually she asked me if I minded if she took off to look for Diego. Sometime after she bounced, her boyfriend Junior appeared.

"Cas-sie, that shit was off the meat rack, yo," he said.

I chuckled as I signed one last autograph. "I didn't even know you were here. Thanks for coming. Thanks for the daps."

"And check it. I got that shit right here." He checked over both shoulders, then flashed his jacket open long enough for me to see the mini video recorder hidden in the inside pocket. "Yo, the other day on my way to the store, I stopped to check out this cat selling mix tapes on the street. He mixes the shit himself, and it's ba-nanas. So we started kickin' it, and I told him about y'all. Got him wide open."

"Seriously?" It had never occurred to me to get us on a mix tape, yet so many heads get put on that way. Maybe because you rarely find sisters on them. "So where's he at?"

"He couldn't make it tonight, but I told him I'd give him a copy of this here," Junior said as he tapped his lapel. "If he likes it, he wants y'all to perform at this little showcase he's organizing at this club in Brooklyn. It ain't no big-name venue, but a lotta young heads roll through and buy tapes if they're feelin' it. Check it, Cassie. He'll even pay y'all a little sumthin', sumthin' to perform. And if y'all rip it like you did tonight, he'll put you on one of his mix tapes." Then Junior barked out a laugh. "Maybe y'all can get on without getting shot and shit!"

Our first paid gig. I threw my arms around Junior and squeezed tight. As I held him, I wondered if this might be a great, even if temporary, compromise between Leila and me. Get on enough mix tapes, labels often come courting, and that possibility would satisfy Leila. Mix tapes also help build a following, which ap-pealed to me since I wanted us to produce our album independ-ently. Perhaps Leila and I could agree to pursue that route for a while—maybe even have Darnell create our own mix tapes in-cluding some of his other clients—and let fate determine our path.

Then Leila turned the corner and spotted us. Junior and I jumped apart, but she just asked if we could bounce. She acted dazed and cranky the entire cab ride home even as I broke down

Junior's opportunity. Two weeks later and she still hadn't recovered, if you asked me.

But I became more ready than ever to work. Every day I raced home from Tower to play that tape over and over, listening to what could be better, where the crowd responded most, the whole nine. I rewrote verses and nagged Leila to experiment with different deliveries.

Meanwhile, the entire time she was waiting for a call that never came. No wonder she was pissed. Homegirl was depressed and I had been riding her, not once asking her what was wrong or if she wanted to talk about what didn't happen that night. Her best and oldest friend acted just like of one of her daddies.

I opened the door to my room. "Leila?" She didn't answer, and I headed toward her bedroom and knocked on the door. I let myself in and she was on the telephone, listening intently to whoever was on the other end. I assumed she had called Diego and parked myself on the end of her bed like I always do when she talks to her boyfriends. Unless they were having phone sex, Leila liked me to listen because it saved her from having to recount every detail later to me.

Leila dropped the phone. "Do you mind? This is a private conversation."

That was a switch, but what else could I do? "Come get me when you're finished," I whispered.

When I left the room, I overheard her say, "Yeah, that was her . . . all in my business and shit." Yeah, it hurt, but what did I expect? She was pissed at me and with good reason. I went to my room and tried to concentrate on tightening the rhyme we were working on when our fight started. I didn't get very far.

About fifteen minutes later, Leila blew into my room like a hurricane. "Look, Cassie, I'm just gonna come out and say it."

I jumped up. "But let me say this first—"

"Before you say anything, I just want you to know—"

"No, Leila, I came looking for you, so you need to—"

"You with 'Don't do this, Leila, you need to do that, Leila!' I'm so fuckin' sick of you tellin' me—"

"Shut up, bitch, and let me apologize already!"

The hardness in Leila's face melted away. "Apologize?"

"Yeah," I said. She looked at me like a little girl who'd broken something she was instructed not to touch. I've apologized to Leila plenty of times and accepted her apologies twice that, but I never felt self-conscious about it until I saw that face. "Look, Leila, we performed so good at Da Corridor, I got hyped about finishing the album. . . . I totally forgot about your whole thing with Diego. Girl, I didn't mean to be so selfish. This wasn't a time to be your partner. I should've been your friend, and I'm sorry I wasn't there for you."

Leila blinked at me, but when I went to embrace her, she stepped away from me. "You ain't gonna wanna hug me when I tell you this. I mean, Cassie, you're like a sister to me, and I know you want this as much as I do. But seeing that we want to go about it in such different ways, maybe it's best if you do your thing and I do mine."

My stomach felt like I was on an elevator going up at sixty miles per hour. "What does that mean?"

"I'm going solo."

That elevator in my stomach plunged. "Solo?" I lowered myself onto my bed. "So Diego was at Da Corridor. He saw how good we were and decided to back you up after all. But not with me." It stung all the more because it made sense. I wasn't shit to him, why should he produce me? And if Leila told me that she wouldn't do it without my blessing, we both knew I would tell her not to be stupid and to take advantage of Diego's help. And we understood, too, that I wished she would turn him down anyway if he wouldn't produce us as a duo, but then that would lead us nowhere. Besides, Leila would never make it and not look out for me. She would feature me on a single or even produce my album. It still burned, but the bite of Leila's news was beginning to fade. And then she continued.

"Diego wasn't there that night, that bastard. But while I was wasting my time looking for his useless ass, I met G Double D."

"The G Double D?" I couldn't believe that she had actually met that Puff Daddy wanna-be. "Explicit Content G Double D?" Explicit Content was the burgeoning hip-hop label under Random Sounds, striving to be what Bad Boy Entertainment is to Arista. As its founder, Gregory David "G Double D" Downs had generated hits and controversy by combing the city's underbelly in search of thug life to translate into gangsta rap. The more Black activists and white pundits slammed him for glamorizing drugs and violence, the louder he bragged that his artists were the genuine articles amidst an onslaught of poseurs. "My roster keeps it real. They just telling stories about what they been through. You have a problem with that, then do something about what's happening in these streets," the man once said on *The O'Reilly Factor*. I got with that, but then G said, "And if you want to go after people glamorizing drugs and violence, go after the prep-school kids talking about doing things they've seen only in the movies." I hoped he'd go deeper than that, especially with Genevieve sitting on the couch next to me sucking her teeth. But all he did was laugh and add, "Ayo, Billy, you should thank me 'cause when I have my boy Hi-Jack in the studio, he's not climbing through your daughter's bedroom window." It would've been a thrill to see someone shut up a fool like O'Reilly if it hadn't been a bigger fool with even more ignorant rants that cast the worst of hip-hop as representative of the entire culture.

Leila had that smirk she gets when she's feeling herself but doesn't want it to show. "He bought me a drink and told me that he'd been looking to sign a female to Explicit Content for a long time, and that I was exactly what he was looking for." A bunch of emotions rushed me and cut me speechless. Excitement. Disbelief. Jealousy. "I said, 'What about my partner? What about Sabrina?' " Leila paused to take a deep breath. "Then G said, 'Look, she's a'ight, but I'm looking for just one female. Atlantic's got Lil'

Kim, Universal's got Foxy Brown, Interscope's got Eve. Random Sounds and Explicit Content need Fatal Beauty.' "

Leila started to pace like a boxer before an easy match. "G Dub ain't trying to deal with no TLC–Destiny's Child bullshit 'cause girl groups blow up and then *blow up.* He said, 'One female and one female only. And any record exec worth his platinum will tell you that if you gotta choose between Sabrina Steelo and Fatal Beauty, you choose Fatal Beauty. Sabrina's nice, but Fatal's ice.' " The more she spoke, the less apologetic the tone in her voice. G Double D had heaped all this shit on her and she was wrapped in it like a mink.

I pulled myself from the bed and walked over to Leila. With as much calm as I could muster, I asked, "And that's when you told G, 'But Sabrina writes all the rhymes.' " Leila glared at me as if she could will those onyx eyes to slice me in half. She spun around and marched out of my room. I trailed her into the living room. "You didn't tell G Dub that I write all our rhymes?"

Leila whirled around and poked a red talon in my face. "No, Cassandra, I didn't, because you don't fuckin' write all our rhymes!"

"Oh, excuse me. You right, I don't write all our rhymes," I yelled back as I flailed my hands in the air. "Only nine out of ten of them. All the good ones."

"G was right. All your talk about not letting some goddamn label control us. Truth is, you want to control me 'cause you know I'm better than you and without me you ain't going fuckin' nowhere."

I don't know what pissed me off more. That some industry bastard was puttin' shit in Leila's head, trying to turn her against me, or that she fell for it hook, verse, and sample. "Since you're all that, you'd be better off without me, then you don't need my rhymes, do you? I'll tell you right now, Leila: If you use even one verse I wrote, I'll sue you, G, and every-fuckin'-body at Explicit Content right down to the muthafucka who cleans out the ashtrays at night."

Panic seized Leila's face. "You can't prove you wrote those rhymes," she said in a hoarse voice that told me she wasn't confident in her own words.

I saw our notebooks strewn across the sofa and picked them up. "You think I'm going to let you keep these? Even if you could take these from me, I have every rhyme I ever wrote in a dozen more notebooks just like these." Then I got up in Leila's face and lied. "I even have every rhyme you ever wrote and trashed."

"Bullshit," she said. But I could tell she wasn't sure.

So I pressed. "Any court will look at the two, compare the handwriting and the style and figure out who wrote what. Your career'll be over before it even starts." That sliver shade of witch in me had taken possession of my soul. I cackled at Leila and dangled the notebooks in her face. "The only place in hip-hop history you'll have is as the illiterate bitch that shut down Explicit Content."

Leila lunged for her notebook and I pulled it out of her reach. The flush in her cheeks told me I was humiliating her, but right then I didn't give a half damn. She'd betrayed me on account of that shit-talking mogul. She knew that she would never be able to get the notebook from me. "I always knew that Ms. Goody-Two Shoes bullshit was an act," she said. "You're the worst bitch there is—one who's ashamed of it and tries to hide it. Me, I'm real, twenty-four-seven. But you don't have the guts to go after what you want like I do. All this talk about independent production isn't about maintaining control. It's about always having an excuse to never handle your business."

I had had enough of her. She wasn't Leila Aponte my best friend anymore. She wasn't even Fatal Beauty my rhyming partner. She was this ugly, nameless bitch on G's jock. Just another half-talented hack on the Explicit Content label. A traitor standing between me and my dream. "Well, the twenty-four-seven bitch better get her ass on over to G's so one of his boys can write her rhymes while she's sucking his dick."

Leila pulled back and slapped me hard across the face. She always joked that our nastiest arguments never turned physical because she did not want to kill her best friend. I'm not going to say that it wasn't possible, because I knew Leila truly believed it, and when folks really believe in something, it damn well is possible. But I also believed that if I ever had to throw my hands up with Leila, I could hurt her bad. I had a good seven inches and thirty pounds on her, and I've seen her mix it up often enough to know what she does and how she does it. I could never imagine Leila wilding out on me like that, but now I found myself in the scenario and realized that I could do her damage because I had no other choice. I never dreamed Leila could ever do or say anything to make me want to do that. But I'm only human and Genevieve raised me to never stay hit, and the little scank had just smacked me like my own mama never did.

I balled up my fist and popped Leila right in her jaw. I'm no Layla Ali, but my punch forced her against the footrest of the lounger. Leila stumbled backward over the footrest and banged her head hard against the floor.

I just stood there frozen by what I had done. Leila turned as red as her nails, more from choking on the tears of her injured pride than her wounded head. I rushed over to her and crouched down to check on her.

"Get out!" Leila screamed as she scampered away from me. "Get the fuck out of my house now!"

What else could I do? I threw all my clothes and notebooks into two large shopping bags and did what she said. I got the fuck out of her house.

CHAPTER 4

D

I rode the subway for three hours. Too anxious to sit, I just leaned against the door with my shopping bags crowded around my feet and stared into the tunnel as if the reason why all this had happened was somewhere in its darkness. Although she made it all sound spontaneous, G had to have been working Leila for some time. At least that's what I wanted to believe. I just couldn't accept that she would sell me out so easily. But if that were true, then she had to have been lying when she made it seem that G approached her for the first time after our performance at Da Corridor. And why would someone of G's stature and steelo be there anyway? The man could scour jails for talent, but he couldn't be bothered with the underground. No matter how I flipped it in my mind, the fact remained that Leila had lied to me.

My train pulled into a station and stalled. The train on the opposite track charged into the station, making the third rail flicker as it screeched to a halt. As I stared at the sparks I thought that this was what it must have feel like to fall on that mutha and get the life zapped out of you.

Although I dismissed rumors that G had founded the label with drug money as the media again trashing a brother for succeeding at the white man's game (I expected that when Leila and I produced our own joint and blew up, a hater at some paper would speculate that we pimped ourselves to get ahead), I always felt G wouldn't know a good beat if Timbaland spoon-fed him a bowlful. And those hoods on his label like Hi-Jack, Primo, and those sick bastards in the 8MM Posse? All they did was put out the same ol' gangsta shit as the next fool. It ain't what I do or prefer to buy, so I can't be bothered with most of it. Not that I don't get caught up in the occasional track. Try as I may, I can't sleep on tight lyrics and sick beats, and more often than not, they come from two things you rarely find in the average hood who aspires to spit— artistry and authenticity. And the last place you expected that was from Explicit Content. Just candy-ass beats and blasé lyrics. I bet if any of those punks at Explicit Content from Hi-Jack on down had to do any serious time, they would hang themselves within a week of lockdown.

After so much aimless traveling, pondering, reminiscing, and even a little crying, I realized that the only thing I could do was follow Fatal's lead. Sabrina Steelo had to go solo. And that's when it hit me to head over to Darnell's. I'd be there so much anyway, trying to finish the album and beat Leila to the punch, why not just camp out there? If Darnell would let me. So I checked the subway map and figured out how to transfer from wherever the hell I was to the N train to Darnell's crib in Astoria, Queens. He wasn't there when I arrived, so I just planted myself on his steps and buried my face in my knees for some more crying and shivering in that wicked March chill.

Neither Leila nor I had a knack for composing music. The schools we went to were lucky to have textbooks where Reagan wasn't still president let alone have any kind of art classes. And neither of us came from homes where music lessons were an option. Being a ward of the state, Leila was the breadwinner in all her households, and let's just say expanding her horizons wasn't exactly a priority to any of her foster parents. As for me, well, Genevieve was not going to waste her hard-earned money on something like that. Class trips to a hospital or zoo or some other place where I might get inspired to pursue a practical career were fine, but she would be damned if I joined a band or a team and got the crazy notion that I was the one in thousands that would actually make a living as a professional artist or athlete. So we needed someone to produce our beats.

We had found Darnell after posting on Internet message boards and interviewing about a dozen cats and even one female. She was tight, but wanted too much money per track, saying that she had to stack her paper now that the industry was so MC-driven and she wasn't a rapper. I really liked the idea of working with another woman, and she was Indian, too, which I thought would make us a hot-looking trio with mad broad appeal. But when I suggested to Leila that we ask her to join us as an equal partner, she wasn't feelin' that idea. "I just met the bitch, and I already don't like her," she said. "She already thinks she's more important than the two of us." I guessed homegirl's rant about hip-hop losing its musicality reminded Leila too much of one of Diego's pretentious lectures.

So one of the guys it had to be, and D was the compromise candidate so to speak. I don't say that to diss him, because he had skills. It's just that I had heard better; we just couldn't afford them. The guys Leila liked relied too damned much on sampling for my taste. I've already got to work on my flow without hearing the familiar bass line of "Don't Look Any Further" and fighting the urge to bust out a verse from Rakim or Tupac or worse, start singing, *Dayo umba dayo, mamba jiayo.* The producers I preferred like that Indian chick were way beyond our budget because originality costs. Now, Darnell used samples, too, but if there was an art to it, he had it mastered, I gave him that. The man can take the elements from three vastly different songs—like a Michael Jackson melody from when he was still Black and sane, a riff by

Charles Mingus, and the Latin percussion from a Marc Anthony joint from his freestyle days—and turn it into something unrecognizable yet hot. And Darnell does not fuck with corny shit like show tunes and commercial jingles and the other nonsense you would hear on an Explicit Content track. When he said, "How many records they gonna make off that tired *Knight Rider* theme?" he won me over.

All the other guys we interviewed were more experienced, but Darnell was the most hungry, the most passionate about his music. The man loved to produce for its own sake. To be paid for it was icing. He cracked us up with the story of his first paid gig when he took over for a DJ at a wedding when the guy got sick with some kind of food poisoning. I joked, "Admit it, D. You did that shit yourself, trying to put yourself on."

He laughed and said, "Damn, I wish I had thought of that."

The others Leila and I had met either wanted exorbitant prices for the sale of their beats or wanted to put expiration dates on our license to them so that after a year, we would have to pay renewal fees. D settled for studio costs and appropriate credit, knowing that in this game cash paid bills but credit generated wealth. Especially in his line of work.

And unlike the others, he even made us rhyme for him. At first Leila complained, "Who the fuck he think he is? Simon Cowell? He's answering *our* ad." But that told me that Darnell was serious about breaking into the industry. I had to convince her to take his *audition* as a sign of business savvy. If Darnell thought we sucked, he wasn't going to cut us any discounts. Instead he would take as much of our money as possible, like those modeling agencies in the back of the newspaper that promise chicks with jacked-up grills that they'll be the next Tyra Banks. If we blew up, he would benefit. If we didn't, he had been compensated for the time spent doing what he loved anyway. So even though I had heard better, I had mad respect for the way Darnell conducted his business. He knew what he had going for himself and was willing to make reasonable sacrifices and take calculated risks to put himself on. I eventually convinced Leila that by working with him, we would be doing the same.

When Darnell heard us flow, he wanted to up the ante. "Let me produce and manage y'all," he said. "And I won't charge you a dime for production costs. I've been making some contacts, and I know I can land you a deal at a major label." After huffin' and puffin' over his *audition*, Leila suddenly got flattered and amped, and I had to cool her jets. As flattered as I was by the offer, the last thing I wanted was to be dependent on anyone, least of all some guy I had just met. And something about signing a management and production deal with the same cat just didn't sit right with me.

The discussion between Leila and me got heated, so we took it outside. We finally compromised on hiring Darnell as a producer for at least four tracks. Once we knew if the three of us could work well together, we would revisit his offer. We even joked that when that time came, she would attempt to talk me into hiring Darnell as our manager and move forward with the demo, and I would try to convince her to keep him on a fee-for-service production arrangement while we finished a complete album. It was all good, though, because we both knew it, and all that mattered at the moment was that we got started. We told Darnell what we decided, and while he was mad disappointed he took it in stride.

Now here I was sitting on D's steps like a bag lady on the subway, hoping to get a few hours' sleep before the po came and forced me to move along.

An hour later I heard my name. "What you doing here?" asked Darnell as he stepped out of some girl's Aztek. He opened the gate and climbed the stairs.

"Long story, D." I sniffed as I stood and wiped my face. Bitch in the car was giving me the evil eye, but I just ignored her. "Mind if I stay with you a few days until I figure out what to do with myself?"

Darnell looked back and forth between me and the Aztek chick, one of those skinny *American Idol* type females with her clingy top, swan neck, and pressed hair. I was sure Darnell would start fumbling to say no, so I started to collect my bags to save him the trouble. But then he reached into his pocket for his keys. "Make yourself comfortable. I'm just gonna say good-bye to my friend and then I'll be right in."

I muttered "Thanks," took the keys, and let myself in. Darnell lives in a two-story, three-bedroom house with his retired mom who's always off on some trip somewhere. I didn't want to be presumptuous, go up the stairs, and drop my bags in the third bedroom. So me and my shopping bags just sat on the couch in the living room and waited for him.

After about five minutes, I heard some female hollering. I peeked out the window and sure enough, Ms. Aztek was reading Darnell something awful. Shit, the last thing I wanted to do was inconvenience him. I debated whether my going out there would make things better or worse. Just as I was about to grab my bags and walk outside, Darnell pulled back from the Aztek, and it sped away.

I jumped up as soon as he entered. "D, I'm really sorry. Give me your girlfriend's number and I'll call her to explain."

Darnell huffed. "Later for that skeezer. What you gonna tell her that I already didn't? If it ain't good enough coming from me, fuck her."

I quickly attributed his remarks to guilt. Maybe I didn't get around, but I knew enough to know that much. "Did you tell her I was one of your clients?"

Darnell gave me this goofy grin. "No."

"Uh-huh. Why not?"

"Man, if I would've told her that I had any female clients . . . Ah, forget it, man. You don't wanna know."

"Yeah, I do. See, that's the problem with you dudes," I said. "You be all deceitful even when the situation don't call for it. You waited until she found out—which was probably inevitable—and now it's worse than it might've been had you just come correct from the get-go."

"Nah, you don't understand, Cass," Darnell laughed in that I-know-you're-right-but-I'm-not-ready-to-admit-it-yet way. "I didn't tell Rochelle I had female clients because I was afraid she would think I was fucking one of 'em. I mean, our shit wasn't all that serious."

"So what's the big deal?"

"The big deal is," said Darnell, "that Rochelle wants me to produce her, and I just can't do that."

For a second, I had gotten so caught up in Darnell's minidrama, that I had forgotten about my predicament. But then the idea of Darnell producing Rochelle brought it all back to me. I felt the anger and hurt swell up my throat. "What is up with these females out here these days? Talkin' about being strong and independent yet the first thing they do is look for some man to do for them what they could do them damn selves? So this girl wants you to produce her just because she's giving you a li'l trim."

"Which I'd consider if she wasn't so wack!" said Darnell. I looked at Darnell to see if he was kidding. "Cass, that girl sounds like Weird Al Yankovic except she's got more bass in her voice."

I burst out laughing. "Darnell, you ain't right."

"Look, if Rochelle was my boo and actually had skills, I'd back her up one hundred percent. But neither of those things is true, and I'm a businessman with a reputation to build and protect. I can't be associatin' my name with some shit that sounds like Toni Braxton on crack." Now I was practically rolling on the floor, and I could tell by the glint through his narrowing eyes that Darnell enjoyed making me laugh. "All that time and money I'd be wasting on skill-less Rochelle, I could be investing in potential hit makers like you and Leila."

Because I had been laughing so hard, hearing her name didn't bother me as much as it could have. But I settled down, taking a deep breath that ached against my ribs. "Darnell, do you think I have hit-making potential on my own?"

"I'm not sure what you mean," he said. But then his eyes traveled over my bags and I could see that he figured the gist.

Still I explained the entire situation to him. He didn't say a word, but the look of shock never left his face. When I was finished, Darnell remained quiet, and I worried that he was searching for a kind way to suggest that I reenroll in the accounting program at Baruch College.

But then Darnell said, "Fuck G Double D and Explicit fuckin' Content. I've heard a lot of ill rumors about them, so if Leila's hell-bent on being down with them, it's probably best that y'all part ways. That label ain't for you anyway, Cassie. You too skilled and too deep."

I wanted to believe that, but I had my doubts. "We can dis it all we want, but for the past two years, everything that Explicit Content has released has gone platinum and then some."

Darnell shook his head as he grabbed some of my bags and motioned me to follow him up the stairs. "Don't mean shit to no one but G Double D. Those cats would be nobody without him, and they have nothing with him. Every one of those thugs in the 8MM Posse signed their deals during visiting hours at Rikers. Niggas didn't even know each other until G bailed them out and brought them to the studio. You know where they get the name of their crew?"

I knew. Some fucked-up movie where Nicholas Cage plays this private eye trying to find out who's behind this snuff film. That's when muthafuckas kidnap a girl and tape themselves raping and killing her. Just the fleeting thought turned my neck into a block of ice.

"Them's some sick dudes, Cassie. First night together they're kickin' it in the artists' lounge at the label's office, trying to get to know each other and come up with a name they all like. Can't find anything in common besides that they're all a bunch of jailbirds, get on each other's nerves, and come two inches off each other's ass, when finally one of them says, 'Fuck this shit. I'm watching a movie.' They all watch this *8MM* shit and love it and boom! They make that the name of their crew and start talkin' about how they gonna take gangsta rap to a whole new level.

"But guess who owns Primo's Bentley? Explicit Content. Hi-Jack not only writes all his own rhymes, but he also wrote most of the hits by everyone else on the label. Guess who owns his publishing? Explicit Content. That crib in Glen Ridge where they all live?" Darnell led me to the last room at the end of the hallway and pressed his shoulder against the door to back into the room.

"It's G's name on the deed?" I guessed.

"Bingo. Look, Cassie, it's foul how you and Leila split, but no matter what happens—even if Fatal Beauty's topping charts and Sabrina Steelo's flipping burgers—you get on your knees and thank God you're not involved with Explicit Content." Darnell placed my bags on the daybed. "From the shit I heard, nothing at that label is what it seems," he said. "And whatever's nice ain't true. All floss, no sauce. Word."

"Like what?" Although I followed hip-hop culture closely, my monitoring of hip-hop *business* never extended beyond researching the legal maneuverings that might affect my bottom line. I couldn't have cared less who was out as the head of this or got promoted to the VP of that, and financial information related to chart positions, sales trends, copyright lawsuits, and whatnot I learned only in articles about particular artists. Plus, the negative gossip delivered in Darnell's annoyed tone comforted me.

"Explicit Content's on the verge still of getting cut by Random Sounds 'cause they ain't making the kinda money they spending, blingin' all over town like niggas own anything," said Darnell. "I'm surprised G even signed anyone new, let alone Leila."

It crossed my mind that if Explicit Content did have financial trouble, perhaps G signed Leila because he believed she could save his label. He saw in her a talent large enough to top charts and break records once he unlatched her from the deadweight that kept her from soaring—me. With that fleeting thought, my funk returned.

Darnell showed me where the bathroom and linen closets were, told me to help myself to anything I wanted in the kitchen, and warned me to stay out of his mother's bedroom and sewing room because the woman had this sixth sense and could tell if someone besides her so much as opened the door and peeked inside her special spaces. "Take a hot shower, get some sleep, and we'll talk business in the morning," he said before he winked at me and closed the door behind him. Thinking about Leila and worrying about where I was going to sleep, I hadn't even thought about how our split would impact our business relationship with Darnell. Like I needed another damned thing to keep me up that night.

So now it was me and my shopping bags crowded on the daybed covered in a lacy comforter that reminded me of a first communion dress. It matched the curtains on the single window and the throws draped over the white dresser and rocking chair. Potpourri pillows sat in every corner of the room like guards instructed to ward off shadows and nightmares. All Darnell's mother's creations, no doubt. The room seemed to be decorated for the little girl she always wanted but never had.

That thought made me draw my knees to my eyes to force back tears. If I could not be at Leila's, I should have been able to go home to my old room in Crotona. It didn't matter that the room didn't exist anymore, that the entire building had been demolished back in the eighties, and my mother had bought one of the new multifamily homes that fill the once-abandoned lots of the South Bronx. There should have been a place for me at Genevieve's. I never should've had to leave Leila's, not on those terms. I shouldn't have to crash at the home of a business associate like some shiftless wanderer who was content to hustle a bed here and a meal there. No, I busted my ass to realize my dreams and never did anyone dirt in the process. At all times I worked my craft and earned my keep. I never expected anyone to give me any-thing just because I was cute, never thought it would be easy just because I had talent. But there I was without home or fam, sitting on a strange bed made for a daughter who never existed, with all I owned thrown in plastic bags from Pathmark and Rainbow.

Good girls ain't supposed to go out like this.

CHAPTER 5

MONEY, MONO & OTHER ILLNESSES

If there's anything more emotionally draining than suffering betrayal, it has to be wallowing in self-pity over it. I fell asleep on the daybed with my jacket and shoes on, using a Rainbow bag full of clothes as a pillow. My ass didn't wake up until three weeks later, no lie. I called out sick the first three days, then just stopped without a thought as to how I was going to explain it to my boss, Roy. Luckily, Darnell overheard one of these conversations and took it upon himself to get this chick he knew who worked at a doctor's office to call Roy and tell him that I had caught mononucleosis, which required that I get ten to twelve hours of sleep. So except to change into sweats, go to the bathroom, and eat Cocoa Puffs, I didn't leave the room, determined to sleep my troubles away. But every time I woke up, I'd remember where I was and why, and I'd roll over and try again. When I couldn't sleep, I'd pretend to, hoping to keep Darnell and our inevitable business conversation at bay. Buried in my core was a faint voice telling me to get up, get clean, and get into the studio. I shut her up by drowning her with Oreos and Coronas.

Then, one morning as I was folding the plastic bags in a daze and stashing them under the bed just like an ordinary person does her luggage, I heard Darnell call for me. "Cassie! Yo, Cass, come quick. G Double D's gonna be on TV." I bolted out of the room and down the stairs. Darnell was sitting in the living room wearing long johns as pajamas and munching on a Pop-Tart. On the screen, Lynda Lopez was introducing G Double D. I dropped myself onto the couch next to Darnell and pulled a pillow to my chest as if to shield myself for an impending blow. J.Lo's sister gassed G a bit about his outfit, although it was the usual ghetto fabulous costume of fur-lined sweats and roped gold, and then finally asked him what was next for Explicit Content.

"We're about to drop the remix of Hi-Jack's latest single 'Color Me Gully,' " he said. Darnell and I both groaned at the title—typical Explicit Content. They started to play the video of the remix as G talked over it. "The track features a hot new artist named Fatal Beauty, and y'all need to check for this *chiquita bonita* 'cause she's taking Explicit Content to new heights." And then Leila filled the screen, her eyes piercing white in the gleam of the strobe light. She rhymed in red shorts and matching stilettos while Hi-Jack grinded on her.

Then Lynda said, "She's good. She's cute."

The camera cut back to G Double D in the studio in time to catch him sneering at J.Lo's sister. "No, your sister's good and cute. Fatal's tight and fine. Recognize."

Even though Darnell sucked his teeth and glared at the television screen, I smacked him with the pillow for harassing me to watch that shit and stomped up the stairs. "Yo, what's that for?" he called after me. "Where you going? Cassie, what'd I do?"

I stormed into the bathroom and blasted on the shower. I stepped under the steamy stream determined to scrub away my funk, physical, mental, and emotional. I poured a fat glob of pink shampoo directly on my crown and dug into my scalp until the lather was so thick the foam cascaded around my back and shoulders like a bubble stole. While still in the shower, I brushed my teeth so hard I spat blood. I gargled and spat hard again as if I had just sucked the poison out of a snakebite.

After I climbed out of the shower, I rummaged through the cabinet below the sink until I found a tub of cocoa butter. I scooped out a big cake of cocoa butter and smashed it between my palms. Then I massaged it all over my body as if I were sealing myself in a protective coating so if the depression should try to creep up and envelop my body, it would lose its grip and slide off me. Caught up in this image, I buttered between each of my toes, under my arms, and behind my ears. I even took another scoop and worked it through my wet hair.

I wiped the steam off the mirror on the shower door. As I caught my breath, I looked at my naked body as its reflection glistened at me. I still wasn't myself, but I wasn't that pathetic chick hiding under D's mama's communion comforter. That voice in my core yelled, "How ya like me now?" and I smirked.

That muse can be a wicked bitch.

I found Darnell working in the studio he had built in his basement. Although I had spent hours in there amidst the metal boxes of dials, buttons, and wires and the walls lined with shelves of CDs and vinyls, it felt like the first time. As a looped beat boomed through his speakers, Darnell sat in his swivel chair with his back to me, flicking his fingers through a sea of colored knobs on his Mackie CR-1604 like an orchestra leader. The man loved his machines, especially his ol'-school Roland W-30 keyboard and his SP1200 drum machine, or his "raw bitch" like he called it because of its beautifully dirty sound. Although technology had improved, he refused to get another keyboard, once telling Leila and me, "If Erick Sermon can do 'The Big Payback' on this in ten minutes, why should I fuck with something else?" Darnell even held on to his Atari computer because he couldn't part with the Band-in-a-

Box software program he never used because it had become obsolete before the man was even born.

The loop ended and he leaned toward his telephone with the speakerphone lamp aglow. "So what you think?" he asked as he hovered over the phone's built-in mic.

A slight cough staggered over the speakerphone into the air. Then a gruff male voice said, "S'a'ight."

"All right?" Darnell said. He picked up the telephone receiver and slammed it back into the cradle. "All right *that*, muthafucka." I snickered, and Darnell turned around with an embarrassed look on his face. "Don't get it twisted, Cass. You don't know how long I've been trying to lose that bastard. Every week changing his damn mind about what he wants. One day he wants to be Pac, the next B.I.G. Like I ain't got no other clients. Speaking of which . . ." Darnell turned to me and motioned for me to pull up a chair by him.

I sighed and walked over to the chair I usually sat in during our studio sessions. I saw Leila's chair and kicked it out of my way. Now Darnell snickered, and I felt stupid. I pulled my chair up next to him. "Look, Darnell, I'm sorry about the way I've been lately, and please don't think I expect you to work for free."

"So what you gonna do?"

I swallowed hard. "I've got no choice but to go solo. I've got the rhymes, maybe enough money to rerecord the tracks we have, edit Leila out of them, and then . . ."

"Whoa, slow your roll," said Darnell. "What if Leila's planning to do the same thing?"

"If she signed with Explicit Content and is recording singles with Hi-Jack and them, why does she need to use our stuff?" I felt fury eat away at my stomach. "Why can't G Double D just put her ass in the studio to record some new shit like every other label does?"

Darnell said, "He can. The question is, Will he?" He shook his head and raised his hands in the air in surrender. "I want to help you out, Cass, but I'm not trying to fuck with G Double D and his thugs at Explicit Content, and neither should you."

"But those are your beats, D," I said.

He stiffened, but then shrugged. "Hey, I got plenty more where that came from, but I only got one head and I like it best without no extra holes in it, know what I'm sayin'?"

"Stop exaggerating, Darnell."

He slid his chair next to mine and put his arm around my shoulder. "Tell you what, Cassie. I'm gonna put my ear to the ground and see what I can find out about what's going on with Leila at Explicit Content, see just how shady that muthafucka is. If it seems G's gonna go in another direction, then we'll use what we've got minus Leila's vocals. If not, we're better off starting from scratch and avoiding any trouble."

I hated the idea of just giving up all that I had worked for and starting over. But I liked less the idea of fighting for it. I wouldn't think twice if it was just Leila. But there was no way I could take her on when Explicit Content—with the Random Sound's organization—had her back.

"I've got some money in the bank," I said. "Not a lot though."

Darnell asked, "So are you still gonna try to record a whole album?"

My heart felt like he had reached into my chest and clamped his fist around it. In three weeks Leila had already cut a track with Hi-Jack and appeared in a video. In the best scenario, I would have enough money to record a demo, land a record deal, and have a label's lawyers squash any disputes with Leila and Explicit Content on my behalf. And O.J. would get his own talk show before that shit happened. I would be lucky if I managed to edit three or four of our songs and sell them next to the DVD bootleggers on the street before Leila dropped an album with all the same cuts. Doing the Wu was out.

"No, D. I gotta go status quo. Put a demo together, get it out, hope a label bites."

"That's what I'm talkin' about," Darnell said. "Fuck Leila and 'em. You do you, get yours on your terms."

Thing was that my terms had always included Leila, and that had changed through no will of mine. You'd think that if I had to go solo, I'd be relieved to be able to do things my way and not have to convince or answer to anyone else. But being abandoned by Leila made the idea of independently producing an album unsatisfying. Overnight the taste for commercial success became much stronger than the desire for artistic freedom. I knew that it was impossible to beat Leila to the streets, but I didn't care. Disappearing for a year or so while I scrounged up the dough to record an independent album was not an option. The only way to rebound from Leila's betrayal and prove that I didn't need her was to stay on the scene. She could drop all the albums and videos she wanted so long as I survived, even if only underground, because that was where the truest hip-hop lived anyway.

I pushed my chair away from the console and stood. "I'ma head to the bank. Once I know how much I have, can we figure out how much more I need and how fast we can get this demo done?"

"No doubt."

"Where's the nearest ATM around here?"

"Go back to Northern Boulevard and make a left. About two blocks down across the street, you'll see a Citibank." I nodded at him and headed for the door. "Yo, Cass," he called after me. I stopped to face him, and he handed me an envelope. I opened it and found a letter forged on the doctor's letterhead and addressed to Roy. "Welcome back, Sabrina Steelo."

Not quite, I thought. But at least I was out of Park and in Drive.

As I walked toward Northern Boulevard, I tried to remember how much would be in the joint checking account I had with Leila. The last time I checked it was the week before we performed for Da Corridor at SOB's. Although both our names were on the checks,

I paid all the bills because Leila didn't want to be bothered with the math. Besides, my gig at Tower Records kept the lights on and the phone connected.

Like I said, Diego paid our rent and stocked our refrigerator. He gave Leila the cash, and she gave it to the landlord and did the grocery shopping. We usually ate dinner out or had it delivered, but either way she always paid for it. When she did her laundry, she always washed my clothes, too. And if Leila took anything to the cleaners or the shoe repair, which was every week with all the leather and suede she liked to rock, she would take my things with her and pick up the tab. Leila hated to clean, so she paid the neighbor's housekeeper to come in every two weeks. When I got on her case about at least doing the dishes because it was both nasty and unfair to have Renata wash them after they've sat in the sink for two weeks, Leila got Diego to buy us a dishwasher.

Leila and I never discussed any of these arrangements. She had been living in that apartment for almost a year before Genevieve gave me her ultimatum. I moved in and things just worked out this way, each giving what and when she could.

We also opened a joint savings account to put money away for studio time even though we hadn't agreed yet whether to go for an album or a demo. I had Tower directly deposit twenty percent of my paycheck into it every two weeks, the rest going into the checking account. Whenever Leila came across some extra cash, she would put it in the savings account. This extra cash usually came from her daddies, mostly Diego. She'd tell him about something she wanted and exaggerate how much it cost. Then Leila would buy it, and sometimes she'd even buy something for me, then put the rest of it in our savings account. Her other boyfriends, Junior (who sold furniture on 33rd Street) and Vance (who owned an art gallery in SoHo), sometimes gave her gifts, and what she didn't want to keep, she'd sell and save the rest in our studio fund.

One time Vance even broke up with Leila because she sold a painting he had given her for Christmas for five hundred dollars.

Even though it looked liked a third-grader fingerpainted it, the ugly thing actually was worth three times as much. Vance found out Leila sold it when he asked for it back because he found the perfect frame for it at some antique shop near his gallery. Leila told me that Vance got so angry, he turned pink and stormed out of the restaurant. The more I tried to convince her that she had done him serious wrong, the harder she laughed. "Fuck that *güero*," she said while kneeling on my bedroom floor and hugging her sides in hysteria. "That's what his ass gets for buying me something he wanted instead of asking me what I wanted." By New Year's, that pathetic white boy had called her to say he had forgiven her and they should start over again. When Leila played his message on the answering machine for me, I was like, "Fuck that *güero*," too. He had everything Leila dished out coming to him and then some.

I arrived at the bank and slipped my card into the machine. When I paid the last round of bills about a month and a half before, we had a little over three hundred in checking and almost four thousand in savings. I punched in my PIN and requested the balance of the checking account. After a few seconds, the screen flashed and told me that I had $512.66 available for withdrawal. I smiled when I saw that there was almost two hundred more in the account than I had thought.

I hit the key to make a withdrawal and paused when the screen read *How much would you like to withdraw? Daily maximum withdrawal is $500.00.* I hadn't gone to the ATM with the intention of cleaning out the accounts. I just wanted to confirm how much was there and cop some pocket cash to tide me over until I figured out what to do. But if my estimate of the savings balance was right, I could record a four-track demo and break off Darnell a little extra for living expenses, especially if G Double D did not use any of our material, forcing us to start from scratch. So I asked myself why shouldn't I empty out the damned accounts? Most of it was my money anyway. I was the one who made steady deposits over the last two years standing on my feet eight hours per day, usually six days a week, while Leila perpetrated like a spoiled housewife, handing me whatever was leftover from her latest shopping spree to deposit.

. So I punched in 5-0-0-0-0 then hit the Enter key. The machine churned out twenty-five stiff twenty-dollar bills into the tray, and I felt nothing but justified. As I stuffed the cash in my back pocket, the first thing I planned to buy was a Metrocard so I could get to the bank down the street from the apartment and close the savings account. Leila was an Explicit Content recording artist now so she didn't need the money, let alone deserve it. Hell, the girl never even had a bank account until I moved in with her, always running to the check-cashing joint to buy a money order when her cash was no good.

Then I requested the balance of my savings account. The machine asked me to reenter my PIN so I did. It churned again and then said, *This account does not exist. Please make another selection.*

I jabbed the Cancel key and the machine spat out my card. I shoved it back into the slot, reentered my PIN, and selected the savings balance option again. The machine gave me the same response. *This account does not exist. Please make another selection.*

"No!" I yelled as I banged on the machine with my fist.

I didn't even notice the middle-aged white woman standing behind me, waiting for her turn to use the ATM until she stepped to me. "I don't think you should do that to the machine."

I spun around and screamed at her, "Mind your fuckin' business, bitch! Just leave me alone!" She gasped and dashed into the bank to get the security guard. I snatched my card out of the ATM and ran the hell out of there.

CHAPTER 6

BROKE(N)

The little bitch had wiped me out, and those fools at the bank let her.

And it wasn't like Leila did it first thing the morning after she kicked me to the curb, either. It had taken her almost three weeks to come in and empty the account. Had I not been lying in bed feeling sorry for myself, I might have beaten her to the cash.

"I want to speak to the manager who was on duty that day," I told the customer-service rep. "If she's not here, you get her on the phone. I don't care if she's at home, out sick, on vacation, or wherever. I'm not leaving here until she explains to me how this could happen."

"Please have a seat, Ms. Rivers," the nervous rep told me. I ignored her, burning my eyes into her back as she checked over her shoulder again and again until she disappeared into a back office. I was too angry to sit. Leila had not only swiped my money, but she had thrown it in my face by leaving behind a stingy few hundred dollars. The heifer manager was going to tell me how Leila could roll in that piece and single-handedly close our joint account without my consent.

But when the rep came out of the back office with the manager behind her, I immediately knew. He was this wiry doofus with a coffee stain on his polyester tie, thick glasses with designer frames that were the in thing five years ago, and a big knot above his right eyebrow probably from opening too many doors into his own noggin. By the time they reached me, the whole scenario had played out in my mind. A customer-service rep told Leila they could not close the account without my permission, so she asked to see the manager, and when she saw this Latino Steve Urkel, Leila dropped her Fatal Beauty charms on him and he gave her all my money.

"Ms. Rivers?" the bank manager said as he extended his hand to me. "I'm George Galán." His name tag actually read *Jorge,* and that made me respect his ass even less. I know the Spanish did a lot of dirt back in the day, but if I were Latino, I wouldn't be trying to whiten my name for nobody.

I brushed Esteban Urkel's hand away from me. "Since when do you let one person close a joint account, Whore-hay?"

"Please follow me, and I'll explain the situation."

"Yeah, you gonna explain this all right."

He led me into his office and motioned for me to sit. "May I get you some coffee or tea?"

"No! I don't want any coffee or tea or a goddamn seat," I said. "I want an explanation and my fuckin' money."

"You have every right to be upset, Ms. Rivers," Whore-hay said as he paced between his desk and the door, "but I'm begging you to please keep your voice down."

In situations like these, that's usually my cue to go off at the top of my lungs. But the tremble in his voice and the way he wrung at the coffee stain in his tie actually made me comply. Still I said, "Look, you either show me where it says that one person can close a joint account without the other's permission or you take me to your supervisor."

Whore-hay rubbed his tie so hard, I thought it might catch fire.

"Ms. Rivers, when Ms. Aponte came into the bank to close the account, she wasn't alone."

"You telling me she walked in here with someone pretending to be me?"

"No, she came with two men. Two, large armed men who claimed to be business associates of Gregory 'G Double D' Downs." I finally took that seat everyone had been offering me. I imagined Leila sitting right were I was, playing with her hair and cracking her bubble gum while the bank manager counted out our savings with two Vin Diesel wanna-bes towering over him. "I tried to explain the bank's policy on closing joint accounts, but . . ." Jorge's hand floated toward the knot on his head as if he still could not believe all this had happened to him. I knew exactly how he felt. "I'm sorry, Ms. Rivers. I'm taking a big chance even telling you this."

Now that was bullshit. Better for him to assume I, too, was one of those Explicit Content thugs who knew how the game was played and come clean rather than risk my telling his boss. Considering the scene I had caused when I came into the bank, he had every reason to think that. "So in other words, I'm ass out."

Jorge didn't have the heart to nod, and oddly enough I appreciated that. I slinked out of the chair and toward the door. "If it's any consolation, Ms. Rivers, your friend kept the checking account open for you. One of the men asked if there were any more accounts to close, and she lied and told him no. And trust me, these aren't people you want to catch you in a lie."

Of course, when I walked into Tower, everyone was shocked to see me. I thought it would take less guts to head over to the job than to walk up to the apartment and confront Leila, but I was wrong. The more I heard, "Hey, Cassie, how're you feeling? What're you doing here?" the harder it was to say, "I was feeling better and happened to be in the neighborhood," instead of bursting into tears. I never came in when I did not have to. I didn't drop in on my day off even if it was payday because my check was deposited directly into those damned accounts, and I knew my stub could wait until I returned to work. And as nice as all my coworkers were, they weren't exactly my friends. Sometimes they'd invite me out for dinner and drinks after work, but I'd always pass because if I wasn't rushing home to write, I was either performing with Leila at an open mic or recording with her in Darnell's studio. And not once had I invited any of my coworkers to any of our perform-ances. I don't know, I just had this thing where I didn't want to ask them to come see me until I knew I'd be quitting the store to rhyme for a living. As I walked around the counter into my boss's office, I regretted not having let these folks more into my life.

"Hey, Cassie," said Roy as he fed a document into the fax ma-chine. "What're you doing here?"

"Feeling better. Rolling through," I said for what I begged God to be the last time. I handed him the letter Darnell had his friend write for me.

"That cute roommate of yours with you?"

"No!"

Roy threw his hands up. "Okaaay . . ."

"Listen, Roy," I said. "If you've got any overtime, I'm down. Seeing as I missed so much work and all." You have to understand how hard that was for me to do. If I had enough to get by, I wasn't down with standing on my feet for more than forty hours per week. I wasn't like Leila, whose hardest activity on a given day is fantasizing about all the name-brand fashions she wants and how to get them without having to get a job. Genevieve always said, "Work hard for what you want and want modest things." And that was how I lived, and what I wanted was to get to the point where my music paid my bills. But if all I did was make music, I couldn't eat. And if I worked for more than I needed to eat, I couldn't make music. So after I moved in with Leila, I took the full-time gig at Tower because it paid enough to keep the heat on in the winter and save money for recording time. But I never did extra shifts or worked my day off because then I would be too tired to write, record, and perform, and what would be the point of that? Now I had no choice.

"I'll keep that in mind, Cassie, but I don't have anything right now," Roy said. "In fact, we're trying to cut back on the overtime because business is slow, you know."

Actually, I didn't, but I guess I should've with what I had read about music industry spokespeople whining about record-low sales. They liked to blame it on CD burners and computer file sharing and whatever, but if you ask me, all they had to do was stop putting out fifteen versions of Britney Spears and *NSYNC like only twelve-year old white girls from places called San This or Mount That buy albums. No matter how big their allowances are, even they get tired of the same shit over and over again.

Roy brought me back to my desperate reality. ". . . so I'd rather do that than lay people off, you know. But with the way things are going, don't be surprised . . ." And without my asking for it, he handed me my latest pay stub.

I looked at it and skipped a breath. My depression had proven to be mad expensive. As I folded the envelope and placed it in my pocket, I shook my head and scoffed.

"What's so funny?"

Not a damned thing, I thought. With the way my life was going, why should a sharp turn from "Aw, shoot!" to "Oh, shit!" surprise me at this point? I had to thank God that at least I still had a job. For now. "Listen, I need you to stop the direct deposits. I had problems with my bank so I'm going to take my money else-where."

Roy opened my doctor's letter and scanned it. "OK, but you should know that it takes some time to process that."

Great. "How long?"

"I don't know," Roy said. "I've never had anyone cancel direct deposit while they were still working here. Usually we stop it because someone either quits or gets fired. But I'll try and find out for you."

"Yeah, but what happens to my money until then, Roy?" I caught the irritated tone in my voice and backtracked with a quickness. Just because my patience had been whittled to a breaking point didn't mean I could afford to scream on my boss. "Never mind. Just let me know what I have to do to stop the direct deposit. If I have any forms to fill out or whatever." I thanked Roy for my pay stub and told him I'd see him tomorrow.

Roy folded up my doctor's letter and placed it on his desk. "Cool, if you're up to it," he said.

Things were way past what I was up to. It was all about what was up to me.

On the way out of Tower, I picked up the *Village Voice* so I could read the help-wanted ads on my way back to Astoria. I circled a few part-time ads, all telemarketing gigs no matter how hard they tried to make them sound exciting and lucrative. I could be ten cents away from homelessness, and I could never make a dime at a gig like that. Even desperation couldn't turn me into a peppy people person. I even peeked at the phone sex jobs. I had seen *Girl 6* and knew that it wasn't what it was cracked up to be, which meant that maybe I could actually do it. I was a performer, right? Wrong.

My first real boyfriend was my last. Kurt was a guy who worked with Junior, and I met him when I went with Leila to visit him at the designer furniture store were he worked. Kurt aspired to rhyme, too, and so we hit it off well. But things got cold after about six months because I realized that Kurt was all talk and no action. On the mic, in the bedroom, you name it. Thing is, I really liked him, too, and I let him be my first. Sex was nothing I thought it might be except painful. It got better as time went on, but it never got good. Not *Jason's Lyric* good. Never a Prince ballad good. On his feet with his clothes on, Kurt was all flowers and candy and could always get me in the mood. But something about getting horizontal and naked seemed to leak all the romance out of him. Sleeping with him was like leaning against a washing machine during the wash cycle. It stirred me up a bit for no bigger purpose. I remember getting more out of rubbing on my pillow of Raphael the Teenage Mutant Ninja Turtle as a kid.

I was so happy to have a boyfriend though after all those months of staying home alone or being a third wheel to Leila and her Man of the Moment. I liked to go out on double dates with Kurt, Junior, and Leila. So even though Kurt always impressed me with his knowledge of hip-hop and made my skin bubble with faint kisses on my neck only to disappoint me back at the apartment, I settled. And I pretended (that's why I rented *Girl 6*). He wasn't a bad guy, I rationalized. He was cute and reliable and we had something major in common.

I quit faking though after the ultimate disappointment—when I realized that for all his talk about becoming a rapper, Kurt never did a damn thing to make it happen. Only once or twice throughout the entire time we were together did I ever read or hear any of his rhymes. I'd ask him and he would get in a funk, complaining that he was working on something hot only to turn on Hot 97 and hear that the latest joint by Jay-Z or 50 Cent sounded just like it and he had to start over again. Whatever Kurt was working on, I couldn't read or hear because he had trashed it once some other rapper on Billboard *stole* his shit.

Meanwhile, I had written about a dozen rhymes while we were going out, and once after faking in bed for a record ten minutes, I asked him if he wanted to hear one of them. Kurt said sure, and I crawled out from under the covers and stood up on the bed and rhymed my heart out for him. I was having the time of my life until I noticed he was looking at me like a weather girl forecasting heavy rains and gusty winds for the Fourth of July weekend and shit. When I finished all he could say was, "Nice, Cassie. With a little more work, you'll almost be as good as Lil' Kim. Don't forget to cut the light."

Kurt knew I hated Lil' Kim and took pride in being nothing like her. I was nowhere near being discovered, let alone blowing up, and already my man was hatin' on my hustle and trying to bring me down. If he was going to treat me like this just for doing what he should be, how was he going to flip when my work started to pay off? So I stopped faking. I never asked him about his rhymes, and he never asked me about mine. Nor did I volunteer to share them.

About two weeks later, Leila called me at work on her cell phone. That alone hinted drama because Diego had bought her that phone and she purposefully left it home all the time when he refused to get one for me, too (since I couldn't afford the service, I successfully convinced myself I really didn't need one, so Leila set on a failed mission to prove me wrong by getting Diego to foot the bill). He wanted to be able to contact Leila whenever he liked, but she wasn't trying to be at his beck and call. But on that day she went to visit Junior and decided to take it with her. She called me from the store to tell me that she had just busted Kurt kissing some female in the storeroom. Leila wanted me to cut out of work, jump into a cab, and come down to the store to help her beat both their asses. I wasn't up to it, and she thought I was crazy. Not that I wasn't hurt. It's just that I was more relieved that it was finally over. I told Leila he wasn't worth the drama and hung up. Yeah, I had a good cry over Kurt, but the whole time I was bawling I was telling myself I had better get it out of my system because I was forbidding myself to shed any more tears over him after that.

I did feel better though when Leila came home and told me that she busted into the storeroom and blew up Kurt's spot, telling the girl he was cheating and that he had a girlfriend. Even better, homegirl stormed out of the store both pissed at Kurt and afraid Leila was going to tear into her behind, so when Kurt tried to run after her, Leila tripped him and he went crashing into this expensive lamp. He didn't get fired for allowing nonemployees in the storeroom, but according to what Junior told Leila, the store manager decided to dock ten percent of Kurt's pay for the next six months to pay for the lamp. That made me feel a little better, and I got some satisfaction when Kurt broke down and called because I was positive he'd add insult to injury and not bother. It felt good to erase his messages and imagine him waiting for my call, but not as much as having Leila go where I really wanted to but couldn't that day.

So the phone sex thing was out. I was never one for positive thinking. Not because I had a hard-knock life. If anything, I had no use for positive thinking because of the opposite. Genevieve Rivers was not going out like that, and for better or worse, I was her daughter. "Positive thinking is for people who have nothing else to get them by," she would say. "And so long as you have a keen mind and a strong back, you should have all you need to get through the day." Well, Genevieve was wrong, because despite my sharp mind and strong back, I had a minimum-wage job and a worthless bankcard. So I gave positive thinking a try on the ride back to Astoria because I had nothing else to do.

Like what Jorge said about Leila hiding the checking account from G Double D's two thugs. So she didn't want to leave my ass out. Maybe Leila wasn't sure if I really wanted the money, seeing how ugly things were when I left and how proud I can be and given that I was gone for three weeks but never touched the account. Or G found out that she had that money, and he made her give it up because, like Darnell said, things were mad shady at Explicit Content. Once G knew the savings account existed, she couldn't hide how much money there was in it. Or Leila probably told him that she wouldn't be able to close the account without my permission and that even if she knew where to find me, she doubted I would agree to fork it all over seeing most of the money was mine. And that's when G decided to have his thugs take her to the bank. Worse, he originally wanted to send his thugs to track me down and force me to close the account and give up all the money on some Suge Knight–Vanilla Ice drama. But Leila convinced him to go after the bank manager instead of me. And before they went, Leila managed to deposit whatever cash she had on hand into the checking account. That's why there was two hundred more in there than I thought. So Leila left me as much as she could get away with leaving me.

Yeah.

Cuando las gallinas mean.

CHAPTER 7

GENEVIEVE SAYS

God don't like ugly, and she ain't fond of stupid, either
Or the way you stalked fame like a psychopathic skeezer.
Said you had my back just to go on the attack
And stab me with your stiletto like a true hood rat.
You couldn't get any more ghetto than that.
You're ultra falsetto, but you can't hold me low
'cause I'm like Beyoncé, I'm a survivor, I'm gonna make it.
With Bri Steez cheese you don't play
And not pay, fo-shay, soon all your fans will cherchez
La femme named Sabrina Steelo.
I fiend to be queen of the hill, yo, and you'd best pray
That I show you mer-cy come Judgment Day.

For the next couple of months, I worked my ass off. Roy did let some folks go, but thankfully I wasn't one of them. He had no reason to question my *illness,* and except for that three-week absence, I had never missed a day of work, was always on time, and otherwise had a solid track record on the job. The layoffs meant more work for less people, so I got my overtime, too. I sensed Roy felt a little sorry for me even though I never told another soul what happened between Leila and me. He had to suspect something though. I changed my address on all my paperwork, I supposedly had suffered this infectious disease, and now I had this desperate need for all the overtime he could spare. He probably figured I now had medical bills left and right to pay. I neither confirmed nor denied, as they say, the whispers in the employee lounge that ended whenever I entered the room. I just ignored the gossip and went about my business that lately took sixty hours per week.

But if not for my coworkers, my twentieth birthday would have come and gone like any other day in April because I doubt Leila would bother to track me down, I had yet to tell Genevieve I had moved, and I never mentioned my birthday to Darnell. My coworkers gave me a small cake and a present. When I unwrapped that beautiful journal, I decided to give myself the birthday present of writing again. I wrote mostly on the subway ride home from work and for an hour or two when I got back to Darnell's. I would be exhausted physically yet too wired mentally to fall asleep. So I often wrote until I fell asleep with the pen in hand and the notebook on my chest. Sometimes I wouldn't even eat, and hunger would wake me in the middle of the night. I'd go into the kitchen to microwave Darnell's leftovers and write again for another hour or two.

I can't front. Most of what I wrote during that time was pure crap. Lots of anti-Fatal shit that made Pac's "California Love" sound like an ode to Biggie. Like a good artist, I could've tried to turn my pain into poetry, but once the venom hit the page I refused to touch it again. I just wasn't there, and that was how it had to be. More than eight hours' sleep or three square meals, I needed to write. Only after I had chipped away the anguish were the worthy verses inside me free to flow again. Writing was self-exorcism, and like I read in this book *The Artist's Way,* I had to be willing to be a bad artist if I was going to become a good one.

It helped to avoid all things associated with Leila. I became Amish and shit. No radio, no television, no nothing except listening to some old albums from Darnell's massive CD collection. He tried to look out by steering our conversations about hip-hop's latest away from the obvious taboo. Occasionally, he'd slip though and leave a copy of *The Source* or *XXL* lying around, which I would pick up and shove to the bottom of the recycle pile before I got tempted to open it and stumble across something about Explicit Content. I walked by newsstands like a zombie, forcing my eyes away from the glossy pages that hung on display. I even stopped reading the newspaper because I was afraid I'd give in to the urge to flip to the gossip page and be punished with a huge photo of Leila with an article touting her as the next best thing in hip-hop. I was on a slow roll with my own stuff and hardly needed to put current fact to recent memory.

Eventually my material got tight enough to go back into the studio, but Darnell and I ran through the money I had saved quickly. So one day he propositioned me after we finished my second new cut. "Cassie, there's a major open mic competition at the 205 Club at the end of June, and you gotta register for it," he said as he lowered the playback of my latest track. "All kinda VIPs are gonna be up in that piece. You gotta cut at least one more track for a demo, get a few copies pressed, and perform the hell outta your best song that night."

"I'm not ready," I said. Every word seemed to scale up the soft lining of my throat and claw its way past my lips.

"Hell, yeah, you ready, girl! And I'm not gassin' you. I wouldn't say it if I truly didn't believe it."

"No way I can have the money in time. Unless I stopped paying rent." I immediately recognized that last remark as something Leila might say, and I regretted it the second I said it.

Especially when Darnell jumped on it like Ben Wallace on a rebound. "Well, Cassandra, you know if we were kickin' it, I wouldn't charge you rent," he said in that way dudes do when saying something they mean but want to be able to front like a joke if they don't get the response they want. So I faked this laugh as if Darnell was just kidding. He took the hint and changed his proposition. "Or you can let me manage and produce you. We'll sign a contract, do it all on the up and up. You focus on making your art, and I handle all the business."

"Meaning?"

"I'll finance your joint in return for part ownership of your publishing and a percentage of royalties. After I recoup expenses, obviously."

I liked that less than the idea of sleeping with him. Don't get me wrong. Darnell was a cool guy. And not bad looking at all. Like an older version of the light-eyed kid who dies in *Light It Up* except his eyes had both the shine and scuff of an eight ball. But sister in this can't, business and pleasure like that, especially one in my predicament. Bad enough I was already sacrificing my process by cutting a demo instead of releasing an independent album. Giving up control over my music in exchange for the money to make it had to be a last resort.

"Let me think about it, Darnell," I said with no intention of doing so. "Our current arrangement may not be ideal, but it works for me."

Darnell adjusted the faders on his Mackie CR-1604 and cut my playback. "To be straight up with you, Cassie, it's no longer working for me. Now, I don't charge you what I could get for room and board seeing we're friends and all, but I've put a lot of work into you and Leila for almost nothing 'cause I believed in y'all. Then Leila bounced on you and she's on the brink of blowing up, and what have I got to show for that? Still, I stick with you, Cass, because I know wherever Leila goes, you can and then some. I just can't afford to lose another year waiting for that to happen."

Unless I was fucking him. Then he'd wait two or three years. Shit, I'd be the one waiting while he tended to his paying customers, most of whom I realized within weeks of living with him were drug dealers with delusions of being the next B.I.G. All cash, no skills. But I decided better to keep such thoughts to myself. "Since we're friends and all, you'll give me until the competition to try and get the money for this demo, right?"

"No doubt. No doubt," Darnell said, voice giddy but eyes hard.

I'd rather give up the whole rap game before I signed away to Darnell any rights to my creative property after he flipped the script on me like that. That'd be as bad as crawling to Leila and begging her to lend me the money. Not that I didn't crawl somewhere else.

Between Darnell's crib in Astoria, Queens, and Genevieve's co-op in the South Bronx, there are twenty-seven train stops. I knew this because I fought to not jump off and turn back at every one. I only hollered on her birthday and Christmas and days like that. A week in advance, I would send flowers in a pretty vase or a gift certificate from someplace like JCPenney, and then I would call on the day in question to see if she got it. Genevieve then would take the opportunity to get on my case about my career or education or lack thereof, and I'd bite my tongue so hard I would start wondering if not telling her off was the true gift.

Luckily, I had not slipped during my funk and remembered to follow through that past Mother's Day. I gave her a call and got the machine. Happy to get off so easy, I wished her a happy Mother's Day and hung up. The second I did I realized that I had not given her my new number. But if I had called her back to do so, she'd ring Darnell's phone out the jack until she finally cornered me and badgered me into giving her an explanation I wasn't ready to offer. I still wasn't, but handling my business had come down to this.

You've probably heard of my mom or would recognize her if you saw her. When she was about my age, she became a star with a breakthrough role in this independent movie. You know those movies where some guy does time, comes home to the 'hood, and tries to stay straight but his friends keep trying to pull him back into the game? *Repeat Offender* is one of those joints except the guy's a gal and my mom played her. Yeah, my mother's *that* Genevieve Rivers.

According to reviews of *Repeat Offender*, my mother was supposed to beat Halle to that historic Oscar. Even the few movie critics who weren't blown away by the film said her performance kept it from playing like a television movie of the week. The fat one with the glasses on TV said Genevieve had "Josephine Baker's beauty, Pam Grier's edge, and Dorothy Dandridge's vulnerability" and called her an actress to watch. When I read that in my mother's scrapbook, I rented a few movies like *Foxy Brown* and *Carmen Jones* and I had to admit that her hype was on point.

But even though she signed with a major Hollywood agency and moved to L.A., my moms never blew up. After carrying her first movie, Genevieve never got to play the lead again. In the eight joints she made, if she wasn't the girlfriend to some Black dude in a crime flick, she was the best friend to the suffering white chick in a tearjerker. Her agent was always pushing white actresses for the juicy roles Genevieve wanted. One of them's even on the A-list this very day, but out of respect for my moms, I'm not gonna tell you the bitch's name. Suffice it to say that Genevieve's right when she says, "She's not an actress but a personality, and the difference in skill required is immediately obvious." She's not just hatin'. It's true. If this A-list chick were a sister, she'd be winding on a roadie in a 50 Cent video.

Anyway, when Genevieve realized that her agent wasn't pushing her like his white clients, Moms started going to auditions on her own. She mingled with mail clerks, administrative assistants, whoever could give her scripts and tell her where to be when. When her agent found out, he dropped her, telling folks she was *arrogant* and *difficult*. No other agency picked her up, and after two years of washing dishes at a soul food restaurant in Watts, Genevieve moved back to New York City, got a diploma in paralegal studies at NYU, and now works for an entertainment lawyer who ain't Donald Passman but heads in the industry know and respect him. In fact, that copy of *Confessions of a Record Producer* I read was his. My moms borrowed it from the office to discourage me, but it didn't work out that way.

I learned all this about my moms only through my own research. Between reading old gossip columns on the Internet and eavesdropping on Genevieve's conversations with my aunt Patricia (she had moved to L.A. with my mother and stayed behind when she met my uncle Marques), I pieced together the truth. Genevieve doesn't even know that I've seen her scrapbook. Once when Aunt Treece's family was visiting for Christmas, she came to Leila's apartment, brought the scrapbook with her, and made me swear that I would not tell Genevieve that she had shown it to me. Aunt Treece's cool, trying to mediate between my moms and me. Telling Genevieve to be more supportive of my goals while trying to make me understand that my moms just doesn't want me to go through the disappointments she did.

If you're wondering about my pops, according to Genevieve, he ain't worth a fleeting thought because he bounced after he knocked her up. Supposedly, he returned for a minute when he got word Moms gave birth. But when he arrived at the hospital and found out I was a girl, he turned back around and left for good. Leila swears my father's one of my mother's costars, a famous director or producer or someone else big in movies. One day she was making me sit through *Glitter* when she suddenly shouted, "The *güero* agent! That's who your father is, Cassie. He did your moms like Mariah's father in the movie, and that's why she doesn't want to tell you who he is." That Genevieve's afraid I'll pack up my shit, move to L.A., track him down and, once he saw that I could rhyme, he'd put me on and we'd become mad tight and famous and all that. Yeah, right. There's no way in hell my father's a white man, let alone someone with bank or connections. My father's probably some dude my mother fucked in the mailroom to get her hands on a script.

That's why I don't think much about the man myself. I got better things to do. Knowing she'll never know who her own father is, Leila was obsessed with this nonexistent search for mine. She never understood how I could not care. If I did, where would I start? Whatever Genevieve knows she won't tell me. She didn't even give me the cat's name. Leila said, "You know when we blow up he's gonna reappear, right? He's gonna want to reclaim you as his daughter. What you gonna do then?" I told her when we got to that bridge, I'd burn it.

Right now I had another one to cross. I made my way toward my mother's new crib in the South Bronx. Folks think this part of the city still looks like a battlefield in the crack wars when the truth is the government's been hooking up this area with new two- and three-family houses and co-op apartments. If you're lucky, a thousand bucks will buy you one of those walk-in closets that fronts for an apartment in Manhattan. In the Boogie Down, a G will get you two bedrooms and a kitchen that doesn't require you to keep your refrigerator in the living room. When the time comes, I'd consider moving back here, maybe even buying a house in this neighborhood. Guess it would depend if Genevieve could be proud to tell the neighbors that the famous rapper across the street was her daughter. Or at least not ashamed. I'd soon find out if she had gotten any closer to that bottom line.

Genevieve doesn't play. The second she saw me through her video screen standing on her doorstep unannounced, she knew I had something important to tell her. I hit the intercom, and a few seconds later she buzzed me into the building without a word. Which meant she felt entitled to command me to take a seat at the kitchen table like a kid coming home to eat after playing in the street all afternoon.

"What kind of tea would you like?" Genevieve said in the same formal tone she asked callers to her law office *And what is the case number on that matter?* She poured filtered water into the stainless-steel teakettle she probably bought with the Macy's gift certificate I sent her for Mother's Day.

I took that as a good sign, so even though I don't drink tea, I asked, "What do you suggest?"

"I have Darjeeling green, Kashmiri chai, Nilgiri black . . ." Genevieve opened the kitchen cabinets to reveal a shelf full of small glass jars with cork lids and neatly handwritten labels with the name of the loose tea it contained. Leila briefly dated this guy who worked for this tea company, so for Christmas I bought and sent Genevieve a gift basket with five different kinds of Indian tea, gourmet cookies, and these cute straws filled with honey. She pulled down a jar marked *Kopili Assam* and spooned a few leaves into a diffuser. I stood up, opened another cabinet, and selected two teacups and saucers. As I lined them along the counter, she asked, "So why would you come here unannounced after not returning my call on your birthday?" Before I could explain, she added, "Your aunt sent you a gift card from Los Angeles, and it gets sent back with 'addressee unknown,' and you call me from a blocked number on Mother's Day. What's going on with you, Cassandra? Tell me the truth and tell me fast. I have a block association meeting in a half hour about that lazy new mail carrier who keeps sticking the wrong mail in the wrong boxes and expects all of us to do this damned job for him."

Genevieve Rivers is a straight shooter and I'm her daughter, so I said, "I need some money." Then I quickly added, "Not a lot. I just want to borrow a few hundred."

"For what?" Of course she wanted to know that, but that hadn't stopped me from hoping she wouldn't ask if I made it clear it was just a loan.

And it didn't stop me from getting annoyed that she asked me that when she already knew the answer. "You know what for, Mom."

The teapot whistled, and it was on. "Cassandra, you did not

come here to borrow money for this rap music of yours. What happened? Did you lose your job?"

"No, Mom. In fact, I've been putting in mad overtime lately. . . ."

" 'Mad overtime'?" Genevieve said as she poured hot water through the diffuser and into the teacup. "Just what is 'mad overtime'?"

"Listen to me. I had to move out of Leila's apartment, which means . . ."

My mother slammed the pot down on the counter. "No wonder when I called you on your birthday the phone just rang and rang and rang. That crazy girl probably recognized my number and didn't want to answer to me. Did one of her roughneck boyfriends get fresh with you?"

I picked up the pot and poured the second cup of tea. "No, nothing like that. Leila got a record deal with Explicit Content, and I wasn't part of it, that's all." I grabbed both cups and carried them to the table. It was hard enough to admit this without my mother staring into my face. When I opened the refrigerator for the milk, I paused to collect myself even though the carton was right in front of me.

"Cassandra, close that refrigerator. Maybe you do that where you live, but don't do it in this house," Genevieve said. I pulled the milk out of the refrigerator while she plunked a jar of sugar and several of those honey straws on the table. We both sat and she continued. "I'm not surprised that girl left you high and dry at the first opportunity, because she's always been a little hustler. Why you refused to see that, Cassandra, I'll never know, because I raised you better than that. Time'll prove though that whatever boat Leila just had to jump aboard without you is bound to shipwreck. Knowing that girl, she probably got herself into some ugly little situation you'll be glad passed you by."

She badmouthed Leila for another ten minutes, and I didn't know what hurt the most. To hear all the terrible things Genevieve always said about Leila again to now agree with most of them. To eat my words when I didn't agree because I was too desperate to defend Leila like I usually would. Or to discover that when Genevieve made unfair exaggerations or said ugly untruths about Leila I still had a small urge to defend her after all she did to me. As my stomach knotted, I remembered why I don't drink tea. I hate it without milk, but I might as well take it with acid as far as my stomach was concerned. Worse of all, it reminded me of how Leila always made coffee for us in the morning—*café con leche* for her, no milk with sugar for me.

Noticing that I had stopped drinking and was rubbing my belly, my mother asked me what was wrong. When I told her, she tried to get me to spend the night. Unable to bear any more rants about Leila or repeat my plea for a loan, I insisted on going home. If I was going to sleep in a room that wasn't decorated with me in mind, I'd rather it be at Darnell's than in my own mother's co-op.

As I placed the dishes in the sink and washed them, Genevieve left the room. She returned and handed me two white caplets and an envelope that contained Aunt Treece's gift card and a check from her for five hundred dollars. "I'm giving you this because you've been making an honest living all this time and you didn't lie to me about what it was for," Genevieve said. "But this is the first and last loan I'm going to give you for your little rap hobby, so don't come back here for any more money unless you're going back to school. And this is a loan, Cassandra. I expect you to repay it in full within six months. But I won't charge you interest. Consider this your birthday present."

I didn't ask what my original birthday present had been. "OK, Mom. Thanks. 'Bye." I pecked her on the cheek and walked out the door.

I was halfway down the block when I realized that I still had not given her my new address and number. I was too busy withholding details about the recent Leila drama to offer that information, and Genevieve was too busy delivering Anti-Leila Lecture No. 1,001 to ask for it. So I just kept on toward the subway.

Even though I already knew there were twenty-seven stops between my mother's co-op and Darnell's house, I counted them again just to be sure. Something that kept my mind off the searing in my belly until the medication kicked in. That and the feeling that even though Genevieve had given me some money without my pleading and even seemed to miss me a little, I still hadn't gotten what I really wanted.

CHAPTER 8

THE ASHANTI PRINCIPLE

I peeked at the judges' table through a hole in the curtain that started as a cigarette burn and had grown into a full-fledged rip, most likely because of other aspiring rappers before me who had done the same thing. Darnell insisted I needed to spend a hundred bucks to enter this bullshit competition only to be judged by a panel of nobodies: an associate editor from that so-called "owner's manual to the streets" *CRED* magazine who resembled Big Daddy Kane in a do-rag, the head of A and R at the vanity label of the latest flash in the pan to go platinum, and this actor who played the same deranged gangsta in every straight-to-video movie set to a rap soundtrack. The worse of hip-hop gone commercial personified in full effect. Even the hostess was this one-hit wonder from the early nineties named Lite Spice who was only gonna come back when her Duran Duran hairdo did. Sometimes that Darnell didn't know whether to scratch his watch or wind his ass.

And because I listened to him, I was backstage at the 205 Club with twenty-four wanna-bes. I could tell who they hoped they sounded like just by how they dressed. Dudes wearing cotton T-shirts like they were made of silk were fixing to be the next Jay-Z, while all the females with denim sets and matching caps were praying they reminded everyone of Missy Elliott. I didn't even want to think what they thought of me in my not-that-mini black leather skirt, black-and-white camouflage sleeveless tank knotted at the hip, and low-heeled gladiator sandals. I should have known this competition was tepid when all you had to do to be down was drop the outrageous fee. No tape, no audition, no nothing. If you had a C-note and were one of the first twenty-five to respond to the call, you could be Coolio reincarnate and get to compete.

The only reason I decided to go through with it was because if I at least placed third I could get my money back. Regardless of the event, the 205 crowd was always large and live, and I knew if I didn't test my new material, I would think myself a coward for days. Me and the other rappers just milled wordlessly around backstage behind fake smiles and side glances. One Angie Martinez type gave me a genuine hello when she caught me looking at her. I didn't mean to stare at her. It's just standing there squinting through her own hole in the curtain and filing her inch-long nails, she reminded me of a timid version of Leila. Relieved that she didn't make a fuss, I wished her luck and turned back to my chosen hole in the curtain.

A few minutes later, a girl with a clipboard and a walkie came backstage, went to each contestant, and scribbled information on an index card. When she got to me, she put the index card she had just filled under the stack and asked, "And you are . . . ?"

"Cassandra Rivers."

She found my name on a list between her cards. "Sabrina Steelo?" I nodded and she grinned at me. "I like that. It's different. How'd you come up with it, if you don't mind my asking?"

"*Charlie's Angels.*" I usually volunteer the full explanation, but I wanted her to go away. Her presence made my participation official, and it bothered me that I was getting nervous about competing alone, bullshit competition or not.

But the girl just wrinkled her nose. "There was a Sabrina in the movie?" She wrote a number eleven on a ribbon with a safety pin and handed it to me. Eleven was good—it was good to fall in the middle. Judges were hard to please at the extremes. At the start of a competition, they're wide-awake with impossible standards. By the end, they're too soft with exhaustion. In both cases, I'd have to dress like Trina but flow like Eve to stand out let alone place.

"No, in the original TV show. Sabrina was the smart one, remember?" I said as I pinned my ribbon to the knot on my hip. "She usually solved the crime."

"Oh, yeah. I watched a marathon on TV Land. The tall, skinny one with the short, dark hair. How come she never wore a bikini like the other, pretty ones?" I was back to wanting her to go away, so I ignored her. But then she asked, "What's the name of the song you're gonna perform?"

"I haven't decided." Which was true. Darnell insisted that I do "God Don't Like Ugly," the rawest of my anti-Fatal joints. He even hounded me to mention her by name, both stage and real, but I didn't want to go there in my first solo appearance. It wasn't typical of me, and I didn't want to misrepresent myself, especially if I came off like the first no-name hater to trash the new raptress two seconds after she reached Billboard's Top 40. I only memorized "God Don't Like Ugly" because I started to rhyme it whenever I felt tempted to read a magazine, surf the web, or otherwise seek information about Leila.

The girl mumbled something and drew a line under my name on the index card. "Well, how do you want to be introduced?" I had given that no thought. Leila usually handled all that, usually off the cuff. She rocked that sound bite shit. She was the style and I was the substance, and remembering that made my jaw ache with anger. "Hello? How do you want Lite Spice to introduce you?"

I stuttered something about being from the birthplace of hip-hop when the Angie Martinez lookalike began to squeal and jump up and down. "Oh, my God! I think I saw G Double D!" Chaos broke as all the other contestants raced for the curtain and began to fight over holes to peek through while the Angie chick tried to pinpoint G's location. "To the right, like four tables in. He's wearing a black suit. No wait. I think it's navy."

When a few of the guys tried to leave backstage, the girl gathering information from us got militaristic. "Don't even think about leaving this area unless you want to be disqualified," she yelled before she went to investigate. Everyone started babbling about how if it was truly G Double D, that would make the entry fee worth it, how you could win even if you lost, and all that. Soon the girl returned and said, "Y'all some lucky people because G Double D is definitely in the house."

Chicks squealed and jumped up and down while dudes clapped and slapped high fives. As I looked for him myself, all I wondered was if Leila was there, too. Was she going to do a surprise performance of her single with Hi-Jack? Or maybe a solo performance of the first track from her album in progress? Hard as I tried, I could not make out G Double D in the crowd, probably because all those late nights writing under the dim lights in Darnell's kitchen had affected my eyesight. And the last thing I felt was lucky.

I searched the backstage crowd and tracked down the girl with the clipboard bragging into her radio about how all the phone and fax calls she had made paid off because a notable like G Double appeared. "You didn't finish taking my information," I told her.

"I know, honey. I'll be with you in a minute."

She tried to turn away from me and I grabbed her arm. "A minute is all I need, so you might as well take it down now." The girl looked at me as hard as I was holding on to her. She slid her pen from out behind her ear. "Get a fresh card." She glared at me but did what I said. "Sabrina Steelo, number eleven. I hail from the birthplace of hip-hop and I'm performing the first single of my independently produced debut called "God Don't Like Ugly." I dedicate it to all the sistas out there who ever survived a bitch like this."

* * *

Having become one of those Erykah Badu–India.Arie types, Lite Spice cleaned up my intro, but it still managed to get the crowd's attention. Luckily, Darnell brought the music for "God Don't Like Ugly" just in case he convinced me to do it. I had two minutes to perform and the clock would not start until I cued the DJ.

So when I got onstage by myself for the first time, I vowed that I would not start until I located G Double D. When I performed with Leila, I never looked into the crowd. The fact that I could not see faces in the audience is precisely what made my stomach tumble. So I would focus on Leila as we crisscrossed the stage, drawing my energy from her. Whether she was with G or not, I needed to concentrate on a face that would stir something deep within my gut besides nervousness.

As I made my way across the stage, I looked in the direction that Leila's shyer twin described. He was at a table surrounded by three standing bodyguards emptying the once full tables behind them. G crossed his legs and clasped his hands around his knee, the dimmed spotlight above him glistening both against the platinum cable chain around his neck and the matching watch on his wrist. The Fendi sunglasses he never rolled without dangled from the breast pocket of his Zegna suit. Within seconds I saw nothing but G Double D. Just as Lite Spice climbed back onstage to check on me, I cued the DJ and launched into "God Don't Like Ugly."

> God don't like ugly, but she loves Bri Steez
> who came to reign on dames like these.
> God don't like ugly, but she loves Bri Steez,
> And I came to reign over skeez like these.

By the second line of the chorus, the crowd—especially the sisters—was with me. Including G Double D. And that's when I decided that whether I won or not, whether Leila was in the house or not, I was going to step to him one way or the other.

The guy that took first deserved it, no doubt, and I'll be checking for him. But some twisted judgment awarded second to this cat that sounded like Mase on helium. No, he wasn't the worst one of all, but I choked him as did four other contestants. I swore they gave me third place on some gotta-have-a-girl-finalist bullshit, which would've sucked if not for the two-hundred-fifty-dollar prize.

That and getting access to G Double D. After giving daps to Darnell's production, collecting my trophy and check, I joined Darnell at a table not too far from where G sat now with three clubrats. D babbled on about how to approach the representative from the no-name label, but everything he said went through one ear out the other as I kept my eyes on G's every move. Lite Spice officially ended the contest and announced open mic, but after the second *American Idol* reject shot feedback through the mic, G Double D signaled for the check. I jumped to my feet and torpedoed toward him.

"Cassie, where you going?" asked D. I ignored him, my feet betraying my heart's warning to stop.

Confusing me for a disturbed fan, one of his bodyguards jumped in front of me. Intent on my mission, I forgot who I was dealing with and tried to step around him like a car jutting out of a sidewalk driveway. For that he grabbed my arm and twisted it behind my back. The pain shot tears to my eyes, but I called, "G!" He ignored me. "Nigga, you better answer me!" He gave me a quizzical look as his bodyguard dragged me from the table. "You owe me at least that much."

At that point Darnell had run up to the bodyguard, "C'mon, bro, you know it ain't necessary to treat the lady like that."

Then G recognized me. As a finalist in the contest or as Fatal's former partner, I couldn't tell, but he surely did. He said, "Let 'er go, dawg. I need to buy this sista a drink."

His thug did as commanded. As I rubbed my arm, I said, "Obviously, you don't learn from experience, no matter how much it costs," referring to the last time G Double D had to pay an "undisclosed settlement" to some cat his guards manhandled in a club.

"I was on vacation when that shit happened," he grunted.

"Sabrina Steelo, have a seat," G Double D said as he gestured to the seat across from him. Still gripping my shoulder, I did as he asked while his trio of hoochies glared at me. "What can I get you to drink, winner? Sky's the limit."

Uninvited and unaddressed, Darnell took a seat and began to speak, but I cut him off. "Why'd you sign Fatal without me?" Before I could stop them, tears were skiing down my face that had nothing to do with the pain inflicted by G's bodyguard. The more I cursed myself for crying, the harder the stream. So I cleared my throat and prayed that it would not crack. "You think I'm such a winner, why didn't you sign me with or without Fatal?" G was about to answer when I motioned him to stop and pointed at his hoochies. "This is a private conversation." Bad enough I was crying in front of G and all these strange hoods and tricks. I was damned if he was going to trash my craft in their presence, too, even if it was all bullshit.

"Ayo, Freight," G called to the guard who had fucked up my arm. "Show the ladies to the limo." His head hooch, who looked just like Alicia Keys right down to the waist-length braids, sucked her teeth. G mimicked her and everyone except me laughed. "If that's how you feel, you can hop the A train, beeyatch." Freight led the women out, then G turned to Darnell. "Thought you said this was a private conversation."

Truth is I really didn't want Darnell there 'cause this was between G and me, but asking him to step didn't sit right with me, either. After all D had done—from letting me stay at his crib to stepping to Freight when he put his hands on me—I felt obligated

to let him stay. Despite my hesitancy to partner with him professionally or personally, the man had proved to be a friend when I
had none. "He stays," I said.

G shrugged and summoned the waitress to order a bottle of
Krug champagne. "Any and every punk drinking Cristal, it's beyond passé," he explained.

Darnell said, "I hear you, man."

I wiped those stupid tears off my face and leaned forward. "Are
you going to answer my question or what?"

"I ain't gonna front, Sabrina. You got skills. Your flow's rough,
but you can work on that. Lyrically, you're tight. Much more than
Fatal."

The waitress came and poured us all champagne. While Darnell and G quickly grabbed their frosty glasses, I let mine sit. "So
why'd you sign her and only her?"

"C'mon, now, it ain't like the girl don't have no talent. She's
lazy is all. The girl's so lazy, sometimes I gotta fight to get the bitch
to eat."

Now that didn't sound like the Leila I knew who loved to brag
that she can eat all her beloved *arroz con gandules* and never gain
an ounce on her size-two frame. But that was irrelevant to this
conversation. "You don't have to tell me she's lazy," I said. "Did
she tell you she wrote all those rhymes?"

"Oh, she told me you wrote most of 'em, but I ain't believed
her," G said. He took another sip of Krug. "I thought that she was
bullshitting me 'cause she wanted to bring you along for the ride.
Now that I've seen y'all do your thing apart, the truth's evident."

His answer shocked me. Why would Leila tell him the truth
only to lie to me about it? Did I piss her off that much? Then I figured she probably came clean after our big fight because she had
to warn him about my threats. And G had no reason to admit that
he came to this knowledge after he signed her, so I let that go. "Still
doesn't explain why you couldn't sign us both."

"Look, Sabrina, I needed a solo female artist . . ."

"So why Fatal instead of me?"

" 'Cause I needed someone who was gonna stand out from all the other sisters already out there without having to invest thousands in promotion to do that." G leaned forward to meet me in the middle of the table. "Quick, Sabrina. Name the top three female rappers at this moment."

I rattled off their names like I was reciting the alphabet. "Lil' Kim, Missy Elliott, and Eve."

An impressed G grinned. "Now what do all those women have in common?"

"Besides the obvious?"

He snickered at my question. "Baby girl, it's so obvious, it isn't."

We sat quiet for a moment. Then Darnell guessed, "They're all Black?"

G Double D clapped once and pointed at him. "There you go. I needed a female who was hot and cute but not Black. I wasn't out there looking specifically for a Hispanic chick. I was open to everyone—Asian, Arab . . . Hell, I would've killed to sign a tight little Pocahontas from one of them reservations upstate and shit 'cause we haven't heard from Solé in a minute. Anyone 'cept a white girl, 'cause I just know every other label's out searching from here to Bubblefuck for the female Eminem. And then I discovered Leila." G poured a few more drops of champagne into my still full glass until it overflowed and dribbled to the white linen tablecloth. "And I couldn't sign you as a duo 'cause that was just gonna dilute her impact and defeat my purpose, know what I'm sayin'? It's business, Sabrina, not personal."

I lurched back and banged my fist on the table. "Don't give me that shit! You didn't just break up a duo, man. You came between me and my best friend." I felt the tears coming again so I grabbed the champagne and tossed it back hard.

"And you fucked with her paper," Darnell added.

I slammed the champagne glass back onto the table. "Tell me one thing, G. If you couldn't sign me 'cause you didn't want to 'dilute her impact,' then why is she on a track by everyone else at Explicit Content? Why haven't you released her on a solo track? If Leila's all that, what's taking you so long to drop her album?"

"Preach," Darnell said.

I wanted to see if G would drop hints about whether or not he was planning to use any of my material. Darnell was right; he did fuck with my paper. If he was going to use my shit, he needed to compensate me. And then if Leila did come out and dominate the charts, I could leverage that to get a deal with another label. Better yet, I would have the satisfaction of knowing that although Leila topped the charts alone, she did not get there without me. Best of all, she would know it and she would know that I knew it.

But G just gave a shady laugh. "Let's just say I'm applying the Ashanti principle on this one."

"Excuse me?"

"I'm featuring her on all these cuts by my other, established artists so that by the time she drops her own joint, everyone will already know who Fatal Beauty is." He raised his champagne glass to take a sip, but then paused as Darnell and I exchanged skeptical glances. "Don't get it twisted. Irv Gotti stole that concept from me when we were playing blackjack in Atlantic City one night, the muthafucka. Reason I ain't blow up his spot is because that's the way it is in this business. My bad for getting too chummy with a competitor and running off at the mouth." G raised his glass as if to toast me. "You keep doing your thing, Sabrina. Learn from your mistakes and emulate the best, and you'll go far in this industry. I hope so, 'cause I like the way you handle yourself and I'd hate to be wrong about you."

That told me all I could stand to know. With unsolicited advice like that, I didn't dare ask about my material. But I couldn't lose face. "You're already wrong about me," I said to G as I jumped to my feet to leave. Darnell grabbed my wrist, but I yanked it away. Then onstage Lite Spice took the mic.

"Ladies and gentlemen, as you know we have a distinguished

guest in the house—G Double D." The spotlight glared over us as the audience clapped and hollered. Darnell pulled me back into my seat. "But the surprises ain't hardly over," Lite Spice continued. "Here to perform their latest single *Spit It to Hit It,* the 8MM Posse"—the din grew as the crowd jumped to its feet and began to stomp—"and the first hip-hop diva on the Explicit Content label"—the roar was so loud I could barely hear Lite say her name. —"Fatal Beauty!"

The rising curtain pulled the crowd to the stage. The three roughnecks of the 8MM Posse did the usual Timbos draggin' bullshit, and then Leila appeared from backstage wearing a purple mesh bustier, low-rider jeans with FATAL and BEAUTY painted down each thigh, and purple calf-high boots with cowboy fringes and four-inch heels. The outfit was pure Leila, but not much else was. She walked toward the center of the stage when it was more her steelo to skip toward a cheering crowd. Her naturally ruby lips and cheeks caked in lavender makeup gave Leila's tan skin a jaundiced hue under the harsh stage light. Instead of spitting her lyrics with punctuating jabs in the air like the Fatal Beauty I knew, she just stood in one spot, gripped the mic with both hands like a pole on a rushing subway, and stumbled over the chickenhead lyrics that I know Hi-Jack put into her mouth. The crowd's excited roar subsided into confused murmurs.

G finally put down the Krug. "What the fuck . . . ?"

After a few random hisses threatened to erupt into a full chorus of boos, one of the posse members pulled Leila behind him and began a weak freestyle. The crowd's positive reaction proved that they much preferred to hear an endless string of nigga this and fuck that than watch a female rapper struggle with weak albeit familiar verses they already knew from the radio. That's why I couldn't get any satisfaction from Leila's embarrassment.

G wasn't feeling it either. I looked for his reaction, and we caught eye. Then he looked away and mumbled, "Maybe I did sign the wrong bitch."

CHAPTER 9

PUNCHANELLA

Despite the weak performance, fans rushed the stage. Explicit Content bodyguards headed to the front to protect Leila from a group of girls squealing and waving posters, CD singles, and even napkins for her to sign. Someone shoved Leila between the bodyguards and the girls crowded around her. The Leila I knew loved to mingle with her female fans, and not just because a flamboyant and foul-mouthed female rapper like her depended on female acceptance to succeed. After speaking to a young girl who approached her after our first Da Corridor event at the Nuyorican Poet's Café for an hour, Leila convinced herself that each and every girl who followed her saw herself in Leila and she felt obligated to connect with them no matter how briefly. "Why else would they be so desperate to talk to me when I ain't shit?" she said. "If fifteen seconds of my time might keep one of them on track or even put a smile on her face for the first time in days, I gotta give it, Cass."

But this Leila didn't sign a single autograph let alone call any of the girls *mamita,* stroke their hair, or compliment their clothes. Instead she looked frightened of them. She stammered an apology and clawed her way behind the bodyguards even as the girls wailed her name and begged for a few more minutes of her time.

Observing this, G rose from the table in an angry fit. He instructed Freight's sidekick to jot Darnell's and my contact information and told us to expect an invitation in the mail. Then, with Freight in tow, he left us behind and made his way to the stage. Darnell turned to me and asked, "Wanna wait? Go backstage maybe?"

If the shoe were on the other foot, the last thing I would want Leila to do was roll up backstage even if it were just to see if I were all right. "Nah, let's go." But I had to get one last glimpse of her before I left. A short, muscular thug from the 8MM Posse grabbed Leila by the arm and hauled her over to G Double D as she stumbled in her boots. When they reached G, the 8MM cat handed her over to him like a dog on a leash.

I couldn't bare to watch any more. "Let's bounce," I told Darnell. And without a final look back, we left the club.

But I just couldn't get what happened out of my mind, either. It bothered me so much that I got blocked. Couldn't write, rehearse, or nothing. So I lapsed and started reading gossip rags and surfing the net, looking for information about Leila and Explicit Content. Somehow G Double D even managed to squash any negative coverage of the performance at the 205 Club. The label's site offered nothing but manufactured hype. Besides stills from the "Color Me Gully" video and shots from the inside of the remix CD, Explicit Content posted only one new photo of Leila—a huge picture of her dressed in a camouflage tank top (in shades of pinks instead of greens) with no bra and a matching skort. Attached to the leg jutting out of the skort's slit, she had a black pistol almost as thick as her slim thigh. The canned bio played up all the negative aspects of her background from her foster care history to her mom's overdose. It even said her father was a "South Bronx pimp," which she'd never told me, so I suspected the label concocted it to make Leila seem harder than she was.

I found not a single interview with her on the site, nothing with Leila's own words. Leila never felt much shame about her past. She felt it was what it was, and what it was wasn't on her. But just as much as she didn't hide her past, I never knew Leila to promote it either, because as she always said, "I ain't trying to keep past shit current." So I wondered how she felt about having all her old wounds on public display.

Then one day a blind item appeared in the *New York Post:*

> What struggling rap impresario is having trouble delivering on the buzz of his latest diva? The once reigning hip-hop mogul was hoping that the feisty femme he discovered underground would return his waning label to its glory days before the criminal exploits of his male artists put him in the red. But insiders say that the starstruck spitfire is more interested in playing Bonnie to one of her labelmates' Clyde than she is in completing tracks for her much hyped yet perpetually delayed debut.

I reread the article three times with different reactions. I just didn't believe it the first time I read it and tossed it aside as unsubstantiated gossip. A day or so later I dug it out of the recycle pile and read it a second time, recalling what Darnell told me about Explicit Content experiencing financial trouble. I wondered if, as the latest artist at the label, Leila had been set up to be the scapegoat for money problems that existed before her arrival. To be honest, the possibility pissed me off, especially since I could not imagine that Leila would be interested personally in any of those animals on the label. Well, maybe Primo, since the girl could not be alone. But the Leila I knew would not let a man come between her and hip-hop. After all, she told me to lose Kurt the first time I told her he seemed uninterested in my rhymes. So even if Primo was the Clyde in question, I doubted that Leila would get involved to the extent that she would sabotage the deal she cut off her best friend to get. By my final read, I felt nothing but smug at the thought that she had dropped me without a blink to go solo with a label that had no bank and now she might even take the fall for its failure.

About a week after the *Post* item appeared, Darnell and I received invitations to the Explicit Content party at the mansion in New Jersey. The front of the invitation mirrored the label's logo—a black and white parental advisory label—with the slogan underneath it in italics. So instead of saying *Not suitable for all listeners* like the real stickers do, it read instead *Not suitable for hatas.* On the flip side in silver letters, it read:

Join the **EXPLICIT CONTENT** *family*
In welcoming its newest member,
FATAL BEAUTY,
And celebrating her 23rd birthday
On Friday the 6th of July
At the **EXPLICIT CONTENT ESTATE**
Glen Ridge, New Jersey

The small print stated that G Double D would arrange for a fleet of limos to pick guests up at the Explicit Content loft in SoHo. Darnell got psyched, fantasizing about who might end up in our limo, the kind of connections we could make, and all that. Then he stopped in midsentence.

"Aw, Cassie, c'mon! You can't even be thinking of not going. Don't take this independent woman thing to ridiculous levels." He put his hands on my shoulders and said, "Here's your chance to let Leila know you gainin' on her."

"No, I'ma go, no doubt," I said. "I just don't want to rely on someone else for a ride." Darnell threw his hands in the air, and I slapped him in the arm with the invitation. "I can't help it. It's the way my mother raised me." I didn't tell him that I worried about having my hair and makeup judged. That I might blow the opportunity of a lifetime because I had no money for the right clothes. Most of all, for a reason I could not explain, the prospect of seeing Leila without knowing whether she saw me perform at the 205 Club and if she knew I had seen her made me uncomfortable. "I wish I knew what's up with Leila at Explicit Content before the party, 'cause I don't know if I should front like I don't know her or what," I said to Darnell. "What if I put my foot in my mouth when talking to some A and R exec?"

Darnell first gave a sympathetic nod but then shook his head. "All ya gotta do, Cassie, is do you. If it ain't about you, hush. If it's all about you, holla. The only preparation you need for that night is to be ready to spit on command." And then, without asking me for money for the deposit, he headed out to order rush copies of my three-track demo for the party that weekend. Sometimes it worked my nerves the way he acted like we were partners, and other times I thanked God I had Darnell in my corner 'cause that's exactly where I would be if it weren't for him. Alone in a corner. And I didn't even know where that corner might be.

Then I decided I had to talk to Leila before the party.

I didn't find the courage to head to the Upper West Side until the last minute. At almost ten o'clock on the night before the party, I finally took the subway into Manhattan. The night I left, Leila had locked herself in the bathroom to tend to her head and never came out to ask me for the keys. She probably had changed the locks, but I thought I'd take a chance that maybe she hadn't, since that kind of housekeeping was never her thing.

The weird thing about walking back into the apartment building was how it didn't feel weird at all. Even though it had been months since Leila had kicked me out and I had moved in with D, it still felt like home. The doorman, Phil, even said, "Cassandra, long time no see! Been busy? Been sick?"

"Yeah," I said to both his questions.

"And how's Leila? Haven't seen her in a while, either."

I let the elevator door close before I could answer. Not that I had an answer. And as I rode the elevator, I guessed that Leila had not told Phil, Renata, or any of the building employees that I no longer lived there. When I arrived on my old floor, I concluded that I was making a big deal over nothing.

I paused in front of the door, staring at the scratchy remnants of the stickers and ornaments Leila and I once put there. One day soon after I moved in with her, I came home from work to find a Trinidad flag sticker on one side of the peephole and a Puerto Rican flag on the other. While shopping she came across the Puerto Rican flag sticker and wanted it for the door, remembered that I mentioned in passing long ago that my mother's family was from Trinidad and decided she couldn't get hers and not mine. I laughed and called her crazy. A week later someone slipped a petition under our door signed by all the people on our floor, protesting the stickers, calling them *an inappropriate blight on the uniformity of our esteemed residence* and insisting that we take them down. Leila figured from the first name—that of the lady who lived directly across the hall and underpaid Renata—who had spearheaded the petition, and she wanted to go pound on her door and curse her out. I convinced her that if she wilded out like that they would get us kicked out of the building. With no other outlet for her rage, the girl stomped around the apartment cursing the neighbors at the top of her lungs in Spanish. I felt so bad about having to repress her rightful anger, I spent my next day off combing mom-and-pop shops in East Harlem and Flatbush, collecting postcards of C.L.R. James and Pedro Albizu Campos, coqui and bamboo magnets, and other knickknacks for Leila to pepper around our flags. All these were gone, and it surprised me that she would remove her things as well as mine. I picked at flecks of glue as I debated my next move.

At first I felt I should knock, but then what if she refused to open the door? I decided to try my key. If she was gonna wild out or call the police or some shit like that, she was going to do it regardless of whether she let me in or whether I let myself in. If my key worked, I could take her by surprise and force her to speak to me. I slipped my key into the lock and it clicked like it had a thousand previous times.

I opened the door and entered the pitch-black apartment. It had never occurred to me until then that she would not be there. I stood in the dark for a moment, alone with my disappointment. Or so I thought, until I heard a male moaning from the living room.

I tiptoed down the darkened hallway toward the living room. Not a single light on, but I knew some man was on the couch getting his. Whether he was getting it from Leila or giving it to himself, I was unsure. So I felt for the switch along the wall and clicked on the lights.

Diego was spread out on the sofa like a rag doll with a woman bobbing her head between his legs. A woman who wasn't Leila. She and Diego yelled and scrambled to put on their clothes. I just stood there and laughed at them until I noticed how much Diego's hoochie looked like Leila—same tawny skin, glassy eyes, and long auburn hair. But she had my height and none of Leila's presence. She just stood in the corner struggling to wipe her chin and put on her tank top at the same time.

Diego shoved his dress shirt into his designer slacks. "Cassandra, what are you doing here?"

"Looking for Leila. Where is she?"

My question confused him. He said something to the girl in Spanish and she trotted out of the room and into the bedroom. "I thought you knew. Leila doesn't live here anymore. She hasn't lived here for months now."

"Where she at, then?" But I already knew. What I didn't know was how it came about until Diego volunteered the answer.

"One day these two gorillas busted into my office and demanded that I break up with Leila and throw her out of the apartment," he said. He seemed so relieved to unload this secret, I ignored his racist comment so he would continue. "So now she lives in Glen Ridge with those gangsters on her label, Explicit Lyrics or whatever the hell it's called."

I searched for a reason to make my visit worthwhile. I asked Diego, "Did she leave anything behind?" At five-nine and a hundred thirty-five pounds, I'd never fit into any of Leila's clothes, but maybe she had left behind some of that expensive makeup that might go with my dark skin or some accessories I could work with whatever I decided to wear on Friday.

"There are some things on the bureau in the bedroom, but . . ." I headed to the bedroom and found his hoochie freshening her makeup at the vanity table that Leila once owned and had given to me. I snatched the compact out of her hand. The color was too light for me, but if I couldn't use it, she sure as hell wasn't going to either, so I shoved it in my pocket. Diego's girlfriend ran from the table like a little kid to snitch to Daddy about *esa maldita morena*. Leila had called me that at times, but it was always love.

I searched through the jewelry box. Leila had taken anything of value, leaving just the costume jewelry, most of which I'd bought for her. Because I was on a tight budget and would prioritize Genevieve's presents, I couldn't afford to buy Leila genuine jewelry for her birthday or Christmas. Instead I would buy her these colorful chokers with matching earrings and bracelets that went with her rainbow of outfits. I thought Leila loved them because she would wear them more often than any of the gold or silver her boyfriends would buy her. I scooped up a handful of necklaces and shoved them into my pocketbook when Diego and his new girlfriend reentered the bedroom and positioned themselves at the bedroom door.

"Cassandra, you need to leave now," he said all macho. I took my time sifting through the jewelry box for the earrings and bracelets. "And give me your key."

I fished through my pocket and found the key. I had no use for it anymore so why not give it to him? But when I saw that smug look on that Leila wanna-be's face, I realized the key had one last use. Some thugs crashed his office and forced him to cut loose his mistress, and the fool still had not changed the locks to his hoochie hideaway? Leila was right—the man was book smart but life dumb, and I decided to take advantage of it.

So I turned and headed toward the bedroom doorway, holding out the key. But when Diego reached for it, I pulled it back. "How much is it worth to you?" I said.

"I'm not going to pay you for what's rightfully mine," Diego yelled. "If you won't give it to me, I'll just change the locks."

"Which is stupid. Why go through all the time and trouble to give that money to a locksmith when you can give it to me now and be done with it all?"

"Get out, Cassandra."

Defeated, I walked out of the bedroom and down the hallway. I heard Diego and his hooch yammering in Spanish as they followed me to the door. When the bitch giggled, I wondered what Leila would do if she were in my shoes.

When I reached the apartment door, I turned around, looked Diego in the eye, and said, "I know who your wife is, too." Leila herself once tried tracking down Diego's wife out of sheer OWC—Other Woman's Curiosity—and realized she really didn't have enough information or know-how to find out who she was. But bluffing seemed to work for her that day at Darnell's.

And it worked for me. After Diego told his girlfriend to go back into the bedroom, he wrote me a check for five Gs and I handed him over the key to the apartment. And to my surprise, I didn't feel the least bit shady about it. In fact, as he was writing the check I told myself that if fate should ever place Diana in my path, I was gonna blow up Diego's spot any damned way. I never liked that racist bastard or the way he treated Leila like a social experiment. Especially the way he—with all his money and connections—replaced her with a new hood rat just when she needed him most, no questions asked. If nothing else, I'd do that just for her.

Even though I had a sudden influx of cash, I didn't run out to buy an expensive, brand-name outfit. Mostly because I had to hold on to as much of it as possible to pay to distribute my demo and similar expenses. Get Darnell off this partnership kick.

But now that I could get the right clothes, I was scared of wearing them the wrong way. Leila always teased me about my sense of style, saying I didn't have one. Not that I didn't keep up with the trends or wore socks with sandals or anything corny like that. She'd complain that I had no signature, whatever the hell that means. "It's not enough to make sure everything's cleaned and ironed and matched *y to' eso*," Leila'd say every time we got ready for a performance. "You gotta do something to make yourself stand out from everybody else who's wearing the same gear." I'd tell her that I did; I rhymed my ass off.

Still, I imagined Leila standing next to me in front of the mirror, replacing the choker around my neck with a scarf or dusting some glittery eye shadow along my cheekbone. "You know all the rules, Cass," I heard her say like she did the night of our last performance. "Now you have to learn the right way to break them."

So I knew that I had to step up my game for the Explicit Content party, but I wasn't sure how. Of course, I spent four hours in the beauty salon getting my hair and nails done. I even got my eyebrows waxed for the first time, something Leila did every other week. But as far as clothes were concerned, I was lost. So I went shopping for an outfit that I thought Leila would buy herself at what I liked to call a hooch boutique. You know the kind of store where every mannequin in the window is dressed like a chick on *Soul Train*.

I walked into this hooch boutique, and I'm not two seconds through the door when this Dominican girl swoops on me talking about, Can I help you? Ordinarily, I don't want help when I shop because usually the last thing they want is to help you. Following a sister around like a tail because they just know you're gonna boost something is their idea of Can I help you? Meanwhile, I can't tell you how many times I've gone into a place like that with Leila, and while the salesclerk helped me to death, she was cramming lingerie into her purse.

I was about to tell this girl that, no, she could not help me, when this silver halter caught my eye. I flipped it around and saw that it was backless save the strap around the waist. Exactly the kind of thing Leila would throw on without a second thought. I could wear it only if it grew a neck and sleeves and turned into black knit.

"I have this really important party to go to, and I have no clue what to wear."

"What kind of party?" she asked with a Dominican accent. "Where is the party?"

"A music industry thing."

She motioned for me to follow her and started walking through the clothes racks toward the back of the store. *"¿Y que clase de música?"*

"Hip-hop."

She lit up. *"Me encanta la hip-hop. Me gusta a ese tipo Petey Pablo y OutKast y . . .¡Primo! ¡Pero ese Primo es un chulo! Si, me encanta la hip-hop muchisimo."*

I was proud to understand what she said and to know she truly meant it. Most of all, I liked that she referred to hip-hop as a female. So I let her help me, after all, to the tune of three hundred dollars of Diego's money.

The salesclerk Yolanda had an older sister named Yeribel who had come to the states five years earlier and did hair and makeup at a nearby salon. She gave me her sister's card and told me to mention her name for a discount. I followed through, and it turned out for the best. Since I had no appointment during wedding season, I had to wait two hours for her to take me, but Yeribel hooked me up on some Tyra Banks shit. That meant impatient Darnell left without me to join the limo caravan from SoHo so I could arrive alone and no one would assume I was there with him or anyone else.

Before I ran out to meet the taxi I called, I took one last look in the hallway mirror of Darnell's house. Yolanda had really hooked me up, especially since I gave her such a hard time. If she had had her way, I'd have walked into that party dressed like a post-Mottola Mariah Carey. Girl held up this fire-engine-red top that looked like two headbands knotted into an X. I picked a mauve blouse with angel sleeves and ruffled collar, but Yolanda wasn't feelin' it. "That say Maria," she said as she folded her hands in mock prayer. "You wear Mariah." We finally comprised on a hot-pink off-the-shoulder top. Yolanda also sold me a pair of low-rise jeans with pink embroidered roses along the cuffs. At her suggestion, I bought a pair of silver sandals with low heels, and I topped it off with a silver choker with a faux tourmaline pendant that I had given to Leila on her birthday last year. I usually avoided pink, but Yolanda said it looked good on me because my skin was so dark and clear. I looked at my reflection and had to admit that Yolanda was right.

So right it scared me although I didn't know why.

Because my driver approached the Explicit Content mansion from a downhill back road, the first thing I saw was the oyster-shaped pool surrounded by several dozen guests in designer jeans and sundresses. Only Mariah Carey dressed in a bikini top and cutoffs sat with some friends at the end of the pool, flicking her toes across the water while sipping from a champagne glass. The 8MM Posse fought over a thick manual while Fat Joe fiddled at a giant steel grill. Before my cab turned the corner, I caught Ja Rule teasing Ashanti, chasing her across the lawn with a shaker yelling, "You don't want no brandy? Why you don't want no brandy? Yo, 'Shanti, what you got against brandy?" I laughed, and for the first time I thought that if all I got from this party was a blast, it'd be worth the forty-five-minute trip. Since I moved from Leila's, I rarely had a good laugh, let alone some fun.

But then the cab turned the corner, and my belly skipped at the sight of luxury cars lined down the street outside the iron gate. An armed guard approached my driver, who rolled down his window and handed him my invitation. The guard inspected it, handed it back, and waved us through the gate.

My driver pulled up the circular driveway overseen by several valets in tuxedos behind a Bentley that had just arrived. The Bentley stopped and out the driver's side climbed Jay-Z. Before a valet could bound over to the passenger side, Beyoncé opened her own door and stepped onto the asphalt. Wearing a simple black tank and jeans, hoop earrings and a bandanna, she was dressed even more casually than Jay but still radiated megawatts of stardom. When she reached Jay, he hooked his arm around her waist, and they trotted up the steps and into the mansion past a massive black flag with a silver X waving in the summer breeze.

"That's forty dollars, please," my driver said.

"OK." I glanced at myself in the rearview mirror and spotted a fleck of stray eyeliner at the corner of my eye. Although Yolanda used only quality brands, my lipstick had already begun to feather and beads of sweat curled the straightened hair on the nape of my neck. Although I had a fifty-dollar bill folded and pressed inside my palm from the moment I left Darnell's, I pretended to scour through my purse to buy myself some time. I even considered asking the driver to take me back to New York City.

Remembering that although I came alone, Darnell should already be there, I flicked off the eyeliner shaving, rubbed my lips together, and wiped the sweat off my neck. Then I paid my driver and climbed out of the cab. In the distance, a fleet of black limousines with silver Xs painted across their hoods parked in front of a four-car garage. As I drew closer to the French doors, the concrete facade could barely contain the sounds of hip-hop music and chatty guests. A doorman—a Black guy about my age—jogged past to open the door for me. "Thank you for coming," he said. When I looked into his face to thank him, his face fell with disappointment. Like he almost wanted to take back his well wishes because I was nobody. I kept my thanks to myself and walked into the house.

I followed a winding hallway lit with chandeliers and spotted with the occasional pairs and trios of guests beaming contact information between their handheld organizers, canoodling in archways, or otherwise distancing themselves from the noisy pack at the main scene.

I eventually arrived at a ballroom teaming with bodies swathed in an array of colors and metals. To my right a half-dozen *Coyote Ugly* sisters—some who even looked too young to drink legally—served up drinks and flirted with guests at a professionally stocked bar. To my left, an ivory spiral staircase led to another floor, but three bodyguards manned the steps to prevent guests from wandering upstairs.

Every face had graced a magazine cover or television screen or at least seemed like it should. The deeper I waded into the crowd, the more invisible I felt. And overdressed as ten dozen girls in outfits a yard of spandex shy of a bikini bounced around while "Spit It to Hit It" blasted through eight megaspeakers that dangled from the ceiling. I stopped halfway across the floor and looked up. The speaker above my head trembled as the song's bass seared through my body. Ugly thoughts of it crashing down on my head when Leila started her verse flashed through my mind. Eyes still fixed on the speaker, I stepped forward and right into Hi-Jack.

"Them shit's off the hook, right?" he said, pointing up at the ceiling with one hand and holding a flute of champagne in the

other. He handed it to me and stepped into my personal space. He
was so close I could smell the stale beer on his breath and the blunt
on his Rocawear terry jersey. I started wondering if enough alcohol
and reefer eventually would cause a chemical reaction to his platinum teeth, and Hi-Jack mistook my expression for interest. "I
had G import the ceiling panels from Australia, right. 'Cause they
specifically designed to keep the music in and all the other bullshit
noise out. I made sure they took everything into account for the
best possible acoustics, know what I'm sayin'? The carpeting and
windows we were gonna have installed, the ventilation system, alla
that." The man was talking interior decorating like he was planning a heist and suddenly I felt as half naked as all the other chicks
in the room. "Girl, don't be rude. Drink that shit," said Hi-Jack as
he motioned toward the flute in my hand.

Even though she never let me go nowhere, Genevieve taught
me to never accept a drink that I had not seen poured with my own
eyes. "I'm allergic to champagne."

"Sometimes people outgrow shit like that," the fool said. "Let's
see." He cackled like a warlock. "All the doctors up in this piece,
you ain't got nothing to worry about."

My eyes zipped through the crowd and I spotted Darnell.
While most of the male guests opted for muscle shirts, baggy
jeans, and chunky watches, D sported a silk shirt, fitted slacks,
and a sleek bracelet. Before I could tell Hi-Jack I had found my
boyfriend, the Alicia Keys lookalike with G Double D at the 205
Club danced into my line of sight, backing Darnell up against the
wall. I thought fast and told Hi-Jack, "Oh, yeah, like y'all need another scandal."

Hi-Jack put a swollen hand on the small of my back and whispered in my ear, "Scandal's my middle name." The skin on my
neck curdled. "At Explicit Content, the only bad publicity's no
publicity, know what I'm sayin'?"

A girlish voice spared my ear from a nibble I knew would turn
sloppy and painful. "Yo, Jack, G's looking for you." And there

stood Leila. Hi-Jack turned and looked to cut her in half. "Om's here! Go see for yourself if you don't believe me," she snapped at him. Hi-Jack dipped into the crowd, and we watched him in tense silence until he disappeared into a doorway under the ivory spiral staircase.

I finally croaked the obvious. "Happy birthday." It sounded more sarcastic than I intended. I was going for no emotion whatsoever.

And Leila gave me none right back. "Thanks." Even with the tension between us, I found her sullenness odd. Despite years of forgotten birthdays and secondhand Christmases, she loved holidays. To have a huge party in her honor swilling with the rich and ghetto fabulous was a fantasy realized. Suddenly, she smiled and nodded in the direction that Hi-Jack just took. "That your type now?"

"Please." I didn't know what else to say because I couldn't tell where she was coming from. She didn't sound jealous, so maybe Hi-Jack wasn't the label mate hinted at in the *New York Post's* blind item.

"You and Darnell kickin' it, then?"

"What?"

Leila sighed. "Good. I don't like him for you. You can do much better, and don't you forget it." She smiled at my outfit and said, "Especially if you're rolling like that nowadays." Her tone was more teasing than sarcastic, like the day she walked me from her projects to my block but less spirited. Not knowing whether to be encouraged or guarded, I waited for her to continue.

"I think it's really fucked up what happened at 205," she said. "You were better than the guy who won. If you had been a guy, that shit wouldn't have happened. And don't even get me started on the fool who came in second. I saw him gassing the chick who was coordinating the whole thing." She rambled on about all the things I'd suspected and had hated myself about that competition. So Leila had seen much more than I ever thought. My first instinct was to apologize about the song, but I squashed that immediately. Why should I apologize when I didn't know if she was trying to make peace or just gassing me like Mr. Second Place did the contest coordinator? And if Leila did want a ceasefire, was it because I impressed G with "God Don't Like Ugly" and that stressed her or because she was on some gracious-starlet-who-couldn't-be-bothered-with-the-also-ran shit? Or was she really sorry for what she did to me?

Then Leila said, "Look, Cassie, I know you had a conversation with G that night, and that's why you're here . . ." She stopped in midsentence as her eyes fell on the tourmaline pendant and then traveled to the matching earrings and bracelet.

Expecting her to claim the costume jewelry, I cut her off. "Where I belong," I said.

Leila held up her hands to stop me, and I noticed that her long acrylic nails were gone. Although she now sported a silver X on black polish over her natural nails, each was clipped and filed to the fingertip. "No, Cassie, you don't. Get that *Stubborn Look* off your face, forget that you're pissed at me, and listen to what I'm telling you."

"So you give me some dap I deserve, and I'm supposed to forget that you stabbed me in the back?" I said. "You'd probably front like you didn't even know me if you hadn't busted your man trying to kick game to me."

She started a heated answer when Hi-Jack and the 8MM Posse left the room under the staircase and headed toward us. Leila turned to me and said, "Watch your back, Cassie. You always be asking questions. Don't stop now 'cause you're desperate to be put on."

Before I could ask her what the hell she meant, Hi-Jack arrived and threw an arm around each of us. "Don't tell me y'all didn't wait to kiss and make up until I came back. I wanted to watch." He and the posse laughed. Leila looked just how I felt: disgusted. She threw his arm off her shoulders and tried to walk away, but Hi-

Jack latched on to her skinny arm with that swollen hand like a baseball mitt on a stickball bat. "G Dub wants to see if our first lady and her arch rival would bless our guests with a little freestyle battle." He pointed to the balcony at the top of the staircase and there stood G Double D looking down at the crowd, ignoring the two women on either side of him competing for his attention with their exotic dance moves while Freight hulked in their shadow. G turned to his left and gave a slight nod. A few yards away from him was the DJ who nodded back and faded out the latest Nas joint into a break beat.

As the 8MM Posse began pushing the crowd back to create a circle around Leila, Hi-Jack, and me, panick clutched my heart. I was always the first to admit that I couldn't freestyle to save my life. In my worst nightmare, I never dreamed that I'd ever be in a situation where that might actually be the case. Everybody who was anybody in the hip-hop industry was there from the top A and R honchos of all the major labels to that New York Knick who'd bankrolled his own album.

A second of hope struck when I remembered that Leila couldn't freestyle either. After I smoked at the 205 Club with "God Don't Like Ugly" and she flopped publicly to the entire label's embarrassment, she had no idea what I had become capable of after we split. Leila was going to find a way out of this because she had so much more at stake than I did.

Somebody shoved a mic into my hand as I tried to catch Leila's eyes. As the crowd drew closer to us and started to sway with the DJ's beat, Leila refused to look me in the face, making no attempt to stop this. Out of nervousness, I called her name, and when she looked at me I finally saw what made her avoid my gaze. Neither confidence nor contempt, I saw in her eyes the last thing I ever thought I would: shame.

"When y'all bitches gonna get to it?" Hi-Jack shouted. He shoved me into Leila, who grabbed on to my top to steady herself. I knew she meant no harm, but feeling more self-conscious than

ever—about my abilities, my clothes, my future, our friendship—
I pushed her off me so hard, she bounced back into Hi-Jack. The
crowd laughed, and I saw the fury of our last fight seep from her
memory under the skin on her face.

Leila whipped the mic to her lips and launched a rhyme that
tore into my gut. Whether to test my skills or to humiliate me, I'd
walked into a public setup. Leila fronted as if they came off the top
of her head, but those words were put in her mouth days, maybe
even weeks, before that night by her label mates in preparation for
this moment. And with lyrics that stung like alcohol on an open
scratch, Leila had to have revealed my every insecurity to those
bastards to serve that up.

> *Well, look who's here*
> *Is it Punchanella, Punchanella?*
> *More like a busted Cinderella.*
> *Gonna leave the ball with no fella*
> *'Cause her gear is less than stella.*
> *Do I see fear*
> *In Punchanella, Punchanella?*
> *Don't get depressed.*
> *Blame yo' moms you're so repressed*
> *And OshKosh for your dress.*

Leila snatched the tourmaline pendant off my neck and the crowd
hollered so loud I couldn't hear the next lines, the only respite I received from the longest thirty seconds of my life. Breathless, Leila
stepped back into the applauding throng and waited for my attack.
I struggled to choose between the flood and the tornado—attempt
to freestyle and surely fail or back down and not freestyle at all.
And for once it was useless to ask what Leila would do if she were
in my shoes.

So I did what Genevieve would. Holding my head high and
steady, I removed the matching earrings and bracelet. The crowd

started to hoot and Hi-Jack cackled, "Oh, shit, it's on now!" I glanced up as G Double D raced down the staircase, followed by Freight, who summoned the other guards and called for backup on his radio.

I approached Leila, grabbed her hand, and slapped the earrings and bracelet into it. As much as I burned to run out of there, I calmly stepped around Leila and walked toward the door. The crowd split to let me pass, murmuring interpretations of my actions.

"She backing down, yo!"

"Yeah, yeah, that's why she gave her the jewelry. She surrendering and shit."

"Naw, naw, naw, man. Look at how calm she is. She's saying she ain't worth battling. Just like the jewelry ain't worth shit, neither is Fatal."

"So why she leaving, then?"

" 'Cause! That's her way of saying, 'Fuck you!' to the whole label!"

"Bullshit! That bitch balked."

I didn't start running until I hit the end of the driveway. Except for the fact that I was going in the opposite direction I had come in the cab, I had no clue where I was going. But that wasn't going to stop me from getting to Queens even if I had to walk all the way there on the service road.

As I trotted past one ostentatious lawn after the next, American flags left from the recent Independence Day weekend snapped at me. My humiliation quickly melted into fear at the thought of some overzealous patriot taking a shot at that strange, dark figure running across his lawn. A carload of assholes rolled up on me, blowing those fake kisses and offering me a ride. I ignored them and hoped that they would go away. The second longest thirty seconds of my life passed before they did. And then another idiot in an Elantra followed a few moments later.

I scooped up a handful of gravel for the third band of traveling predators who soon approached in a white limo. Rock bottom meant they were a bunch of hormonal ushers leaving a wedding and offering to *console* me instead of the 8MM Posse chasing me down and forcing me to return to the mansion. The limo slowed beside me. I waited until the jerk in the passenger seat had rolled his window down halfway before I heaved the gravel at him. I reached down for another pitch when I heard Darnell yell, "Cassandra, what you doing? Girl, get in here before some lunatic out here nabs your ass."

He climbed out the passenger side, opened the back door for me, and followed me into the backseat.

"Cassandra . . ."

Before he could say more, I broke into tears. Darnell pulled my head into his shoulder and stroked my hair. The gentleness of his touch unlocked something in me, and I collapsed onto his chest, sobbing tears through to the skin under his silk shirt all the way to Queens.

CHAPTER 10

CLOSER

The next afternoon I woke up and found a note on the night table from Darnell. It read, *Let's talk. Dinner tonight at six.* Like I had any desire to leave this house again. Or anyplace to go if I did.

But remembering what had happened during the last time I hid in bed, I got up, took a shower, and went downstairs. There I paced the living room while reliving the previous night's horror. In front of me, I could see Leila again, bobbing her head and spitting her verses. Above I felt the massive speaker rain bass on my head while the swanky crowd buzzed around me. The hot tar of the service road burned under my feet as the gravel cut into my palm. I worried that time would never lessen the intensity, that the memory would always conjure these nasty emotions surely as if it were happening all over again.

I could not bear the thought that my career had started and ended over the course of two weeks for hundreds to witness. So instead I sifted through every bad memory of my seven-year friendship with Leila, attempting to pinpoint what I had done to make her turn on me so foul. But no argument was ever as ugly as the one before she kicked me out, and that was after she had already betrayed me, and I still had yet to figure out what I had done to make her do that. But when G Double D approached her, she asked about me and admitted that I wrote most of our rhymes. I realized then that I might never find out, and I wondered if this was how it went down between Foxy and Kim.

But that led me to reconsider what Leila had said and done before G had commanded us to perform at the party. She came to me just as Hi-Jack was about to get too acquainted. With more men than fingers to wrap them around, Leila was never prone to jealousy. And she knew I would never hook up with the likes of Hi-Jack. As a matter of fact, neither would she. Leila had multiple types and she dabbled occasionally in roughnecks, but they were always poseurs and she knew it. She always suspected that her father was the dealer who got her mom hooked, so she never messed with a guy who *worked* as they say.

Then she teased me about seeing Darnell only to seem relieved that we hadn't hooked up. Leila liked to flirt with him— complimented him on his clothes, sat on his lap and whatnot—but she never took him seriously. Darnell was too tame for her and she too wild for him, and they both knew it.

And I remembered the shame on her face. Even though she thought nothing of abandoning me to sign with Explicit Content, Leila did not want to battle me even though she knew she had the upper hand. And yet she had to be complicit for her label mates to write verses that cut so deep. That puzzled me most of all.

The Leila I knew made entrances. She took advantage and created scenes. My mother once said that Leila craved drama no matter what hell it wrought because eighteen years of clay-colored walls, paper trails, and stone-faced officials had taught her that was the only way to remain of any consequence. She said this to me the first time I brought Leila home. Genevieve came into my room to turn down the radio and found Leila in her heels standing on my bed rhyming along with "Not Tonight" remix of "Ladies' Night," matching her flow from Angie Mar to Missy E and all the sisters in between. After telling me she didn't want her in our house anymore and bringing me to angry tears, Genevieve said, "Some people are like sharks, and they have to keep moving lest they die," my mother said. "But that little girl is something altogether different. She's had a loud life and knows no other way to live." Which only made me want to hang out with Leila even more, because we were living the proverbial quiet existence and I wasn't feelin' it.

The Leila I knew would have floated down that spiral staircase rhyming like a boxer throwing punches on his way to the ring for a title bout. At worst, she would have ambushed me like she did in the locker room in junior high school. At best, she would have challenged me herself for all to hear. Leila *was* a shark; if she truly wanted a piece of me, I never would have seen her coming until she took her first bite.

The back and forth drove me into the street buying ever city newspaper I could find. I took them back to Darnell's and scoured every inch, searching for some clue. The setup was so obvious, the witnesses so prominent, there had to be some coverage of what happened. I found it wedged in a full-page spread in the *New York Daily News*. After suggesting that G Double D threw the *lavish soiree* to counter talk that Explicit Content's financial problems were on the rise, the reporter focused on the major players that were there—who was wearing who in terms of both fashion and passion. And then he spent exactly 132 words writing the obituary of my short career:

> And perhaps to stave off rumors surrounding her continually postponed debut, rapper Fatal Beauty (née Leila Aponte) challenged an unsuspecting guest to an impromptu freestyle competition before the other 200-plus attendees. The

Latina lyricist took one searing verse to dispatch her overmatched opponent—referred to only as Sabrina—who opted to walk out the door rather than return the heat. Some like rapper 50 Cent raved the much-hyped pixie's skill. "Shorty truly chased that [girl] out of here," he said. "If you gonna do battle, bring that sh—!" Still others like Busta Rhymes were less impressed. "She was nice, but she really ain't had no competition. Battling that little girl was like having Oscar de la Hoya fight Rico Rivera." When asked who was Rico Rivera, the dread-headed rapper replied, "Exactly."

The article went on to say that people were expecting Lil' Kim to arrive and hoping that she would take on Fatal. But Kim never showed, and Fatal herself soon disappeared after getting reprimanded by Hi-Jack for snubbing a group of female fans. Shortly after I *opted to walk out the door rather than return the heat,* she was last seen heading up the stairs wrapped up in Primo, who's supposed to be Explicit Content's answer to Ja Rule, a rapper who got it in his head that he can sing. The last thing the reporter wrote about Fatal: *With one hit already under her belt and another climbing the charts, let's hope Fatal Beauty's debut hangs around longer than the diminutive diva did for her own birthday party.*

I was tearing the article to shreds when Darnell walked in carrying several department store bags. He looked at my sweatshirt and jeans and said, "I knew you wouldn't be ready."

Embarrassed to be caught hating on Fatal, I grabbed all the newspapers and brought them into the kitchen. "I'm clean, I'm dressed, what?" I said as I dropped the stack onto the recycle pile. "It ain't even six yet."

"Girl, where you think I'm taking you?" Darnell said. "When I say I'm taking a woman out to dinner, I don't mean to the Chinese takeout joint down the block. Lucky I know you like I do. Go change." He held up a Henri Bendel bag. I recognized the name only because Leila and I could not walk down Fifth Avenue without her dragging me in there. Within minutes she would buy some foundation or lipstick just to waste the next hour pining over dresses designed by muthafuckas with no last name, flipping over the price tags and mumbling, "Shit, Diego don't keep my ass that good."

I gave Darnell a dirty look, snatched the bag, and went upstairs. At first, the whole thing offended me. How the hell did Darnell just know I would be sitting there in my street clothes? What other way was I supposed to be dressed after the dreadful night that I had? My name wasn't Liza Doolittle and Darnell was no Henry fuckin' Higgins, so he needed to excuse the shit out of me for not fetching my mink stole from the furrier because he said he was taking me to dinner.

But as I placed the bag on the bed and began to peel away the tissue paper, I started to feel like Jada in *Set It Off* when that fine banker takes her to this ritzy boutique and buys her a gorgeous evening gown before whisking her away to this upscale party. Amidst the tissue paper was a swirl of pink silk with a tag that read Betsey Johnson. I slowly lifted the dress out of the bag as if it were as fragile as a spider's web. It had a handkerchief hem and was encrusted with pearls along its trim straps. Not even in the publicity shots from her short film career did Genevieve ever wear anything as exquisite as this.

I quickly pulled off my street clothes and slipped the dress over my head. It clung to my breasts yet leaned away from my thighs as if it were sewn especially for me. For the first time I understood why even though Leila shopped as if she were paid a grand for every bag she collected, she was never happier than when Vance or Diego bought something for her themselves. Hell, Junior made nowhere near the money they did, but I watched Leila lose her mind over a tank top that said BOY BEATER that he picked up for her at a street fair. She washed it by hand every other day because she liked to wear it whether she planned to see Junior or not. I went into the bathroom and twirled in front of the full-length mirror and discovered the romance of a man buying you something to wear on his own accord, especially if it fit you to a tee and suited your personality. Not only was he saying that he got you, but he liked what he got.

Later I would understand that Darnell succeeded in earning my trust by taking it one step further. He hadn't bought me a dress according to who I was. He chose a dress that spoke to who I wanted to be, knowing who that was even when I hadn't admitted it to myself. Darnell merely followed G Double D's advice to emulate the best.

Darnell took me to a Latino restaurant in the Flatiron District called Patria, which is *motherland* in Spanish. That's what Leila told me after the first time Diego took her there to amend for going to Vance's gallery pretending to be interested in buying an engagement gift for his *fiancée, Leila.* When Leila insisted I tag along on their dates, we never wound up in a ritzy place like Patria, that's for sure. So after he already had dropped over two hundred dollars for dinner, Leila asked if she could order something to take home. Diego said yes, and Leila preceded to rack up another eighty dollars ordering dinner and desert for me because "not only did poor Cassie have to hear me fight with Vance over your bullshit, she had to listen to me bitch about you for an hour after that."

So I had heard about Patria but had never been there until that night. In the beginning of our relationship, Kurt took me to a few so-called romantic restaurants. But they all seemed to unpack romance from a cardboard box of dim lights, murky wine bottles, and somber music. At Patria's, romance hummed through the yellow walls, the orange flowers, and ruby drinks. The bar swarmed like a hive with twenty-somethings in every shade of brown. The sisters dared to rock chartreuse shoes, the brothers unafraid to laugh from their bellies. The Cinderella fantasy never spoke to me, maybe because it was too different from my reality. But if there ever was a fairy tale for 'round-the-way girls of the 2K like me, this had to be it.

Darnell gave his name to the hostess. She immediately seated us at a table by the window and handed us menus. I think Darnell noticed me stiffen when I saw that the cheapest appetizer was seven bucks. "You worry about what you want to eat, and I'll worry about the bill."

"How you know I'm worried about the bill?" I said. If push came to shove and homeboy's credit card bounced, I had a few hundred dollars in my pocketbook. Not that I wanted to spend it on an expensive meal, but I was prepared to if necessary.

" 'Cause I know you, Cassie," he said. The hottie waiter who looked just like that Latino dude on one of Leila's soap operas (not the Spanish dude who's married to that annoying white girl but the fine Puerto Rican guy with the weird name from *New York Undercover*) came and asked if we would like to start with drinks. Not being much of drinker, I asked Darnell for suggestions. He smiled and asked the waiter to bring us mojitos and then ordered black lobster empanadas for himself. After he goaded me into ordering an appetizer, too, I settled for the salmon soy seviche, seafood marinated in citrus juice and spiced vegetables depending on the country.

When the waiter left, Darnell said, "I've got some news for you about Leila and Explicit Content." I could not tell by his expression whether this would be news I would want to hear. So I launched into all the doubts and theories that had plagued me since I awoke that day. He listened patiently while I rambled until the appetizers and mojitos arrived. The smell of the mint leaves floating in the glass caught my attention and so I took a sip. That drink was as stiff as starch and rang my head like a bell.

Taking advantage of my reaction to the mojito, Darnell said,

"Cassie, check it. It turns out Leila might not have a real contract with Explicit Content."

I thought the rum had already affected my hearing. "She doesn't? How can that be? She's already recorded two songs with Hi-Jack and the 8MM Posse and is supposed to be working on an album. The Ashanti principle, remember?" I sunk my fork into the salmon and a slice of avocado, jammed it into my mouth, and immediately went for more.

"You know that girl you saw me dancing with?" Darnell said. I hadn't given her a second thought the night before when I saw her bumping against Darnell. But now the mention of her made my face burn. I took another sip of mojito and just nodded at Darnell, afraid that my voice would expose my sudden jealousy. "G signed her to a modeling contract."

"Modeling contract?"

"Yeah, she wanted a record deal as an R&B singer, but G told her that he was expanding in other areas and wanted to sign her to his new management agency. Called it Explicit Talent, specializing in models and dancers for videos, tours, and whatever."

The idea sounded less far-fetched than I'd initially thought. If represented by someone who knew the game like G Dub, sisters with extraordinary looks, genuine talent, and a legitimate desire for an entertainment career would avoid getting exploited. Meanwhile, artists would know they had true professionals on their project and not have to worry about being chased by hoochies out to trap them. But what the hell did this have to do with Leila?

Darnell answered my question before I could ask it. "So G signed that girl Monica to a one-year quote-unquote develop-ment deal." I put down my fork. From raiding the law library at Genevieve's office, I knew such deals were often mad shady. "I ask her about it, and get this bullshit, Cass. All it required the label to do was provide her room and board and some pocket money. Meanwhile, she has to appear wherever G asks her to, and if she 'proved' herself, Explicit Talent could extend her contract for another year with all the terms of a traditional management agreement."

"She doesn't get paid for her assignments in that year?" I asked. It never ceased to shock me how some folks can be so hungry for wealth and fame that they signed away their best gifts to the first bidder without consulting an expert. If you ever wanted a strong argument for pursuing a career strictly for the love of it, this was it. Problem was, too many people confused their love of wealth and fame for the thing they hoped would bring it. "Somebody's copping those fees. In a year, G could make a killing off of her, and she wouldn't have shit to show for it," I said.

"Exactly," said Darnell. He leaned forward and put his hand on mine. "I'm thinking maybe G ran a similar game on Leila. No advances, no royalties, not even an agreement to record and release a single album."

The waiter returned to take our orders and Darnell asked him to give us a few more minutes. My head spun from the mixture of the mojito's rum and Darnell's revelation. Suddenly, I heard Leila's voice cut through the whirlwind in my head. *Watch your back, Cassie.* I pulled my hand away from him. *You always be asking questions.*

"What's wrong?" asked Darnell.

Don't stop now 'cause you're desperate to be put on.

I reached inside for the courage to ask him if he was still trying to be down with Explicit Content after what happened to me even though those past few months he had treated me better than my own best friend. He gave me a roof over my head, encouraging words, and a shoulder to cry on. Darnell took my hand again and looked me in the eye with a bittersweet smile. "I think Leila done got herself into some shit. And maybe she's trying to keep you out of it."

The notion comforted me if only for a second. The Leila I knew had no qualms throwing up her hands for me no matter how big my enemy, sometimes even fiending to stand up for me when I

would rather let things go. But this new Leila was the scorpion riding on the frog's back. "If that were true, why would she set me up
in front of all those people?" I asked. Overcome with the memories of the previous night, Darnell told the waiter to bring the duck
leg with sweet plantains for him and the churrasco for me and to
keep the mojitos coming.

"For a lot of reasons. I don't know," Darnell said. "She gets offered a bogus record deal, one she knows you would've seen
through had she come straight to you with it. But she couldn't do
that because G Double D had already convinced her to drop you.
But then you catch his eye in an amateur contest the same night
she falls on her face. Next thing Leila knows, you show up at
what's supposed to be her official entrée into the record industry.
If you ask me, Cassie, the way Leila's acting makes total sense.
When you feel guilty, you do shit. Then when you're afraid your
guilt's showing, you do some other, contradictory shit." The
waiter came back with two more drinks and set them down between us. "The bottom line is that girl doesn't want you anywhere
near that label, Cassie. Maybe she's embarrassed for you to know
how she fucked herself up and maybe she wants to keep you from
getting caught up in the same bullshit. Or maybe she doesn't even
realize she fucked up and thinks this is all going to work out for her
just like G said and doesn't want you to have any part of it. Just
add this to the list of things you might never know."

"So what am I supposed to do now?"

Darnell took a sip of his mojito, then said, "Do you, and let
what happened with Leila go."

Sounded right, but I had no idea how to do that. My face must
have given that away because Darnell handed my mojito to me and
said, "All you have to do tonight is enjoy your meal."

After the best meal of my life, Darnell and I took a cab back to
Queens. Because of a fender bender on the FDR Drive, we prob-

ably would have gotten home quicker had we taken the subway. But I wouldn't have had it any other way 'cause Darnell and I really got to know each other better. He asked me about how Leila and I had become friends. It surprised me how easily I talked about her. Not that I didn't ache here and there, and oddly enough the pleasant memories seemed to hurt more. I don't know if what Darnell had told me over dinner had an impact, but I seemed to be out of tears for Leila.

Talking about Leila eventually led Darnell to ask me about my mother. As comforting as it was to talk to him, I was tired of talking. Or more like tired of having drama to relay. So I deflected the question by asking, "No, I've said enough. You tell me about your mother. If she lives with you, how come I haven't seen or heard from her all this time? You got her locked up in the attic or something?"

I was joking, but Darnell became serious and looked out the cab window. Just when I thought I had killed our conversation, he turned back to me and said, "She's away. In rehab." Between her gambling jaunts and rehab stints, Darnell had been a latchkey kid for as long as he could remember. In the sixth grade, he had gotten thrown out of a private school when his moms lost his tuition on a trip to Atlantic City. Worse than transferring him to public school in the middle of the year, his mother sent him in his old school's uniform. The kids teased him for wearing the same gray slacks and burgundy tie every day instead of the baggy jeans and expensive sneakers they did. But their mothers loved it so much they started pushing the school for a dress code. And who was at the front of the battle but Darnell's own mother, perpetrating as if D's getup was some kind of intentional statement. The battle of the dress code divided the parents, and that's when the kids went from teasing Darnell to beating him up. Eventually, the principal threw his hands up and said the parents could send their kids to school in whatever they wanted whether it was a uniform or street clothes. "And to top it off," Darnell said, his hand rubbing my knee, "they didn't even choose one like the one I wore." Instead they chose navy slacks and ties, and Darnell never fit in at that school.

So the summer before Darnell started junior high school, he started robbing. "I'm not proud of what I did, but I was in a whole other space back then," said Darnell. "My pops stopped paying child support, but he wouldn't give me the money. My moms got the house in the divorce, so unless she wanted to sell it, welfare was out. She's not a terrible person, Cassie. She just has a problem." His eyes begged me to believe him, and I did. "I wasn't trying to end up in a Leila situation, you know, so I just did for self."

Doing for self meant he went from snatching purses from old ladies on their way to the supermarket to slipping into people's houses and grabbing whatever of value he could find. One day during Christmastime, he broke into someone's basement and found boxes of hidden presents. But the second he got in, someone upstairs apparently heard him and started to head down to the basement. Darnell grabbed the nearest box he could lift, stole back out the window, and ran up the driveway. The owner of the house saw him and gave chase, but luckily, Darnell was a young kid with a big lead. When he got home, he unwrapped the gift and discovered that Roland W-30 keyboard. He decided to keep it, trading the criminal life for a musical career.

The cab pulled up to Darnell's. He climbed out of the backseat and offered me his hand. I took it and he helped me out of the cab. Not that I make a big deal if a dude doesn't open the door or pulls out a chair for me. I got two functional arms. But when a dude offers, I do notice and appreciate. With so many busters that can't be bothered, those little gestures always set a brother apart.

Darnell opened the gate for me. I walked past him and up the stairs, searching for the keys in my pocketbook. Such an everyday thing to do, and it made me so happy. As I turned the key in the lock while D held the screen door open for me, I realized that Darnell's had become home, and he like family. No, something different. Better.

We walked in, and Darnell headed for the stereo. He found a quiet storm on the radio and asked me if I wanted something to drink. I said to surprise me, and then I stretched out on the sofa like I saw my mother do in one of her movies. Darnell went into the kitchen and checked the messages on the answering machine as he found and rinsed wineglasses. The first two messages were from clients wanting to touch base with Darnell about their projects. The third one was left by a woman calling on behalf of G Double D.

"This is Miss Om calling for Mr. Gregory 'G Double D' Downs. I'm trying to reach Cassandra Rivers, or Sabrina Steelo. Miss Rivers, Mr. Downs would like to arrange a meeting with you."

She left two numbers where I could reach her to confirm—a line at the offices of Explicit Content and her pager. D stood in the doorway between the kitchen and the living room, a wine bottle in one hand and two glasses in the other. "Wow, Cass," he said. "What are you going to do?"

"What do you mean what I'm going to do?" I said as I snatched a wineglass from his hand. "Go down to his record company so the clowns on his roster can punk me some more? Forget it."

Darnell poured wine into both of our glasses. "Maybe the dude just feels bad about what happened and wants to apologize. Make it up to you in some way," he said.

Instead of waning over time, my embarrassment over what happened at the party seemed to grow. "If I was a dude, he wouldn't want to apologize. He wouldn't want to make it up to me. If I were a dude, he wouldn't give a fuck." I took a big gulp of wine. "Everything Leila said last night was scripted down to the last word. . . ."

"He might not have known that. . . ."

"It doesn't matter," I said, my tongue tripping over itself. "It doesn't matter, and it's all right. Leila needs his fuckin' charity, but I don't. So to hell with Explicit Content." I raised the glass as if I were toasting the condemnation.

"So you're just going to ignore him, Cassie?" Darnell asked again. "You're going to dis Gregory 'G Double D' Downs?" He shook his head, smiling in disbelief. I stood up and wobbled past him into the kitchen. I looked at the telephone, reached out, and pressed a button on the machine. Nothing happened. "Cassie, what are you doing?" I hit another button.

You have erased all messages.

I looked at Darnell who was giving me this crooked smile. "That's what I'm doing," I said. "That and . . ." I gently placed my hands on Darnell's cheeks and pressed my lips against his. I felt his warm tongue slip past my lips as he put his hands on my waist and pulled me toward him. I had forgotten what it was like to feel the hard warmth of a man against my hips. It both excited and scared me, especially in my compromised state.

But just as I was going to pull away, Darnell did.

"What's wrong?"

"Nothing," he said as he grinned down at me. "You just erased all my messages but everything's cool." Before I could apologize, he kissed me again, and my stomach fluttered like it did every time I stood backstage, except this time the quivering trickled down my belly and pooled at the top of my thighs. I pulled away.

"I know we've been friends awhile, and tonight was the best night I've had in a long time, but . . ."

"You're not ready for this," he finished. He kissed my forehead. "It's all good. Everything in its time."

I've heard that before from dudes who have tried to mack me, all so sure they're gonna eventually talk their way into my panties. I let them know right away I had no intention of giving them any play. They never believed me, but learned soon enough.

But when Darnell said it, I believed it as much as he did. So I didn't say anything more. I just kissed him again.

CHAPTER 11

PRESSURE

Dpressed me to quit my job at Tower Records so that we could work on my album full-time. Although he had made a few connections, he decided to hold off on distributing my demo until I arrived and he could introduce me. But then Leila devastated me, I bailed, and Darnell chased after me. "With all the work we've done on our own already? If we can produce a tight album, we might be able to get a distribution deal without giving up much," Darnell said. "You've convinced me, boo. We gonna do the Wu." And he wanted to do so as soon as possible while his contacts were fresh.

I cringed at the thought of executives tossing my CD into their wastebaskets once they recognized my name. "But when you tell them who I am, they'll remember me as the girl who backed down from Fatal at her party," I said. "Why would they be interested in me?"

Darnell just laughed at me. "Girl ain't done shit yet and already your head all swole. Cassie, nobody in the industry cares about that shit. Freestyle's for the street. Industry heads have already forgotten that shit."

"Yeah, what if you run into the one person who hasn't?" I said, trying to soothe my singed pride. "What then?"

"I play them 'God Don't Like Ugly,' and the whole party incident becomes part of your backstage lore," said Darnell. "When your joint's the most requested video on TRL while Fatal still hasn't released shit, all the critics'll be like, *Once publicly humiliated by Fatal Beauty, Sabrina Steelo has redeemed herself into stardom while her much-hyped rival has faded from the scene as quickly as she exploded onto it*. Or some shit like that."

We both laughed, but then I said, "I'd rather forget the whole thing, but, yeah, if 'God Don't Like Ugly' doesn't get us a deal, it'll at least get us a meeting."

"The track can get us deal, but . . ."

"But what?"

"They have to recognize who you're talking about," Darnell said. "You have to call out Fatal by name. And when they hear the other cuts and realize you're a bonafide talent and not just some hata with a novelty record like Sporty Thievz, they'll sign you." I hesitated and he made a proposition. "Let's just do a rough cut to see how it sounds. I'll foot the bill for it. If you don't like it, we'll use the original."

I figured it couldn't hurt, but I didn't quit my job right away. Especially when we used the rest of Diego's money to rerecord "God Don't Like Ugly" and another track, even though Darnell told me not to worry about rent, utilities, and all that. He said he got some work through the contacts he'd made at the party, and that he had enough for all we needed. Still I was hesitant not to have my own money.

Not long after, though, I did quit. The day Eminem had dropped his new joint, to be exact. Nothing against Em. I mean, I don't like his rhymes about women. Especially the ones he's related to. And least of all that he puts his little girl on his filthy-ass records only to front like father of the year and shit. But white boy or not, the man has skills, which is exactly why how he uses them pisses me off. Anyway, after waiting outside for hours in the August humidity, folks had stormed the store with their bad attitudes, and we eventually ran out of his joint. Of course, some people got belligerent.

One moron called me every kind of bitch as if I had the last CD stashed under the counter just to torment him. I ate it but not on some the-customer's-always-right-bullshit. I held my tongue because muthafuckas out here be crazy. Who's to say he wouldn't be waiting for me outside at the end of my shift. Shit, I didn't have to say a word, and he could still be out there. That thought just infuriated me even more, so I walked into Roy's office and gave him two weeks' notice. I was tempted to quit on the spot, but after all I had been through, I knew better than to burn bridges.

He tried to convince me to stay, but what happened had inspired me on many levels. I wanted to get on the subway and write a song about dudes who hid their emotional baggage by lashing out at the women around them whether they're Eminem or that twisted brother in the store. I wanted to get into the studio and produce an album that would cause sisters to storm Tower Records on release day. Most of all I wanted to go home to Darnell and bitch about what happened so he could say or do something to lift me back up again. Turned out, though, he needed me to do that for him.

I knew something was wrong the second I arrived because the front door was open. With all the expensive equipment and first-hand experience with burglary he had, Darnell didn't play that. Even with the AC busted at the peak of summer, D clamped all the windows and doors shut.

"Darnell? D, you here?" I dropped my pocketbook on the sofa and then thought better of it. I picked it back up and tiptoed toward the basement. "D?"

The basement door was wide open, too, and I could see that the light was on. I slowly went down the steps. The first thing to catch my eye was a CD case on the floor at the foot of the staircase. My stomach fluttered 'cause Darnell is very meticulous when it comes to anything that has to do with his music. Not only does the man have all his CDs, tapes, and records organized into a database on his computer, he even invested in one of those bar code wands like they use in the library.

I picked up the CD. The cover was cracked so badly, I couldn't tell whose album it was. I opened it—Foxy Brown's debut joint *Chyna Doll.*

Then I saw the second broken CD. And the third. And then the trail of cracked covers leading to Darnell, sitting in a whirlpool of broken plastic cases, shredded liner notes, and discarded silver discs. In each shaking hand, he held half of a vinyl record. He pressed the broken halves together and bore his blackened eyes into the center as if he could weld them into one piece again by sheer will. Every case that held his five-thousand-plus CD collection had been cleared, some even toppled to the floor.

But they did the worst damage to Darnell's equipment. Someone had thrown his Phillip 107MB monitor onto the floor with enough force to shatter the screen. A hard blunt object had been slammed repeatedly into both his 16-track Mackie mixer and reel-to-reel analog recorder. And Darnell's beloved Roland keyboard and Atari computer—both gone.

"Oh, my God!" I rushed a few steps toward him. The crunch of plastic under my boots made Darnell gasp.

"Stop!"

I froze in place. I wanted to comfort him, but the only way to get to him would be to trample over the remnants of his prized collection.

"Darnell, what happened?"

His looked up at me and snickered. "Explicit Content happened, that's what." I took another step forward, and he yelled, "Don't!" I started to pick up the CDs scattered about my feet.

"Cassie!" I jumped, and Darnell whispered, "Please just leave everything where it is. I'll take care of it."

I dropped on the last step. "Why, Darnell? Why would they do this to you?"

"Because you dissed G. He thinks it's on account of me."

"Why would they think that what I did had anything to do with you?"

" 'Cause you stepped to him hard at 205, Cassie," D said as if he were in a trance. "Then, when he reaches out, you blow him off without even hearing him out. . . ."

There wasn't a hint of accusation in his tone, but guilt took over me. "Darnell, I'm so sorry." He didn't answer me. "D, if I had known he'd do something like this, I would've sat down with him. I just didn't see the point of—"

"Look, Cassie, I gotta go through all this shit to see what I can save. . . ."

"Let me help you. . . ."

"I want to be alone."

So all I could do was leave the man be. With the CDs I had picked up still in hand, I made my way to my room. I placed the broken cases on the bureau and sat on the bed useless. Why the hell did G go after Darnell over my decision to dis him? Were they really after me and decided to mess with D because I wasn't here and he wouldn't tell them where to find me? Did Darnell let them think it was his decision to dis G in order to protect me? Why would G Double D wild out because I didn't want to deal with him after he had chosen Leila over me?

I went back and forth between outrage and guilt. On the one hand, where did that muthafucka G Double D come off messing with Darnell over something I did? Don't get me wrong. Just because I handle mine doesn't mean I'm trying to box with Freight. But the way G got to sistas by intimidating the dudes around them was pissing me off. Like the way he got Leila to move into the Explicit Content mansion by sending his dawgz to Diego's office and making him force Leila out. Was all that even necessary? Was Darnell going to walk into my room any second now to put me out?

On the other hand, I never should have been at Darnell's long enough for something like this to happen. We had little more than a fee-for-service association, but the man took me in when my best friend kicked me to the curb. Instead, I took advantage of Darnell's hospitality even when I knew his feelings for me were starting to change. If anything, I held him suspect for wanting to have my back. And that didn't stop him from treating me like a queen when I hit rock bottom. For all that the man got nothing save my drama. I should have gotten my act together and moved elsewhere months ago.

Darnell knocked on my door and let himself in. Before he could speak, I asked, "How're you doing?"

"I'ma be all right. It's just CDs and equipment. I can always replace it," he said. I knew he was fronting. It would take thousands to replace his equipment, and until he did, he just might need that Tower job I quit. And the CDs, tapes, and especially the records had no price tag. Those were Darnell's soul.

I stood up, took Darnell's hand, and led him out of my room down the hallway to his. I picked up the telephone on his nightstand and dialed 411. A computer voice asked me what city and listing. "Manhattan," I said. "Explicit Content." Within seconds the voice gave me the number and offered the automatic dialing option. I took it, but as I waited for someone to pick up at the other end, Darnell grabbed the telephone from my hand.

"Cassie, I can't let you do this."

I gently took the phone back. "Darnell, I have to."

"Look what that crazy muthafucka had done to my studio!"

"All because I didn't return his damned phone call." Anger overrode my fear. Like Genevieve always said, I despised being afraid, and I became infuriated with G Double D for trying to intimidate me. Like it or not, I had to face him if I wanted it to stop at vandalism. And I knew of no other way to make amends to Darnell. "I have to meet with him, Darnell. If not to fix things, to keep them from getting worse." I hit the Redial button. As I waited for someone to pick up on the other end, I felt Darnell wrap his arms around my waist and bury his face in my neck.

"Explicit Content."

"My name's Cassandra Rivers. Mr. Downs asked me to call to arrange an appointment." The pause that followed made me wonder if the receptionist knew precisely what led to this call. She transferred me to G Double D's personal assistant named Jen. When I got her on the line, I said, "Just make it for whenever." She told me she would put me on hold while she checked G's schedule. Darnell's warm breath on my neck helped me resist the urge to slam the phone back into its cradle.

Jen returned and said, "Mr. Downs has an opening tomorrow. You can meet him here at one." She confirmed the address and I hung up.

Reading my mind, Darnell said, "I'll go with you."

I appreciated that he said that, but I knew I had to meet G alone. I had to earn his respect like any of the male rappers. Not that it would guarantee against future rampages when G didn't get his way, but it was the only strategy I had other than trying to out-thug him.

I turned around and put my arms around Darnell's neck. He leaned his forehead against mine, and I looked up toward him. "I'm sorry, Darnell." My voice cracked, but I forced myself to continue. "I never should've stepped to him at 205. I should've just—"

Darnell stopped me with a firm kiss against my lips. I dragged my hands from around his neck to his jaw, leaned forward, and kissed him back. As Darnell pressed against me, he parted his lips and grazed his tongue where my lips met. I felt a pull down the center of my body as if the tip of his tongue were connected to the nerve between my legs. Our tongues met between our wet lips, and I leaned backward. Following my lead, Darnell gently laid me across his bed.

As we continued to kiss, Darnell wound his hips between my thighs, which absorbed the warmth of his hardness and channeled it throughout my body. Wanting to kiss him harder, I sat up slightly, but Darnell bore his weight against me. I fell back onto the bed only for him to sit up over me. He undid the buttons of my blouse and sunk his moaning face between my breasts. I longed for him to kiss and touch my nipples. Sure that he was teasing me, I ran one hand across his head while leaning forward as best as I could to undo my bra with the other. My bra sprung forward, and Darnell sat up to pull it down my shoulders and toss it over my head. He cupped my breasts and squeezed gently. I let out a moan, and Darnell squeezed again harder. So hard I gasped in pain.

Darnell stopped and moved his hands to the button of my jeans. He popped it, yanked down the zipper, and tugged the waistline down past my hips, dragging my panties along. I raised my hips while he stood at the edge of the bed to wriggle my jeans across my legs and off my feet. I took that moment to say, "While you up, get a condom."

"You're not on something?"

"No!" I yelled. Then, hoping to save the mood, I joked, "What you take me for?" His assumption offended me and he knew it, but I was too hot not to give him the benefit of the doubt. So I felt relieved as he hurried to the night table for a condom. Even if I were on birth control, I wouldn't have told him so. Not the first time. Leila taught me that as a way around the AIDS conversation when things had gotten to where I wanted it as much as the guy did without having to take any stupid risks.

As Darnell rolled on the condom, I hoped for more kissing and touching before going to the ultimate. So I pulled my legs together, swung them to the side and pulled myself so that I knelt on the bed. I pulled Darnell's head toward mine. As we kissed, he ran his hands down my back. With fingertips calloused from all his hours at the boards, Darnell kneaded my ass.

Then he pressed against me until I was lying on the bed again. He pried himself between my thighs and dropped my ankles onto his shoulders. Darnell pushed into me, and I exhaled with the anticipation of future strokes. He clamped his hands over my breasts and pumped into me. The friction of his rough palms rubbing against my nipples made them swell into an aching hardness and my breath quickened. I rolled my hips against Darnell until I felt his thrusts create that spicy pressure with a mounting rhythm. Placing my hands over Darnell's, I squeezed my breasts with a matching pace. Sensing that it was getting good to me, Darnell leaned forward and bucked faster, slamming his hard thighs against me and groaning in my ear.

Feeling his back tense, I lowered my hips to slow him down. But as if his hips were chasing mine, Darnell dropped his and pinned mine against the bed with such a force, my legs flailed open. He drove into me, barreling toward an explosion. So I went for mine, sinking my fingers into his shoulders and locking my ankles around his waist. I pounded my hips furiously against Darnell, but just as I started to boil, Darnell threw his head back with a howl and collapsed on top of me.

As he laid on me and caught his breath, Darnell kissed my cheek and stroked my breast. I couldn't help but thinking *Oh, now?* Which made me laugh.

"What?" said Darnell. He pulled up so we could look into each other's faces. He brushed my hair off my forehead and kissed it. "What?" He looked so sweet all I could do was smile. I closed my eyes and followed the sensation of his fingers tracing my hairline. Then I heard him say, "I know. 'Bout time, right?"

Without opening my eyes, I said, "Yeah. About time." And it wasn't a terrible start in the least. I got closer that first time with Darnell than I ever did with Kurt. So I promised myself there would be more times, each better than the last until I really could say "About time." Darnell fell asleep, and my fantasies of those better times kept me company. They eventually gave way to visions of Darnell and me on video shoots and talk shows. But industry dreams led to thoughts about the one man I did not want in my head and my meeting with him the next day.

CHAPTER 12

NEGOTIATIONS

I arrived at the Explicit Content loft in SoHo about fifteen min-utes early. The second the elevator door opened, the smell of chronic and the bass line of Primo's old cut "Latin Don" wrapped around me and pulled me through a pair of tinted glass doors with a giant silver X painted across them. The entire office was decked in black and silver. Even the walls were black, as was the matted carpet and drawn curtains. The glistening silver fix-tures in X formation from the lamps on either side of the leather couch to the chandelier that hung from the ceiling only empha-sized the darkness. Even the framed awards were black and silver, and I wondered if they had stashed all their gold records in a closet because they disrupted the pattern.

The little color came from the posters of the Explicit Content artists who still wore black and stood against silver backdrops. In his poster, Primo wore a black suit and silver tie and held a cigar. Hi-Jack snarled in his picture to display all the platinum in his mouth. And Leila posed with her hands tugging at the straps of a black camisole, showing off her silver nail polish.

I approached the receptionist and said, "I'm Cassandra Rivers, and I have an appointment with G Doub—Mr. Downs." She nodded and asked me to make myself comfortable while she checked to see if G Double D was ready to see me.

I took a seat on the leather couch. On the table in front of me, instead of the usual Black magazines and industry trades, there were dozens of laminated sheets of articles about Explicit Content. That's right, not the magazines, just the label's coverage reprinted from them. And everything was there. Not just album reviews and artist interviews either. I first read Hi-Jack's jailhouse *Vibe* interview with Shelby J. Lee after his arrest for sexual assault on a sixteen-year-old girl backstage during a concert.

Shelby J. was one of the fiercest journalists on the hip-hop scene, sometimes going where even some of the male writers didn't dare tread. As paid staff for *The Source*, she wrote that a gangsta rapper named 3K (as in three strikes) showed up for his interview three hours late, pissy drunk. Shelby documented all his drunken rants and predicted his career would last as long as it took him to clear a Magnum forty because his debut album was just as nauseating. When the magazine ran the piece, 3K drove over to the magazine's office building in his Escalade, called her on his cell, and dared her to come down and say what she wrote to his face. Never expecting her to show, 3K opened a bottle of malt liquor while he continued to call the office and harass the staff. Next thing he knew, Shelby J. knocked on his window wearing a bulletproof vest, shaking an aluminum bat, and calling him everything but a child of God. When the cops arrived, they arrested 3K for menacing, driving under the influence, and a host of other crimes. Later, Shelby's prediction materialized. 3K's first album went gold, but his sophomore disc tanked. Hip-hop never heard from 3K again until he made the news when cops answering a 911 call for domestic violence went to his apartment and found enough narcotics to charge him with intent to distribute. After that incident, Shelby gave *The Source* one more year, then set out on a freelance career where she pursued interviews on her own and sold them for top dollar to the highest bidder.

But Hi-Jack proved to be a tough case for Shelby. No matter how hard she drilled him, he denied he forced the girl or knew she was underage. Mind you, Hi-Jack has two kids with two women who were under eighteen when he got them pregnant.

The other publicity on the reception area table followed suit. The column Juan Gonzalez wrote, blasting Primo for grabbing his dick at the crowd from the Explicit Content float during the Puerto Rican Day parade. (At the time Leila kind of defended Primo saying, "Just because some sorry-ass females let it slide 'cause he's a famous fool don't mean everyday fools out here got license to put their hands on any ol' Latina they see.") There was even a printout from the Smoking Gun Web site, from when it published the rap sheets for all three members of the 8MM Posse, not to mention all the ink Bill O'Reilly generated blasting G Double D for knowingly signing three convicted felons. Those I tossed aside without a second glance. Hi-Jack meant it when he said the only bad publicity was no publicity. The label had more pride in the bad press of everyday tabloids than any positive review in *Rolling Stone* or *Billboard*. And there was so much of it, I didn't realize that I had been waiting for over an hour until the receptionist buzzed me through a door and told me to head to the last office.

When I reached that office, I knocked on the door and let myself in. Sitting at the desk, punching away on a two-way, was a Korean chick with a deep tan and peroxide-blond straight hair. Most Asian females who do that shit look ridiculous, but somehow she worked it. She jumped up and walked over to me with her hand extended. "Hi, Cassandra. I'm Jennifer Om." She gave my hand a firm shake. "Make yourself comfortable, and G'll be with you once he's done with his current appointment."

I sat on the couch. This office, too, kept to the black and silver scheme, but at least it had promotional material on the walls, including enlarged album covers. The only Explicit Content artist not represented on Jen's wall was Leila, and I found myself feeling a little sorry for her.

From a door at the end of the room behind her desk entered the short, muscular guy in the 8MM Posse who goes by Chaos or Catastrophe or something like that. He waved a stack of head shots at Jen and dropped them on her desk. "These are the models G approved."

"Yeah, but now that this shit's fallen on me, he gave me final say," said Jen. As Chaos or whoever hovered over her, she quickly flipped through the photographs, casting an occasional one to the side. She handed the ones that made the cut to him, but he grabbed the castaways and flipped through them.

"Damn, Jen, it's sad the way you be hatin' on your own peeps," he said. "You only took out the Oriental bitches."

Jen glared at him and snatched the rejected photos back from him. "Trust me, if I were hatin'," she said, "I'd keep them in." The intercom on her desk buzzed and she picked up the receiver. "Bring 'er in now? OK." Jen stood up and motioned me over to her. As I walked over to her desk, the 8MM guy grabbed the head shots off her desk and bopped out the back door, cursing under his breath.

"Give me one more minute." She reached under her desk and pulled out a large shredder. Then Jen grabbed the stack of head shots of the Asian models and quickly turned them into confetti. "OK, let's go."

She led me through the back door that Chaos/Catastrophe had just used. It led to a narrow corridor and after a few angular turns, we found ourselves in front of the tinted doors. Jen continued past the main elevator bank through another hallway and into a service elevator. Using a key, Jen opened a latch and punched in numbers on a keypad, and we rode to the basement. When the doors opened, I saw rows of cardboard boxes, some marked *Promotions* in thick black marker. I followed Jen through an aisle of boxes that led to a vault door. "Stay right here, and G will be with you in a minute." Then she disappeared. Just like that. Like Keyser Söze and shit.

I stood there by myself amidst the boxes wondering if I might find press kits for Leila's album in them. My curiosity got the best of me, and I took a step toward a stack. Just as I was about to give into the urge to pull back the flap on the top box, I stopped myself. Genevieve always said, "Every time you mind someone else's business, you're fixing to let them mind yours." Then I looked up and found the security camera. As I turned in place, searching for others, the vault behind me clicked and the door crept open. Freight stood in the doorway, a silver gun with a thick handle in his waistband. He motioned for me to enter. I sucked my teeth at him. What the hell did he take me for, standing in a giant safe and asking me to come in?

I stood my ground until I heard G say, "C'mon, Cassandra, I don't have all day." I entered and discovered that this giant vault was G's office. On the left side of the room stood more stacks of *Promotion* boxes. Installed in the right wall were a dozen security monitors that covered all the Explicit Content offices as well as all the elevators, the street in front of the building, and a parking lot. An entertainment system held every mogul's plaything, including a sixty-inch television screen on which G and Freight watched a homemade audition video as some girl jiggled her behind in the center of a gymnasium. Like the reception area, only an occasional touch of silver gleamed in the blackness of the decor. I felt like I had fallen into a giant well.

G Double D sat behind a massive desk holding some papers in his hands. Nothing else was on the desk except for a giant paperweight in the form of an X and a gun just like Freight's. G motioned me to sit in the black leather chair across from him.

"So, as you might've guessed, Cassandra, I decided that Explicit Content should sign you after all. In fact, I want your album to be our next release," he said. He slid the papers in his hands across that island of a desk toward me. "Take this to your attorney, and he'll confirm that this is the standard agreement for new artists."

I just stared at the sheets on the desk. None of this made any damned sense. I wouldn't be sitting there had they not messed with Darnell, but he made me an offer that I *could* refuse. Why have his boys tear up Darnell's crib when all he wanted to do was offer me a legitimate recording contract? Then I remembered what Leila told me at the party. *Watch your back, Cassie. You always be asking questions. Don't stop now 'cause you're desperate to be put on.*

But all the unanswered questions I had about what had happened to Darnell evaporated in the sound of Freight's heavy breathing just feet behind me. Instead I decided first to front like this was a typical negotiation and hoped G's propositions would confirm just that. Then perhaps I would know the if, when, and how to steer the conversation toward the attack. "You want to sign me as a solo artist or are you teaming me up with Leila again?"

G laughed like I was some little kid who had just told a silly knock-knock joke. "Nah, Bri Steez is definitely a solo artist."

"But my album's gonna come out before Leila's?"

"Ain't that what you want?"

Hell yeah, but I kept that to myself. Instead I picked up the contract and asked, "Is that in here?"

G leaned forward, licked his lips, and said, "No, but it can be." I sat back in my seat, wanting to put as much distance as possible between us even though the desk kept us far apart. "What's up, Cassandra? You step to me at 205 and read me for signing Leila and not you. Now I offer you a contract and you frontin'."

I still did not dare bring up Darnell, but I couldn't come off soft either. " 'Cause you signed Leila on some bullshit, and she's yet to come out with her own album. Why should I believe you gonna sign me all these months later on the promise that my joint's gonna be the next release? And I'm not even recording with her."

Freight jumped in front of my chair and yelled, "What you talking 'bout *some bullshit?* What you heard? You disrespectin' G?"

I threw my arm across my face and drew my knee to my chest. By *some bullshit* I meant what D told me at Patria's about Leila probably having a bogus contract. But the fright curdling under my skin told me better not to admit that. Afraid not to answer at all, I was about to repeat the reasons G gave me for signing Leila over me when G jumped to his feet. He yelled, "Ayo, Freight!" like he was disciplining an unruly watchdog, and just like one, Freight sunk back into his corner of the room.

G retook his seat and then grinned at me. "They told me you were smart." Before I could ask him who was they, he said, "Your skills cannot be denied, and you know what else? I liked the way you handled yourself at my party. Mad respect."

Freight chimed in, "Any other chickenhead would've started wilding out, fucking up shit and ruining the party."

"But in addition to talent and intelligence, Cassie, you got class," G said. "Pride. Discipline."

His words made my chest swell, but I had to ask. "And Leila?"

G Double D clasped his hands as if in prayer. "Leila's struggling. We're having a hard time getting her to produce."

"So why aren't you putting us back together?"

"Is that what you really want?"

His question threw me big time. I expected him to gas me more than he must have Leila when he approached her at SOB's. Or that he would ask me to write rhymes for her so she could finish her album once and for all. It never crossed my mind that if I wanted to reunite with Leila he would allow it.

But I was past wanting that. Leila and I were rivals now. She was to blame for that, and there was no turning back. They say success is the best revenge, and at that point, nothing would have been better than signing to Explicit Content and beating her to the street. I imagined what the tabloids would write about Fatal Beauty's *overmatched opponent* then.

All that would be sweet if the contract was right. Unlike Leila, I wasn't going to be so hungry and sign any sheet of paper shoved in my face. I knew that there were some things I would not be able to negotiate. But there were some things I could.

I lifted the contract off the desk, folded it, and tucked it in my purse. "I'ma have my lawyer look at this, but I already know I want some other stipulations added." G waited for me to continue. "Like I do want it to say that my album has to come out before Leila's. And I ain't gonna do no ghostwriting. If I write for any-body, I want proper credit. And royalties."

G smirked. "Fair enough."

"And I don't want to perform on no one else's shit but my own. And I certainly don't want something I'm working on for my joint being handed over to someone else." I had read somewhere about shit like that going on, which is why some artists who are con-stantly writing and recording never release squat. I'd be damned that be me, especially because G's handing my tightest lyrics over to Leila. And after what they did to Darnell, I knew I had to bring him on, yet look out for his beats lest his best hooks wind up on Primo or Hi-Jack's album instead of mine.

G Double D strained to keep that smirk on his face. "Cassan-dra, coming to Explicit Content ain't just signing to a record label. It's joining a dynasty. And fam look out for one another, which means we all have to wear more than one hat. You just don't come to Explicit Content, do your thing, and be out. Besides, it's in your interest to appear on some tracks with our more established artists before you drop your debut."

I couldn't really argue with that last point, but I had to protect myself as much as possible. So I said, "Yeah, I know. The Ashanti Principle. But if that's what you're gonna be working in my case, then work it just like that, G."

"Meaning?"

"Meaning that any cuts I do with someone else gotta be on my joint, too. I don't want to be doing three, four tracks that sell everyone else's shit, but every time I'm going into the studio to work on my joint, I'm starting from scratch. Every time I work, I want to be making progress whether I'm getting paid or credit."

G Double D leaned back in his seat and drummed his fingertips on the desk. "I think we can work something out."

Then I got bold. "And I want my publishing."

In his corner, Freight howled like some thug Santa, and G joined him. I knew I had gone too far the second I said it. But G was being so accommodating, I thought I had nothing to lose. After holding my own in my first negotiation, I had just come off like a Girl Scout selling cookies. I hated that they were laughing at me, but I figured I deserved it, so I ate it, trying to hide how pissed off I was at myself and at them. Then it got worse.

"You got a lotta demands for someone who ain't feelin' Explicit Content." He turned to Freight and said, "Ayo, what did Leila say Cassie said about us?"

Freight snickered and said, "Said we produced nothing but candy-ass beats and blasé lyrics."

"Yeah, yeah, yeah." G clapped and laughed. "And I was nothing but an Irv Gotti wanna-be who wouldn't know a good beat if . . . oh, yeah, if Kanye West force-fed me."

"Naw, if Timbaland spoon-fed you a bowlful," Freight corrected him.

"Yeah!" He looked into my frozen face. "My line was funnier." Luckily, he continued because I had no idea what to say to him. "Cassandra, Cassandra, Cassandra," G Double D said as he opened a drawer and pulled out a flask and two shot glasses. "You too smart to not know that's a deal breaker. But I ain't mad at ya, baby girl." He poured a clear liquid into the two glasses and pushed one toward me. "I admire your hustle though, and out of that admiration, I'ma offer you a nice advance. How's two hundred fifty thousand sound?"

My heart raced at the sum, and I paused to regain my cool. "Sounds standard, but I'll take it."

G roared. "You and me, we gonna get along. With a head like yours, we should get you on the ground floor of some upcoming ventures soon, no doubt."

I thought the celebratory shot was a bit premature, let alone any conversation about starting talent agencies or fashion lines. But after showing my ass, I wanted to regain some ground. And bringing up Darnell at this stage in the game was out.

So while I reached for the glass, I didn't sip. I didn't want to perpetrate like the deal was done. At least not until I saw G toss his back first.

"So who's your lawyer?" G asked.

Thinking quickly, I answered, "Ed Hayduk."

"Day-um!" growled Freight.

"You unsigned but got Hayduk as representation?" G squinted at me. "How you swing that?"

"Like you said," I replied. "I got hustle." The look on his face told me my answer didn't satisfy him, but I wasn't trying to embroil myself any deeper in this lie than I had to. "Look, I got a personal connection to him. I got a chance to play my stuff for him, and he was feelin' me. Said anytime I needed representation to holla."

G nodded, clearly impressed. "All right, baby girl. My people will call your people. We'll do lawyers." He raised his shot glass. "And to all them other clichés." He threw his head back and tossed the drink down his throat. Then he looked at me and waited for me to do the same.

I leaned back and poured the liquor down my throat. Aguadiente—this Colombian drink kinda like anisette. Leila probably turned him on to it. She loved that shit. Me, I never did like my alcohol sweet. G snickered at the face I made, and before I could protest, he poured me another.

"Nah, man, I'm not trying to get on a subway back to Queens all fucked up."

"Stop by Jen on the way out, and she'll give you money for a cab."

I stood to my feet. "That ain't gonna show up on my tab, right?"

G Double D and Freight laughed. "This girl's a trip," he said as he poured another shot of aguadiente. "Ayo, if Eve's a pit bull in a skirt, then Sabrina Steelo's like a Doberman in high heels. Nah, Cassandra, this ride's on the house."

The vault door clicked loudly and slid open. Freight stepped aside to let me pass. Just as I was about the walk out, G called my name. I turned and he raised his shot to me. "Bri Steez, welcome to the Explicit Content dynasty."

I nodded and rushed out. When the elevator arrived on the floor of the reception area, Jen was waiting for me by the glass doors with a hundred dollar bill. When I expected her to ask me to get a receipt or sign something, she winked at me and said, "Keep the change."

The second I hit the street, I hailed a cab and told the driver to take me to 31st and Park Avenue South. I had to get to Ed Hayduk's office before Explicit Content called. And although I knew the odds were against it, I prayed that Genevieve was out for a late lunch.

After chitchatting with the front receptionist about how long it had been since she last saw me and how much I had grown and all that, she waved me into Hayduk's office and I found Genevieve at her desk, clacking away at her keyboard as she juggled the constantly buzzing telephone lines. Her chignon and navy suit were as crisp as they must have been first thing that morning. Genevieve stared at me with surprise as she handled one call and quickly switched to the next. I took a seat and flipped through an old *Billboard*.

It surprised me to see my mother on the phone since she was a paralegal. She had started as a legal secretary but worked her way up. Until I started high school, I would take the train into Manhattan after school every day and hang out in my mom's office until she got off work. Once, Hayduk told her that if she went to law school, he would lighten her workload and would consider hiring her when she passed the bar. Genevieve wasn't having that, saying she was too old. I put my two cents in, tugging at her skirt and saying, "You ain't old, Mommy." She'd swatted my hand away, corrected my English, and told me to stay out of grown folks' business. Funny, at nine years old I was supposedly too young to stay at home alone and participate in adult conversation, yet I was old enough to take the subway by myself into Manhattan.

Genevieve finally had a moment of silence to turn to me and ask, "Cassandra, what are you doing here?"

"Hey, Mom," I said. "I have something that I hoped Ed could look at for me." I fished the contract out of my pocketbook and handed it to her. "Actually, some changes are going to be made to it, but it's supposed to be a standard agreement. I just wanted to see if it was all on the up and up before I signed."

Without taking her eyes off me, Genevieve took the contract from me. She scanned the first page and then flipped to the next one. Then she looked up at me. "Who else is on this label Explicit Content?"

I resisted the urge to roll my eyes. Genevieve always prided herself on staying on top of pop culture and whatnot, having been a movie star for a minute and working for a respected entertainment lawyer. Problem was that my mom didn't read any entertainment magazines, watch videos, surf Web sites, or subscribe to e-letters like Davey D's or the Electronic Urban Report or anything like that. All she knew about the music industry—especially hip-hop—was whatever made the six o'clock news, and any head'll tell you that the only time hip-hop got any prime-time play was when some rapper got himself into some bullshit.

So before I answered I prayed that none of the Explicit Content cats had managed to run afoul of the law recently. "Um, Primo,

8MM Posse . . ." Genevieve didn't seem to recognize their names, and I knew better than to mention Hi-Jack. His name alone would get her in a huff. I definitely didn't mention Leila, although I did get a bit mixed up when she didn't recognize the name of the company. On the one hand, better for me if Genevieve didn't remember that Explicit Content was the very label that had come between Leila and me. On the other, I couldn't help getting a little heated that she didn't, wondering if she had heard a word I had said to her in her kitchen that day.

But I knew better than to expect Genevieve to congratulate me on my potential accomplishment. She handed the contract back to me and said, "Well, Cassandra, I don't know how I feel about your asking my boss for any favors. I've been working here for over seventeen years, and I've never asked him for any free legal advice. Not even when I bought the co-op."

"Mom," I interrupted, struggling to maintain a patient tone. "If the deal's legitimate, I'll get an advance, and I'll be able to pay him, OK?"

"And what if it isn't legitimate?" my moms shot back. "Then the man has wasted his time. Time that could've gone to paying—"

I got fed up and yelled, "Then you look at it!"

Genevieve blinked at me with surprise. "Excuse me?"

"You read it, then," I repeated. "If you won't let me ask Ed to look at it, then you do it."

"Cassandra, I am not a lawyer."

"Didn't you just say you been doing this for over seventeen years?" I said. "By now you should at least be able to spot a bullshit contract when you see one."

"You watch your mouth . . ." The telephone rang and Genevieve picked it up. "Law office? Please hold." Her face told me that Explicit Content was on the other end.

I got mad anxious. "See, Mom, I told them Ed was my lawyer—"

"Cassandra, I don't believe you!" Genevieve said. She clicked back to the telephone. "I'm sorry, Mr. Hayduk's unavailable. Would you like to leave a message?" She reached for a pen and message pad. "Oh . . . then why don't you just fax the contract to us?" My moms gave Jen the number and hung up. Then she grabbed me by the arm, pulled me out of the office and down the hallway to the ladies' room. She checked under the stalls to be sure we were alone and then she went off.

"How dare you tell some record label that you're represented by this firm!" she hollered.

"I did it so they wouldn't try to play me!" I yelled back. I'm not one to scream on my moms, but I had had enough of her tripping. I couldn't care less at that point that she hadn't blown up my spot on the phone. "Is that what you want for me? You so against what I'm doing, you'd rather I get caught out there by some record company? That would make you happy?"

But Genevieve just said, "Cassandra, I am not falling for your melodrama. I know you know better than to think I want to see you hurt. But if this rap thing isn't something you can do honestly, then perhaps you shouldn't be doing it at all."

I didn't know what to say to that. As far as I was concerned, my shit was as honest as it could be in this game. What legitimate business in America didn't have its racket? And if anyone should know about hustle, it had to be my mother. Half the movies she did, she got on her own without her shifty agent's help. But then again, when he found out, her career was over as quickly as it started. Hustle too much, and your ass can wind up in handcuffs, maybe worse. Don't hustle enough, and you get stuck. So stuck you might as well be in cuffs anyway. So I stood there, leaning against the sink and trying not to feel sorry for myself. Or my moms.

I finally asked, "So why didn't you blow up my spot?" She gave me a frustrated look and I rephrased my question. "Why did you tell her to fax over the contract if you're not going to read it or show it to Ed?"

"Because . . ." Genevieve started. After a pause, she said, "Because I don't want Ed to find out what you did."

Knowing that was a convenient lie, I pressed. "But now they're just gonna call again, expecting to speak to him and negotiate or whatever."

"We'll deal with that when the time comes." She turned me around and shoved me toward the exit. "Now we have to get back to the phones and intercept that fax."

Since she said *we* I stopped pressing.

My moms looked over the contract that Jen had faxed and said it did seem like a standard agreement. But she wanted to be sure and decided to ask Hayduk to read it after all. I gave her my number in Queens, and Ed himself called me, confirming that the contract was legit and that I'd do no better as a new artist on another label. I ran my discussion with G in his office by him, and Ed said, "The conditions you're requesting are unusual, but hey, if he's amenable to them . . ." But he said to forget about keeping all my publishing. That even if I gave up all my other demands, G would expect to own much of those rights.

I had tried to keep my contract negotiations with Explicit Content on the down low until I could break it to Darnell. I had every intention of putting him on, and I would have done that even if G's dawgz hadn't trashed his studio. I just didn't know which was stronger for Darnell—his hunger or his pride. And I had to wait until I had a scored a deal before I took the risk of finding out.

I almost had until I got stuck on the publishing rights for over a week—long enough for Darnell to intercept a message Ed left for me describing G's latest offer. I finally had run to Barnes & Noble to buy my own copy of Moses Avalon's book and remind myself of what he had to say on the matter. When I returned to the house, I found D in the kitchen listening to Ed's message with his arms tight across his chest.

When the message ended, Darnell glared at me so hard, I dropped my eyes to the floor. Before I could explain myself, he said, "Nice to know that when you're selling me out, you're still T-crossin' and I-dottin' over some industry standard shit. I'm out tens of thousands of dollars of collectible vinyl and studio equipment because of you, and you're haggling over publishing. And you dog Leila." Before I could speak, he pushed me out of his way and stormed off to the basement.

When I reached Darnell, he was sweeping shards of compact disc and broken vinyl into a dustpan. He had stacked his destroyed equipment into the farthest corner of the room and thrown an old sheet over it. Next to it was a massive pile of discs and wax— whole, broken, and scratched. Every time I offered to help clean and reorganize those past few weeks, he would snap at me. I figured that my sincere offerings only hurt him more, and not wanting to make matters worse, I eventually quit. I watched him empty the dustpan into the wastebasket, then return the broom and dustpan to the closet. Although I had followed him without knowing what to say, watching him gave me an idea that I hoped would make it right.

"D, if this deal goes through, I can replace your equipment. And I can put you on. We can continue to work together just like we have been and finally reap some benefits." Darnell walked over to me with a look that made me feel like an exotic animal in a cage. "It's a legitimate deal, D," I continued. "I've got it in writing that my album has to be the next release so long as I deliver material on time. I need you to make that happen. And I'm not like Leila. She stabbed me in the back and never looked back." Pain gripped my throat, causing my voice to crack. "I would've never done that to her. Like she figured since she had been so good to me up to that point, it was cool for her to do me like that when it mattered most. But it's because Leila had been so good to me, I never could've left her behind the way she did me. And because you've been so good to me ever since, no way am I gonna do that to you."

Before I could regain control over myself, I was crying hard from both my memories of Leila and my guilt over Darnell. I tried to apologize, tell him that I was sorry and that I promised to make things right, but the sobs made it impossible to speak. Darnell pulled me to him and I wept the rest of my apology.

As hard as it was, I conceded to G's final offer regarding my publishing rights and made an appointment with Ed. While Genevieve hovered over us, we e-mailed legalese back and forth to the Explicit Content attorney until we came to a mutual agreement. An hour later the label sent a messenger over with the contract. When I signed the second copy and returned it to him, the messenger handed me another envelope. I opened it and found my advance—a check for two-hundred fifty Gs. Not even five minutes later, G called me at Hayduk's and told me to clear the coming Friday. "We gotta update all our promotional material, starting with the Web site," he explained over the speakerphone. "So I just arranged a photo shoot for you."

Excited as I was, I played it cool. "All right, but don't go hiring no stylist or makeup artist or whatever for me. I got my own peoples." I wasn't going to let the label do anything for me I could do myself and give them excuses to start deducting my royalties before I had any.

"A sista always gotta be doin' it for herself," joked G.

I laughed. "You know how I do."

"Then we gotta get you right into the studio. You debut live at NV the Saturday of Thanksgiving weekend, ya hear? So mark your calendar and let's get to work."

I looked up and caught Genevieve staring at me. Her mouth smiled, but her eyes were worried. She dropped her head to scribble the information about my debut on a pad that I hoped she would transfer dutifully to her PDA tonight. True, I never believed she wished for me to fail. But I also knew that she hated being wrong, least of all when it came to me. Still she had helped me, and I vowed not only to pay back her loan with interest but also to break her off a little something extra for herself as soon as my check cleared.

CHAPTER 13

CEASEFIRE

Yolanda and Yeribel were no joke. I give myself major daps for asking them to style me for my first photo shoot. It even turned out that Yoli was going to the Fashion Institute of Technology at night, and she used her employee discount at the boutique to buy pieces that she would pull apart and re-create into original designs. Not only did the girl have skills, she knew how to make me look hot without hooching me out. Oh, she would push me to show *un poquito de* cleavage, *un poquito mas* leg. But she respected my comfort zone and designed for me so well that I really didn't need all that to stand out.

And at the risk of sounding stereotypical, nobody does Black hair like a Dominican chick. I never went to a Black stylist who didn't grease the shit out of my hair, and one time I went to this Rican woman who took over three hours to do it because she couldn't focus, gossiping with this one, commenting about whatever was going down on Dr. Laura's show with that one. (Not the scanky one on the radio but this Peruvian lawyer who's like a cross between Ricki Lake and Judge Hatchett. I knew this 'cause that

was Leila's favorite show, and when I made the mistake of confusing her with the other one, she jumped to school me about how the
Latina Dr. Laura speaks out for women who have been abused,
exploited, or otherwise dissed, unlike the other one, who likes to
blame women for everything terrible that happens to them just because they *are* women.) Yeri knew how to style my hair whether
she blew it out straight or let it dry into its natural curl, and it never
took her more than an hour and a half.

The night before the shoot, they came over to Darnell's, Yoli
carrying a suitcase of clothing and a portable sewing machine and
Yeri toting a professional makeup kit and a bag of hair products
and styling tools. The Segui sisters were twilight babies for their
aging parents, and they left the Dominican Republic to earn
money, get an education, and eventually bring their parents to the
United States. Although Yeribel was older, she worked full-time at
the salon and styled hair on the side so that Yolanda could go to
F.I.T. first. I thought that mad generous and I told her so. As she
untangled my freshly washed hair, Yeri said to me, *"Mira, Cassandra, te digo* I know what I want to do and I know I'm going to
do it no matter what. *Pero* this one I have to keep my eye on her.
Otherwise . . ."* In the mirror, I saw Yeribel flourish her hand like
a helium balloon fluttering away.

On her knees at my feet while pinning the hem of the pants she
asked me to try on, Yoli just huffed. *"Ay, dejate de esa baina ya,"*
she said between pins in her pursed lips. "I know what I want to
do, too."

"Si, yo se," Yeribel told her sister. *"Pero no tienes disciplina y
haces la cosas a medias."*

I reached for my school-taught Spanish. "Yolanda doesn't have
any discipline and does things by . . . socks?"

Yeribel laughed at me in that kind way that Leila always did.
"You almost got it. Yolanda wants to do things by *half*."

"I do not!"

"Cassandra, you understand very good."

"*¿Como ella va entender cuando tu estas exagerando?*"

"Cassandra understand me just fine," Yeribel insisted. She leaned forward so I could see her face and said to me, "*A quien esperar y sufrir puede, todo en su tiempo le viene.*"

I looked down at Yolanda, who had no interest in helping me figure out what her sister had just said. My mind grabbed at the words I recognized, and then I translated and strung them together. Who, to wait, to suffer, all, time, comes. The closest saying in English leaped at me. "Good things come to those who wait?" I guessed.

Yeribel beamed with regard. "Yes, he who has patience has the world." We both smiled at the other's reflection in the mirror, satisfied with both our translations.

When I knew there'd be no way I could replicate their magic on my own at the photography studio, I asked them to come with me. Yoli became so I excited I thought she'd shatter into tiny pieces. Although she tried to play cool, I could tell Yeri was amped, too.

So rolling into the photography studio with the Segui sisters made me feel like a professional who had been doing this for the longest. And while we weren't mad close just yet, it was all love. None of that fuckin'-Spanish-girls-this and *jodía-cocolas*-that Leila and I had to deal with when we first got tight. It was mad cool to have girlfriends again. And even if we hadn't been cutting up in their apartment during the fittings or on the car ride to the studio, I felt better not having to deal with the Explicit Content people for the first time by myself.

We arrived at the studio a half hour early, introduced ourselves to the photographer—some dude who went by Gold and was supposed to be the next Ernie Paniccioli and had already shot several covers for *Trace*—and got to work putting myself together for the shoot. Yoli broke out this sunlight yellow halter top that I never would have worn let alone bought, but I had to admit that it made my dark skin glow. Yeri swept my hair into a smooth French twist and made me up with a natural look that played up my full lips and large eyes.

"Watch out, Tyra," Yeri said.

"Yeah, right," I cracked.

"*¡Ay, no!*" Yoli agreed. "She's prettier than Tyra. *Sin los ojos verdes y las cenas grandes,*" she explained, as she pointed to her eyes and then cupped her breasts. "Tyra who?" I doubted that, but I could tell she was sincere so I laughed along with her sister.

Almost as if she were cued, this white girl with dreads and an Explicit Content baby T turned the divider dragging a travel bag on wheels. She looked me up and down and hollered, "What are you doing?"

"Excuse you?" Yeri said and went back to adjusting the sequined bolero she had draped around my shoulders to see how it worked with the halter top.

"No, excuse you," the girl said. Then she turned to me. "Are you Cassandra, Sabrina, whatever?"

"Why?" I snapped.

"I'm Andi Quinn," she said. "I'm your stylist."

"But I told G I wanted to use my own people," I said.

Andi just rolled her eyes at me. "I style all the Explicit Content artists." She groaned at the bolero and reached out to pull it off.

Yoli slapped her hand away. "*¡Quita!*"

Andi looked at me and waited for me to command Yoli to back off. I remembered the red vinyl gym shorts and skyscraper heels Leila had worn in the "Color Me Gully" remix video. "You heard her," I said to Andi. "*¡Quita!*"

Andi huffed into a corner with her cell phone while Yoli and I laughed. But then Yeri hushed us in that older-sister way. "*Mira,* Cassandra, maybe we should let her work with you. We don't want to get you into any trouble with the label."

I knew she was right. I was having so much fun getting glam for my first photo shoot, I had forgotten who was paying for it. And with all he had to think about, G probably just forgot. But I wasn't trying to let Andi have her way just like that either. I called her back.

"Wait, G, she's calling me," she said.

I can't lie. The sound of his name got me anxious. "Look, it's cool if you take over from here. But I don't want to take off my makeup and I'm not wearing anything I didn't bring."

"Well, it's not like we have time to start over anyway," she muttered.

Andi got back on the phone. "G, we settled it. Yeah, see you in a bit."

Yoli, Yeri, and I exchanged nervous glances. "G's coming over here?" I asked trying my best to sound more curious than concerned.

"Well, now he is."

It took all I had not to smack the bitch. And Yoli looked exactly how I was feeling. For their own sakes, I turned to the Segui sisters and said, "Why don't y'all go have lunch, do some window shopping, whatever. When I break to eat, I'll call you so you can bring me back something." They took the hint and my money but not before Yeri gave Andi a fuck-with-her-and-deal-with-me look.

The second they were gone, Andi rushed to undo their work. She yanked off the bolero and applied this porno red lipstick over the deep plum shade Yeri had chosen for me. She undid my hair and did God-knows-what since there were no mirrors. I didn't like any of this shit, but I was trying to go with her flow. But I drew the line when she shoved all of Yoli's designs aside, opened up her travel bag, and asked me, "What color are your panties?"

"Say what?"

"Do they match the top you have on?"

"No," I said, making it obvious how stupid I thought the question was.

"I have something that should work," Andi said, but I didn't know what she meant until she yanked out a bright yellow thong with silver lightning streaks out of her bag. Then she pulled out a black micro-mini.

"I said I want to wear only what I bought with me," I said. "My stylist broke more than a few nights designing clothes just for me."

Andi looked me up and down as if I hadn't said a word. "What are you? A size eight?"

"A ten," I said. Wanting to make her feel stupid, I added, "Tall."

"And that's why your legs are gonna look fabulous in this," she replied in this two-and-two-are-four tone that made me wish she hadn't bothered with the empty compliment. She was no Segui. "That skirt's way too long, Cassandra."

"The slit's almost to my hip!"

Now the heifer was looking at me like I was three years old. "So what's the difference if you wear this?" she said, waving the micro-mini at me. The difference was that my skirt flowed like a curtain while hers hung like a wristband. Andi came at me with the thong and skirt, and I backed away like they were a stun gun and pepper spray.

"I said I'm not wearing that."

"Yes, you are," said a familiar voice behind me. I turned and there G stood in a rust Stacy Adams suit and those Fendi sunglasses. In a tone so tight, it hurt to hear, he said, "Cassandra, put the skirt on and get out here already."

My face burned with the heat that pierced through his dark frames. I stood there for a moment, glaring at him. Then I snatched the thong and skirt. I grabbed my waistband and was about to yank down my skirt when I stopped. "Do y'all mind?"

G gave this sick grin and disappeared around the divider. I turned to Andi, who was still standing there with this smug look on her face. I put my fists on my hips, and she finally got the hint and bounced. Maybe I didn't have the courage to refuse to wear those skimpy clothes, but at least I had managed to hold on to some dignity by insisting I change alone.

The set consisted only of a black leather sofa draped in leopard skin throws positioned before a matching backdrop. I thought it was mad cheesy but kept that to myself. After what had just gone down behind the divider, I decided to pick my battles.

My pissy attitude worked for a minute. G sat there shaking his head as Gold shot a whole roll of me sitting on the sofa with a scowl on my face and my legs and arms crossed tight. "Always the tough chick," G said. I just ignored him. "Ayo, Gold, loosen her up. Dudes ain't gonna be feelin' that ice princess shit."

"OK, Cassandra, let's go for something softer," Gold said. I uncrossed my legs but kept them pressed at the knees and dropped my hands into my lap. I wasn't trying to give him a hard time, it's just that I never had my picture taken professionally outside of class pictures, never mind with someone like G in the background hawking me behind his sunglasses. Andi's tugging at my clothes and hair between shots just made me even more ornery. "OK, Cassie, I want you to imagine that you're sitting at the Staples Center in Los Angeles. It's Grammy night and you've been nominated for, like, ten awards." I rolled my eyes, but a smile began to gurgle in my throat.

"Fuck that," G said. "She got twelve nominations. My girl's gonna leave Lauryn in the dust." I chuckled. "Ah, you like that. I like that, too." He stood up, pulling off his sunglasses and handing them to me.

I put them on, and Gold snapped a few photos. Then he said, "And 50 Cent just finished reading the nominations for Best New Artist and is now tearing open the envelope. And the winner is . . ." He paused for such a long time, I closed my eyes and, swear to God, I could see it. I saw the stage, I saw Fiddy, I saw him tear open the envelope. And instead of Gold, I heard Fiddy say, "Yeah! Sabrina Steelo! My girl!"

"There you go!" Gold said as he popped flashes in a fury. "You have a fantastic smile, Cassie. Great cheekbones. Keep smiling."

"That's what I'm talkin' about," said G.

So I started to get into it. I grabbed one of the leopard throws and wrapped it around my head like a hood, and Gold rushed in for a few close-ups. Then I propped my chin into my hands and grinned like a schoolgirl. Gold snapped away. He ran out of film, and while his assistant exchanged rolls with him, I got the impulse to stand on the sofa and perch myself on its back.

That's when all the other Explicit Content artists rolled into the studio—Hi-Jack, Primo, the 8MM Posse, and Leila. I could tell by the way she avoided my gaze that she knew I was there. While the guys drifted over to G to give him pounds, Leila dipped behind the dividers, and Andi went to join her, saying to me, "You're gonna be OK without me, right?" I just sucked my teeth at her, and she disappeared behind the screen.

Gold noticed something in my expression because he snapped away. "I like that contemplative look," he said. "Just tilt your chin slightly to the left." But with all those male eyes on me, I soon lost my groove. Yolanda and Yeribel saved me when they returned even though I had yet to call them. Yeri raised two white paper bags to let me know that she had brought me lunch. I signaled for them to wait for me behind the screen. As they crossed the room, Yoli noticed Primo and began tugging at her sister's sleeve. Primo noticed Yolanda and blew her a kiss. Yoli giggled, and Yeri grabbed her arm and dragged her out of Primo's sight. Primo whispered something to Hi-Jack, who snickered and offered him a pound.

Then G said, "Yo, Cass, give the PMS thing a break already." The guys cracked up like he was Chris Tucker and shit.

I decided not to pick that fight. Instead I forced a smile and said, "That ain't PMS, kid, that's hunger."

G and the guys laughed. Then he said, "All right. Why don't you take a short break? And I mean short, 'cause these muthafuckas got an appointment at the studio."

I couldn't get behind the divider fast enough. There I found Leila trying on the bolero and chatting up Yolanda and Yeribel in Spanish as if she'd known them forever. The three of them were going at it so fast, I couldn't catch a single word. My first impulse was to use Andi as an excuse to send their asses home. But I'd never clued them in on what went down between Leila and me, so why should I punish them for being as nice to her as they had been to me?

So I grabbed one of the deli bags and a chair and sat in the corner. I pretended to be too into my chicken cutlet hero and lemonade to notice what the three *amigas* were up to, and the Segui sisters were too busy fussing with Leila's hair and clothes to be checking for me. Since the clothes and makeup they brought was for me, they had a hard time finding something that looked right on her. And truth be told, that comforted me.

At one point, Leila pulled off her sweatshirt and shocked me with her gaunt frame. She'd always been thin but healthy. From where I sat, her profile resembled the spine of a spiral notebook. G had said he had to hassle her to eat, but he never said why and I never asked. I wondered if the label had a chef at the mansion who made food she didn't like. But then again, Leila had tried just about every kind of food during her time with Diego and seemed to like it all. The sight of Leila's rib cage was so painful even Yolanda and Yeribel paused.

And Leila noticed. She rushed to throw on a royal blue blouse. Well, on me it would have been a blouse, but on Leila it hung like a short tunic. The blue made the veins on her neck stand out. She said something softly to Yoli and Yeri, and they began to talk quickly over each other as if they were trying to reassure her. I had enough of being kept in this linguistic ghetto, but before I could ask them what the hell they were talking about, Yoli told me they would be right back and they disappeared.

So Leila and I were behind the screen alone. I gnawed at my hero while she picked imaginary lint off the blouse. She looked straight at me and then at the sandwich half that still sat on the deli bag flattened across my lap. Her eyes blazed with starvation. Even though I was full on breaded chicken and sweetened lemonade, I actually could feel Leila's stomach growling in pain as if it were my own. Almost as if she knew that, Leila asked me, "If you not gonna eat that . . ."

Then I saw it again. The same shame I caught on her face when she dogged me with those canned rhymes at the party. We had not seen or spoken to each other since she and her dogs set me up, yet she stood before me with a face sunken by hunger and asked for half my lunch. I had no idea what, if anything, she knew about my record deal, but I thought maybe she had come to accept that I was now part of Explicit Content. Or maybe G Double D told her she had better make nice with me. Maybe both. Or something altogether different. I couldn't figure it out.

So I decided to be the bigger woman. I picked up the second half of my sandwich and offered it to her. The way she hesitated, I could tell it was the last thing she'd expected me to do. That she was afraid that she would reach out for the sandwich and I would jump to my feet and beat her pallid ass. I stayed still as if Leila were a squirrel in the park and the sandwich was a nut. She forced herself to look me in the eye as she took the sandwich out of my hand. Leila jammed her teeth into it, tearing off a big chunk and chewing furiously. She was about to take another huge bite when someone rapped hard at the divider. Leila jumped and hid the sandwich behind her back.

"Ayo, y'all need to get out here so we can finish this thing and head to the studio," G said from behind the screen.

I tossed my cup into the deli bag, balled it up, and threw it in the trash. Right before I crossed to the other side of the divider, something told me to look behind me. I caught Leila stuffing the rest of the sandwich into her purse.

"Ya'll bitches need to get out here NOW!"

I stood there watching Leila when I felt a thick hand on my arm. I turned to find Hi-Jack with his hoof on me. I yanked my arm away. "Don't be grabbing me!" Then I walked around him and toward the set.

The 8MM Posse were slumped across the sofa while Primo chatted up Yolanda in the corner. Starstruck, Yolanda played a weak game of hard to get as Primo sweet-talked her in Spanish while Yeribel stood close by and stern to make her disapproval obvious. Primo handed Yoli a business card and headed back to the set. The second his back was to them, Yeribel snatched the card from Yolanda's hand and tore it up. They began to argue in hushed Spanish, and when Gold shot them a look, Yeribel took her sister's hand and led her outside. All I heard as Yeri pushed Yoli out the door was Primo and *tigere*.

As Primo retook his seat on the sofa's armrest, G Double D consulted with Gold. Then he spotted me and said, "OK, Sabrina, I need you where you were sitting on the back of the seat." I took a last look behind me, and now Hi-Jack had his claws into Leila as he whispered harshly in her ear. She shoved him away from her and came to the set. I climbed onto the sofa and prayed that the 8MM thugs would keep their hands to themselves.

"Where do I go?" Leila asked G.

G pointed at the 8MM Posse and said, "Y'all need to stand behind the sofa, behind Sabrina. Hi-Jack, Primo, y'all sit on the couch on opposite sides of Bri. Fatal, you sit between Hi-Jack and Primo at Bri's feet. Ayo, Andi, change Primo's shirt. There's too much red on that side."

We took our places, and Gold shot a roll of film. Then G said, "OK, y'all dudes clear out for the studio. We're gonna take some of just the ladies." Where I was seated, I didn't know if Leila was upset to not be rolling to the studio with them. On the one hand, it seemed like G had her album on the perpetual back burner. On the other hand, I couldn't stand being the only female rolling with Hi-Jack and them. Either way it would've bothered me.

The guys left and G turned his attention to Leila and me. "We need some really hot shots of y'all together. Let's start with a few just where you at." So like a totem pole, I stayed at the top of the sofa while Leila kept at my feet. Although I couldn't see her face to know how she felt about that arrangement, I had an urge to suggest that we switch places for a few shots. But then G said, "Bri, you're like some pliers and shit. Open up."

"What you mean *open up?*" I said afraid that I already knew.

G walked over to me on the sofa. "I mean . . ." Just as he clamped his palms on my knees, Leila jumped between us. "What the hell you doing?" He shoved her, and she fell back. Then he grabbed my knees and tried to pry my legs apart. I fought to block him, and as I did I saw his gun in his waistband as his suit jacket fell away from his body. Then Leila sprung between us. G shoved a thick finger in Leila's face. "Stay out of this, Leila."

The Leila I grew up with would have turned pit bull and torn that finger off his hand. Instead she wedged herself between G and me. "You knew that wasn't her steelo when you signed her," she said through her teeth. Her eyes still fixed on G Double D, Leila told me, "Cassie, go sit down there." Relieved to get away from G, I did what she said. Leila took my old spot on the sofa and said to G, "You gotta have some coochy shot on the Web site, I'll do it. Just leave Cassie alone." Yolanda and Yeribel reentered the studio with a small drugstore bag and immediately picked up on the dramatic vibe. In a calmer tone, Leila said, "The stylists are back, so lemme take five minutes to adjust my gear, and then we can take all the pictures you want. OK?"

G unwound. "OK. Five minutes. That's it."

Leila turned to me and said, "Cassie, come with us so Yeribel can freshen your makeup." But I immediately knew she just didn't want to leave me out there alone with G. And I didn't want to be left alone with him, so I followed her behind the screen.

Then Leila took charge. She told Andi, "Find me some underwear and shoes that go with this top." Happy to be needed, Andi jumped to it. "While you're at it, find some pants for Cassie to wear." Yoli spun Leila around as she hooked sewing pins in strategic places while Yeri changed my lipstick, removing that streetlight red and reapplying the pretty plum she'd originally chosen for me. Leila, Yeri, and Yoli talked in hushed Spanish although this time the Segui sisters seemed worried and Leila reassured them. As Andi handed me a pair of jeans and I pulled them on, Leila quickly dropped and stepped out of hers. The second G yelled, "Y'all bitches get out here now," we were ready to roll.

Leila marched to the sofa and climbed on top of it. She thrust her hips forward and stretched her skinny legs forward as if she had done this a thousand times. Then she smiled and winked at the camera. Gold snapped away at her. Then Leila hiked up the top and dropped her knees open, revealing a sliver of royal blue between her legs.

G turned to me. "What you waiting for? Get into the picture."

So I took a seat between Leila's feet and struck ladylike poses while Leila vamped for the camera. G said, "Yeah, that's hot. That's what I'm talkin' about. Y'all are two badass bitches." Andi played yes girl, but Yolanda and Yeribel stood in the back looking as if they had just stumbled on an accident and were hoping to hear news about survivors. Although I could not see Leila's face, my gut told me that she had no more smiles for the camera.

CHAPTER 14

ONE-TWO, ONE-TWO

About three the next morning, Darnell finally realized I wasn't in bed and found me in the kitchen. When I told him what had happened at the photo shoot, I left out that G had put his hands on me. I didn't want D to wild and make matters worse. I just wanted to forget the whole thing. But that meant not telling how Leila had my back when G crossed the line. Hiding that bothered me more than keeping what G did from him. But I did tell him about Leila and the sandwich and how every time I turned around some dude on the label was pushing her around and she was taking it.

Darnell sat down next to me at the table and rubbed the small of my back. "All these females out here trying to be put on—you included—and G chose her. The man believed in her, bankrolled her, and now she can't finish that album. If Leila's got drama at the label, it's because she's not backing up all that talk. Leila's choking, Cassie, and there's nothing you can do about it."

I got a bit heated. "So if I get nervous under the pressure and have trouble completing my album, it'll be all right for G, Hi-Jack, and them to put their hands on me?"

"No, but you're not listening to me," Darnell answered. "After putting herself out there like a solo artist and agreeing to those bullshit terms, Leila ain't cutting it. You don't need to worry about that, though. You got a legit one-album deal to prove your-self, and if there's anything I've learned about you these past months is that Sabrina Steelo don't choke under pressure. And when you do have a bad day, ain't nobody gonna put their hands on you unless they want to tangle with me." Then D took my hand and said, "Maybe you need to put a brother on so he can look out for you."

I squeezed his hand. The idea of bringing Darnell to Explicit Content had appealed more to me every day. Long before we started kicking it, we were putting it down together with hot re-sults, so why not? After all I'd seen I especially liked the idea of having a man in the studio who would have my back. But after watching Leila handle her business at the photo shoot, I didn't doubt her ability to deliver like D did. She was quite capable of doing whatever she had to do whether she liked it or not. Always has been. Something else was going on between Leila and the label, and that was what really was keeping me up.

When Jen called me with the date of my first recording session, I pushed for a meeting with G Double D before reporting to the studio. She resisted, saying that G was mad busy and that I'd have an opportunity to speak with him at the studio.

Annoyed with her gatekeeping, I said, "Look, it's important that I speak with him before then."

"Well, what's all this about anyway?" Jen shot back.

Not expecting her to ask me that, I just snapped, "It's per-sonal!" I knew her responsibility was to buffer G from bullshit artists who wanted to waste his time, and that was no easy task. But as an artist on the label, she had no call to mind my business.

"Look, the best I can do is a late dinner after your session," said

Jen. "And dinners with G are always a gamble. That's when he's most likely to cancel."

"Fine," I said. "I'll take my chances."

First thing I did when I awoke that morning, I called my bank to check my account balance. My advance cleared, so I wrote a check to Darnell for five grand and left it on the night table. That way if my dinner conversation with G was canceled—or worse, failed—it would soften the blow. And if G granted my request, the check would be the icing on the cake I would deliver that night.

I had hoped that my first recording session would be a solo track and brought my best rhymes in case. But like I expected, I came to perform on the remix of Primo's latest single "But Can You Feel Me?" Initially recorded and released as a hip-hop ballad, G wanted to quicken the tempo and extend the rap segments for the clubs. I arrived at the studio to find Primo warbling in the recording booth while Hi-Jack and the sound engineer, Bokim, made adjustments at the board. I let them know I had arrived and took a seat behind them.

As Hi-Jack played with potential beats for Primo's remix, he'd come up with something hot only to cast it aside for a generic melody. The better the beat, the quicker he disposed of it, especially if Bokim showed it any love. Like Hi-Jack was terrified to be unique. My distaste for the man wouldn't allow me to sleep on his skills. If the dude kept his hands on the boards and off underaged chicks, he truly could give Dre a run for his money. But realizing that beneath the public menace was a cowering artist only made me lose more respect for him. Why should I feel compassion for Hi-Jack when he was doing it to himself?

I hoped Primo would surprise me, too, but nope. With caramel skin and ink-black hair, Primo was fine to women of all kinds. So much that I had never noticed the three faint scars he had across his right cheek before that day. I figured they retouched his album covers or only shot him from one side. Not that they needed to. Like Seal's childhood scars, Primo's imperfections only accentuated his beauty while making him seem attainable. Leila once said, "Nothing's sexier than a man whose fly enough to want but not too fly to get," but only when I saw Primo up close in the studio did I understand what she meant and why she would hook up with him.

But Primo's only talent ended with looking good. He didn't outright suck, but he didn't shine, either. And like most mediocre singers, G often teamed up Primo with rappers or, worse, let Primo rhyme himself. In fact, Primo fancied himself an MC first, but my guess was G Double D signed him just to say he had a Latino R&B singer on the label as if Maxwell wasn't out there doing his thing.

As I sat behind Bokim and listened to him edit Primo's vocals, I remembered the first time I heard him on the radio. I had tagged along on one of Leila's shopping sprees when they played his record. "You hear this?" I said as I pointed upward toward the store's speakers. "J.Lo with a dick."

Leila scoffed. "Then his *pinga* better be as big her *culo* if he wants to last a minute."

Lost in this memory, I laughed so loud that Bokim spun in his seat to hush me as nicely as possible. I nodded in acknowledgment of his patience, and then to keep myself in check, I cracked open my notebook. Now that I had heard Primo's song, I concentrated on modifying one of my existing verses to work with it. I grew bored with that after fifteen minutes, so I tried to pen some new lines. A half hour later, the door opened and in stepped the 8MM Posse and Leila. The Posse members each gave me stiff nods and rolled past me into the studio. The only seat available was next to me and Leila took it.

"Hey," she said.

"Hi."

Within minutes those boys turned the recording studio into a frat house. Hi-Jack gave Bokim a lunch break and summoned Primo from the recording booth. The second the door closed behind Bokim, each member of the Posse busted out with two forties and Primo lit a blunt. I glanced at Leila, who looked as annoyed as I felt. I bet this carousing on G Double D's dime was routine for them, and they didn't think enough of Bokim to invite him.

Hi-Jack shoved a beer bottle in my face. I started to refuse it when I felt a tug on my cuff. I looked over to Leila, who caught me square in the eye and then motioned toward the bottle. Hoping none of those bastards had any communicable diseases, I faked a swig and passed the bottle to Leila. Then I watched her do the same. When she handed the bottle to Primo, it had lost only five drops since it left Hi-Jack's bloated paws.

Then the blunt followed, and Leila and I repeated the fraud. Leila never got high on account of her moms's history and all. Me, I smoked occasionally on the social tip. But I wasn't comfortable around these wildcats sober so I certainly wasn't going to risk my right mind around them.

Before we knew it, two dudes in the 8MM Posse almost came to blows over some bullshit. The skinny one with the lazy eye called the Black dude in the Joe Boxer commercials a punk for dancing around in his drawers on national TV. Leila and I exchanged silent grins. The first time we saw the commercial, we had a major disagreement about it. Leila thought the Black Joe Boxer—or the BJB as we started to call him—was downright adorable. For once I agreed with my mother; the man's a modern-day coon.

Eventually, the short Posse member with no neck—I mean, homeboy probably spent fourteen months on lockdown piling Franky G muscles on a Darryl Hughley frame—jumped to his feet and got in the skinny guy's face. "Why you frontin', son? If you had been offered that nigga's loot, you'd be skipping across the screen in your skivvies your damned self." He started hopping around like a member of the Lollipop Guild on *The Wizard of Oz*. The guys roared, and OK, I cracked up, too. But Leila sat there as if at a wake. Just as I pulled at her sleeve to ask her what was wrong, I learned.

"Yeah, muthafucka? Let's see you put on a show with my foot up yo' stocky ass," the skinny guy said. "Let's see you dance then, muthafucka."

Stocky got in Skinny's grill. "I'll dance on you, nigga, after I cap you for even thinking about coming out your face to me."

What could've been an interesting conversation about the kind of image the Black Joe Boxer was perpetuating quickly deteriorated into some macho name-calling, chest-bumping nonsense. I don't know who was more stupid. These fools for threatening to cap each other when they essentially agreed that the BJB was a high-paid clown. Or me for believing for a second that they could discuss something meaningful like intelligent adults. To think I almost added my own two cents knowing Leila would leap into the fray. But then the fray turned into a brawl, so the third Posse member with the split lip had to push the muscle-necked one outside to cool off while the lazy-eyed one stayed behind with the rest of us.

Finally Bokim returned and Primo went back into the booth to lay down his vocals. Downing a forty and smoking a blunt did nothing for his mediocre singing. If anything, they cost Primo the little control of the limited range he had. Hi-Jack cursed under his breath and banged the board with frustration.

I peeked at Leila out of the corner of my eye, and the girl truly had a smirk on her face. You'd think she'd be embarrassed for her man. But then again, Leila has always been straight up with and about her men. Although I doubted she would be as quick to criticize anyone at Explicit Content as she might Diego or any of her other boyfriends, I knew she wouldn't gas any of them if they didn't deserve it either.

Leila caught me looking at her, and I shifted my gaze to the open notebook on my lap. Primo cracked a note, and Hi-Jack cursed up a storm while Bokim sighed and rubbed his temples. When I heard Leila snicker, I forced a cough to hide my own snickering. Leila reached for my pen and scribbled across the bottom of my notebook.

You called it. I gave her a confused look. She picked up the pen again. *J.Lo with a dick.*

Now I couldn't help but giggle. And that got Leila started. Soon we were having a poorly repressed fit until Hi-Jack turned in his seat. "You bitches think this shit is funny?"

"I'm just nervous about performing," I said. "The longer I sit here, the worse it's gonna get. Sorry."

Hi-Jack jumped from his seat and headed into the recording booth. Bokim needed a smoke and stepped out of the studio. Leila and I burst out laughing, the most authentic impulse either of us had since signing with Explicit Content.

Then I had to go spoil it. I leaned over to Leila and whispered in her ear, "So just how big is he?" Leila never felt self-conscious about discussing her men's dimensions. If anything she loved to crack me up with her assessments. Diego was average, but he loved to go down so Leila liked to wind him up and let him go. Despite all the stereotypes about white boys, Vance was huge, but he was also insecure and klutzy. With the constant encouragement and direction he needed, sometimes Leila couldn't be bothered. Junior was short and stubby, but the brother learned to work what he had, which was why Leila kept him around no matter how often he flaked. When she caught up with him, he proved to be worth it.

But when I asked her about Primo, Leila shut down on me. Not in an offended or angry way. More like I had busted her in a lie of some kind.

Before I could ask her what was wrong, Hi-Jack opened the door to the recording booth. "Cassie, you're on. I'ma work with you while Primo takes a break." He pointed at Leila and said, "Leila, go downstairs and get Primo some tea for his throat."

Leila sucked her teeth but rose to her feet. I don't know if she was annoyed with the errand or disappointed that she would have to wait longer to hear me do my thing. I found myself scowling at

Primo as we walked past each other in the doorway of the recording booth. Why couldn't the dude get his own damned tea? Too busy making a scene of clearing his throat, he didn't notice my stank attitude toward him.

So I slipped on the headphones and kicked a few yes-yes-y'alls, I-said-a-hip-a-hop-you-don't-stops and in-the-place-to-bes while Bokim adjusted the sound. I wished Leila could hear me keep our ritual alive. We always warmed up that way before we recorded, our way of giving homage to the hip-hop predecessors and to remind ourselves of that day in Crotona Park when we realized we had found a partner in rhyme.

Then Hi-Jack cued me and I spit my new rhyme while waiting my turn.

> When Bri comes marchin' home
> (A'ight, A'ight)
> Don't call me out my name
> And question my return
> 'Cause I learned to play the game.
> Like Perón, I never left you.
> Like Pac, still got around
> Stealin' stars out the sky
> With my Tims still on the ground
> Surfin' the Tats line
> Splashing colors over grays
> Casting light over gloom
> And bringing better dayz.
> Home's where the heart is
> And my heart rides the E.
> I know you feel my flow
> But can you feel me?

Since the verse was new to me, I stumbled here and there, but I forged ahead. I used to stop in my tracks and apologize a thousand times, but over the past few months Darnell broke me of the habit. I waited for Hi-Jack to give me some kind of feedback on the rhyme, but he said nothing about it. Take after take, he just told me where to start or to adjust my speed. I finally asked him about the rhyme.

"What about it?"

"I mean, you think it works?"

He sneered at me and said, "Yeah, yeah, yeah, Punchanella, it's a'ight." Then he turned to Primo and Bokim and cracked, "Bitches always be needing reassurance and shit." The three of them laughed, and I fought to pretend that I didn't hear or care.

Then G Double D entered the studio, and they forgot me. After G gave Bokim a pound, Hi-Jack pulled him into a corner. Within minutes Primo crossed the room to join them. The sound was cut so I couldn't hear them, but it looked as if Hi-Jack and Primo were trying to lobby G from opposing viewpoints. Then the discussion became so heated no one noticed that Leila had reentered the studio with a paper bag. She tried to get Primo's attention so she could hand him his tea, but he barked at her, pointed to a seat, and went back to his argument with Hi-Jack and G.

That pissed off both of us. I motioned for Leila to come into the booth. She pulled Primo's teacup out of the bag and placed it on a seat. She walked past the three of them into the recording booth. They were so involved in their dispute, they didn't even notice her. Leila pulled another cup out of the paper bag and handed it to me.

"Thanks," I said. Other than offering me some booze and smoke I didn't want or need, Leila was the first person on the label to check for me. I tore a rip into the plastic lid and took a sip. Coffee with sugar, no stomach-tearing milk. Just like I always took it. I finally asked, "What the hell's going on out there?"

"Another creative fuckin' difference," Leila answered. She pulled a stool next to me and sat down.

"So how long before they start wailing on each other?"

Leila sucked her teeth. "You can set your watch by that shit." I laughed and she joined me. "When Earl and Jason turn on Keef, it's half-past seven."

"When who turns on who?"

"You know. The dudes in the Posse."

"Oh," I said embarrassed. I had never admitted that I couldn't tell one from the other. They looked nothing alike but shared the same thug attitude so I avoided hanging around them long enough to learn their real names or distinguish one from the other. But I realized that I had better do so before any of the guys on the label noticed I couldn't and start drama over it. "So the skinny one with the lazy eye . . . ?"

"That's Earl. Or Third Eye."

"Third Eye?" I scoffed. "Like he can see into the future or something?"

Leila smiled and shook her head. "His third eye is the barrel of his gun."

"I guess it's no wonder he can't see when No-Neck's about to go off and diffuse the situation?"

"No-Neck?" Leila laughed. "You mean Jason?"

"Whatever."

"Although he goes by Cryciss." Then she spelled it for me and we rolled our eyes in agreement. "And the last one's Keef."

"Keith?"

"His mama named him Keith, but with that busted lip, he's got a lisp. So it comes out Keef, and that's what we call him."

At least his own mother hadn't sunk to ghetto extremes on him. "How did he bust his lip?"

"Some dude in jail caught him in the face with his own shank," explained Leila. "Don't buy his peacemaker act. Keef's going right back in the second the guy who did that to him hits the streets." And by the look on her face, she hoped to be far away when Keef and his enemy came face-to-face again.

I didn't want to think about it either. Hi-Jack, Primo, and G Double D were still heated, so I walked over to the window that

separated Leila and me from Bokim. Boy was thoroughly annoyed, leaning on his elbow as he glared at G Double D and them
arguing. His face clearly read *Simple niggas*. Just because Bokim
got paid for his time regardless didn't mean he wanted it wasted.
That was the kind of person I always liked to work with. So I
tapped on the window and motioned for him to give us a beat.

I checked the mic. "One-two, one-two. Bri Steez in the place to
be." I pointed to Leila. She put a hand to her chest and a question
on her face. I waved for her to continue.

Leila pulled her stool closer to the mic, adjusted it, and said,
"Yes, yes, y'all, you don't stop. Fatal's gonna rock the mic until ya
drop." We looked at Bokim as he grinned and shook his head.
Yeah, he thought it was corny, but he still liked it.

So for the first time in months, Leila and I rhymed together. We
may have well been back in our living room on the Upper West
Side, me stretched along the Natuzzi sofa and Leila cross-legged
in the matching chair. Our chemistry remained on point, and the
next thing you know I was freestyling. Not great, mind you, but
not bad either. Every time I spewed a lyrical gem, Leila would
point to Bokim as if to say, "You got that?"

Then I pointed to Leila to let her know she had next. She shook
her head wildly and tried to back away from the mic. I grabbed her
hand and pulled her back, and we were giggling like little girls
playing tug-o'-war. Bokim became all teeth, having fun for the
first time all day. Eventually, Leila got back on the mic, and after
some lame warm-up lyrics, she started to freestyle. And while
Leila wasn't particularly good, she wasn't bad at all. To be honest,
she was better than me, and it became my turn to check to see if
Bokim had caught all her best lines, and he would pump his fist to
confirm that he had.

Leila barreled on, and I got out of her way. Her eyes sparkled in
a way I hadn't seen since that night of our last performance at Da
Corridor. She had met G Double D there, and instead of finding
inspiration, Leila had lost the joy of rhyme. In the recording booth

with me trying to freestyle, she rediscovered it. Leila took to the mic the way a homeless person accepts a bag of leftovers with a tentative humility that quickly gives way to a ferocious hunger.

Just as Leila kicked the flow back to me, the beat abruptly stopped. Leila and I looked through the glass and G Double D now was at the boards giving Bokim instructions. Hi-Jack and Primo huffed to each other in the corner where G had abandoned them. G leaned into the mic at the boards and said, "Cass, Leila, I need you take the verse from the top." Bokim restarted a beat that Hi-Jack had discarded.

Leila panicked. I grabbed my notebook and flipped to one of the verses I had tinkered with while waiting for Hi-Jack to put me in the booth. I quickly changed some words to suit Leila, tore it out, and handed it to her. I covered the mic and whispered to her, "And if you mess up, don't sweat it. Just keep going." Leila grabbed the sheet, and her eyes darted down the page as she tried to make sense of my scribble. Her face relaxed with familiarity.

Loose from our brief freestyle session, I delivered the first verse perfectly. Leila swooped right in behind me, rhyming without a hitch as if she had written it herself and had weeks to memorize it. I bet it helped that she recognized it some from our past sessions.

From the Boulevard South
To the Ave Chest West
Jumped the elevated sub
To spit with the best.
From the Points Hunt
To the Hub's Point,
From South Bronx bricks
To the SoHo joint,
From the PJ Adams
To the Manse Glen Ridge,
I had to cross more
Than the GW Bridge,

> *And you'd never believe*
> *What done crossed me.*
> *So you can bop to the beat*
> *But can you feel me?*

After the first take, G Double D seemed pleased. "Let's do it one more time a little different," he said. "Just so we can have something to play with."

"Maybe a little more laid-back?" suggested Leila.

"Yeah, same pace, less energy," said G. "Give it to me on some Snoop Dogg, I-could-give-a-fuck shit."

So we did it once more, and just like that our recording session ended. Leila leaned over to say something to me when Primo busted into the booth. "Leila, let's bounce already," he barked as if she had kept him waiting. She looked to me, then back at Primo. "Let's go!"

Leila climbed off the stool and gave me a hug. "Thanks," she said. She walked to the door and then stopped to turn around. "Yo, Cassie? The Black Joe Boxer rocks."

"Please," I said, pretending to be offended. "Boy be coonin'."

"Don't be such a playa-hata," she said with a big smile across her face.

I grinned back at her. "Stop being an ass kisser." Before Leila could respond, Primo grabbed her arm and pulled her through the door. I was about to shout him out when G came into the booth.

He said. "You hungry?"

I was famished. "You payin'?"

He snickered and motioned for me to follow him. As I gathered my things, I saw Primo and Hi-Jack back in the corner conferring, their eyes fixed on Bokim as he gave Leila daps on our session. I should have known that just as Earl and Jason squash their beefs by turning on Keef, Primo and Hi-Jack had made a tentative peace based on a common rage at someone else. It was the Explicit Content way.

CHAPTER 15

G'S DIDDY THEORY

itches always be needing reassurance and shit. Hi-Jack's voice echoed in my head as I mopped a sun-dried tomato across my plate. Although we had arrived at Orso with no reservation, the host whisked us by the line of theater heads and sat us right away. Except to order his grilled scallops, seafood risotto, and a bottle of Lis Neris, G Double D never stopped his rant about how long it took to record Primo's remix.

Not a word though about how Leila and I saved the remix. With both of us on the track, G told Bokim to whittle Primo's vocals to the chorus. I don't recall that being done before—having female rappers lead while a male R&B singer did backup. Just the novelty that fueled G's executive decision, no doubt, but that didn't make our contribution any less worthy of recognition, you know.

"Drinking and smoking so much in the goddamn studio," G complained. "Just last month Cryciss spilled a half bottle of St. Ides on the mixer. And who had to replace that shit? Me, that's who. I'm trying to expand, and these niggas squandering my cap-

ital on blunts, booze, and bail bonds instead of generating rev-
enues by making records. From now on, no drinks or herb in the
studio. Nah, fuck that. From now on, nobody in the studio unless
they on the track."

That comment opened a window. "Yeah, but if Leila and I
hadn't been there today . . ." I stopped immediately, disgusted
with myself for trolling for his acknowledgment. Still I knew if I
had been one of the guys, he would have fallen over himself to slap
my back and give me a pound. I hadn't forgotten that our dinner
was no gesture of appreciation but just another scribble of lead in
his calendar that I had to badger Jen to get. And if I hadn't thrown
down in the studio this afternoon, he probably would have canceled dinner to seduce an aspiring singer he had just met on the
street or to get a last-minute eyebrow trim or some shit like that.

As if he had read my mind, G suddenly said, "Cassie, you saved
me today." It must've been obvious that he took me off guard, because he leaned across the table, placed his hand over mine, and
said, "Thank you."

I'm ashamed to admit how much that meant to me then. So
much that it never crossed my mind to secure daps for Leila. Probably because I took credit for drawing her out of whatever artistic
funk the papers kept writing about. If she finally was putting it
down the way G expected her to when he signed her, all praise was
due me.

And in that uncanny way of his, G then said, "And for a minute
there I thought you were gonna go diva on me."

"Me?" I replied with genuine shock. I knew I was confident in
my skills, and that sometimes that confidence rubbed others
wrong. While that never stopped me from knowing my worth, I
was no diva. If anything, I took pride in being my true self no matter the circumstances. And yeah, sometimes that meant being a
bitch. You can call me a bitch whenever, because in this game,
bitchiness was often justifiable. But don't call me a diva, because I
was never about stepping on someone else to get to where I wanted

to be. I figured that if I truly belonged there, that wouldn't be necessary. "Why you gonna say something like that?"

" 'Cause of all the trouble you were giving me at the photo
shoot," said G. "You didn't want to use the label's stylists. You
made a fuss about the clothes, the poses. Like you've been in the
game for more than a minute." He summoned the waiter to refill
the wine carafe, most of which he emptied by himself long before
the appetizers arrived.

Some choices words got caught in my throat. Not letting him
hooch me out at the photo shoot made me a diva? So fuckin' be it.
I bet if Primo or Hi-Jack refused something, they earned respect
for being their own men. But let Leila or me even suggest that
we're less than enthusiastic about G's directives, and we were difficult. Emotional. On the rag. Didn't understand the business.
Whatever.

But I knew I couldn't go there and get what I wanted. So I held
back my true sentiments and opted for another approach. "I didn't
mean to be difficult," I said. "This is all new to me, and while I'm
trying to learn how to play the game, I'm not trying to become
something I'm not. After all, you signed me, not some Lil' Kim
knockoff, right?"

"I feel you," said G.

"And to be real honest with you, G, I'm having trouble truly
feeling part of the label. I mean, first you sign Leila without me.
Then you sign me just to try and remake me into Leila."

G interrupted, "That wasn't what I was trying to do. . . ."

"I want to trust you, but . . ." I took the first sip of my wine,
hoping to hide any expression that might give away my feelings.
Although every word I said was true and my tone sincere, I was
afraid that G might hear past them to my false intentions. "Look,
that's why I wanted to have this conversation before the recording
session. I'm ready to put it down, G. Represent Explicit Content
lovely and all that. But I need a few things from you to help me do
that."

As if to prove I had his full attention, G put down his half-filled wineglass and pushed it across the linen tablecloth toward me. He laced his gold-encrusted fingers around his knee. "What you need, Cass? More money? Some new clothes? A car?"

G would think it was about that. Those things are what he could and was willing to provide. I took a genuine breath and said, "First, I want an opportunity to look out for my people." He broke into a twisted smile I couldn't read. Either he thought I just perpetrated like the diva I had just denied being or he respected that I wanted to bring up my crew. I had to snort at the second thought. Even if I were one to roll that deep, I barely had the numbers for an inner circle let alone a full crew. "I'm not talking about no entourage or anything like that. And I'm not saying you should put folks on the payroll who can't do nothing for me. I mean, for us. The record company."

"So what are you saying?"

"I'm just asking that you give my people a chance to prove themselves. They're good at what they do. They'll earn their ends."

"Like who?"

"Like Darnell, for one."

After exhaling with a cross between a sigh and a chuckle, G leaned back in his seat. "Darnell," he repeated.

"Who's a kick-ass producer and you know it," I said, the words rushing past my lips. I kicked myself for coming off like the gung-ho girlfriend. Reaching for a sesame breadstick, I shrugged and said, "You've already signed two of the artists he's worked with, so I'll let that speak for itself." I snapped the breadstick in two and hoped I sounded a bit more nonchalant.

G took a breadstick half out of my hand and said, "I had planned to produce your album myself, Cassie." He bit into the breadstick while his eyes hooked into mine. "I'm talking real hands-on. In the studio with you every day, overseeing every track just like I did today." Grinning and munching, he flicked a crumb from his chin with his pinky as if I had just pointed it out to him.

His earnestness took me back. If the rumors of Leila's bogus contract were true, he certainly wasn't doing that for her. The news both concerned and flattered me. On the real, I never thought much of G's production skills. His talent was limited to knowing the right hit of yesteryear to sample and resell to record buyers too young to recognize, too nostalgic to mind, or too resigned to protest. Nowadays, a muthafucka drops by the studio midsession, listens to a few seconds of a track-in-progress, says something like, "Speed it up," walks out never to return, and gets production credit and royalties. Even when the head of a label handpicked his roster instead of leaving it to A and R execs, he rarely produced albums no matter what the liner notes might say. Darnell was the superior producer by far, but as the CEO of Explicit Content and executive producer of my album, G Double D would be damned if my debut flopped. He'd make Random Sounds pull out all the stops to promote it properly.

But had G made the same promise to Leila when he approached her at Da Corridor that night? Would I care if Jim Farber dismissed my album as over-produced tripe so long as it sold a quarter million units its first week? Would strong sales buffer me from the diva accusations and other kinds of *hands-on* interference with future albums?

G interrupted my thoughts. "You know what, Cassie? You're right. I signed you 'cause I liked what I saw and heard. It's not like when I saw you at 205, I thought she reminds me of so-and-so or she sounds like whatserface. I shouldn't be fuckin' with your essence, I should be tryin' to highlight it." Then he stopped in contemplation. "I've got some big plans for you, Cassie, especially when we drop Primo's remix. I'ma try and get the Neptunes to produce a single for you. In fact, I got a meeting tomorrow at Elektra at the end of the week, and I'm going to see if I can get Missy to record a track with you." The waiter arrived with our main courses and set them down before us. When he left, G continued, "I had set it up for Leila, but let's be real. She ain't ready. And I can't go in there proposing no collaboration with an artist who's not good to go."

Once I had secured work for Darnell and the Segui sisters, I had hoped to get the story on Leila. But even though I had yet to close those deals, I had to flow with the conversation. "So what's wrong?" I asked. "She was pretty tight in the studio today."

"If I knew, I'd fix it," G said with no hint of despair, only a trace of aggravation bordering on indignation. Like Leila had the audacity to fall short of his expectations as a show of contempt rather than from a bout of insecurity or a block in creativity. "She talks a big game, that little girl. But she don't back it up. And she ain't exactly a team player."

I had no idea what he meant. "You're not thinking of dropping her, are you?" And I truly didn't know what I hoped he would say.

G laughed as he straightened up and dove his fork into his pasta. "You'd like that, wouldn't you?" Before I could protest, he said, "Sorry, baby girl, I'm not dropping Leila. I got too much invested in her already. She may not be bringing what I hoped, but she's got her value at the label. She hasn't cost me yet, and in time I think I can bring her around. Maybe you can help me with that."

With all his misgivings about Leila, his discontent with the men on the label, and his regard for Explicit Content as a dynasty, I felt I really had no choice. I had no problem with that, though, so long as he looked out for me. After my first studio session, G saw I could bring out the best in Leila, and I knew my self-interest didn't lie in doing her like she did me. If anything, I could increase my own value at Explicit Content by being the team player that Leila wasn't once I figured out what that meant to G. "Whatever you need, G," I said.

He must have expected me to resist because my compliance took him aback. "Are you sure, Cassie?" he said. " 'Cause Explicit Content's a family business, and we're planning to expand into some other ventures. For now the label's the business, and the roster is the family. Which means that no matter what goes down between family members, all aspects of business are top priority. You want to prove your loyalty to me? Always put the bottom line first."

Truth be told, I didn't know what the hell G was talking about. Every boss wants his employees to show loyalty to the company, but more seemed involved here than minding studio time as if we paid for it ourselves or keeping our creative spats out of the press. I pondered a way to get clarification without revealing my ignorance when G's cell rang. I usually hated it when someone answered their phone when I was breaking bread with them. Only in an emergency should a telephone call override a face-to-face, but when G took the call, I felt relief from the unrelenting tension beneath this dinner conversation.

"You got G," he said. "I'm having dinner. Why can't you deal with it?" Then his tone quickly switched from annoyed to defensive. "What you mean he's headed over there now? See, that's why you muthafuckas live there and I don't." He waved to get the waiter's attention and then motioned for the check. "Yeah, yeah, yeah, I'm on my way now." He hung up the telephone in disgust and turned back to me. "Cassie, I'm sorry, but I've got to head out to Glen Ridge to handle some business. Please stay, finish your meal, order whatever you like." The waiter came by with the check portfolio in hand. G flicked him a credit card and told him, "Let the lady have whatever she desires and call her a cab when she finishes."

The waiter nodded and turned to leave when I motioned for him to stop. "I'd like my pasta wrapped to go please." He took my plate and started for the kitchen when I grabbed his wrist. Peaking over my shoulder at the day's special, I said, "And let me get an arugula salad, the grilled chicken marinated with lemon, garlic and rosemary, and the hazelnut crème brûlée." I finally let the exasperated waiter go, and G laughed.

"Damn, baby girl, you can eat." Then his grin fell into a lopsided sneer. "That's sexy as hell."

A queasy feeling swelled in the pit of my stomach, but I had to ignore it and handle my business. "Mind if I ride with you to Glen Ridge so we can finish our conversation?" I said. Then I reached across the table and placed both my hands over his. "If you're sincere about giving me what I need, don't say no." If you had asked me at the time what the hell I thought I was doing then, I probably would've told you that I was just being Genevieve Rivers's daughter. But Genevieve Rivers's daughter never would have ordered a second meal or flirted with G Double D, let alone insist on accompanying him to Glen Ridge. I don't know exactly when it happened, but at one point I was less Genevieve Rivers's daughter and more Leila Aponte's best friend.

As a matter of fact, only Leila Aponte or her best friend would know to steer away the conversation on the limo ride to Glen Ridge from business to personal matters. With my leftovers and takeout cradled in my lap, I waited for G to make a series of calls on his cell before I attempted to speak.

The first was to Jen. "Ayo, Jen . . . Yeah, yeah, yeah, I know, but that's not what I'm calling about. First thing tomorrow I want you to set up another photo shoot for Cassie. And a little press junket for Primo's remix . . . Nah, just for Cassie, heads know about Leila already. All right." He groaned. "I'ma handle it now. You worry about what I asked you."

He made his last call to Primo, and after he gave him an ugly cussing I'd rather forget, I said, "G, can I ask you something?"

"What?" he said as if his patience was running on empty when here I came—another self-absorbed artist on his label—with another demand.

"You live the kind of life that many dream about," I said. "So what does a man like you dream about?"

For once the man I always knew to worship his own spotlight the way ancients revered the sun cast his eyes away like a shy schoolboy. "Damn, in all the interviews I've done over the years, I don't think anyone has ever asked me that question." He rubbed his chin between his thumb and forefinger as he contemplated an answer.

"But that doesn't mean you never thought about it, right?" Of course, he had. Genevieve always said that no matter what it seems, no one had everything and therefore, everyone wanted something. And nine times outta ten, those who had the most wanted the most, especially if they doubted they deserved all they had or knew they came by it in less than legitimate ways. And that ain't hard. For all the talk about merit in our society, brilliantly branded mediocrity will propel you on the top of the heap much faster than old-fashioned quality. And like any other phenomenon born on the margins, when hip-hop adopted the same formula, it went from subculture to mainstream. In my mind G and Explicit Content epitomized this, but I planned on being the exception.

So G's answer to my question floored me. "In my dreams, Cassandra, I'm on the mic. Onstage or on-screen. On the cover instead of in the liner notes."

"No."

"For real."

"You own your own label. Put yourself on." Against my better judgment, I started to laugh. I couldn't help myself. I mean, wasn't it that simple? "Diddy did it, so what's stopping you?"

But G wasn't laughing. "What's stopping me is the most important thing of all."

"What? It ain't money. It ain't connections. And it really ain't time, 'cause you could make that if you really wanted to." As quickly as I found myself laughing, I stopped, truly stumped.

"Talent, Cass," G said, staring out the window at the yellow tiles as we passed through the New Jersey Turnpike. "I just don't have the talent. And don't tell me that a man in my position doesn't need that. Hell, that's even more reason why I need it. If I gotta discount my albums or buy them myself to make the charts,

I ain't got no business making them." He turned back to me with the grin of a teacher about to spring a pop quiz. "Cassandra, you're a straight shooter. Give me your honest opinion. What do you think of P. Diddy as a rapper?"

I hesitated, trying to recall if G was a fan of Diddy or not. When I couldn't, I decided to go with the truth after all. "That's exactly what he is. A rapper."

G suddenly clicked on the light in the backseat. He examined my face, then snickered. "You say that like it's a bad thing."

"Ain't no vice, ain't no virtue."

"So what is a virtue, Ms. Steelo?"

"To be an MC," I said with so much conviction, I could feel my own eyes radiate. "To be lyrically brilliant. To always have something to say worth listening to without repeating yourself. To want to do this every day whether you earn ten thousand a year or ten million. To treat hip-hop like a privilege or a legacy and not some temporary hustle until a more lucrative racket comes your way like selling bootleg DVDs or pushing weed on the street corner."

"Oh, you on some Ronin Ro shit," said G in a tone light with affection. "I guess you believe gangsta rap is destroying hip-hop, too."

I said, "Ain't helping none." Ordinarily, I'm like a cat in a corner with her eyes fixed on the mouse hole when someone defends gangsta rap. Some of it had rhyme, some of it had reason, but it had become the all and all of hip-hop because of labels like Explicit Content that released little else, as if nothing more lived in the 'hood. My fingers itched to count off all my well-rehearsed arguments, but I held back until I found an answer that allowed me to maintain the ground I made yet be true to what I believed. "I know it sells, but you know what, G? You signed Leila, then you signed me, and as different as we are, neither of us is about that. So I'm thinkin' you're looking to try your hand at selling something else. Like why're you asking me about Puff?"

"See, I got this theory about Puff." G leaned forward and

clasped his hands, his face twisted with the anguish of an impending confession. His demeanor became so somber, I squelched my
impulse to quip *First the Ashanti principle, now the Diddy theory.*
G stared at me for a long pause as if waiting for assurance that he
had my fullest attention. So I turned toward him, draping my arm
across the backseat and drawing my legs under me until my knees
sank into the soft leather. Satisfied, he continued with the rhythm
of Cosby imparting a lesson to one of his sitcom children.

"I don't believe Puff's first love is producing. I think he always
really wanted to rhyme. But he ain't even have the confidence to
get on the mic let alone the courage to do his thing in front of a
whole buncha people. 'Cause the glory in hip-hop ain't in the
recording studio, Cassie, you know this. Being a recording artist is
a means to an end, and that end is doing your thing live, 'cause
that's where the love is. But Puff couldn't do it so he took to the
background—producing—which is the next best thing. Can't be
the fury on the mic? Then be the fuel behind it.

"Then B.I.G. got killed, and my man was truly devastated. All
that bullshit about Puff caring only because Biggie was his best-
selling artist or being involved in his murder is just that. Bullshit.
Personally, I think the nigga's weak on the artistic tip, making
more money nowadays off being famous than doing what he did to
become famous in the first place. But saying Puff ain't have no
love for B.I.G. that didn't have ends attached? That's some hatin'
to the extreme." For a moment, I dropped his gaze because I was
one of those people who believed that.

"Puff was so devastated when B.I.G. got killed, Cassie, the
brother's pain was so deep, it surpassed whatever fears he had of
the mic. So genuine was his grief over Biggie's death, it, like . . ."

". . . suffocated his insecurities about being a rapper," I finished.

"You feel me?" G said, and I realized that while I probably
wasn't the first person he ran down this theory to, I obviously was
the first to take it seriously. "So Diddy did what an artist does," he

continued with an advocate's conviction. "He poured his feelings into his art. My man was in too much pain to worry about, *Does this verse work?* or *Is this flow tight?* All he's thinking about is paying proper tribute to his boy and to heal hisself. Then he hooks up with Faith, Sting . . . releases the song and it blows up.

"But let's be real, Cassie. That song coulda sounded like a garbage truck at three in the morning, and it still woulda been a hit, 'cause nigga ain't the only one mourning the loss of B.I.G. But Puff mistakes the track's success for his. Yeah, it came from the heart, and no, he ain't do it for the money. But he performed that shit live, folks lost they mind, and he got it in his head *Yo, all these years I was afraid to pick up the mic, and damn, I actually got skills.* And now you can't tell the nigga shit. Maybe deep down inside Puff knows he ain't all that, but what does that matter? He got millions of people and dollars telling him that he's good at what he really wants to do. Don't expect him to stop.

"But that's the difference between Puff and me, Cassie. I know I ain't got that gift, and that's enough. No amount of units sold gonna tell me I got what I don't. And I'm all right with that. Shit, I take pride in accepting my limitations 'cause I ain't without my talents. Not that I've been making the most of them, which is why I started looking to expand beyond the music. But that's about to change, thanks to you.

"After you stepped to me at 205 because I signed Leila and not you, Cassandra, I realized that I shouldn't be wasting the abilities I did have because they weren't the ones I would've chosen. And that's why I signed you. Now, I know you think just because I'm trying to tweak your appearance here and there, I'm trying to change you. Make you more like Leila. But that couldn't be farthest from the truth. There's nobody at Explicit Content like you and never has been, and I'm not talking just artistically, either. When you left the party like you did, I knew you were gonna be a star. I said to myself, *She ain't going nowhere. She can't even imagine giving this up. She knows she ain't ready so she's gonna go make*

herself ready. And while she may not come back here, she showing up
somewhere tomorrow doing her thing better than she did it yesterday.

"You just don't know what you have. You feel entitled to it and
all it brings. Hell, even obligated to use it. That's what you taught
me, Cassandra. Your album is my call to step up my game as an executive and as a producer. And that's what I'm gonna do."

G reached over and chucked me under the chin like a coach
does his star player, and I found myself longing for more. His
words captured every motivation I had for the path I had chosen.
What I could never explain to Genevieve. What I always believed
separated me from Leila. What I suspected Darnell might have
understood but was never sure because his ambition made it difficult for me to know if he really got me at that level. And try as I
did, there was nothing more left for me to say on the matter.

And in that way of his, G said, "Not that I regret anything I've
done to date or might do in the future. I mean, get as moral majority as you wanna be, the fact remains is that gangsta rap made
these white folks take notice of what niggas had to say. Shit, not
just white folks, but people all over the world."

Taking the line he threw me, I launched into my canned dia-
tribe against gangsta rap, relieved to be on safer ground. Arguing
that hip-hop went global long before gangsta rap exploded and
challenging him to describe the benefit of having an international
stage just for us to act the fool gave me cover. It kept me from crying with that intense joy that validation brings. That and imagining what it would be like for G Double D to kiss me.

CHAPTER 16

FRAGILE

When we arrived at the mansion, Hi-Jack and Cryciss were outside sharing a thick blunt and animated conversation. Through the tinted glass, I couldn't tell if they were having a harmless debate or verging on a fight. I learned quickly that when it came to the Explicit Content crew, a broken line existed between the two through which the artists dove from one side to the next. G Double D had only one leg out the backseat when Hi-Jack and Cryciss rushed the limo.

"Yo, G, I'm telling you this cat's buggin'," said Hi-Jack, pointing to Cryciss, who pulled on the joint and then offered it to G. "He gonna blow this whole deal for us."

G refused the joint so Cryciss passed it back to Hi-Jack. Even though I didn't want any, it pissed me off how they rendered me invisible. But eventually I became more amused at how they could be at each other's throats and blow the same stick.

"You need to stop trippin', son," Cryciss told Hi-Jack. Then he hitched himself to G's other side and said, "G, you know me. That's why you brought me in, right? You know I've been in this game for a minute." I scoffed, thinking Hi-Jack probably never said about any of the guys, *Niggas always be needing reassurance and shit.*

G gestured for both of them to quit. "All I want to know is if Om's still here." He started up the driveway toward the house with Hi-Jack and Cryciss nipping at his heels like excited pets, a pinscher on his left and a bulldog on his right. Resisting the slight urge to remind them of my presence, I shadowed them.

"No doubt, on accounta me," Hi-Jack said.

"Nigga, stop bein' all melodramatic," Cryciss shot back.

G said, "I'm here now, so both of y'all shut the fuck up." He pushed his way through the French doors and down the main hallway. Just as he was about to enter the parlor, he turned to Cryciss and yelled, "Muthafucka, didn't I tell you to smoke only in the family room? Get any ashes on my Kerman carpet, I'ma bust your ass for real. Shit cost me over nine hundred dollars."

"I told him," Hi-Jack said. Then I guessed to save Cryciss's ass and G's carpet, he snatched the blunt from Cryciss. The last thing I saw and heard before the three of them disappeared into the parlor was G extending his palm for a handshake and saying, "Mr. Om, thank you for waiting."

I stood in the hallway with the leftovers in my hand, debating my next move. The fellas were so engrossed with their business argument, they had forgotten that I was there. Of course, I was mad curious to follow them to learn exactly what preempted my dinner with G Double D, especially since the name Om rang a bell. But then I realized that if she were home, I might finally have a chance to be alone with Leila, and that became my priority.

Having been at the mansion only once before and only in a ballroom full of people, I experienced some trial and error in finding that ivory spiral staircase leading to the bedrooms. I walked into what seemed like two separate dining rooms albeit one seemed much smaller than the other. I also found two kitchens, one a Martha Stewart fantasy that I knew Genevieve would love. A kitchen for people for whom cooking was an expensive hobby like a photographer's darkroom or a pilot's hangar. Then I came across what had to be the service kitchen with more hardware than an auto shop. This one was clearly built for the so-called help to get their hands brittle.

I made so many turns, I lost my sense of direction. Afraid to accidentally stumble into the parlor where G and the others were meeting with this Om guy, I strained to listen for male voices. What I actually heard was a group of females chattering. Thinking Leila might be among them, I followed it.

The girlish sound led me to a doorway. The second I opened the door, a pungent vinegary smell hit me in the face. Holding my nose, I stepped into the landing of a descending staircase and listened. A feminine and vaguely familiar voice said, "You need to take a break, fine. But I want the rest of you to know that taking a break can mean losing a break. You want to make money in this business you need to hustle always. . . ." I saw a shadow approaching the stairs and zipped back through the doorway. I went far enough down the hallway and ducked into a utility closet. I cracked the door open to peek through and caught the weirdest scene.

Through the door in a huff came the girl who had danced with Darnell at the party and resembled Alicia Keys. Clad in a black terry-cloth towel, she lit a cigarette and leaned against the wall when Jen came through the door behind her. Jen wore a surgical mask around her neck and carried what I presumed was an emery board the size of a playing card in her hand. She snatched the cigarette out of the girl's mouth and got in her face, lecturing her in a low growl while jabbing the card inches from her face. I could catch only pieces of their conversation. *You wanted to be down, Monica, and this is part of the game* Jen said at one point while the Alicia look-alike said she couldn't help it if the smell made her sick or something like that.

Puzzling together everything I knew—or thought I did at the

time—I concluded that Ms. Thang had decided to sign with G's new modeling agency after all, despite the questionable terms of her contract. Now she had pissed off Jen, who was heading the agency by refusing to model nude and bitching about the smell of whatever beauty products they had provided. Just another sister too hungry to heed the fine print and now wanted to complain. Jen managed to get Monica to tow the line, and they disappeared back through the doorway.

Only when I slipped out of the utility closet did I notice the music. Faint and familiar, I slowly circled in place trying to pinpoint where it was coming from. It led me back through the service kitchen. I walked across the kitchen to a door and opened it, discovering the pantry. One empty shelf after the next lined the walls while several rows of cardboard boxes sat in the center of the room. I closed the door and listened again. I walked to the other side of the service kitchen and found a small doorway leading to a plain and narrow staircase. I climbed a few steps and paused. The source of the music came from somewhere up those stairs.

And as I climbed the steps, the music grew louder, as if it wanted me to notice and follow it. Within seconds I didn't have to strain at all, and I recognized it instantly: a song by Angie Martinez called "Every Little Girl." Unlike "Dem Thangs" or that "Suavamente" joint she did with Wyclef, you wouldn't know it from radio. I recognized it because it was Leila's favorite cut from Angie's first album. One of her favorite tracks period. Angie's verse slowly pulled me up the staircase.

> *Overall, it's a rough business*
> *It could stop even you*
> *There's people that gonna say things that's not even true.*

When I reached the landing, I recognized at the far end of the corridor the spiral staircase that led to the ballroom. As I stepped into the corridor, I found to my right the banister over which G Dou-

ble D had presided Leila's coming-out party. To my left were a series of doors, identical in their plainness. I crept down the hallway
until I came across a door that was ajar.

> *How 'bout the one that goes,*
> *'Yeah, she goes with him.*
> *He bought her the car, the ice, the clothes, and rims.'*

When I peeked in I saw Leila sitting cross-legged on a bed and
burying her face in her hands. As if she could feel the weight of my
stare, she looked up and straight into my eyes. A jolt of surprise
flashed across her tearstained face.

Just as I was about to run into her room, she said something to
someone I could not see. I backed up a few steps, ready to flee
down the back staircase, but no one came through the door. Instead the music became louder, The Product G&B singing the
chorus as if to coax me to stay and listen. Observe. Witness.

> *To every little girl, on every block*
> *that's comin' of age tryin' to reach the top*
> *I said no matter who you are,*
> *You can reach the stars*
> *But never forget, how fragile you are,*
> *'Cause a girl is fragile.*

I tiptoed toward the door until I caught Primo's angry voice beneath the song. I couldn't make out what he was saying, but Leila's
eyes relaxed as if she felt safer now that I stood nearby undetected,
like a guardian angel. Remembering how she had behaved during
the photo shoot when we broke for lunch, I motioned toward the
leftovers in my hands and then I pointed toward a Chinese lacquer
cabinet. Just like I couldn't see Primo but knew he was in her
room, I knew Leila could not see the cabinet from where she sat
but understood what I intended to do. Primo yelled at her to pay

attention to what he was telling her, and I stole across to the cabinet, dropping to my knees and stashing the leftovers in the last drawer.

"Cassandra! Yo, Cassandra, where you at?" I crawled to and peaked through the banister and saw G Double D stride to the center of the ballroom flanked by Hi-Jack and Cryciss. I jumped back from the banister so if he looked up he wouldn't spot me. "Ayo, Leila turn that shit down! Cassie, where the hell are you?" Then I dashed across the corridor, down the back staircase and into the servants' kitchen.

"Cassandra!"

"I'm in here."

"Where the fuck's here?" Hi-Jack said.

Angry to hear his voice, I spit back, "The fuck I know. I don't live here." I relaxed a bit when I heard G snicker. In a few seconds, he, Hi-Jack, and Cryciss came through the door.

G threw up his hands with the exasperation of a parent with a rambunctious child. "How'd you end up in here?"

"I don't know. I was trying to find the bathroom."

"All you had to do was ask somebody," said Cryciss in a tone far from hospitable.

"Y'all were handling some urgent business, and I didn't want to interfere."

G extended his hand to me. "Come. I'll show you were it is." I walked over to him and took his hand. As he led me out of the kitchen, Hi-Jack and Cryciss gave me such dirty looks, it took my all not to stick my tongue out at them like the teacher's pet.

"Yo, G, you chillin' tonight?" asked Cryciss.

G sighed. "Might as well," he said as if he really did not want to.

"A'ight. Need anything, you know where we at. Holla." Hi-Jack and Cryciss followed us for a few more paces and then turned off down another corridor.

G led me out the main entrance into a September breeze. We

walked off the driveway, and he waved for the driver and yelled, "You're done for the night." The driver nodded, locked the limo, and headed up the driveway. "Ayo, hold up," G stopped him. "Get Cassandra's food from the backseat."

I tugged at G's arm. "Oh, I brought it in with me." I panicked at his obvious next question.

"Where is it?"

"In that kitchen," I said thinking quickly. "I didn't know how long we were going to be so when I saw the refrigerator . . ."

"We're staying over." G pulled out his cell phone. "You want me to have someone bring it to you?"

"No, that's all right." I thought of Darnell pacing in his studio unable to work because he knew I was with G and had yet to call. Not out of jealousy or even worry, just restless to know if I'd scored him a producing contract for my album. And that thought bothered me. "Can I borrow your phone, though, so I can call Darnell?"

"I already got Hi-Jack taking care of that." Questions cloaked with anxiety and anger raced through my head as we walked across the lawn toward a smaller house on the estate. Had I done anything to make G think I wanted to stay with him that night? Did he buy everything I had told him, or did he suspect I was sneaking around the mansion? If I wanted to go back home, would he hold me against my will? Was Leila OK? Was she able to get to the food with no problem? Would Hi-Jack really call Darnell, and if so, would he try to create drama between us? Where the hell was G taking me?

"Yo, G, this bathroom an outhouse or something?"

G flashed me a smile as he fished in his pocket for a set of keys. "When I crash out here, I stay in the guest house. If I stayed in the mansion, them muthafuckas would never give me a moment's peace." We arrived at the house, and G slipped the key into the lock. "I figured you'd appreciate some privacy as well."

He opened the door and stepped aside so I could enter. The second I walked into the guest house, I knew it was much more my steelo than that cavernous mansion. The place was decorated like the set of a Black family sitcom. Bright lights shone over smoky woods tailored in earth tones. Except for the lamps on either side of the plush sofa and the modest television sitting on a worn cart that looked handmade, little in the room hinted of cosmopolitan life. This was the kind of living room that project kids and tenement brats like Leila and me tuned into every night on prime time and went to bed dreaming we might one day move to, family and friends included.

In my *Family Matters* fantasy, Genevieve met and married a nice man who looked like Denzel Washington and treated her like a queen and me like a princess, the little girl he always wanted but never had. This man had an older son who doted on me, too, buying me black Barbie dolls and chasing bullies away. And he had cute friends who always had crushes on me. We lived in a house in Yonkers that looked just liked the one that Aunt Treece and Uncle Marques had in Los Angeles. My new father bought me a car and trusted me with lots of freedom, so I drove across the border every day into the Bronx to pick up Leila and my other girlfriends so we could drive back to my house and work on our rhymes in my studio in the garage.

But in Leila's daydream, both her parents were alive. Her mother was a schoolteacher, and because of that, Leila never had any trouble in school, although she never said if it was because her mother tutored her or the principal let her slide because of her mother's position. Anyway, Leila's father worked for a bank and wore tailored suits and shiny shoes to work. They had plenty of money and all the furniture to show for it, but they moved out of the projects only to settle in a Mitchell-Lama building in the 'hood instead of buying a house. The only part of Leila's fantasy that rang true was that she had dozens of aunts and uncles with kids of their own who visited every weekend. In real life, Leila did have quite a few aunts and uncles on her mother's side, each with two or three kids. The state had tried to convince them to step up as Leila's guardian so she wouldn't have to go into foster care, but none did.

And in Leila's family fantasy, I lived with her. When she told me that, I got into a little snit. "Why you got me living with you like my mother abandoned me or something?"

Leila's initial response was defensive. "I ain't say she couldn't come." We both knew my mother had no place in her dreams, especially since no love flowed between them. Then she became angry. "At least you're in my shit."

"You're in mine!"

"The same way I am now." Her skin turned pink, and I wondered if she was only getting angry to avoid becoming sad. I tried to apologize, but she cut me off to say, "Forget it. Why fight about something that could never happen? Let's go to the Virgin on Union Square so I can boost the new Mary J. Blige CD."

G's voice interrupted my thoughts. "Cassandra, are you OK?"

I was and I wasn't. I felt instantly comfortable there, and that bothered me. I had always wanted to cozy up in a room like this, yet I felt guilty. And even a little frightened. "I like your place," I finally said. "I wanted to grow up in place that looked like this."

"So did I," replied G. "I like the finer things in life, but them things ain't always the most expensive on the shelf, know what I'm sayin'? All that shit in the mansion is for *them*," he scoffed.

My next thought hung so heavy in my mind I had to release it. "Have you ever . . ." I had difficulty finding the words for the emptiness that crept up on me. "Ever been homesick for a place where you've never lived?"

"All the time," said G, and I understood why I felt compelled to share my sentiment with him even though I barely knew him. "That's what they call romanticism. Nostalgia's when you miss what you had or knew. Romanticism is when you yearn for something you only wish you had or think you know."

G's official bio mentioned a year at Hunter College before he

discovered Hi-Jack on the subway, but I'd figured he did more
hoochie hounding than book bending. I had to smile. "Scared of
you."

G Dub grinned back. "You should be." He pointed down a
short hallway. "The bathroom's over there."

I never had to go, but I had to make like I did. Besides, I wanted
to see as much of the place as possible. Sure enough, I walked into
that same down-home decor in crème, beige, and gold. The gold
fixtures glistened with cleanliness, and the mirrors above the sink
and on the doors were spotless. I slowly pulled back the beige and
gold shower curtain to find a massive tub made of immaculate
porcelain. Breathing in the faint odor of the curtain's new vinyl, I
opened the closet door and grabbed as many of the beige towels as
I could. Like I always did as a little girl helping Genevieve pull
clothes out of the dryer, I plunged my face into the laundry-fresh
softness and inhaled deeply.

G banged on the door. "Cassandra, you all right in there?"

I jumped to stuff the towels back into the closet and prayed the
door wouldn't creak as I closed it. Then I reached over to the toilet and flushed. "Yeah," I said, sure that my annoyance seeped
through that single word like an ink spot on looseleaf. I turned on
the faucet to wash my hands even though I hadn't actually used
the toilet. But I decided to put the running water to use and
pumped a generous spurt of liquid soap into my palms. The loose
foam trickled through my hands into a dark gray swirl down the
drain. Bothered by the sight, I squeezed more soap into my hands
and scrubbed up another lather.

G knocked on the door again. "Cassie, I have something for
you." Now both annoyed and preoccupied, I reached for the knob
with my soapy wet hands and flung the door open. G stood there
with a thick black bathrobe folded under a wicker basket of bath
products. "I thought you might want to take a long, hot bubble
bath before turning in."

It had been years since I'd had a bubble bath. Between working and performing and dodging Leila's boyfriends, I never had the time. Every once in a while Leila would treat me to a Saturday at the Lancôme day spa, but nothing compared to soaking in heated solitude until your skin puckered like a cinched waistband. G could have just handed me two tickets to a Black Star reunion concert, and I wouldn't have been happier. I took the bathrobe and basket from him and said, "You're sweet, G. Thanks."

"Yeah, keep that shit to yourself." Before I could catch his expression to figure out if he was serious or playing, he pulled the door shut with a decisive thud. I shrugged, placing the basket on the toilet seat, turning off the sink faucet, and twisting open the one in the tub. I peeled off my clothes as I surveyed the products in the basket. Bubble bath, foot scrubs, facial masks, all by expensive brands. No matter how often I told Leila that the products at Rite Aid or Duane Reade were no different, she insisted on buying them and putting me through smell and touch tests. "All these companies have their ghetto equivalent," I would argue as she rubbed a ritzy moisturizer into the back of my hand. "Genevieve told me that the same company puts one line in Saks under one name and then puts another line in CVS under another. Meanwhile, the stuff ain't that much different."

Leila shoved my arm up so hard, she clocked me in the face with my own hand. Giggling at her blunder, she said, "Smell that. Do you smell that? Don't tell me that smells just like the shit you just bought at CVS, OK?"

I sniffed the supple area on the back of my hand. The fragrance was nicer than my drugstore brand but not so much better it was worth copping to it. Instead I said, "Whether you pay five dollars or fifty, none of that shit's gonna make you prettier or richer or happier, anyway. All you paying for is the belief that it does."

"So then why not pay more?" Leila said. "Just because they might be running a game on us is no excuse not to try. And if you gonna try, you might as well believe."

I opened the bottle of bubble bath and poured it into the running stream. As I waited for the foam to build, I unfolded the robe. A black article of clothing fell to the tiles. After hanging the robe on the hook behind the door, I leaned over to pick it up. G had given me an Explicit Content T-shirt size extra large. It was black with a giant silver X down the back, of course, and a parental advisory sticker across the front with the label's slogan underneath: *Not suitable for hatas.*

I smiled and draped the T-shirt over the basket. Then I dipped my toe into the bathtub to test the water, which fell enough degrees below unbearable. I eased into the tub, melting my way into the bubbles. I leaned back, closed my eyes, and tried to lose myself in the soft crackling of the foam engulfing me. But all I could do was fixate on my hands.

I poked them through the thick white sheath. My fingers already had begun to wrinkle. Although my palms were a glowing taupe from my recent scrubbing, I wondered what kind of bacteria still lurked in the crevices of my lifeline. I rewound my day trying to recall what my hands had undergone. Scribbling across my notebook. Gripping the mic. Sipping coffee from a paper cup. Holding a thick fork at the restaurant. Steadying myself along the banister of the back staircase. I had spent the entire day in the recording studio, for the most part sitting in a chair and waiting forever to get into the booth. I washed my hands at the restaurant before dinner, and didn't remember the water being so dark. Then I rode back with G to the mansion, which, despite all the spoiled roughnecks that lived there, always seemed pristine. For the life of me I couldn't figure out when and how I got my hands so dirty.

I started to rub bubbles between my hands when the bathroom door crept open. Wearing a black bathrobe exactly like the one he had given me, G swept in. With a disarming nonchalance, he casually stepped out of his matching slippers, dropped his robe, and settled across from me in the tub. He strode in and I let him, all without a word, as if we did this every night. I knew if he had been Hi-Jack or any of the others, he never would have made it to the tub. But this was G Double D. And I didn't let him join me just because he was the head of the label. We both knew that even though I hadn't given him an invitation, he wasn't uninvited.

"Everything OK?" I asked. "Took care of all your business emergencies?"

"Oh, yeah," he said, his voice already lazy with relaxation. "Turned out not to be too big a deal after all. It's just Hi-Jack and Cryciss. They've got real different approaches to business. Jack, he high-strung. Real cautious. A detail-oriented guy who reads the fine print first, know what I mean? And I like that. Now Jason, he's ambitious. Takes risks. And I like that, too. So I put them both in charge of my latest enterprise on some checks-and-balances-type shit." Then G snickered. "Even though they be stressin' the hell outta of me sometimes over nothin', bickering like Fred and Ethel Mertz." He leaned back and closed his eyes, and I envied his ability to unwind so easily.

"So what enterprise is this?" I asked just to keep him talking and find an opportunity to be that team player.

Without opening his eyes, G drawled, "We're still trying to decide between one luxury car detailing service or a chain of parking garages."

I laughed. "Parking garages? I thought y'all were talking about starting a clothing line or maybe opening a restaurant."

"And be like every other muthfucka out here? I'm trying to grow, not just maintain." G opened his eyes. "Which do you think we should go with?"

"Aw, G, I don't know nothing about cars. . . ."

"Give me your gut feeling."

"The chain of parking garages."

"Really? That's what Hi-Jack thinks. He'd rather we go for the no-frills, multiple locations thang," said G. "But Cryciss likes to bling-bling, so he'd rather we have the one flashy place and deal only with the rich and the beautiful."

Once I got past the irony of sharing a position with Hi-Jack, I said, "Well, I don't know what Hi-Jack's rationale is, but I say go with the chain of garages and put them in 'hoods where folks need 'em. Make the rates affordable, too."

G Double D sat up with pure interest. "Go on."

"This is your first venture after the label, right?" G nodded and I continued. "So go with something that builds your following. Even other celebrities who are feelin' Explicit Content are gonna buy only one or two copies of an album, right? But if you provide a needed but affordable service to the average Joe? When he's done buying an album for himself, his girlfriend, his cousin in the military serving wherever and not to mention bigging you up to all his boys, you're talking thousands of albums right there. Multiply that by all the spaces you offer. How does that compare to the few luxury cars you're gonna service at a time?"

"But we're talking about wealthier clientele here, Cass, which means more expensive services," said G in a tone that was less challenging and more curious as to what my response would be.

"Yeah, and these fuckin' celebrities expect to be comped for shit they can afford to pay for."

"True," said G. Then he snickered. "Guilty as charged. I haven't paid for a Knicks ticket on the floor in over a year."

I sat up with so much excitement, some water splashed over the side of the tub. "You open a luxury-car detailing service, you're gonna have to give away as much business as you make, only for their fickle asses to flip to the next famous cat who decides to bite your shit. But the dude in the 'hood who sleeps better at night 'cause the ten-year-old Altima he relies on to go to work every day is safe and sound in your garage? That's a fan for life, G."

G rubbed his chin as he pondered my words. "Om'll go for that. He was frontin' like he was neutral, but I think he wanted to go the low-key route, too."

That name again. "Does he work for the label?" I asked. "His name's familiar."

"Oh, he ain't with the label," said G. "My personal assistant,

Jen? That's his daughter. The guy's a self-made millionaire. Imports. When I started Explicit Content and hired her for pennies, my man flipped, talking about he didn't send her to Wesleyan to be nobody's assistant. They didn't speak for almost two years, until I blew up and paid Jen what she was worth and then some. So they made peace, and when I told her I was looking to expand into other industries, Jen told me that her pops might be able to hook me up with some loot."

"Damn, you really believe in keeping it in the family," I said. "So Papa Om likes him some hip-hop, huh?"

G laughed. "Papa Om will follow the do-lo wherever it leads. Thing is, I need more capital than what he's got to make this fly, and I gotta find it soon before he pulls his offer off the table. Word is, he's talking to some cats at another label." Under the water, his hand tweaked my calf. "Hi-Jack'll be happy though. Maybe it'll even compensate for your being here with me. He gotta thing for you, you know."

Yeah, I knew. I've known ever since the third grade when I came home crying with a skinned knee and Genevieve explained that Danny Rodriguez tripped me in the school yard because he had a crush on me. That the cutest boy in class had shown he liked me by hurting me angered me so much, I forgot that I had always liked him, too, and busted his lip in gym class the next day. I carried on with my crocodile tears like it was an accident, but I had aimed the wooden handle of my jump rope right at Danny's grill. Hi-Jack was Danny Rodriguez all grown up into the thug life and just like in the third grade, I couldn't be bothered.

"So's that why you really signed me?" I asked G. "To keep Hi-Jack happy. Leila for Primo, me for Jack . . ." I already knew the answer, but I wanted to hear him say he brought me to Explicit Content to appease no one but himself. Not even Leila.

As G pulled himself toward me slowly, I felt his hand float up my thigh. With his other hand, he grasped the back of my neck and drew my face toward his. As we leaned into each other, his tongue slipped between my lips, his fingers grazed between my legs. He stroked me until I sensed a wetness more warm and silky than the surrounding water. G slid his other hand from my neck and down my hand, resting it over my hand and squeezing it like a first boyfriend assuring a less experienced girl that he genuinely cared. Beneath the water, he dragged my hand forward and clasped it around his bulky shaft. The heft of his manhood crashed me back to my senses, and I jumped to my feet so quickly, G reeled backward on his elbows to avoid getting kneed in the face.

"I'm sorry. I can't," I said as I scrambled out the tub for the robe. "I'm with someone." I tied the robe so tight I cut my breath short. Nor did I bother to loosen the tie, feeling unworthy of smooth breathing. I turned around to face G, expecting to see a look of rage. But he leaned back in the tub like a sunbather under the perfect ray. His crooked grin only made me feel guiltier. "I'm sorry, G," I said again. "I never should've let you in here in the first place."

"I'm not gonna chase you, Cassie," he said. "You and Mini Me ain't for each other, and you know it. If it'll make you feel better to go through these motions with Darnell. It's all good. I can wait until you're ready. And when you are, you'll come to me." I honestly couldn't tell if he was romancing or threatening me. But I didn't care either way. If he was romancing me, I was playing Darnell dirty. If he was threatening me, well . . . I had already gone too far, and I had to leave.

G lifted himself out of the tub, and I forced myself to look away. "If it'll make you feel better, you can even stay in the guest room."

"I think it's better if I went home . . ."

"Already dismissed the driver."

". . . or stayed at the mansion."

"You're staying here with me, Cassandra," said G. He opened the bathroom door and nudged me through it. "Come into the master bedroom, go into the guest room, crash on the sofa, whatever. But you're not leaving here tonight." He handed me my clothes in a pile topped by the Explicit Content T-shirt. After placing one last kiss on my cheek, he turned down the hallway and disappeared into a room.

I stood there for a long time, waiting for him to come out after me, but he never did. I finally trekked down the hallway and found the guest room. Relieved to find a lock on the door, I quickly shut it, changed into the T-shirt, and crawled into the bed. As I pulled the sheets to my ears, I knew G would honor his word. At least for the night.

But I tossed for most of the night with guilt and worry. To be innocent meant to be decent and that meant avoiding any and every compromising situation. But I was decent and imperfect, and if G wanted to force himself on me, I probably would not have been able to stop him. And if I went public, what would people just like my mother say? That she followed him home instead of going home to her waiting boyfriend. That she took a bubble bath in his house and allowed him to join her. That she pursued him in a club after placing third in a two-bit talent show.

My mind wandered to Leila and how people had called her a slut behind her back all through school. How even when I envied her for having her pick of men, I still judged her for choosing more than one. Meanwhile, she was more honest than any playa out there and never made me feel unusual because I was choosy. She once said to me, "Look, Cassie, ain't no thing. My freedom to say yes comes along with your right to say no. Can't have one without the other." And yet we were both coiled up in bed crying on the luxurious grounds of Explicit Content.

If I had had a way that night, I would have stole out of the guest house, snuck Leila out of the mansion, and hightailed it back to New York. But I was stuck. I wanted desperately to leave, but I could not leave without Leila. Even if I eventually found my way back to Darnell's or even Genevieve's, I just knew Leila was trapped there. How could I break her free of Explicit Content without getting deeper in myself?

CHAPTER 17

VINTAGE VINYL

I awoke the next day to find a cleaning woman scrubbing the bathtub in the guest house. G had left without a word. I washed up in the sink and asked the woman, "Do you have a plastic bag I could use?" Although she seemed surprised, and even a little embarrassed that I'd spoken to her, the woman handed me a white garbage bag used for office wastebaskets. After helping myself to the vanilla body scrub and after-bath oil in the wicker basket, I headed straight for the mansion. To be honest, I'm not crazy about vanilla as a flavor or a scent, but Leila once told me vanilla was an aphrodisiac, and I needed all the help I could get when facing Darnell after this fuckup.

When I arrived at the mansion, the front door was locked, so I rang the bell feeling foolish. A butler I had never seen before—a white guy with a familiar but uncommon accent—opened the door and announced me even though I had not identified myself to him. "Miss Steelo," he said.

I had a bad case of morning crankiness, so I mumbled, "That's *Ms.* Steelo," handed him the plastic bag, and walked in past him.

"I'm sorry, ma'am," he said. Then he announced me again. "Mizz Stee-Lo." I heard a chorus of male laughter erupt down the hallway, and I followed it. As I did I pinpointed the butler's accent and figured he must have arrived recently from Ireland and probably settled in Woodlawn in the Bronx before landing this job and moving to Jerz. I'd barely glanced at the cleaning lady and had assumed that she was a light-skinned Latina, but she was probably an immigrant from Europe, too. Obviously, G thought it cute to hire white people as the help. Leila always believed that if so-called minorities ever got on top, we would never do white people they way they did us because we knew how painful it was. "I mean, there'd be a few people we'd fuck over like the Klan, just to send a message to others like 'em," she explained, "but knowing what it's like, we would treat them better than they ever treated us."

I thought it was bullshit and I told her so. If we ran the world, we would do them worse than us, and on a subconscious level white people knew it. That's why whenever one Black family too many moves into a neighborhood, the white families put up *For Sale* signs like candles on a birthday cake. They had no problem moving into Harlem or Bed-Stuy so long as they could buy the best house in the 'hood while the so-called minorities around them were broke as hell. But they weren't feelin' living side by side with Black and Brown people who had just as much money as they did, especially if they were on their way to outnumbering them. Not that I believed we'd do white people harm out of vengeance either. It's just after seeing how they ran things for so long, we wouldn't know how to do otherwise. And given how much dirt we did to ourselves with white people calling the shots, I could hardly imagine not digging in our heels if we were in charge and had white folks under our boots. It amazed me how after all Leila had to survive, she believed that people—no matter what color—were good at heart. But I guessed that's because no matter what she had experienced, she still was. As I walked toward the voices mocking the butler's accent, I became more dedicated to getting Leila the hell away from these cats at Explicit Content.

I turned into the large dining room and found the entire crew except G, including groupies and other hangers-on, sitting around the table. Although it was after one in the afternoon, the spread included waffles, bagels, and other breakfast dishes. Wearing the tourmaline pendant and matching earrings, Leila said, "Hey, Cassie." She pushed her untouched plate away from her and smiled, letting me know she found the arugula salad and chicken dinner in the Chinese lacquer cabinet.

Primo stood up. "Ladies and gentlemen," he said in a botched Irish accent. "I present Ms. Steelo." The entourage applauded and Primo took a bow.

Leila mumbled, "Y'all need to leave Patrick alone." But they ignored her.

"Don't quit your day job, bro," hollered Earl.

"Yeah, man. Colin Farrell, you ain't," added Hi-Jack as the Alicia look-alike Whatsername stood behind him and massaged his shoulders. At first she made me nervous, staring at me as if she recognized me. But then I relaxed by convincing myself that she remembered me as the female Darnell left her to chase after during the Explicit Content party and attributing her intrusive eyes to nothing more than OWC. Hi-Jack and Third-Eye slapped high fives while Cryciss brooded in a corner, chewing on a sausage link while a groupie draped across him like a tinsel on a Christmas tree cooed in his ear, failing to console him. Before he left for the day, G must have informed them that he had decided to go with Hi-Jack's garage chain.

Hi-Jack then waved me over to him and patted the empty seat beside him. If he ever had any problems with my "hooking up" with G, he was over it. "What's up, Punchanella?" he said with all the warmth Darnell might call me boo. The guilt of not going home returned with such a force, I dropped into the seat next to Hi-Jack.

"Stop calling her that," Leila said. Primo grabbed a piece of toast from the basket and brought it to Leila's lips. She gazed at it for a second only to shove his hand away.

Primo banged his fist on the table. "You're wasting away to nothing from that bullshit you girls catch when you think you too fat and don't fuckin' eat."

"You don't catch an eating disorder. It comes from guys like you," she said. "Just leave me alone, OK? I'm just not hungry." She peeked at me over Primo's shoulder and then the mystery concerning her appetite unraveled. Even when she ransacked the refrigerator at three in the morning, Leila was always down for pancakes soaked in maple syrup and a mug of *café con leche*. She loved her body as she felt all women should, no matter their size. She hated diets and the quacks who created them. The Leila I knew skipped meals only when she didn't like what was being offered.

Or was afraid to eat it.

"What you want to eat, Bri?" Hi-Jack said. "We got French toast, waffles . . ."

"I'm not hungry," I said, praying that my aching belly would not groan in dissent. "Y'all headed back into the city anytime today?"

"No doubt. No doubt," chirped Hi-Jack as he swiped a piece of French toast through a pool of syrup. "We got much business to conduct. Ain't that right, Jason?"

Cryciss looked like a pit bull about to lunge. "Fuck you."

Everyone laughed at him except for his groupie, Leila, and myself. Cryciss was taking this loss so hard I wondered if it had cost him some status or position with the label. I even worried if he might make me suffer the consequences, but quickly pushed that idea out of my head. G Double D wouldn't allow it. Neither would Hi-Jack. G said that business was top priority at Explicit Content, and Jack rolled by that credo. If Cryciss ever wanted a secure position in G's inner circle, he had to get with that program and kill the childish pouting when he did not get his way.

Primo said, "Yo, Bri, what's up with those honeys at your photo shoot?"

I looked to Leila to see if she minded Primo's question. She just dug a blunt nail into a stain of dried egg yolk on the linen table-cloth. Knowing Leila like I do, I figured she did mind, although I could not tell why. "What do you mean by what's up?" I asked. If Primo wanted to go on the prowl, he had best find himself another hound dog to sniff out prey.

"G told us you had crew you wanted to look out for, and Leila and me, we was thinking they'd like to work with Andi or Jen." He nudged Leila in the arm with his elbow for confirmation, but she just scraped at the egg stain with greater determination. After get-ting along so well with Yoli and Yeri, why was she against them coming to work for the label? And why couldn't she just say so? Or did she suspect Primo's interest in Yolanda was more than profes-sional? I used to be able to read Leila like a horoscope, knowing within seconds how the day would unfold. Not being able to do so had crossed far past frustration. It began to hurt. A lot.

But I had to follow through on what I began. While I scoured my pocketbook for their business cards, Primo asked, "So, like, that Yolanda girl. What she like? She gutter and shit?"

Initially, I hadn't a damned clue what the hell he meant, and then figured he wanted to know if Yolanda as a stylist could create that look. I doubted it, which was the reason why I liked her so much, but I really didn't know and decided not to blow up her spot. "She can do anything." I found the business cards and reached across the table to hand them to Primo. "You can keep those."

Leila looked at me as if I had blurted out her darkest secret. She had given me that look only once before, and I had never forgotten it. We were play fighting in the pool at St. Mary's Park, splashing water at each other and calling each other stupid names. Leila had zapped me with a doozy—a multi-hyphenated string of kinder-garten silliness that had me laughing so hard, I thanked God we were in the shallow end. I punched the water and yelled, "Yo mama!" I meant only to concede the fight the way some kids cry, "Uncle," so when Leila froze, I thought at first that I had splashed some dirt floating in the water into her eyes. Only when I saw that look on her face holding a pain that ran much deeper under the surface, I understood the impact of what I had said. "Oh, my God, Leila, I'm so sorry. I didn't mean it," I said over and over. Each and every time I did, she said not to worry about it, that she knew I didn't mean anything by it. I knew she was sincere, but Leila's expression of resigned anguish haunted me for weeks.

Leila tried to rise from the table the way she scrambled out of the pool that day. Primo grabbed her arm and pulled her back down. He whispered something in her ear. Then they both rose and left the dining room to take their disagreement elsewhere.

"Bri, you gonna ride with us into the city?" Hi-Jack said.

Some folks take great amusement in observing another family's funky dynamics because it somehow made them feel better about the dysfunctions in their own. But Darnell's fury would be nothing compared to the Explicit Content family drama, and I preferred to go home and deal with him than observe any more of this confusing madness. "Yeah," I said. "Let's ride."

Hi-Jack pushed himself against the table, stood up, and said, "Ride or die."

Primo, Leila, and the fringe contingent stayed behind while Hi-Jack, the 8MM Posse, and I climbed into the limousine and headed for New York. Cryciss glared at Hi-Jack and me from where he sat with his group across from us. I tried my best to ignore him by striking up a conversation with Hi-Jack about his next album. I figured that being a female in his as-good-as-it-gets graces was a rare experience that I should work to my advantage.

But Keef got himself into a tizzy over rumors that the cat who sliced his lip in prison was back on the street. He calmly plotted in graphic detail what he'd do to the guy should he see him.

"I'ma, like, take that nigga, strip 'im buck naked, then bend his ass over a stool and shove a hot poker—"

"Wait, wait, wait! First ya gotta take the poker, right? And coat that shit in alcohol, yo," said Earl. He fed Keef's rage with such twisted suggestions I immediately knew that the idea of naming themselves after that Nicholas Cage movie came from his wicked imagination.

They went on for twenty horrifying minutes, when not to be outdone, Cryciss eventually yelled, "Muthafuckas, that ain't gangsta!" He then proceeded with an unsolicited critique of Keef's scheme that, of course, led into another shouting match with Earl about what would work and what wouldn't, what was soft, what was gully.

At one point, Keef muttered, "Damn, where Bokim at when you need 'im?" and the three of them roared with a laughter that made me shiver despite the warmth of that fall morning.

Hi-Jack shouted, "Y'all need to calm the fuck down. Niggas wilding out while a brother's trying to maintain a civilized conversation here."

They quieted down, and he turned his attention back to me and continued from describing his vision for his next album to unloading his first baby mama drama. "Yeah, I get around, but don't get it twisted," he said as he thumped his chest. "That bitch Trudy? That's my heart right there." And I believed him in that way you don't question a man who comes to sob on your shoulder after socking his wife in the kitchen for not having dinner ready. He wanted every track on his new joint—whether a radio-friendly party single or a bloody thug tale—to reference something Trudy would recognize. A sample from the first song they'd danced to or the name of their favorite restaurant. Maybe even add skits based on true incidents from their volatile three-year relationship. Trudy was the one who had stuck with Hi-Jack when he was writing rhymes by day and hustling his Brooklyn street corner at night. But that wasn't what earned her Hi-Jack's love (if you can call it that) as much as that she waited dutifully to get pregnant until he blew up. And when he dealt with his anxieties over impending fatherhood by sleeping with a sixteen-year-old after a show (who immediately wound up pregnant), not only did Trudy stay, she was raising that girl's child, too.

I nodded at Hi-Jack, pretending to be moved and wondering if Leila had heard this story. Leila came to mind because she was the one person who could shame me for thinking Trudy was a fuckin' idiot. Hell, I wouldn't even admit what I thought of Trudy for staying with Hi-Jack to anyone but Leila. And for that privilege she would have me feeling guilty for not seeing the girl as anything but a victim in short order.

I missed Leila so much at that moment that Hi-Jack misread my silence for sympathy. He mentioned experimenting with live instruments on his next album. It was the first thing he said that genuinely interested me and I asked him to tell me more. Jack rambled about the musical intricacies of the last albums by The Black Eyed Peas and the Roots the way a fourteen-year-old boy babbles about the levels of his favorite video game.

The shit was hilarious if you really think about. How often do you hear of the gangsta rapper who admits to aspiring to be more than another Iceberg Slim or Al Capone? Yeah, they might cop to admiring those cats, or go as far as comparing themselves to them in their lyrics, but no, there's so much more to them than that. Just like every average Jill claims to have been Cleopatra in a past life, despite the dirty mouth and sharp edges, every thug on a mic is truly Common inside.

Maybe it's not that funny after all.

Although Hi-Jack was eager to drive me home, I insisted on riding with them to SoHo. I made some excuse about wanting to do some shopping. I even faked window-shopping along Broadway for fifteen minutes, checking over my shoulder, expecting the limo to turn the corner any second. When I felt sure that the guys had gone about their business and forgotten about me, I jumped the N train at Prince Street to Astoria.

I expected to find Darnell sitting in the living room ready to give me hell, but he wasn't there. "D, you home?" I peeked in the kitchen. He'd left no notes for me on the refrigerator, and all five messages on the answering machine were old. Even though I usually shied away from the machine since I'd accidentally erased his messages that day, I replayed them not knowing what I should hope or even expect to hear. The first three were old messages from Darnell to me, letting me know where he was and when he intended to be home, making me feel worse for not showing him the same courtesy.

D, it's Jack. The session ran late. Then we went to get something to eat, blasé blasé. Anyway, Bri's here at the mansion, and since it's kinda late to be going back into the city and shit, she's gonna crash here. We'll drop her off tomorrow on the way to the studio, so don't, like, wild out or nothing. Peace out.

The machine's time-date stamp said that Hi-Jack left the message a little after one this morning. While I still felt guilty for not calling myself, I had more hope that Darnell's absence meant that Hi-Jack's message had sufficed.

I'm calling for Cassandra. This is Yoli. I could barely hear because in the background, Yeribel was throwing a fit. *Mira, Cassandra, Primo just called me at the store, and I need to talk to you. It's very, very important.* Llamame, *please.*

Although the sound of her accented English comforted me, Yolanda's voice lacked the excitement or gratitude that I had anticipated. I bet Primo calling her at the boutique offering her work with Explicit Content created drama with her current boss. Maybe she got fired and called in a panic needing assurance that Primo's offer was a legitimate opportunity. But I had to iron one wrinkle at a time, so after checking all the bedrooms upstairs for Darnell, I headed for the first place I should have looked.

The second I opened the door that led to the basement studio, I knew he wasn't there either, but I went down anyway. After lining the spared records and discs along the shelves in no particular order—replacing a cracked case as needed—Darnell had tossed all the broken records and orphaned CDs into several cardboard boxes and slid them into a corner. He neither had the time nor the heart to deal with them.

So I thought I could make up some for my mistake by going through the wreckage and reorganizing whatever I could salvage. I even became inspired to sift the rubble for something valuable that I could replace, not only as a mea culpa but also as a token of appreciation for all Darnell had done for me since I moved in six months ago. I found a pen and pulled some sheets of paper out of his laser printer so I could make a list to take with me to the used record stores in Times Square.

I sat in Darnell's swivel chair and rolled over to the boxes. Darnell had thrown crumpled or torn liner notes in one box, the orphaned CDs in the second, and the broken vinyl in the third. I spent the next hour and a half smoothing liner notes and placing them in alphabetical order. Then I shifted to the box of loose discs and remembered that I needed empty jewel cases to place them in until I figured out if any of the remaining liner notes matched.

When I stood up to look around the studio to see if Darnell had any cases left, I noticed that he already had replaced his computer monitor. At the time, I didn't know squat about recording equipment except that it's expensive. But I did remember that before G's thugs wrecked his studio, Darnell owned one of those old-school monitors that resembled a television. Now he had one of those Apple flat screens that were all the rage, which must have set him back at least two grand. As I opened the closet door, I smiled at the thought of how happy he must have been to bring it home.

To my left an entire carton of jewel cases sat on top of a much larger cardboard box. Darnell must have ordered the cases wholesale and had them shipped to the house. When I picked up the box, I caught a glimpse of the shipping label on the box beneath it. It had a giant silver X on a black background. A feminine hand scrawled Darnell's name and address across the label in silver gel ink. I dropped the carton of jewel cases and pulled back the flap. Buried in sheets of bubble wrap, I found rows of carefully packed vinyl records in plastic covers. I lifted a handful and stepped out of the closet into the light so I could read them.

A twelve-inch of "Eric B. is President" with "My Melody" as the B side. And not the one released in 1987 either. This was the original release by Zakia a year before Eric and Rakim signed with 4th & Broadway. With the pyramid on the cover.

Boogie Down Production's debut joint "Criminal Minded" on B-Boy. Mind you, not Landspeed's 2001 best-of rerelease. I knew from the typo on the cover that this copy was pressed in the first run.

Another twelve-inch—"Beat Bop" by K-Rob and Rammelzee. That's right—the joint that Basquiat did the cover art for. I traced my finger over the blackboard etching of "New Yoke, NY," remembering the day Darnell bought it.

Leila and I were waiting for him on his doorstep, thinking he had forgotten about our session. Just as we were about to bounce, he came running up the street waving this flat package like an honor student on report card day. Darnell gently slipped the album out of the plastic shopping bag, and Leila squealed and hugged him as if he had just become a father. I read the cover and finally admitted that I didn't get the fuss. "I've never heard of these cats. They're some kinda one-hit wonders?"

"The track's a classic, but that's not all," Leila said, her gentle tone allowing me to save face. "The cover. It's by Basquiat. That makes it worth at least a grand." She looked to Darnell for confirmation.

Still breathless from his run, he said, "More. I've been saving for months. Thank God, it was still there." Then Darnell kissed the record and held it up to the sky.

I ran back to the box, dropped to my knees, and quickly flipped through the rest. Not a single one a piece of mundane wax casually collected at flea markets and yard sales for pennies and lint. These records were the foundation of a true aficionado's collection. The archive of a generation. Classic material.

A trip back to the box of broken vinyl confirmed my next suspicion. I grabbed the first ripped disc I saw. The left side of the label read *Kwa* and underneath it *Ownl*. With Darnell coming home at any moment, I felt like a *Wheel of Fortune* contestant trying to solve the puzzle before my time ran out. I scoured the box for the matching half and sure enough, the broken record was Kwame's "Ownlee Eue." I dug through the box and found a several albums with a gold stamp that read *For promotional use only. Sale or transfer is prohibited. Must be returned on demand of record company.* With the exception of a few debatable keeps, the box represented the dregs of hip-hop. Now, I would have saved the twelve-inch of Zhigge's "Rakin' in the Dough" produced by maestro Salaam Remi and only a liar pretends to not dig the *uptown bounce* as well as the Original Flavor album if for nothing else but the Jay-Z/Damon Dash connection, but other than that, the box contained a peanut gallery of novelty acts, failed experiments, and one-hit wonders of moderate success. Like the publicity cuts, most found their way into Darnell's library at all simply because they were free. When I inspected the CDs in the next box, most had a hole punched neatly through the serial number or had been branded with the same promotional stamp. One cutout after the other.

When I dug deeper into the CD box, I noticed that many of the albums actually were recent and popular, so their presence in the rubble marked something else. Unlike the vinyl, the technology and currency made them easy and inexpensive to replace. They were merely calculated additions to the rubbish.

No wonder Darnell refused to let me help him clean after G's men wrecked his studio. Because every new addition became an opportunity to flaunt his collection, and my command of hip-hop was so strong he could not afford the risk. If I had sifted through the wreckage, I might have noticed that anything of true value in his beloved collection—monetarily and sentimentally—had escaped unscathed the wrath of G's henchmen. And my understanding of his tastes might have made me realize that only music Darnell deemed of questionable worth or at least easily replaced landed in the path of destruction.

I sat on the floor before Darnell's makeshift altars of sacrifice to the demons of hip-hop in utter disbelief. Then I remembered the equipment—the shattered monitor and cracked keyboard I had seen strewn across the floor with my own eyes. The missing Roland keyboard and Atari computer. Could Darnell really sit by while G's dawgz destroyed his raw bitch?

Afraid of upsetting him, I'd avoided the basement ever since the attack. And since we had not worked on my album since I had signed with Explicit Content, I never had a reason to head down there. Unless he replaced his equipment, he could not produce for others. But I wrote him a check only the previous morning. It was impossible for him to acquire the cash to replace the new equipment so quickly.

I jumped to my feet and rushed over to Darnell's console. Thrown by the sleeker technology, I recovered my pen and paper and jotted down the make and models of his new equipment. In addition to the Apple flat-screen monitor, Darnell had replaced his analog recorder with a Tascam 8mm digital recorder and his supposedly incomparable raw bitch with an Akai 3000 drum machine. As for the mixer, he stayed loyal to Mackie and just upgraded to a 1604-VLZ.

Unable to check my curiosity, I switched on the mixer. As if operated by a ghost, the faders began to slide into position. I hopped back and watched until they stopped. In awe, I inched back to the console and hit play. "God Don't Like Ugly" boomed through the speakers with every sound element perfectly in place.

I snapped off the mixer and scoured the closet for something to answer the suspicion bubbling inside me. I had no idea what I was looking for, just that I would know it when I found it. In the corner of the closet, I spotted a short stack of magazines. I grabbed the first one—a Sam Ash catalog—and begin to flip through it. I walked it over to Darnell's console and began to compare make and models. His new recorder alone set him back five grand. The new Mackie fully automated digital 8 bus console with motorized faders and on-board signal processing cost D another six. Altogether his new equipment cost three times more than the check I had given him only twenty-four hours earlier. When I turned the catalog over to its back cover and saw the address label, it made better sense: *Jackson Hightower c/o Explicit Content, Inc.* and the SoHo address.

So the attack on his studio was staged, probably to make me sign with Explicit Content. Which meant that Darnell had to have gotten down with G Double D beforehand. Leila knew something was up and tried to warn me at the party.

Suffice to say, I had no trouble re-creating the mess Darnell had concocted.

CHAPTER 18

A WOMAN'S WORTH

Despite my rage, I knew I had to perpetrate like the guilty girl-friend. I combed the kitchen cabinets and found enough in-gredients to make spaghetti and salad. As the pasta boiled, I ran upstairs to take a quick shower.

When I reached into the bag for the vanilla body scrub, my fingertips brushed against a wispy strand of metal. I grasped whatever it was and pulled it out of the bag—the tourmaline pendant. I flipped the bag over and dumped its contents along the bathroom rug. Besides the two bottles I dropped in there, the matching tourmaline earrings spilled out. Suspecting the bag was mine, Leila had taken them off and slipped them inside. We were cool.

I changed into one of Yolanda's outfits—a sleeveless mock turtleneck in cherry red, the ankle-length black skirt with the slit to my hip, and knee-high leather boots with the French heel. Not conservative enough to overlook but not too sexy to suspect. Al-though I knew I had a costume jewelry set that better matched my outfit, I put on Leila's instead. Somehow I thought it'd get me through the night. I hurried back to the kitchen and found Darnell pouring tomato sauce from a jar into a pan.

"S'up, Cass?" he said as if we did this every day. The second time in as many days that a man had done that to me.

"Hey."

D eyed my outfit. With neither a frown or a smile, he said, "You look nice." He opened a drawer and pulled out a large spoon.

"Thanks." He turned on the burner and began to stir. I walked to the dishwasher and pulled out plates and utensils while Darnell reached toward the spice rack for the oregano. As I set the table, he spiced the spaghetti sauce. The silence finally broke me. "Look, Darnell, I'm sorry, OK?"

He lifted the spoon to his lips and tasted the sauce. " 'Bout what?"

"You know." Darnell turned to me, his brow wrinkled. I wanted to yell at him to stop fucking around, but instead I said, "Last night."

"Oh." He tapped the oregano jar over the bubbling sauce. "No big thing. Hi-Jack left me a message, and then G called me this morning."

"He did?"

"Yeah, he wanted to know if I could swing by the office this afternoon so we could talk about my producing a few cuts for your album, so whatever you said or did last night worked." Darnell opened the bottom cabinet, poked his head, and rummaged through the pots and pans.

My heart tightened into a knot. "What the hell is that supposed to mean?"

"Hold up, I can't hear you." He straightened up with a sieve in hand. "What'd you say?" Just as he was about to place the sieve in the sink, I snatched it out of his hand.

"I said what the fuck is that supposed to mean?"

Darnell looked at me as if I had just slapped him for no reason. "Cassie, what's up with you?" He threw up his hands and calmly said, "Yes, when you didn't come home or call, I admit, I was upset. But I've been in this game for longer than a minute, Cassie, so I understand how it goes." Darnell returned to the stove and poured the hot spaghetti water into the sieve in the sink. "We'll forget the whole thing happened, OK?"

But just what did he think we were forgetting? Did he believe I slept with G to get him a producing contract? If so, why wasn't he losing his fuckin' mind? Even if I could accept that Darnell set me up with G Double D so he could convince me to sign with Explicit Content, I refused to consider that sleeping with him was part of the scam. Not after Darnell and I became involved.

As I watched him pour the sauce directly over the strained spaghetti as he tossed it in the pot, I wondered how less forgiving he might have been had G not offered him a production deal. Living with Leila, I'd had plenty of opportunities to learn how to see past a scorned man's cool. I knew when a man's silence screamed accusations and how to translate blunt, nonchalant statements into cries for reassurance. A man who cares about a woman enough to be angry with her when he believes she's done him wrong gives her at least that much. This wasn't the case with Darnell. He deprived me of any of that because he truly didn't give a fuck. For a man who supposedly cared so much for me as a lover, he hadn't asked a single question about my night at the mansion. Not who else was there and where I slept. *Even a man who's afraid to learn the truth wants to know it—if he truly cares,* Leila always said. Now that he had what he wanted most, Darnell couldn't have cared less that I spent the night with the head of the label. And the romantic overtures and the attack on his studio and perhaps even the humiliating episode at the party were all part of the ruse. For all I knew, he had delivered me to Explicit Content and the deal was his reward.

Maybe all these sordid possibilities made me say what I did next. "If you're so upset with me that you don't want to talk about it, maybe I should just pack my things and move into the mansion." As upset as I was with Darnell, I really didn't want to do that at all. As bad as it looked, I knew the drama hidden under his roof was nothing compared to what would surely come to light if I went live in Glen Ridge. And I understand now that at the time I wanted to stay despite everything, because I hoped that if I did his feelings for me would prove real over time.

Darnell snorted as he kept stirring the spaghetti. Then he looked at me. "One thing I always liked about you, Cassie, is that no matter what went down, you refused to be a drama queen," he said calmly. "Yeah, you had your moments when you'd get emotional, wild out a little, but only when you thought someone underestimated your worth. I can relate to that, Cassie, believe that." He walked over to the table and picked up the two flattened bowls I had set. Darnell pulled a large pasta fork out of the drawer, scooped some spaghetti out of the pot, and dropped it into a bowl. "We both know what the other wants most and what it takes to get it, so let's not create drama over it."

But I didn't know, and his little soliloquy didn't cut it. Had I not discovered what I did, his speech might have shamed me. "So I'll go pack, then."

I turned out of the kitchen and into the living room. Behind me I heard him say in that same calm voice, "That's how you want to do this . . ." As I walked across the living toward the stairs leading to the second floor, I heard silence behind me. Then the bowl of spaghetti whizzed by my head and crashed into the wall before me.

I spun around in time to see Darnell charging toward me. Before I could dodge him, he tackled me onto the sofa. "What happened last night, Cassandra? Did G do something to you? Did he touch you?" He grabbed my chin and squeezed so hard I thought his fingers would puncture my jaw. "Did any of them muthafuckas touch you? They run a train on you? Because if they did, I swear to God . . ."

"Darnell, you're hurting me!" I cried as I tried to pull his hand off my face. I fought to sit up, and he finally scampered backward

EXPLICIT CONTENT 219

on the sofa. I wanted to cry out, but instead I swallowed so hard it felt as if I had ingested a baseball. After all the vicious things he said to me, I refused to trust him with my tears.

Darnell ran his hands across his head, inhaled hard, and looked at me with watery eyes. "Is that what you wanted, Cassandra?"

You and Mini Me ain't for each other, said G, *and you know it.* The worst thing about it is that I still didn't know where I stood with Darnell. Or where I wanted to go with him. If I could go anywhere with him. I still couldn't tell which was real—the sudden tantrum or the calm question. Nor did it register to me at the time that it took no time from when I learned Darnell was not the man I thought he was for me to unravel into the perfect woman for him. And I didn't like her.

So I ran upstairs and locked myself in my old bedroom, where I felt safe enough to release my tears. When I walked to the dresser to get the tissue box, I found the broken Foxy Brown CD on my bureau. I tossed it in the trash and then looked in the mirror. Before my new clothes and pampered hair, my reddened eyes fell immediately on the tourmaline pendant. I returned to the bed and peeked under it where I'd stowed away the plastic bags that I had used to pack my things when I left Leila's. I grabbed them and took them to the master bedroom. I threw my Yoli clothes and notebooks into them, knotted them closed and carried them into the hallway.

Then I went downstairs to find Darnell. Sure enough, he was in the basement editing "God Don't Like Ugly," trying to splice some of Leila's sloppy recordings from old recording sessions the three of us did together with the new version where I dissed her by name. I headed downstairs. He jumped when he first saw me and then tried to play it cool. I made it easier by ignoring the sleek new equipment. "What do you think?"

"You think G's going for that, seeing how we're both on his label now?"

Clearly, the man never thought of that. He smirked at me and said, "You never know. G's all about the gimmicks. The thought of having two rival MCs selling answer record after answer record for Explicit Content just might make his dick hard." Then he laughed, and I forced myself to join him. Then Darnell stopped and said, "Perhaps we could work on it here first before we take it into his studio. You know, after you rewrite it some. Not make it obvious that its about Leila after all, if you want."

So that's how the dog throws the bitch a bone, I thought. I just nodded. "Thanks." I started back toward the staircase, but I couldn't resist. I turned around and said, "I'm glad you've been able to afford to replace your equipment so quickly."

"Yeah," Darnell stuttered. "My old clients have been hanging on, coming through. And not to mention that sweet check you left me. Thanks, boo."

"Just trying to keep my promises," I said. I hated playing dumb. I never respected women who did, never believing it could ever be necessary. Now I understood. "I don't know anything about this kinda stuff except what you've taught me, but this new shit looks mad nice."

Darnell shrugged. "It ain't my stolen Roland or my raw bitch, but it'll have to do."

"I'ma let you get back to work." I went back upstairs and waited to hear music. D eventually began to work on another track from my demo, and I crept back to the bedroom. From there I called Jen and asked her to send a car for me. Within the hour, a black Hummer with a silver X painted on the hood pulled up in front of Darnell's. I slipped down the stairs with my bags as he continued to work in the basement. I threw my bags in the back and jumped into the passenger seat.

G grinned at me and said, "Back so soon, baby girl?"

"Shut up, G."

He laughed as he sped off down the street.

*   *   *

After a month, I became convinced that living under the same roof actually served to keep Leila and me apart. Although I asked to be in the mansion with everyone else, G put me in the guesthouse, where I stayed in the same room as I had that first night. I'd tag along with Hi-Jack or the 8MM Posse when they rode to and from the city, whereas Leila would drive in with Primo even though the limo had plenty of space for all of us. I passed my days often with G, putting in long hours at the studio and preparing for my up-coming performance at NV. However, he rarely came home with me, if at all. When he did stay at the guesthouse, he usually fol-lowed a few hours later, always crashed in his own room, and left before I would wake. So for weeks I spent nights there by myself, scared to be alone but even more afraid of going to the mansion.

But I still made an effort to go there every day to feed Leila and wait for an opportunity to be alone with her. Although I ate in the city, I always brought home an extra meal for Leila that I hid in the Chinese lacquer cabinet on her floor. I'd go into the mansion to front nice with the fellas and then excuse myself. With Leila al-ways with them, I knew no one would follow me. So I'd sneak up to her floor and hide the food in the Chinese lacquer cabinet. Every time I got away with it, my hope rose that one day some-body would let down his guard, and she and I would be able to steal a moment alone.

But that never happened. We were never alone for more than a few minutes at a time and always with someone else from the label within earshot. Never enough time for the kind of conversation we needed to have. In fact, Leila was never alone. She was always in the shadow of one of the guys, usually Primo or Hi-Jack. I would come home from the studio and drop by the so-called family room. When I peeked in, I'd see Leila with Primo's arm curled around her while he and Hi-Jack got high. The first time I saw that, it bugged me out, because Leila doesn't get high on account of her moms. Yet there was Leila trapped with them in a roomful of smoke, the smell clearly making her sick and triggering bad memories. That was when I first realized that even when I wasn't around, Leila was never alone.

Every time I thought of a way to communicate with Leila, I discovered how vigilant the guys were in preventing it. When I finally got a cell phone, Leila no longer had one. Like all the Explicit Talent models, she had an alphanumeric pager.

I considered sending her a letter, thinking no one would think I'd be writing to someone at the same address. But luckily I tested it out by sending a Halloween card to my family in LA, telling them the great news about my new record deal and giving them the Glen Ridge address. The card of congratulations that my aunt Treece sent me, however, got intercepted and rerouted back to the Explicit Content office in SoHo. I learned that Jen instructed the butler, Patrick, to collect the mail and Express Mail it back to the Explicit Content office, where she proceeded to sort and open it. I didn't dare ask Patrick to give me my mail directly because I didn't know his story. What if he relied on G to stay in the country and was loyal to him?

But I complained immediately about the mail one night when Jen came to the mansion and handed me my open mail. "You ain't supposed to be opening up other people's mail," I said. "Don't you know that's a federal offense?"

Jen looked at me as if I had grown a third ear on my nose, then doubled over laughing when Primo walked in on us. He demanded to be in on the joke, and Jen told him I was tripping about the mail. Primo choked back a smile and said, "Yo, Cassie, we's all fam here."

"My fam has never invaded my privacy," I said. And it's true. Genevieve never opened my mail or listened to my telephone conversations and neither had Leila, even though we shared everything with each other.

"What you getting that's all so private?" Primo asked. His menacing tone put me off, and I guessed it showed because he softened up. "Look, ma, it's for your convenience. Any bill you get, Jen's gonna take care of it for you. You like that, right?" Before I could answer, Primo scoffed, "Oh, I forgot. You paranoid that the label's gonna charge you with some questionable recoupment and cut into your royalties." He and Jen laughed again at my expense.

"I wouldn't be the first artist that's happened to," I said defensively. "Don't hate on me 'cause I'm trying to mind my business."

Primo said, "So you wanna handle your own security, too? When you blow up, you want these lunatics out here to get your address and send you whatever-the-fuck to the house? Jenny's just looking out for you."

Now I was the one to laugh. "Yeah, Explicit Content pays Jen to sniff out anthrax and open letter bombs and shit."

"Now you're minding my business," Jen said with no humor whatsoever. Then, with a toss of her peroxide tresses, she huffed past me to track down the others and continue her deliveries.

"Don't sleep," said Primo. "Jen's gangsta. You should see the piece she keeps behind the counter at the office."

"Does that mean I'm going to have to get one to keep her nose outta of my shit?" I thought he was teasing me, so I just was talking shit. I should have known better than that.

When things jumped off, it became mad easy to forget the drama and run with the hype. After G Double D heard the "But Can You Feel Me?" remix, he got amped about shooting a video as soon as possible. When he mentioned it to me on the way home from the studio one night, I leaped at the chance to request we hire Evita "Vi" Martinez, the first female director to make serious noise in music videos. But even though Vi had been nominated for several awards for her work with Floetry and Mystic, G wasn't feeling my suggestion.

"She kinda artsy for a party song, Cassie," said G. "If she'd want to work with Explicit Content anyway."

His second point had merit, but I refused to concede because I knew beneath his first reaction hid a resistance to hiring a woman. "That's exactly why this video's gonna stand apart from all the others," I said. "And it's got to, G, 'cause that cut's gonna be my introduction to the record-buying public. My joint can't be the same ol' rapper-in-a-wind-tunnel or hoochies-in-a-nightclub shit we've seen a thousand times before."

"You talkin' like a video ain't nothing but a commercial for the track, Cassie, and you wrong. When a kid drops fifteen bucks on a CD 'cause he liked the video, it's because the video sold the artist not the song," argued G. "That's why some labels drop a mil or more to shoot 'em." That fact blew me away. Genevieve's first film *Repeat Offender*—a ninety-eight-minute joint made in the late seventies—cost a fifth of that. I found it hard to believe that the cookie-cutter videos that looked exactly the same cost the same to shoot as a feature-length indie joint. "Random Sounds is on my ass, so we can't spend money to make money anymore," G continued. "Your joint's not only gotta be tight, it's gotta be cheap, 'cause you're a new artist. An unknown entity. Unproven. I'm sorry, Cassie, you're nice on the mic, no doubt. But on the market, you ain't Missy Elliot just yet."

I let his dig slide. "Ain't that more reason to go with a director like Vi Martinez? No way she's gonna cost as much as those dudes you be working with. Them niggas be making action joints now with Ice Cube and LL. What kinda budget do you think they're gonna expect from you now they've gone Hollywood? Shit, half the budget'd probably go into their own pocket. Have you peeped Vi's shit? It's all about concept, G. She's gonna give you more for less, I know it."

"All right, all right. Damn!" G said. "We'll send her the track and have her send us her reel and a treatment." Then G gave me a long look and started to laugh. "I knew you'd be trouble. That's why I ain't sign you first."

"Just 'cause I want folks to watch my joint and know I ain't the lead hoochie just 'cause I gotta few lines?" I joked. "You ain't right."

G grew solemn and nodded. "You right. I ain't."

G liked Evita Martinez's reel but still wasn't sold that her style suited Explicit Content. Primo agreed with him, and of course, Leila with me. That all changed when Vi e-mailed her treatment, but not before some drama went down between Primo and Leila.

Primo created the concept for both the original "But Can You Feel Me?" song and video. In the words of the ballad, the man wanted to know if the woman he's kickin' it with can see past his good looks and deep pockets and understand his truest feelings, even the ones that may unnerve her. A video that depicted Primo as a man with less confidence in love than he did in career not only would have been true to the song but also original and hot. Instead, Primo went for the gully cliché and played a drug lord who fell for a schoolgirl who never suspects a thing. Visually, it ripped off 50 Cent's "21 Questions," right down to the police raid that forces Primo to dump kilos of product down the toilet. But instead of having Megan Good help him cut and flush, he has Jessica Alba standing in the doorway staring at him wide-eyed with shock.

At a meeting in the conference room at the SoHo office, Primo pitched the same concept for the remix video with a ludicrous twist—a love triangle where Leila and I competed for him. Because the remix had a dance tempo, he suggested we move the locale from his character's Hampton estate to a dance club—and drug front—he owned in Brooklyn. "And instead y'all already know what I do and are down with it," said Primo, "so it's more about which one of y'all I choose. Which one of y'all's willing to go the furthest to have my back." It had no relationship to the lyrics Leila and I added, and he thought himself a grand conceptual artist for imagining an ambiguous ending. "But when the video ends, y'all are like standing in front of my desk insisting that I choose on some Brandy–Monica type shit, and just as I'ma 'bout to choose, the camera fades." All that when G had relegated his part in the remix to the chorus.

G actually considered that garbage, and while Leila and I protested and fought with Primo, Jen walked in with Vi's e-mail. He took it but barely glanced at it at first, just watching the three of us hollering at one another like a kid at a circus.

"I ain't gonna front like I've never done stupid shit because of some guy," said Leila. "But I haven't stooped to fighting a female over a dude since the seventh grade. So I ain't gonna do it now, even on some video, especially with my best friend."

Her words shocked me into silence. Although we'd remained congenial over the previous weeks, our inability to speak prevented the resolution that I thought necessary to be at peace, let alone become friends again. Until that moment, I realized that I never thought I would ever hear Leila refer to me again as her friend, let alone her best friend.

Primo seemed blindsided by her words, too, as if Leila fired the opening salvo of a completely different battle. "*Mami*, it's pretend," he cooed at her, caressing her arm. "And if it were real, you know I'd choose you, right?"

Leila flapped his hand off of her. "I ain't asking you to choose nobody. Y'all muthafuckas think you got me all caught up in this piece, controlling everything I say and I do . . ."

"Ayo, Leila, calm down," G finally said. Then he began to scan the e-mail.

". . . y'all don't own me, no matter what the fuck I signed. *I'm* choosing this time. And unless you're gonna drug me up and prop me up on the video set like some kinda Kewpie doll, I'm not doing this shit." Leila looked at me, her eyes begging for me to have her back yet understanding that she did not deserve it.

I said, "Neither am I. The concept's not me, it's not her . . . it just ain't us."

"And y'all don't have to," said G, waving Vi's treatment, "because this concept here's bananas."

Vi did her research. She didn't stop at listening to the song and watching previous Explicit Content videos. In a brilliant risk, she wanted subdued emotion to play against the upbeat rhythm to reinforce the song's message. The woman actually read our bios and studied the lyrics for ideas to also highlight our backgrounds.

In Vi's video concept, Leila and I were independent rap stars from the Bronx on the road who find ourselves afraid to trust the people fawning over us and yearning for the 'hood where the people know and feel us for who we truly are. Primo represented the voice calling us home, and his chorus narrated alternate scenes of Leila on the tour bus and me in my hotel room, each reminiscing of simpler days in the 'hood when we did funny things like drying our laundry on the radiator and buying leather on layaway. At the end of the video, Leila and I simultaneously decide to make a pilgrimage to the old neighborhood, and we each end up at the Big Pun mural on 163rd Street and Westchester Avenue at the same time. Each sees the other and finds comfort knowing that someone else does understand.

We shot the Bronx segment first on a beautiful day in early October. Word had gotten out about the video shoot, and when our car pulled up at five in the morning, a mob of school kids already waited behind police barricades across the street from Pun's mural. The crowd consisted mostly of young girls who wanted to see Primo, screaming and waving his Explicit Content T-shirts, CDs, and posters. However, quite a few fans came for Leila brandishing homemade signs that read *Welcome Home, Fatal* and *We Love Fatal*.

When Leila and I stepped out of the limo, the kids applauded and screamed her name. She waved and blew kisses to them. They called her over, but Jen had the bodyguards usher us into a trailer where Andi awaited us. Leila hopped into her styling chair, and Andi got to work on her makeup.

As I waited my turn, I looked out the window at the antsy crowd and sulked. Because I had not dropped anything yet, none of the signs or posters spoke to me. It ached to return to my old 'hood and not be recognized. So I vowed to leave known to those faces who cut school to see a superstar. "I'll be back," I said, and rushed out the door before anyone could stop me.

I made it halfway across the street when I heard someone call my stage name.

"Sabrina!"

I turned around, and a Chinese woman in her early thirties sporting a baby blue FUBU sweatsuit and matching Sketcher boots caught up to me. She extended her hand and said, "Hi, I'm Shelby J. Lee, and I was wondering if you would mind giving me a few minutes for an interview, maybe take a photo or two." My surprise barely registered when she addressed it. "The J's for Jun, and well, you don't care what Shelby's supposed to be English for. So can I have few moments?" Before I could answer, Shelby dug a palm-sized digital recorder from her pocket and angled it under my chin.

"Sure," I said.

"Great. Just give me a second," she said. Shelby turned around and waved toward a car parked at the corner. A Chinese guy hopped out of the passenger side, carrying a professional camera, and jogged over to us. "Sabrina, this is my husband and partner Nick Zhao."

"How ya doin'?" he said as he snapped a photo.

I couldn't have scripted a better scenario. There I stood in the middle of my old neighborhood being interviewed by Shelby J. Lee, the Big Pun mural on one side of the street and a mob of would-be fans on the other. And I had it all to myself.

Shelby said, "So Sabrina, you're the latest artist on the Explicit Content label, second woman—"

"First Black woman." Some kids across the street recognized that I might be a VIP and began to point. From the corner of my eye, I saw them ask each other *Who is she?*

"And you're back on your ol' stomping grounds to shoot the video to your first single. It must feel incredible."

"It does. I'm mad proud to come back here for my first joint," I said. Nick continued to take photos of me as I spoke, changing his angle to capture the kids or the mural behind me. "Most folks nowadays wait until they blow up, do a dozen video shoots in mansions and on yachts and whatnot. Then try to come back to where they come from and front like they down, when it's really about *Oh, look, how far I've come*, shitting on their 'hood. I'm not about that, that's why I'm here now. These fans here don't know who I am just yet, but they will soon, and I hope they remember I came back from jump."

Shelby seemed impressed with my comments. She said, "And you're not the kind of person who comes to mind when they think of a rapper from this area. Salutatorian at South Bronx High School, no criminal record . . ."

The sista really did her homework. "Yeah, and you're never gonna catch me acting like something I'm not, all hard and gangsta. I mean, I don't take shit, but I don't start it either, you know." I laughed.

But Shelby didn't join me. "So why sign with a label like Explicit Content, Sabrina? As someone with such a positive background, don't the rumors about the label bother you? Any truth to the rumors that Explicit Content engages in criminal activity?" Nick's flash exploded in my eyes, but I reeled more from Shelby's question. Within seconds I went from stunned to angry. ". . . drug trafficking, gun running . . ."

"No!" I yelled. "Every time you turn around, the media's talking about some federal investigation into a rap label, but you know what? Po going after Tha Row and the Inc., and coming up with nothing but allegations. Why don't they allege up Pac's and

B.I.G.'s killers?" Even as I surprised myself with my avid defense of companies I did not know, the principle fueled me into a heated tirade. "If a brother criticizes Corporate America, he's just a lazy nigga who don't wanna work. If a brother works for Corporate America, he busts his ass for twenty-five years so some white boy half his age can steal his pension, maybe do a few years in Club Med Correctional *if* he gets caught, and make another million or two selling his story. Sells it to the same media, mind you, alleging Irv Gotti did this, Suge Knight did that, Gregory Downs did the other thing, because if a brother *joins* Corporate America and beats the white boys at their own games, well, he must be a criminal."

"You're absolutely right, Sabrina," Shelby said. "The media and the criminal justice system are rife with double standards against people of color. But does that mean the rumors about Explicit Content are untrue?"

"Yes!"

The vehemence of my response took her aback, but Shelby recovered quickly. "And if they were true, would you still feel obligated to defend the label because of the biases in media and law enforcement?"

I stammered for an answer when the kids behind me began to shriek. We all turned in time to see Primo climb out of an Explicit Content limo. Girls in the crowd screamed his name, and some even cried. Anticipating a bold move by a crazed fan, the police closed in toward the barricade.

"Fuck!" Shelby yelled, knowing that Primo's arrival signaled the end of our interview. Her husband, Nick, rubbed her shoulders and assured her that what she already had was solid. Then Shelby shot past me and ran over to Primo, dogging his heels and sticking her recorder in his face as he bustled toward the trailer.

Nick fished out a business card and handed it to me. "Sabrina, thanks for your time. When we place it, we'll be sure to send a copy over to the label." I took the card without a word. "Hey!" Nick yelled. He ran over to Shelby, who had gotten into an argument with one of Primo's bodyguards. I headed back to the trailer, and the last thing I saw before I went inside was Nick standing between the guard and Shelby saying, "I don't give a fuck. Do not touch my wife!"

I entered the trailer and all eyes were on me. Besides Andi and Leila, Primo and Jen stood there, too. Breaking the awkward silence, Leila rose from Andi's chair and said, "Your turn, Cassie."

I took the seat, and Andi started on my makeup. Jen said, "So, Cassandra, what went down between you and Shelby Lee?" I ran it down for her, although the conviction of my responses paled from the experience of being caught off guard.

"Fuckin' bitch reporter," mumbled Primo.

Jen snapped, "She's just doing her goddamned job." Her defense of Shelby made me feel worse about the interview. Whenever I had read a Shelby J. Lee clip before that day, I gave her daps for asking the hard questions. I never called her a hata or questioned her motivations. But when she blindsided me, all kind of ill things came to mind that I'm too ashamed to admit now. The worst thing about it though was that I wholeheartedly believed everything I told Shelby when I said it. Not five minutes later and passion faded into doubt.

"You just saying that shit 'cause she one of your own."

"Fuck off, Primo."

"Fuck me? She ain't supposed to be talking to nobody without clearing it through publicity. When G finds out, he's gonna have a fit."

Leila took Primo's hand and led him to the door. "Let's sign some autographs while Cassie gets ready."

"Thank you!" said Jen. Leila and Primo left and she turned to me. "He's right about that, Cassie," said Jen. "In the future, do not speak to any reporters until they've run their request by our publicity department. We can't protect you or the label if you don't, OK?"

"OK. Jen?" The question in my mind was how true were my

answers to Shelby. But that was not what came out of my mouth. "Did I fuck up bad?"

"No, honey, if it went down as you said it did, you actually handled it pretty well. Shelby Lee's a muckracker not a gossipmonger, but guys like Primo can't see past their own egos to know the difference and act accordingly. Not that they would know how." Jen smiled and patted me on the knee. "I wish all the others were as quick on the draw as you."

Although I know she meant it as a compliment, it didn't feel like one.

Once on the set, I soon forgot about the morning incident. A video shoot ain't more than a bunch of hurry-up-and-wait, but I loved this one because we were outdoors on a beautiful day, and the fans stayed with us until sundown. When the po threatened the underage kids who were cutting school, they cracked us up with the holidays they invented to convince the cops they had the day off.

Vi had Leila arrive at the mural first. As she stared at the mural, I came in from the right. Then we were to make eye contact and connect. That direction proved difficult for both Leila and me. We had a hard time looking at each other for more than a second without breaking the gaze and cutting the moment.

So as the crew situated the camera for another shot of a closeup of Leila over my shoulder, Vi adjusted her direction. "Leila, Cassie, I want you both to look at this wall as if for the first time. Rediscover it. Nothing else exists but this mural. Take as long as you need, and whatever feelings come up are perfect, so just sit with them."

My eyes traveled down from the Yankee insignia on Pun's ski cap, down the bridge of his nose to his full lips. A silver microphone served as the _I_ in BIG PUN spelled in purple letters outlined in gold. Leila reached out to touch the wall, her nails short and bare. She traced a finger down the center of Pun's goatee, and said, "He's one of the lucky ones."

I tried to make sense of her bizarre statement. "Because at least he broke through before he died?"

Leila shook her head. "Because he died of a heart attack. In this industry, a guy dies before the age of thirty because some other cat caps him. I see this wall and it reminds of a dozen more just like it. Only difference is that those guys ain't famous." She dropped her hand from the mural and looked at me. "You know, Cassie, you always worried about what hip-hop was coming to, and I'd act like you were crazy. I thought, yeah, some knuckleheads be out here generating friction, but hip-hop's bigger and better than ever. But . . ." She waved at the wall. "Like look what graf's come to, Cassie. Graf used to be about telling heads *We's here!* Now it's about saying *We're gone.*"

I nodded. Then I said, "Or *Drink Coca-Cola.*"

And Leila belted out a laugh like I had not heard from anyone in ages. A flash of bliss from a previous life. And whenever Leila laughed like that, I lost it, too.

"Cut." Leila and I turned to Vi in disbelief. We'd had no idea the camera had been rolling that entire time. Vi winked at us. "Perfect."

And the kids across the street jumped and cheered in agreement.

CHAPTER 19

GOING SOUTH

Even though the original version of "But Can You Feel Me?" only peaked on the hip-hop charts at number seventeen, the remix rocketed to number two in its first week. No way would we ever take number one with Jay-Z coming out of retirement to bury the hatchet and record a single with Nas, but how could I hate on that? Especially when the remix also debuted in the top ten on the dance charts, and a few weeks later it crossed over and appeared at number six on the pop charts.

Then the media flurry began. The small junket that G had Jen arrange for me became a full campaign. Calls poured in from everywhere, requesting interviews and appearances, so for the next week or so G had a Town Car and driver assigned to me personally to usher me between studio sessions and publicity events. I thought it unusual to never go with Leila and even Primo, but Jen explained that it enabled us to cover more ground. The label assigned a publicist to me named Katz, who never left me alone during interviews yet ignored me on the rides to and from them, yelling into his cell phone to hound the guys to make their appearances on time, nag his assistant to send faxes and e-mails, complain to Jen that he needed more staff and G to make the guys respect his authority, and argue with his girlfriend about why he was coming home late yet again.

Shelby J. Lee's profile never materialized, and no one ever brought it up. Given the attention the rest of the media gave me, I figured one of two things. Either my answers to her questions were not juicy enough for her to dive in with a big splash, or I got so much exposure that Shelby decided to leap off the bandwagon. For whatever reasons, I presumed she killed her own story, and it relieved me.

But it never left my mind. So I found the nerve to approach Jen about it. One morning before leaving the office for an interview with *Spin,* I waited until Katz left the room to get a press kit and said, "Jen, you never told me what I should do if someone does start asking about . . . you know . . . rumors and shit."

I expected Jen to become defensive, but she blew me off like dust on a book. "Don't worry about that. Katz'll handle it. That's why he's there. Besides, most of these reporters know now that going there can mean terminating the interview and losing access to the entire roster."

While I understood the rationale behind terminating the interview, I had to avoid that. My career had roared out the gate, and my visibility had multiplied. No way I could afford to get a reputation with the media for being a difficult or flavorless interview. And while I thought a label-wide ban an extreme punishment for inquiring about rumors, that policy stood outside my control. Besides, that would take affect only after the damage to me might have been done. "No, Jen, I need you to school me. I don't want some white boy speaking for me. Whatever he can say for me, I can say for myself."

Jen stared at me and then broke into the warmest smile. "You're right. And you already know what to say."

"I do?"

"Sure, G loved the answer you gave at the video shoot that day. He told me he was almost sorry Shelby didn't publish it. We both thought that if she had, it might've actually won you some fans."

G had never told me that, but it carried a special weight to hear it through Jen. Like it held more truth coming from someone else, especially the woman who served as his right hand. Only thing sweeter would have been to hear it from Hi-Jack, whom G had signed before he even hired Jen.

"That's even more reason why I gotta know what to say if someone like Shelby presses," I said. "What do I say when asked point-blank about . . ."

"Cassie, just tell them what you know."

"I don't know anything. G talks about expanding beyond the new label, starting new ventures, seeking capital." Then I remembered that Jen's father and G had been negotiating about the chain of parking garages, but I became uncomfortable admitting that level of knowledge about her family's involvement in possible enterprises, especially since I had yet to hear if the deal had occurred. I grew frustrated with the entire topic, tired of thinking about it, even resentful that it cast shadows on my new fortune.

Jen read the frustration on my face and put her hand on my shoulder. "Cassie, just be an artist. Leave business to us. And for God's sake, enjoy your celebrity."

So I put the issue to rest and did as she advised. I ate at restaurants with journalists who paid more to buy me one drink than I had paid for entire meals back in the Boogie Down. When I walked into a hotel suite for a press junket, a buffet of wine, cheese, and fruit awaited me, and yet every fifteen minutes a guy with three hairs on his chin and probably less on his nuts would ask if he could fetch me anything else. I stopped worrying about my appearance because Explicit Content always kept a makeup artist on hand. Eventually, I built the confidence to handle most interviews alone, so Katz spent less time perched at my shoulder and more time in the corner hissing into his cell phone. Sometimes after a particularly long day, a hotel treated me to a full session at its spa.

And industry writers proved to have little desire to grill me about Explicit Content. I wondered if it had to do with being lazy, kissing ass, or running scared. The few who wandered into sensitive territory asked throwaway questions about my mom. On account of her fame, Katz pressed me to mention her in my bio, but I insisted he remove any references to her. Still, reporters found out that Genevieve Rivers was my mother and wanted to know things like what she was doing now, when she planned on returning to acting, did she support my choice of career, and shit like that. The questions were harder for me to answer than they realized, but only one picked up on my discomfort or at least made an attempt to explore it. He asked me, "Seems like you don't want to talk about your mother."

I said, "I just don't want anyone to think I'm trying to ride my mother's coattails. She's an actress, I'm an MC, and I want to make it on my own, you know. That's the way my moms did it, and that's how I should do it, too."

My answer satisfied him, and Katz escorted the next reporter into the suite. I requested a break and went into the bathroom. Despite my effortless escape via clichés, that brief exchange took more out of me than any fear of potential questions about Explicit Content's alleged criminal enterprises.

The outbreak of fans that followed the media flurry soon took my attention from any nagging doubts. After my first junket at the Plaza Hotel, I found three high school girls waiting for me in the lobby. Not that I knew that when I saw them. I just caught the maître d' grilling them and wasn't feeling it. Those sisters were just sitting there chatting quietly, but this muthafucka rolled up on them and asked them to leave. I knew if they had been three white girls, no one would've said shit so long as they weren't making a scene. So I stepped to him and said, "Excuse me. Is there a problem here?"

Before he could say anything, the petite one with shoulder-length cornrows leaped to her feet and said, "Oh, my God, it's her! It's Sabrina Steelo!" Then the three of them started to squeal and jump so I had to hush them. Like robots they settled into stiff postures and silly grins.

I reached into my pocket for a twenty to give the maître d', and then I thought, *Fuck that. Reward his ignorance?* Nah, I'd only give him the cash if I knew it would make him feel as small as he tried to make my fans feel. "You may go now," I said. He huffed at me, but bounced. The second he did, the girls rushed me to autograph their CDs and ask a thousand questions.

My favorite moment came when the chubby one with the Leila nails said, "Lemme ask you something. Where your family from? Like they from here, or from the islands, or what?"

"My mother's people are from Trinidad."

"I told you!" she yelled at the third girl with the thick glasses. She tore open her jacket and pumped out her chest to show off her T-shirt of the Trinidadian flag, and began to strut. "Trini in the house, holla!"

And with every appearance, the crowd of waiting fans multiplied. They burned the request lines at the radio stations and video shows for my joint. Soon my publicity jaunts included radio interviews (G's doing) and surprise visits to random high schools during lunch hour (my idea).

Eventually, my schedule became so busy, I stopped trying to create opportunities to speak alone with Leila, but I never lost hope that one would appear. I knew the time would come when these muthafuckas would drop their guard, and I had to keep my eyes and ears open to take advantage of that moment when it presented itself. I prepared for that moment but not all that came with it. Especially after what went down between G Double D and me.

He broke his promise. At first he met me in the studio and oversaw my recording sessions. He stopped every so often to parlay on his cell, and sometimes disappeared for two or three hours. But for the most part he worked with me as he said he would at Orso. But that ended before it became routine.

One day G spent twenty minutes in the studio with me and then ran out to the SoHo office. I knew he would not return. The second he abandoned the session, it went to shit and I felt that I had wasted ten hours of my life. The driver picked me up at eight that night, and I climbed in and said, "Could you take me to the office please?"

He looked at his clipboard and said, "I'm sorry, miss, but I am not authorized to do that."

"What do you mean authorized?"

"According to my itinerary for the day, I'm to pick you up here and return you to Glen Ridge."

"Well, I need to go the office."

"Unless I receive authorization from security, Ms. Om, or Mr. Downs, I cannot do that, miss."

I fished into my pocketbook for my cell phone. "Damn, I know G's gotta keep a close eye on the bottom line, but this is ridiculous." Then I held up the phone to my lips and said, "Call G." The phone dialed his direct line.

"G Dub."

"It's Cassie. I know you're mad busy and all, but can I swing by there for a few minutes on the way home?"

"Whatever."

When I arrived, Freight awaited me at the elevator. Like Jen had my first time there, he led me into the service elevator, used a key to access the basement, and escorted me to G's office.

The smell of herb hung in the air as G rubbed his eyes and collected papers scattered across his desk. I took the seat before his desk and waited for him to acknowledge me. He dropped the papers in a manila envelope and handed them to Freight. "Give these to Jen."

"Jen's still here, too?" I asked.

"Jen don't go home until I go home," G said, as if I should know better. I wondered if all those nights he failed to come home, he spent with her. The possibility made me uncomfortable, and I became uneasy with that discomfort. "How'd your session go today?"

"Garbage," I said. "Don't mean to bitch, Whatshisface is a nice guy and all, but he just don't run unless you ride him. So either you got to come through, G, or hire someone else." I preferred that he honor his word to oversee production of my album, but G released such a long exhale throughout my complaint, I felt guilty for stressing him. "How 'bout Bokim? We worked well together in the past, and . . ."

"Bokim's out of the question. He fell out with Hi-Jack and them, and I don't have the time or patience to be courtin' a nigga, playing mediator or . . . Are you ready for me to holla at your boy?" he said, referring to Darnell.

Some things you don't know until you have to. But not only did I have an album to finish, I had made a promise. "Call him." Still disappointed that G broke his own promise and punted to Darnell, I stood up to leave.

"Ayo, Cassie, why don't you hang out a bit?" asked G. "I'm just gonna be another hour or so. We can ride back to Jerz together."

"I'm real tired, G. I've been busting my ass, and I need to crash." I reached the door and smiled over my shoulder. "Unless you want me to get all erratic in front of some reporter, start stripping and shit . . ." Even Freight laughed at that. But then I stopped and turned, "Hey, G, when am I going to do TV?"

"When you finish your album," he said. "Don't you want your first television appearance to be a solo?" Of course I did. I wanted my first live appearance at NV on Thanksgiving weekend to be a solo, too. That meant putting in extra hours at the studio and producing a worthy cut. I thought I'd crash on my feet at the very thought.

"Then I really need to get some sleep," I said. "See ya whenever."

"Take the day off tomorrow."

"Can't."

"You don't gotta choice," said G. "Sleep late and then be here by noon. We'll have lunch and then we can go get ready."

"For what?"

"We're going to the Source Awards."

I had no idea what G meant by getting ready for the Source Awards because before I could ask, Freight grunted, "G need to work," and yanked me out of the office. He escorted me to the car, and the driver took me back to Jerz. So excited about going to the show, I almost busted into the mansion to ask the others if they knew what G had planned. Just as I hit the door though I remembered something that stopped me. I had forgotten to bring Leila something to eat.

So I headed to the guest house, where sleep evaded me. I lobbed from one side of the bed to the other from guilt over Leila to excitement about the Source Awards, which were only two days away. Imagination overrode morality, and I fantasized about performing at the ceremony. Of course, I knew in reality that I would perform "But Can You Feel Me?" with Leila and Primo, but I controlled my imagination and it wanted Sabrina Steelo solo. I closed my eyes and telecasted it across my mind.

Vivica A. Fox hosts the show and in her earthy way, she introduces me. "I don't know about y'all, but I've been waiting too long to hear from this sister again. She's talented, intelligent, and just straight up gorgeous. Here to perform her first solo track from her debut album off the Explicit Content label, y'all better show much love to my girl Sabrina Steelo!" The opening melody to "Boogie Reign" plays, and I walk onstage in a Lady Enyce denim jumper with Paul Green boots in black nappa, and a matching Kangol 504 in the spirit of the song. Some heads cheer while others hush them so they can catch my lyrics.

Remember the glory of our humble start.
When heads tagged on walls, then ran from cops.
Caps once spun, but now they just peel
On some bullshit 'bout keepin' it real.
All praise due to Herc, Flash, and Bambaataa
But you don't even think to call 'em Godfather.
With ease a peeps sped way past Phase 2
And wound up as a RIP thrown up by Tats Cru.
We had a five so furious, they holeshot Vin
A three so treacherous, they made heads spin
A four so funky, they plussed one more
A Mel so mellow, he burned the floor.
From Hills of Sugar and Wells of Rock
Our spot gave birth in pops and locks.
Silly little gangsta, you must've forgot
Who spawned this art we call hip-hop.
But just where did you say you from, son?
Compton? Chi-Town? Hotlanta? Brooknam?
Kneel five times to pray and thank the ancestors
And face forward Bronx 'cause that's Hip-Hop's Mecca.

Gone worldwide but still just a rookie
You coulda never jumped off
Until they up jump the Boogie.
Bri knows her roots run deep past fame
You now reap long sowed by Boogie Reign.

Heads nod as I flow. I bounce to the edge of the stage so I can make
eye contact with the stars. The eyes of old souls regardless of their
true age gleam with approval of my message. Younger cats miss the
references, but the flow directs them to school themselves at the
first opportunity. Rush whispers into Kimora's ear, compliment-
ing my skill. Missy pumps her fist in the air and Mos Def wants to

collaborate. P. Diddy smirks with envious wonder—why didn't he sign me? Busta's jaw hangs into his lap with recognition—that little girl grew up into a heavyweight.

Even all the right heads hate but with much respect. Deep inside they admit that their confusion reflects both their shallowness and my profundity. They don't like my point—if they even get it—but they can't sleep on my skills.

> *But now Scarface gets all your respect*
> *Before him y'all dive to genuflect.*
> *Niggas before Tone on their knees bent*
> *Meanwhile muthafucka's only pretend.*
> *How'd you catch that tragic affliction*
> *Where you give daps to a cat of fiction?*
> *How dare thou takest on a false idol*
> *Then wonder why you're suicidal.*
> *So go say hello to your little friend*
> *While Ms. Steelo breaks it down again.*

> *Gone worldwide but still just a rookie*
> *You coulda never jumped off*
> *Until they up jump the Boogie.*
> *Bri knows her roots run deep past fame*
> *We only reaped what was sowed by Boogie Reign.*

I spit the refrain one last time even though the music has ended, and the kids in the balcony chant along with me. The crowd rises to its feet for a standing ovation and cameras pop like the Fourth of July.

I walk backstage, and waiting in the wings to present the next award are Allen Payne and Nia Long. Although we have never met, Nia opens her arms and hugs me with a sisterly warmth. A tear of pride forming in her eye, she holds my hands in hers and says, "I hear you're Trinidadian, too." Then she flips to a Creole accent. "Fah true?" I grin, and Nia hugs me once more, whispering in my ear, "After the show, you come to the fete and fire one with me, eh?"

I say, "Of course, doods."

And just before she heads onstage, Nia calls over her shoulder, "OK, don't you do a back back on me now."

Her copresenter Allen is slow to follow, lingering to put his arms around me and nestle a kiss on my cheek. "Beautiful," he says in my ear. "In every way, just beautiful."

The sound of G Double D entering the guest house woke me from my sleep. When I heard his footsteps enter the hallway, I sat up in my bed and called him. G opened the door to my room and peeked in.

"Why ain't you asleep?"

"G, what do you think about my performing 'Boogie Reign'?"

"Yeah, I like that track for the album. Needs work, but we can turn it into a good cut." G cut a deep yawn and stepped back to close the door.

"Not for the album. At the Source Awards."

He stopped and tipped his back through my door. "The Source Awards?" Then G exhaled. "Aw, baby girl, you're not performing at the show. Shit, I wasn't gonna go my damned self, them muthafuckas ain't show me no love this year. But tonight I decided to take you 'cause you've been working so hard."

A blaze started in my stomach and shot up to my cheeks. "So what'd you mean by getting ready?"

"You know, spend the day at the salon, shop for a hot dress, things like that."

As nice as it sounded, it sat far from where my head ran to in those last few hours. "OK. That's cool. Thanks, G."

"All in due time, Cassie." I expected and wanted him to leave, but G stood his ground. He knew he had disappointed me once again and pondered how to make it right. G reached into his pocket, pulled out a roll of cash, and peeled off ten hundreds. He laid it on my nighttable and said, "Before I left I had Jen call the manager of the Red Door to have them fit you in tomorrow. Go get yourself some well-deserved pampering. Go shopping. Then you fly with me to Miami for the show, have yourself some fun. Then, when we come back, you go back into the studio inspired and re-laxed, and we see how it goes. If things flow and we find a single, maybe you can perform solo at NV."

G Double D flashed me a fatherly smile and started toward the door. "If it's gonna flow, you need to be in the studio with me like you promised," I said.

G looked at me and said, "Fine."

"G?"

"Ayo, Cassie, a brother needs to get some sleep, you know."

"One question."

"And it can't wait until tomorrow?"

"While you here."

"What?"

"What's wrong with 'Boogie Reign'?" I took so much pride in that cut, aspiring to be the one to put the Bronx back on the map with my ode to the artists—from the uptown DJs to the breakers—who created hip-hop. "With some work, couldn't it be my first single? I really think . . ."

"No, Cassie, I'ma be real with you. 'Boogie Reign' is a nice cut, and I'm even thinking about going with an ol'-school electric-funk sound with it, like maybe Planet Patrol or Soul Sonic Force. You probably don't know . . ."

I remembered that sound from the tapes that Leila had copied for me throughout junior high school. "Yeah, yeah, I know. Some Tommy Boy shit. G, that would be so hot!" A charge sparked be-tween us, each being impressed with the other's knowledge of the vintage sound. Like Darnell, G had almost seven years on me, but we all were supposed to be too young to know, let alone appreciate it. Even the sample addicts tended to skip the hip-hop crates and opted for post-1985 R&B to lift.

". . . but Explicit Content is never gonna release it as a single," G said. "Maybe we'll get it on a soundtrack or compilation or something, if the right opportunity presents itself, but you're going to have to trust me, Cassandra. 'Boogie Reign' ain't for radio, let alone a lead single."

"Why?"

G gripped his head. " 'Cause it's too . . . Cassie, your releases gotta have broad appeal, and the only ones who're gonna be feelin' 'Boogie Reign' are ol' diehards and maybe kids from the Bronx. You fuckin' with *Scarface,* too? Cassie, you know how niggas in hip-hop feel about that muthafuckin' movie."

I pulled the covers up to my chin and slammed my head onto the pillow. From the doorway I heard G say, "You mad at me for giving you my honest opinion? 'Cause I'm not takin' no angry female to the Source Awards."

I hated his logic about "Boogie Reign," but I also knew he was on point. "I'm not mad at you, G. We're both tired. We'll talk tomorrow."

I waited to hear the door open and a crack of light from the hallway to fall onto my wall. Instead G said, "When we get back from Miami, I'ma be in the studio with you like I promised. We're going to work it out, produce you a multiplatinum debut." Then I felt G place his hand on the back of my shoulder, then press his lips against my temple. I fell asleep to fantasies of walking down the red carpet at the Miami Arena waving to screaming fans while holding on to G's arm.

CHAPTER 20

DOWN AND DIRTY

G canceled lunch on me the next day, but at least he called before I left the mansion to let me know. He had planned to meet with Jen's father for breakfast, but Papa Om had to postpone for lunch. Knowing how much G wanted to close that deal with him, I cut him slack.

When I arrived at the Red Door, the receptionist immediately alerted the manager to my arrival. He offered me a glass of merlot and led me to the back, where two women waited for me. For almost an hour, they both massaged me—one working the deep tissues all over my body with the other concentrating just on my feet. After the massage, they led me to another room, where I received a European facial including a vegetable peel and seaweed mask as well as a French manicure with silk tips, a sea-salt pedicure, and a full leg wax.

Just as they began to do my hair, I remembered Yolanda and Yeribel. Guilt dampened my mood when I realized that it had been weeks since they had called. I considered canceling the hair-styling session and heading over to Astoria. What better way to make amends to the Segui sisters than to reappear to ask them to style me for the Source Awards? But then I realized that I could not go to Queens without G Double D finding out. What if he thought I really went to see Darnell? I had no reason to do that, especially when I knew I would see him soon. But that might be exactly why G might think I would go see him.

I decided against taking the risk. I rationalized that other opportunities would arise and when they did I would take care of them. Then it struck me how, after all those times when I had no money for such luxuries and Leila insisted I go with her to the salon and treated me, she never crossed my mind even as I got my nails wrapped for the first time like she always did. I tried to rationalize that guilt away, too, but it didn't budge for the rest of my visit to the Red Door. I eventually dodged it somewhere between buying my dress and finding the perfect shoes for the Source Awards.

G planned a whirlwind trip to South Beach. He had Jen book a hotel suite, but we were not to spend the night. It just served as a private place to rest and prepare for the show. We arrived in Miami a bit after three in the afternoon. G dropped me off at the Ritz-Carlton to run some errands. Our suite had a king-sized bed and windows that ran from the floor to the ceiling. I slipped into a plush terry-cloth robe and walked onto the balcony to peep the view. Not only could I see the beach, I also saw the Atlantic Ocean. Too excited to nap as I had originally planned, I unpacked all the beauty products given to me at the salon, went into the complete bathroom, and prepared for the show.

When I opened the bathroom door clad in a large towel, I found G lying on the bed, wearing his Sean John sweatshirt and jeans and yammering on his cell phone. Giving me not a glance or a word, he picked up his overnight bag, strolled right past me into the bathroom, and locked the door behind him. I moved my makeup and clothes to the half bathroom and got ready, intent on making him notice me the next time he saw me.

Thrilled to be relieved of my old fall clothes, I stepped into my awards dress. I had chosen a magenta sundress and found a pair of Manolo Blahnik sandals the same color with a spiked gold heel. I also bought a gold Kooba clutch. When I unpacked and put on the gold jewelry set Genevieve and Aunt Treece had bought me for my sixteenth birthday, it seemed too much. So I took off the necklace and bracelet and kept the earrings. I decided to make a statement and left my hair in its natural curl but applied pomade flecked with gold dust to make it sparkle. After two attempts to replicate Yeribel's technique with my new makeup and still thinking I resembled Miss Potato Head, I washed my face one last time, trusted the palette Yeri had chosen for me, and applied it with a light hand. I surveyed myself in the mirror, and while I thought I looked fine, I still felt like Leila always said: I played it safe.

I walked out of the bathroom and paced around the bed. Then I noticed G's Fendi glasses on the nightstand. I barely tried to resist temptation and snatched them. Just as I stood in front of the dresser mirror with them on, G stepped out of the master bathroom. He wore a marble gray Everett Hall suit with loose legs and wide shoulders that reminded me of old-style Hollywood. A huge diamond studded his ear, and he smelled of CK One.

Embarrassed that he'd busted me trying on his sunglasses, I offered them to him. "I was just . . . Leila's always saying . . . I felt like I was missing something."

G took the glasses from my hand and slid them onto my face. "Baby girl, you ain't missing anything." He led me to the suite door and opened it. As I walked past him into the hallway, he said, "Not a damned thing."

He took me to another hotel called the Savoy for dinner, where we ate at a restaurant called the Strand. I swear half of the celebrities slated to appear on the Source Awards ate there, too. Although spread across several tables, all the Crunk Brothers dominated one corner. Lil Jon made a loud toast to the Dirty South, and several of the other patrons in the restaurant tapped their silverware against their wineglasses in agreement.

Then we took the limo to Miami Arena. I heard the fans screaming before we rolled up at the red carpet. G stepped out and the crowd roared. He offered me his hand to help me out of the car. Just when I almost climbed out of the backseat like a tomboy, I remembered what Genevieve told me about *how a lady dismounts a vehicle. She does not plant one foot on the curb and pull the opposite leg out after it like she's doing the Electric Slide.* Then I did as she had demonstrated to me that day. I slid across the seat until I was as close to the door as possible, pivoted so both my legs swung out of the car and with my knees close together, I stood up and out of the car. When the crowd cheered my name, I waved to them and laughed at the thought of them congratulating me on a perfectly feminine exit. G offered me his arm, and I hooked mine threw it. Flashes popped incessantly as we walked down the red carpet toward the arena entrance.

A reporter jumped in front of us with her mic and cameraman. "G Dub, are you and Sabrina an item?"

G stopped and leaned into the mic. "Now, wouldn't that make me a lucky man?" he said. "Doesn't she look fantastic?"

"Absolutely," the reporter said. "Sabrina, who designed that gorgeous sundress?" I told her and she said, "You are absolutely stunning tonight. Have a great time."

G and I thanked her, and as we walked away from her, I overheard her say, "That was the ever-dapper Gregory 'G Double' Downs, CEO of Explicit Content, with his up-and-coming star Sabrina Steelo looking gorgeous in a Fushá design by Marie Claudinette Pierre-Jean, wife of rap star Wyclef Jean, who we're also expecting to see tonight. . . ."

I appreciated G in a new way that night. It irked me when

celebrities lied about being together, especially when they were. I understood not wanting to put your love life on blast, especially when celebrity hookups often failed as fast as they started. There's never an excuse for that Bennifer nonsense, but when some famous dude fronted like he didn't know a woman he was fucking, I found that shit downright disrespectful and vowed to never put up with it whether I was famous myself or not. Acknowledge me, then change the subject. If he told the media, "We're just friends" and then expected to swing over to my crib at two a.m., we'd be less than friends in a minute. G rolled like a true gentleman on the red carpet. He didn't make me feel cheap by suggesting he was hittin' when he wasn't, like Primo probably would, or responding like the idea repulsed him because he wasn't, like Hi-Jack might.

I caught a glimpse of us in the glass doorway before we entered the Miami Arena. Peeking over the bridge of his sunglasses, I took a longer look at our reflection. We did look mad hot together.

G brought Darnell into the studio as soon as we returned from South Beach. Darnell'd come in there and speak to me only when he had to. No "What's up" or "How you doin' " just "Give me that line again" and "Come in a little quicker on that verse." He even tried to drag the poor engineer into it, asking him repeatedly if he thought the sound was off in a tone that suggested the engineer agree with him. The wuss would, and I'd have to do another take for nothing. Bokim wouldn't have been down with D's nonsense, and I missed him. But he never returned after that first session, fed up with the bluntin' and bickering, I guessed.

Darnell pretended to be professional but still came off like a kid in the schoolyard giving his crush the silent treatment. G picked up on the tension right away and tried to ignore it. As did I, until Darnell started frontin' like a perfectionist and asked me to redo the chorus for the third time. I ripped off the headphones and yelled, "You for real?"

D scowled at me through the glass but tried to retain his cool in front of G Double D. "Time's money, Cass. Give me the chorus one last time."

So that's the way he wanted to play it. "No, time's *his* money," I said, pointing to G. "Not yours." Then I looked at G. "Mr. Downs?"

Although he had been patient throughout the session, I could see that G reveled in the opportunity I gave him to pull rank. I had to give him daps, though, for not overplaying his position. Instead of blasting Darnell the way Hi-Jack might've, G gave him a brotherly pat on the shoulder and said, "Sounds good to me, D. Let's move on."

Now Darnell turned his scowl on G. He stood up and slammed his chair into the console. "Fifteen," he yelled at me through the booth. Then D gave G Double D a final once-over and stormed out of the studio.

G and I caught eyes, his glimmering under the dim light of the studio. At that moment, I knew he would be coming home with me that night.

For most of the way, we drove to Glen Ridge in G's Hummer in a silent power play as if the first to speak would lose the upper hand. Slick bastard he is, G raised the stakes by shutting off the radio. Unbeknownst to him, I held on by clutching Leila's food on my lap.

Yet G and I both knew that what was going to happen would regardless of whether we spoke a single word to each other. A multitude of questions rushed through my mind along with Leila's warning. *Don't stop now 'cause you're desperate to be put on.* If nothing else, I had to know what this meant to him so I could figure out what that might mean for me.

"G, did you tell Darnell what happened between us that night I stayed at the mansion?"

"No," he said without hesitation. "Because nothing did happen."

I smirked at the smart-ass. "Yes, it did. And you probably said nothing to Darnell in a way that told him everything."

G shook his head. "I told you that I wouldn't chase you. That when you went through whatever you had to with Darnell, that you would come to me. And you did." I considered asking him how he knew I wasn't going through the motions with him. Then I debated confronting him about my discovery in Darnell's closet to see how honest with me he was willing to be. I even considered telling him that he didn't have me yet just to fuck with him. But for the most part, I sat in silence, trying to convince myself that the only reason I went with him was to get answers to my questions.

G took his turn to put a question to me. "You know, Cassie, you remind me of that James Cagney movie. Are you an angel with a dirty face? Or just a dirty rat?" He started laughing, and if we had not been doing seventy-five on the New Jersey Turnpike, I might have jumped out of the Hummer. "Aw, baby girl, don't look at me like that. I know you know more than you let on 'cause you a smart girl. A real smart girl. That's what I like about you. Ain't too many sisters like you in this game. Who can give as good as she takes. Make a contribution instead of looking for a donation." G zoomed from the fast lane onto the exit ramp in one rush. "But you're a good girl, too. You fancy yourself a badass, you want to stomp with the big dogs, but you're a good girl. With the direction I'm taking Explicit Content, I'm fixing to be the biggest dog there is, Cassie. And if you want to roll with me, you gotta stay a good girl and still become a badass, ya feel me? You gotta be an angel with a dirty face. So what I need to know from you is this: How down and dirty do you want to be?"

"Like I told you before, G," I said. "Whatever you need."

G drove straight to the guest house. When I put down Leila's dinner to take off my coat, G took it upon himself to pick it up, take it into the kitchen, and slip it into the refrigerator. Lost for a believable excuse to take it back out and bring it to the mansion, I stood in the doorway staring at him. Just as I thought that maybe I could steal out during the night when he was asleep, I caught that glimmer in G's eyes telling me that he had no intention of letting me go anywhere that night as if he could read my mind.

"What do you say we pick this up where we left off?" he asked as he motioned toward the bathroom. "Except let's take this to my bathroom."

G motioned for me to go ahead of him. I walked into his room, and just like the Explicit Content offices, the furniture was black and the fixtures platinum. The black fireplace resembled a cave, and the silver industry awards that jutted along the mantel looked like icicles. Wondering if any gold trophies G might have won were thrown in a box in Darnell's studio closet, I entered his bathroom.

G's bathroom spanned the size of a child's bedroom and contained almost as many toys. An entire wall consisted of silver shelves that held an array of hi-tech gadgets for personal grooming from an electronic razor to a paraffin wax heater and even a compact stereo system. At the farthest corner stood a professional massage table next to a caddy of oils and scrubs. In the opposite corner sat a pedicure station just like at the Red Door, with a massaging chair with the remote in the armrest and the footrest in a tub that bubbled. In the center of G's bathroom was a large, black Jacuzzi. I walked over to it and turned it on. As the water gushed and rose, I opened the closet and found a bottle of bubble bath. When my hand started to shake as I poured the bubbles, I just emptied the entire bottle in the tub. For a moment I sat at the edge of the Jacuzzi, gazing at the whirlpool as the rush of water swirled the pink lotion in a frenzy of bubbles. Finally, I stood up, peeled off my clothes, and slipped into the tub.

G entered wearing a black bathrobe and carrying an open bottle of Krug champagne and two glasses. He handed the bottle and glasses to me, and I made a production of lining them along the tub so I wouldn't stare at G as he dropped his robe and stepped into the bath. He found a remote at his end of the tub and pointed it toward the stereo. I expected to hear a hip-hop ballad by Mary J. Blige or even that corny love song on Primo's last album, but instead a soothing Sweetback instrumental flowed out of the speakers into the air.

I reached for the champagne bottle, filled both glasses, and offered one to him. As he accepted the glass, G noticed my hand shaking. I quickly dropped it in a fortress of bubbles, but he reached under the water and pulled it back to the surface. G tilted the glass and gently poured champagne over my hand, rinsing away the bath bubbles. Then he brought my hand to his lips, kissed the tip of each of my fingers, and then slowly licked the champagne off them.

When he finished, I reached for my own glass and slid toward him. I traced my fingers down his forehead to his chin. As I did, G closed his eyes and leaned his head back. I straddled him, then gently poured the champagne over his head. The sweet liquor cascaded down his brown nose and pooled between his full lips. I leaned down and pressed mine against his, and our tongues toasted with the champagne that trickled between our parted lips.

When G wrapped his arms around my waist until his hands weighted down my shoulders, I crossed my arms behind his neck and cradled his head against my forearms. He raised his hips and pressed them against my parted thighs as he pulled me down into his grinding pelvis. I started to grind along with him, arching my back so he could draw my dripping breast into his wet mouth. G circled his tongue around and around one nipple while kneading the other breast with his hand. When I moaned, he dragged his tongue across my chest to the other nipple to suck on it as he rubbed the breast he just left. Then my moans came from a deeper place, and G gently pushed me away from him.

He lifted himself up to his feet as I sat back in surprise. As he stood over me, I stared up at his thick erection wielding above me. Before I could speak, G offered me his hands. I slipped mine into his and he pulled me to my feet. Then he pulled me into him for a long kiss. G hoisted me up until I wrapped my legs around his waist and then carried me from the Jacuzzi to the massage table.

I rolled onto my stomach, my body tingling with melting bubbles and sexual yearning. Soon I felt G's oily hands gliding up and down my back, pressing harder against my skin with every stroke. The scent of roses danced under my nose as he dribbled massage oil across my ass and down each of my legs. The oil tickled slightly as it oozed down my thighs and between my legs. With his large, strong thumbs, G dragged circles from the small of my back down the back of my thighs to my calves. Then I felt his slick palms float up my legs and burrow between my inner thighs at my knees. G rubbed slowly up my thighs.

With every deepening breath, I parted my legs slightly until G dipped two oily fingers into my wet pussy. He pressed against my inner wall until I felt a sharp sensation that I never had before. I gasped, and as if that was the sign he had been waiting for, G rubbed that spot until I whimpered with pleasure. Like a cat in heat, I lifted myself onto my palms and drew my knees to my chest and rocked against his thrusting fingers.

Suddenly, G pulled out his fingers and turned me over on my side and sank his face into my pussy. He flicked his tongue across my clit while I curled my head with every stroke. Then G reached across for the caddy and pulled out a condom.

Just as he tore it open, I sat up and yanked it from his hand. This time I pushed him back far enough for me to lean over and lower my mouth onto his head. G placed one hand on my shoulder to steady me and gripped the back of my head by the hair with the other. Now he growled like a panther as I bobbed my head maniacally up and down his shaft.

When G came to that brink, he pulled out of my mouth and shoved me backward. I dragged my soaking bottom to the edge of the massage table and splayed my legs open as wide as possible. G slid himself inside of me and pressed his oily palm against my pubic bone. As he thrusted into me and rubbed the heel of his palm against my clit, I found myself at that familiar point I had never gone beyond with Darnell or Kurt. Recognizing that I was about come for the first time with a man deep inside me, I grew a smile with roots deep between my legs. When G's repeated strokes finally shattered my core, my preorgasmic moans turned into ecstatic laughs. Soon he cried out with his own release, laughing right along with me.

He whispered in my ear, "Yeah, Cassie, you're a good girl." Then G lifted me off the massage table and carried me into the bedroom. And I thought to myself, *About time.*

A few hours later, G and I laid in his bed tangled up in each other. As he buzzed with sleep with my head against his arm, I scanned around his room. When my eyes adjusted to the dark, I made out the huge poster of Al Pacino as Tony Montana in *Scarface.* Snippets of our conversations buzzed around my head like annoying mosquitoes. *What can I get you to drink, winner? Bri Steez, welcome to the Explicit Content dynasty. Your album is my call to step up my game as an executive and as a producer. I can wait until you're ready, and when you are, you'll come to me. How down and dirty do you want to be? Yeah, Cassie, you're a good girl.*

Before long, hot tears rolled down my face. To do what I had to do, I had to let G think it was all about him. But how could I go this far, and it not be about him?

CHAPTER 21

MISSING

As usual, G left before I woke up the next morning. I washed up and got dressed in G's bathroom so Scarface wouldn't stare at me. After getting the food I left in the refrigerator, I headed to the mansion.

"What's up, Patrick?" I said to the butler as he opened the door. I had become friendly with him, as I had with Lynn, the housekeeper of the guest house. So friendly I knew that they were carrying on a secret affair. I mean, neither were married or had lovers back in Ireland. They kept their relationship a secret because Patrick was afraid G would fire them. Or worse—the fellas would start bothering Lynn as another way to harass him. It pissed me off how those idiots prohibited anyone in that crib from being happy, including themselves.

"Don't ask, Cassie," he replied. Before I could ask for an explanation, I heard Primo hollering down the hallway. I crossed the threshold, but Patrick blocked me from going any farther. "Maybe you should come back later." I read concern on his face, but it only compelled me to walk around him toward the ruckus.

As I headed toward the parlor, I heard Leila's soft voice attempt to calm him down. But Primo just yelled louder. "No offense, Leila, but now you know why I didn't want any fuckin' females on the label. And instead of defending that shit, you best watch your back. Next thing you know, your album stays on the back burner while hers gets on the fast track."

"True that," Cryciss said. "I told G, too, about not signing any bitches."

I turned into the parlor, where Primo stood in the center of the room, having a tantrum for the entire house—Leila, Hi-Jack, the 8MM Posse, the Explicit Talent models, and the rest of the entourage. He bopped over to Cryciss and jabbed his finger in his face. "Yo, don't be calling her a bitch, all right?" he said referring to Leila. "I told you about that shit."

"And what about me?" I asked to make my presence known.

Leila started to speak, but Primo hushed her. He spun around to face me, but before he could say a word, Hi-Jack jumped in. "Yo, Cassie, what track's gonna be your first single?" he asked.

"I'm not sure." And that was true. Darnell still pushed for "God Don't Like Ugly," but seeing I was in a different place now than when I wrote it, I hoped to convince G to scrap the song altogether. He had yet to decide, but now that we were kickin' it and better tracks were coming to life in the studio, I believed I'd have my way. "We haven't decided yet."

"You hear that?" Primo said to Leila as he pointed at me. "We. We haven't decided yet. Since when does a new artist have any say in shit like that?"

Then Third Eye asked, "OK, so what you've been working on in the studio?" Not only had G kept his word about working with me every day, he had also stuck to his decision to ban onlookers from the studio. The guys swung by on occasion on their way to or from their own sessions at other locations, but G would stop production, kick it with them in the lounge for a while, and then send them on their way before heading back into the booth with me. Because I focused on my album and didn't socialize too much, no one really knew how my joint was progressing. But then again, for all the talk about family, no one bothered to ask me. At least not until that point, but then it felt like an interrogation, and I wasn't feelin' it.

Having nothing to hide, though, I answered honestly. "We're playing around with two songs from my demo, and I know 'Boogie Reign' is gonna make it to the album. . . ."

"And what else?" interrupted Keef.

Genevieve's daughter did not play this shit. "You handling my promotions now?" I barked at Keef.

Cryciss said, "Yeah, figures she'd say some shit like that."

"Fuck that," Primo said as he sauntered toward me. "Let's get to the bottom of this shit right here. Have y'all been fucking with 'But Can You Feel Me'?"

Then Leila answered the question my facial expression must have posed. "G told him this morning that instead of releasing the remix now, he's gonna save it for your album." With that, I landed back to square one trying to read her. I could hear her strain to keep her voice neutral while she eyed the brown paper package in my hand, but I couldn't tell if she was angry with me for not bringing her food the previous night, pretending not to take sides to throw off Primo and the guys, or trying to hide that she actually believed I knew that G had given me Primo's song and maybe even sexed him into it.

"I don't know nothing about that," I said. "This is the first I'm hearing about it."

"I told you," Leila said to Primo, and I sighed with appreciation for her support.

Cryciss snorted. "Just 'cause she says so? Y'all know she's a fuckin' T-crossin', I-dottin' . . ." He interrupted himself with his own laughter, and Earl and Keef snickered with him. My face burned as I tried to recall where I had heard that expression before. Then I remembered—Darnell. Tired of having to mediate our conflicts, yet too impressed with his skills to fire him, G sent him to work on the 8MM Posse's album-in-progress. Obviously, I had become a topic of conversation in those studio sessions. Nice to know they were bonding at my expense.

To my surprise, Hi-Jack said, "If shorty says she ain't know, she ain't know. Y'all wanna keep harping on shit beyond your control, go right ahead, but I'm outty." After this declaration, he stood up and crossed the room. As he passed Primo, he told him, "Man up, nigga. You been lost that track when you couldn't throw down in the studio, and you know it." When Jack reached the doorway, he squeezed my arm and winked at me. "Later, Cass."

And like puppies chasing their mother's tits, the 8MM Posse got up to follow him. Cryciss said, "If it were me . . ." Then his words trailed into a hiss.

"Word," said Earl. He gave me a sarcastic wave. "See ya, Mariah. We'll tell Tommy you said hello." He and Keef snickered like the brats they were, and the three of them were gone.

I looked at Primo and said, "I really didn't know, Primo. I'll just tell G that I don't want your track on my joint, OK?"

Primo glared at me. "Don't think just because you're fucking him, you're gonna have your run of shit around here." He pushed past me and out of the parlor.

Of course, Leila had to follow him. On his angry stomp toward the car, Primo dusted her without looking back. Leila took advantage of those seconds to take the package from my hand, kiss me on the cheek, and say, "It's gonna be all right." On the way out, she handed the food to Patrick, and said, "Put this in the refrigerator in the service kitchen for me, please." As soon as the package exchanged hands, Primo stopped to yell over his shoulder.

"Hurry up!"

Hi-Jack and the others had already left in his ride. Even though he has his own Bentley, Primo the divo insisted on taking the limo. So he, Leila, and I climbed in. She asked me questions about the album with genuine interest, and I believed she did it for my benefit and not Primo's. Then I asked about hers.

Primo yelled, "Don't you worry about her album."

So we rode the rest of the way to New York City in silence.

At the studio G told me that not only did he intend to put the "But Can You Feel Me?" remix on my album, he wanted me to perform it when I opened for the 8MM Posse at NV that coming Saturday. Maybe my pussy wasn't whipping material or G had more resolve than I thought, but he said to me, "Here's the deal, Cassie. We either go with 'God Don't Like Ugly' or 'But Can You Feel Me?' You decide.'

In other words, I had to choose whether I made my live debut sharing the stage with Leila or appearing solo with a diss to her. No matter how much we softened "God Don't Like Ugly," she knew the origins of the song. Leila never said a word about it to me or anyone else at the label, as far as I knew, I figured out of guilt. But now that we were cool again, to go forward with the track would be a slap in her face. On the flip side, performing "But Can You Feel Me?" would create more static between Primo and me, not to mention Cryciss and the others. Primo's second album was selling like space heaters in dog days so he desperately needed another release. A hit that showcased him, increased his airplay, and boosted his chart position, and that remix wasn't it.

And yet doing that song also would be the ultimate gesture of reconciliation to Leila because Hi-Jack was right—that was a Sabrina Steelo and Fatal Beauty joint now, featuring Primo and not the other way around as initially planned. Although Leila had appeared already on three singles as a featured artist and desperately needed a solo release, a performance like "But Can You Feel Me?" would return her to the public eye. A successful single on which she played a key part might cause G to reassess Leila's value. It could only help her in this bizarre situation she was in at Explicit Content, and after all that went down, that would do my heart good. And let me be real straight up—as the only two sisters on a roster filled with members of the he-man women-haters club and shit, whatever helped Leila helped me. That is, if I were willing to gamble that when push came to shove, Leila would have my back and not betray me again.

Darnell entered the studio. He gave G a pound and nodded at me. Then he said, "Cass, call your moms. She keeps calling the house looking for you, asking about Thanksgiving dinner. I'da given her your new number, but I don't have it." I felt a momentary pang in my heart for him. What was he going to do for Thanksgiving dinner? I chased away the sympathy with a vision of him visiting his mother wherever she was getting help for her gambling problem. Or maybe he had rekindled his relationship with Ms. Aztek. "Oh, and that Dominican girl keeps calling you, too. She thinks I'm trying to keep between y'all 'cause I can't tell her how to reach you."

Eager to get to work, G interrupted. "So what's it gonna be, baby girl? You gotta decide now so we can finish the instrumental for Saturday's show."

"Let's go with 'But Can You Feel Me?' "

D exhaled. "You sure, Cassie?" Although he always favored "God Don't Like Ugly," I heard no defeat or resentment in his tone, only worry. Darnell understood that my choice was risky much better than I did at the time. And while I appreciated his concern, I remained too angry with him to show it. After all, he dogged me behind my back to the fellas, and that hadn't exactly increased my popularity with them.

"Did I stutter?" I swung open the door and headed into the recording booth.

Genevieve and I planned to have dinner the Wednesday before Thanksgiving. With some of the money I gave her, she booked a flight to LA to spend the holiday weekend with my aunt Treece and her family. It hurt that she had never asked me if I wanted to come. Trying to give her the benefit of the doubt, I figured she just assumed I could not go because of my performance at NV that Saturday. But that only made me wonder if she had any intention of flying back in time to see me perform. Then I realized that even though I thought about it every day, I had not talked to Genevieve much at all, let alone reminded her of the event. Or even given her a ticket. I should have been happy that we were having some kind of holiday dinner together before she left, but it only made me sad.

To cheer myself up and prepare for Genevieve's scrutiny that night, I got two tickets to the show from Jen and headed to Astoria. I arrived at Yeribel's salon a half hour before opening time, but as is always the case with fantastic hairdressers in the 'hood, five other women were already there. I didn't worry about being late for my recording session though because I knew Yeri would look out for me.

Or so I thought. Yeri arrived with a flash of a smile for all the regulars except me. Thinking that she didn't recognize me, I called her name and waved. The girl just scowled at me and turned to unlock and lift the awning. The other customers rushed the door, and I elbowed my way ahead of the fray and plopped myself in Yeribel's chair. She took her time making small talk with the others before asking what they wanted done. I've been in enough Latina-owned salons to understand that two manicures, one relaxer, an eyebrow wax, and another wash-and-blow-dry were before me. I figured the manicures and the eyebrow wax would have to wait for the nail technician to arrive, so Yeri would wash the relaxer and place her under the dryer for a deep conditioning while working on me.

Turned out she was buying time until the second hairstylist— the owner of the salon—arrived so she could pass her off to me. Yeri said something to her in Spanish, and the owner grinned plastically at me. Now, I'm not one of those sisters who gets bent out of shape when Hispanic folks speak Spanish in front of me and not just because I've picked up a lot of it over the years. I don't think

it's right for Black folks to hate on other people who want to maintain their native tongues. As far as I'm concerned, that made us almost as bad as white slave traders back in the day who killed our
original languages.

But I knew when I was being played in any language and wasn't
having it. So I grabbed Yeri's arm as she attempted to slip by me on
her way to the shampoo sink. "Yeribel, what's up?" I said.

"Go with her," she ordered as she pointed to her boss. "The big
star goes with the best you can, right?"

It hit me that she might have seen the Source Awards on TV
and knew that I had gone somewhere else to style myself for the
show. But I caught myself before I apologized, because I remembered passing on their digits to Primo. So I stopped feeling sorry
and started getting angry. "I hook you up with my label like I said
I would, and this is the thanks I get?"

Yeribel ripped a string of Spanish curses, and every head in the
place turned in our direction, jaws dropping into the centerfolds
across their laps. The owner interrupted her with a reprimanding
tone. Yeribel huffed and marched into the back. I followed.

I found Yeri in the waxing room, crying so hard I was afraid she
would heave herself into a seizure. The sight of her so distraught
curbed my anger, and I pulled a step stool to her feet and tried to
pry her hands from her face. "Yeribel, what's wrong?" She shook
her head violently, but I couldn't tell if it was because whatever
was upsetting her was too terrible to say or she was too angry with
me to share it. As weird as it felt, I asked, "What did I do?"

"*Mandaste a ese susio Primo a buscar a mi hermana . . .*" she
began.

Although I understood every word she said, I remained confused. "Yeah, he was supposed to call you and Yolanda about
working with a woman named Andi or maybe Jen," I said. "They
work with G's new modeling agency. I thought y'all might like
that."

Before I could say another word, Yeribel slapped me across the face. I was too stunned to hit her back. Nor did I have time to ask her why, because her boss, coworkers, and even a nosy customer with an aluminum cap plastered against her wet head piled into the room.

Yeribel's boss said, "I don't want any trouble here. You have to go. Don't come back and don't send anyone else from your so-called company, either."

As I made my way to the front door, I made some quick calculations. Ever since Explicit Content came into my life I kept getting smacked around by people who were supposed to care about me as well as thrown out of one place or another. And to my knowledge all I had done was try to make a record and look out for my people. My ambition led me into this twisted world where my best intentions resulted in explosive situations. How much worse was it going to get? I walked out the door and was about to turn the corner when Yeribel came running out behind me.

"Please tell Yolanda to come home!" she screamed. A lust for vengeance burned in her dark eyes. Her boss chased after and grabbed her. Yeribel fought her so hard, she tumbled to the ground, overcome with hysteria. Northern Boulevard shoppers stopped to stare at the commotion. Not standing to be a part of it, I ran around the corner, but Yeribel's words chased after me. "Tell my sister to please come home!"

Just when I thought I knew everything about Explicit Content. Somehow they had gotten to Yolanda. But I swear to God I had no idea where she could be.

I took my mother to Patria's for Thanksgiving dinner that night and hit her off with five hundred dollars in cash for her trip. "And buy something for Ivy and Kerwyn," I said of my two younger cousins.

"Thanksgiving is for reflecting on what you already have and not about fixing to get more," Genevieve said. "How about I save the money for Christmas? I know Patricia will appreciate our not sending the kids the wrong message."

"OK, Mom." I picked at my dinner roll, trying to remind myself how fortunate I was compared to those around me. Hi-Jack suggested that on Thanksgiving all the artists go into the 'hoods where we planned to open garages and give away free turkeys to poor families. Afterward, G would host a Thanksgiving feast at the mansion for artists, staff, and their families. His own mother had died several years ago of lung cancer, he and his pops were estranged, and he had no siblings, so I guessed we were all the family he had. Darnell planned to visit his mother in rehab, while Cryciss and Earl said that after visiting friends in jail, they were hitting the clubs. Primo intended to bring his mother from Brooklyn to G's dinner, so Leila had resigned herself to spending another day in Glen Ridge. And Yeribel had no idea where Yolanda was and probably had the awful task of calling her parents in DR and pretending Yoli was doing last-minute shopping for their holiday meal.

"Cassandra, why such a long face?" Genevieve asked.

"Just wish I could go with you to LA."

"Well, they're coming for Christmas, so you'll see everyone then. Kerwyn's already excited about it, bragging to all his little hip-hop-crazy friends that his cousin is Sabrina Steelo," Genevieve said. She laughed and said, "His sister told him, *Fool, that's the same cousin who stuffed you in the dryer when you were seven.*"

"I did not stuff Ker in the dryer," I said. "Ivy did that and tried to blame it on me." I never missed my cousins more than I did at that second, and believe it or not, it crossed my mind to bail out of the performance at NV so I could go with Genevieve to LA.

I should have followed my instinct.

CHAPTER 22

A DEVASTATING DEBUT

O n the night of my debut performance at NV, G and Hi-Jack
went to meet with Papa Om and got caught in traffic. With
all the other things weighing on my mind, his absence made
me only more nervous. I thought Leila would be disappointed,
too, as this was her chance to get G to put her album back on track.
But she seemed eager to go forward with the performance whether
or not he was there. "The show must go on," she quipped backstage as she reapplied her lipstick in a compact mirror.

The stage manager poked in his head. "Ten minutes."

Whether Primo always meant to wait until the last minute to
blow up our spot or decided to take advantage of G's absence, I'll
never know. But after going through the motions—arriving at NV
on time and going through the sound check and the rehearsal—the
dude stood up and said, "I'm not doing this." Nobody else seemed
surprised by his announcement except for Leila and me. "I'm not
singing backup to these bitches."

"Oh, shit," said Cryciss with a mischievous grin. "It's on now."
Muthafucka probably put Primo up to it.

Leila rushed over to Primo. "*Papi,* how you gonna do this to me now? You know what this means to me."

Primo shoved her away from him. "I be looking out for you, then you go side with her. Now it's, '*Papi,* how could you?' " he said. "Go 'head and do your thing, then." Then he glared at me as if to dare me to do anything except stand there.

And for a long while that was all I did. Then the manager returned. "Sabrina, Fatal, five minutes," he said, and he disappeared again.

Then the solution hit. If this is the way a man like Primo oper- ated, then I had to call a woman to do the job. I said, "Leila, what's the name of that girl that runs with Jack again? The one that looks like Alicia Keys?"

"Monica?"

"Do you know where she's at?"

Leila hesitated slightly. "She's probably at the mansion. Work- ing with Jen. You know, the modeling thing." She seemed uncom- fortable articulating that supposedly common knowledge.

I whipped out my cell and dialed Jen's number. When she picked up, I said, "What's up, Jen?"

"Business as usual, the usual as business," she said.

"Monica there?"

"Yeah. Why?

"Cool, 'cause we have an emergency situation here at the club, G's running late, and I need you to step up big-time."

"No doubt. What's up?"

"Get Monica flied up and down to NV ASAP. How long do you think that'll take?"

"Mmm . . . forty-five minutes?"

"Forty-five?" I repeated. Leila leaped at my cue and went to tell the stage manager about the delay. "Thanks, girl. You the only real Jenny from the block." Jen laughed and we hung up. I knew that barring car trouble, an accident, Jersey State Troopers, and other traffic hazards, she would see to it that Monica arrived at NV in forty-five minutes if not less.

Now it was my turn to look at Primo as if I dared him to do something. He cursed under his breath and bounced. Keef and Earl took off after him, but Cryciss stayed behind, eyeing me up and down. "Respect," he said.

Behind me I heard Leila managing her end of the drama lovely. She let the stage manager bitch about holding up the show for an hour, the crowd growing restless, and all that jazz. When he paused his rant to take a breath, Leila put a comforting hand on his shoulder and said, *"Papi,* when's the last hip-hop concert you went to that didn't start an hour late?"

Monica arrived looking as if she stepped right off the cover of *Essence.* When the manager brought her backstage, she was wound so tight I thought she might spring at any given second. "Have you heard the 'But Can You Feel Me?' remix?" I asked. She shrugged and looked around as if she wanted to be anywhere but there. "C'mon, Monica, if you don't know this joint, Leila and I have to teach it to you mad quick. We gotta get on that stage before muthafuckas start to wild out. Are you down to sing or what?"

She just blinked at me. "You called me down here to perform?"

"Yeah," I said, annoyed by her confusion. "That's what you do, don't you?"

Monica squealed and jumped up and down, finally showing the enthusiasm I had been expecting. Then she threw her arms around me and hugged me tight, as if I were her long-lost friend from elementary school. "Thank you, Cassie," she said, her voice with a tearful undercurrent. "Thank you, girl." That I didn't expect. I figured she walk in there flossing on some 'bout-time-y'all-recognized-my-skills attitude. I thought she didn't even know my name, seeing as I never remembered hers.

"So you down for this?" I asked.

"Are you for real?" she said. *"This* is what I do." She knew the lyrics, and Leila quickly ran her through the song.

When we were ready to take the stage, I bypassed the stage manager and even the show's MC by taking the mic and asking the crowd, "All y'all ready to get explicit?" The crowd roared back at me through the closed curtain. "I don't know, ya'll. That sounded kinda subtle. We don't do subtle, so I'ma ask you again. ARE YOU READY TO GET EXPLICIT?"

The audience screamed, and the club DJ started the tape of "But Can You Feel Me?" The recording opened with Primo saying *I know you like what you see, baby, but can you feel me?*, and the ladies screamed at the sound of his voice. Then the curtain rose and Leila, Monica, and I strutted to the edge of the stage with mics to lips.

Leila said, "Fatal Beauty's in the house, but don't call it a comeback." Then she pointed to me and said, "Show some love for my girl Sabrina Steelo with the infectious flow on this, the night of her very first show." I smiled so wide I thought my face would split. She had prepared that intro and planned to surprise me all along, I just knew it.

"And introducing our sister in song Moni Keys," I said improvising a stage name for Monica. "And we have no doubts that you like what you see, but what the ladies of Explicit Content need to know is . . ."

". . . CAN YOU FEEL ME?" the audience hollered.

A few asswipes sporting 8MM T-shirts started catcalling Monica. Leila sashayed to their end of the stage and rhymed over them like a *santera* doing incantations. She mesmerized them long enough for Monica to take center stage to sing Primo's chorus. That girl wailed. Even the crowd's deafening roar of approval couldn't drown her out. She owned that shit. We all did. Together the three of us ripped it, walking off the stage with the audience's heart in our hands.

While the 8MM Posse took the stage after our set, Leila, Monica, and I hugged in the wings. As exhilarated as I was, I kept thinking about who was missing. By any chance, did Genevieve fly back so she could be out there? Why hadn't I found the time to call back Yolanda and Yeribel? Had Roy and my former coworkers at Tower heard the promo on the radios and rolled through? Did Darnell put his feelings aside and show up? Had G arrived in time? I felt Leila's small hand rubbing the center of my back as she buried her forehead in the crook of my neck, and I filled with an immense gratitude for her presence. If only one person could be there for this big moment in my life, of course it had to be Leila. Even if the others had arrived, no one but Leila could understand what the moment meant to me.

I lifted my head, wiped a tear from my cheek, and tried to smile. I said, "Let's go mingle with our public, shall we?"

"I don't know, Cass," Leila said, surprising me. "The fellas are still doing their thing. Going out there after a performance like that might be a distraction." I could see in her eyes though that she was fiendin' to swim in the love of her fans.

"Fuck the fellas," I said. Monica laughed, and no more needed to be said.

The three of us headed to the floor. Without fanfare, we worked our way into the crowd. As folks recognized us and requested autographs, we eventually drifted apart. Still we kept an eye on one another, and at one point I looked over toward Leila and caught her hugging a girl who, despite her hemline and heels, was too young to be in a place like NV at that hour. For a moment I felt perfect. But the feeling soon vanished, and as I continued to sign autographs and pose for pictures, I looked over my fans' heads in the crowd for anyone I knew who could make the feeling return.

Suddenly, Keef's voice boomed over his cordless mic from the stage. "NIGGA!" At first, I thought this was some asinine attempt of his at call-and-response or improvisation or some shit. Why else howl something like that in the middle of 8MM's set? But then Keef flung the microphone into the crowd like nunchuks and dove off the stage. Before long he and some cat were fistfighting with murder in their eyes. Whether to break up the fight, protect their boy, or just for the sick pleasure of it, Cryciss and Third Eye leaped off the stage and joined the melee. As the crowd flooded toward the mesh of thrashing Black bodies, I immediately searched for Leila. She was looking through the crowd for me, too, and just as she called my name and I spotted her, Keef squeezed off the first shot.

Heads screamed and swarmed around us. I grabbed Leila's hand, and we dashed through crashing bodies and flying chairs toward the nearest exit. Just as we reached the emergency door, we heard another gunshot followed by a wave of shrieks. Although we made it outside, the chaos had already spilled into the street. From a distance, we heard the sirens of police cars blaring toward us. Leila and I ran into the street and tried to hail a cab, but we were among dozens also fleeing the shoot-out at NV.

"Leila! Cassie!" We turned to the voice. Monica yelled from the sunroof of the Explicit Content limousine. Leila and I ran toward it and climbed into the backseat, and it tore off down the street just as the cops arrived at the club.

We were the only three in the ride, but no one said a word about turning back for any of the others. Leila asked Monica, "Are you OK?" And with that question, Monica fell into uncontainable sobs. Leila crossed to her side, pulled Monica's head into her lap, and stroked her hair.

Monica's sobs were unusually heavy, and I became uncomfortable. "C'mon, Monica, everything's cool. Everybody'll get back to the mansion in one piece. You'll see." I really didn't believe that, and it turned out that Leila and Monica didn't want to believe that, either.

"That's it, Cassie," Leila said as she continued to stroke Monica's hair. "We don't want to go back."

And I knew that. What I didn't know was exactly why. "What the hell's going on with the label?"

"It's a front, Cassie," said Leila. "Explicit Content is a dope ring." Leila broke it all down on the ride back to Glen Ridge. Although Explicit Content was a legitimate independent record label that Random Sounds had acquired, G's initial investors *were* a group of crime lords, and the plan was always to eventually expand into a drug operation. The chain of parking garages in the 'hood that I recommended G create were to transport heroin to and from the supplier. And the modeling agency Explicit Talent? Filled with girls who prepared the dope for sale on the street in the mansion's basement.

When G signed Leila to the label, he expected her to attract and recruit girls to work the drug mill with promises of modeling contracts and record deals. He wasn't just looking for someone who *was hot and cute but not Black* for the label. G heard those gutter rhymes Leila performed with me at SOBs, saw how she carried herself, made all kinds of assumptions, and approached her. They chatted, and G thought he found someone who would be down for the dirt as well as divahood. "And I was so desperate to be put on, I played gully," Leila confessed. "Really gully."

Then she signed a bullshit development deal, and G put her in the studio immediately. When her visibility and popularity started to rise, G wanted her to scout female fans for the mill and told her he wanted her eventually to manage it when not recording, the way the guys on the label ran other aspects of the traffic. "Find me girls just like you," he told her, meaning pretty, hungry, and alone. But Leila refused. To punish her, G put her album on indefinite hold and leaked to the press that she was a problem artist.

So Leila told G she wanted out of Explicit Content, but G just clamped on tighter. He felt she knew too much to let go, especially after she struck such a hard-core pose only to balk when the time came to get gutter. That if someone with her upbringing felt so righteous about the label's other ventures, nothing would stop her from going to the police. So he stooped to other ways to break her spirit.

They began to lace her meals with that date-rape drug Rohypnol, and every other day she would wake up next to Hi-Jack or

Cryciss with no memory of the previous night. She figured it out and refused to eat anything prepared at the mansion or offered her by anyone on the label. As Leila started to waste away, Primo grew concerned and stepped in. The guys backed off on her sexually but continued to drug her food occasionally, sometimes for no other reason than to fuck with Primo. "Bring him down a few notches for becoming Prince Charming and coming to the bitch's rescue," said Leila.

In an effort to smooth tension between her father and G, Jen took over the mill. She told G he might cultivate some more loyalty and strengthen the operation if he delivered on some of his promises to the girls. Explicit Talent was born, and Jen eventually found the girls legitimate print and video work as an incentive. They earned assignments—and opportunities to escape the mansion for a few hours—by working efficiently in the mill and making themselves available to the male artists, their entourage, and whomever else they saw fit.

Then Cryciss came up with the idea that G expand Explicit Talent into an escort agency. Right before I joined the label, he had convinced G to make the girls available to well-heeled clients in entertainment from rap stars to label executives. The concept flew as these men rationalized to themselves that they weren't hiring prostitutes but just paying for a professional service that ensured their one-night stand didn't evolve into baby mama drama or a rape case. Because she looked so much like Alicia Keys, they frequently asked for Monica, and when Jen had dispatched her to NV that night, she thought I had intended to rent her to someone at the club to curry some kind of favor.

When I asked Leila to what extent Darnell was involved in all this, she said he knew about the drug operation from the get-go, but she doubted he knew about the prostitution ring. Through Primo, Leila eventually learned that while she and I were working with him on our demo, he had already been presenting himself as our manager to G Double D. It was Darnell who convinced G to check out the Da Corridor event at SOB's the night he met Leila. But then G had signed Leila only, double-crossing Darnell out of a production deal on the grounds that D had pitched him a duo.

Whether D knew the true reasons why Leila wasn't cutting it as a solo artist at the label, she didn't know. Leila did know that Darnell continued to front as my manager and told G Double D he'd regret not signing me. "Not just 'cause you're good, Cassie," said Leila. "You're diligent with yours. He knew he'd get a hit album out of you fast and get the money he needed to keep the label afloat and expand his ring." Darnell knew that I wouldn't sign a contract without having a lawyer review it, and he worked that knowledge to his advantage. G believed that to get to me, he had to get down with Darnell, so they concocted a plot to make me sign. Leila had no idea what they had done, but she knew they had been scheming ever since I placed in that contest at the 205 Club.

"Let's just say Darnell wanted to be sure that my loyalty to him ran deeper than my desire to get a record deal," I said, "and leave it at that."

"Maybe that's how he started, Cassie," she said. "But he really fell for you. Primo told me he almost lost it when you took up with G. Them two had a big fight, and he came to Primo mad upset. . . ."

I didn't want to hear nothing about that then. "Why the hell are we going back there now?" I said. "Let's just tell the driver to turn around and drop us off somewhere else." I crawled to their side of the limousine and began to bang on the glass separating us from the driver.

Leila grabbed my fist. "Where am I going to go, Cassie?" she said. "Home with you to Genevieve's?"

"Why not?"

"Forget it." She stopped stroking Monica's hair to press her palm against her own tears like a child. "The driver won't do it anyway. He's under strict instructions to go only where G, Hi-Jack, or Jen tell him to. We've got no choice but to go back."

CHAPTER 23

MALDITA MORENA

We arrived at the mansion in time to catch G Double D and Hi-Jack dashing out of the house. The gals and I climbed out of the limo, and Jack immediately spotted us. I heated at the sight of G as he barked orders into his cell phone.

He marched over to us and said, "What the fuck happened, man?"

"We don't know," said Leila.

"What the fuck you mean y'all don't know?" yelled Jack. "Weren't you fuckin' there?"

I said, "Look, Jack, after our set we went to the floor to parlay with the crowd, and before we knew it, Keef jumped off the stage and started fighting with some dude in the audience."

"And then somebody busted off in the club," added Monica. "And we got the hell outta there."

G finally hung up his cell and turned to us. "Jack, let's go. They got Keef down at the precinct." Then he looked at me. "You and I need to talk," he said like a frustrated parent.

"You damn right about that," I said.

"When I get back, alla y'all better be in that house," he said. Then he and Hi-Jack jumped into Jack's Navigator and tore off. Like obedient children, Leila and Monica hurried toward the mansion, but I just stood in the driveway staring angrily at the Navigator until it disappeared from sight.

"C'mon, Cassandra." When I looked toward the house, Jen stood in the doorway. Leila and Monica already had disappeared into the house. I took my time walking up the driveway. Jen eyed me as she waited in the doorway. As I walked past her into the house I said, "And you must be Carol."

"Glad to see at a time like this you got jokes," she said.

I headed toward the parlor and found Primo guzzling a forty as Leila and Monica talked excitedly over each other to recount what went down at NV. By the row of empty bottles lined beside his Tims, he had headed straight to the mansion after he stomped off like an impetuous child and had been drowning his frustrations in St. Ides since.

Jen appeared behind me in time to catch the tail end of Leila and Monica's rehash. She said, "How much you wanna bet it was Shane?"

"Who's Shane?" I asked.

Primo said, "How you gonna be down with Explicit Content all this time and not fuckin' know who the hell Shane is?"

"Maybe because I'm too busy doing my job and minding my own fuckin' business," I shot back. Then I turned to Leila for an explanation.

"Shane's the cat who shanked Keef in prison," she said.

"And I blame you," Jen told Primo.

"What?" Primo tried to rise from the sofa but was too drunk to find his feet. "Yo, Jen, how you gonna put that shit on me when I wasn't even fuckin' there?"

"Because your ass never should've left the club, that's how. G wasn't there, Hi-Jack wasn't there, Cryciss was there to perform. You shoulda been a man and kept your ass there to handle business. But no, you jetted like a fuckin' little boy runnin' away from home because Daddy didn't let him have his way." The longer Jen read Primo, the more she transformed into a female Asian version of G Double D. Her peroxide locks up in a high ponytail and nails that Leila would envy, Jen got up in Primo's grill. I found myself admiring her, for she had no fear of him. And not just because he was drunk or her father had ties to the label. She was as gangsta as Primo had warned me, and by throwing his tantrum that night, he gave her the opportunity to prove him right. My respect for her ran as deep as my fear, and I momentarily had overlooked that she was reading Primo for not taking charge of the crew on the assumption that he should have, not because he had the least to do that night or had seniority on the label, but only because he was a man. Just four hours earlier, she thought I had taken over in G's absence and had no problems heeding my directions.

Monica broke my attention to the fight when, irritated by the constant hostility, she threw up her hands and sauntered out of the parlor. Too embroiled in their argument, neither Jen nor Primo noticed. Nor did Leila, who attempted to get between them.

Primo got predictable. "Don't think 'cause your pops throws a few duckets around here, you G's right hand and shit."

"A few duckets, son? Try half a mil," yelled Jen. She grabbed the forty out of his hand. "My pops paid for your advance, muthafucka. My pops got your mama outta Red Hook." The way her eyes blazed as she towered over Primo's sloppy form, I swore she was two seconds away from clocking him in the head with the beer bottle.

Leila got between Jen and Primo. "¡Coño, ya, basta! Don't you think we've had enough drama for one night? And as far as we know, this episode ain't even over. For all y'all know, Keef or somebody's dead!"

Jen said, "Serves him right, jumping off the stage in the middle of his set over some old bullshit. . . ."

As the three of them argued, I snuck out to trail Monica, and like Leila said, the evening's drama was far from over.

*   *   *

Monica slipped away quickly, but something told me not to call her name. I wandered through the mansion before I decided to re-trace the steps of my second visit to the mansion. Chances were that she had returned to that vinegary room in the basement that I had seen her and Jen come from when I was searching for Leila.

It took a few moments, but I eventually found that door that led to the staircase. I opened it and heard Monica excitedly recounting what had occurred at NV, occasionally interrupted by an equally agitated and girlish question.

"So, who fired the gun?" someone asked as I slowly made my way down the steps.

"Girl, we ain't stick around to find out. As a matter of fact, the second I heard Keef yell, 'Nig-ga!' and saw his ass in the air like one of 'em flying squirrels . . ." Monica paused as her listeners gig-gled, chuckling herself. "I seen him in the air, and I was heading for the exit. I ran outside, found one of the cars, and stood through the sunroof to look for Leila and Cassie in the crowd. Thank God, I spotted them when I did, because when the driver heard the po-lice coming, he wanted to tear outta there, and I was like, *No, you can't leave my girls,* but I don't think I would've been able to keep him from burning rubber if I hadn't seen them. You know how that is."

With every step, more gradually came into view. I first saw a sea of bare legs in various shades of brown standing around Monica as she sat on a stool with her back to me. Then the ends of black terry-cloth towels like the one I saw her in that day came into view. When I reached three steps from the bottom, I noticed that some of the girls held up their towels by clasping beepers to their breast-bone while others stood in their underwear. I arrived at the last step and their entire bodies appeared.

Whether dressed in towels or underwear, all two dozen had sur-gical masks either hanging around their necks or sitting on their heads. I had seen almost all of them before on someone's arm or ride. They were all Explicit Talent models or Explicit Content groupies, which over time had become one and the same. The large room was furnished like a wealthy family's den. In addition to a complete entertainment system with a sixty-inch-screen television and megaspeakers, the room also contained a fully stocked bar in one corner and large pool table in the other.

Yet in the farthest corner from the staircase stood things that I had never seen in a place someone might call home. A row of four long tables were lined up near the wall, each made of glass and dusted with white powder. While the majority of the girls had gathered around Monica to hear about the night's drama, two remained at one of the tables, yelling their questions across the room. The girl facing me pounded a plastic bag of the powder, breaking it up while it remained sealed. The other, with her back to me, measured what seemed like grounded chalk onto a triple-beam scale. At the foot of every table sat boxes labeled *Promotions* like the ones I'd seen at Explicit Content headquarters, with plastic bags of tiny vials filled with powder. I was hit with that nagging sense you get when you come across a new situation that still strikes you as familiar. And then I realized that I had seen something just like this in one of my Allen Payne movies—*New Jack City*.

When the woman weighing the chalk looked up as another girl tossed another question at Monica, she noticed me. "Cassandra!" All their eyes were on me with shock. The woman walked over to me and pulled off her surgical mask. Yolanda. She pushed her way through the others and threw her arms around me. I could feel her tears dampen my neck. "*¡Ayudame!*" she whispered in my ear.

"The star's slumming," one of the others said sarcastically. The deadness of her eyes told me she did this by choice. Still her comment shamed more than angered me.

Monica said, "Leave her alone. She didn't call me to pimp me. She let me sing." And her eyes sparkled with adulation so unnatural, I began to shake. In a matter of seconds, I went from pariah to messiah, as the women flocked around me. As they started tugging at my clothes and fighting for my attention, I felt like I was trapped in a scene from a zombie flick. "Sabrina, hook me up please. Bri, you got to put me on your next joint. Sabrina, I've saved up five thousand and, I swear to God, I will pay you to let me come into the studio with you. Please, Bri, please!" Their pleas carried much more than the typical hunger for fame and wealth. In their voices I heard a desperation for independence, to escape, a way out. They weren't hounding me to put them on; they were begging me to set them free. Until that moment, I had never thought I'd ever hate my stage name.

The entire scene freaked me out. The night had started with my professional debut with Leila and I reunited and flawless and quickly had disintegrated into a gangsta rap cliché of dangerous proportions. And until G Double D and Hi-Jack returned from wherever they ran, it was far from over.

I broke free from the wrenching hands and ran upstairs. When I hit the landing, I crashed into Jen. For a moment, we stood eye to eye, and I tried to match the intensity I saw in hers. She heard the girls giggling downstairs and shoved past me, yelling, "If I don't count at least seven-hundred glassines, everyone's getting docked." But before I could disappear through the door, she stopped and called after me. "Don't even think about hiding out in the guest house. When G gets back he wants everybody in the parlor, waiting, and that includes you."

Primo had already fallen into a drunken doze by the time I returned from discovering the basement mill. Leila was staring out the window longingly at the string of expensive cars lined along the driveway. "Leila," I whispered, and she jumped. "Here's our chance to jet." We both ran to Primo and patted him down for keys to his Bentley. "Why didn't you just go?"

"I was going to, but I couldn't leave without you."

"You crazy?"

"They'd probably think you let me go, and God knows what they might do to you for that. Don't sleep, Cassie, just 'cause—" She stopped immediately, probably realizing how sick I was of the assumption that I expected special treatment because I slept with G Double D. "If something would've happened to you because I ran, I wouldn't have been able to forgive myself."

"Why didn't you call the police?"

"And have them think we're part of all this shit?" Leila grew annoyed with me. I'd been hip to the entire drama for only a few hours, but she had been searching for a way out for months. "After all these *pendejos* have put me through, I'm not going down with them over their dirt on top of it all."

Just as we were about to roll Primo over to see if his keys were in has back pocket, we heard Jen in the hallway cursing out Monica. We jumped into the love seat as if we'd been sitting there all along. When they entered the parlor, Monica was crying and sporting a busted lip. Jen clutched Monica in one hand and had a .38 special in the other. She shoved Monica toward the couch next to Primo.

"We're all going to wait right here until G returns and gets down to the bottom of all this shit."

And wait we did, until almost eight in the morning.

When G Double D and Hi-Jack returned, they had Cryciss and Earl with them. All of us, save Primo, jumped to our feet and expected to hear the worst. "Oh, my God," said Jen. "Keef."

"That stupid nigga's still on lockdown," G replied as he strode back and forth across the parlor. "The fuckin' judge wouldn't cut him loose 'cause that dude's on life support. And you know what? I'm all right with that shit 'cause I don't have money to be wasting on a million-dollar bond when we've got shit to move! That son of a bitch is a goddamn occupational hazard. You all are." When he saw Primo sleeping with his mouth hanging open, G hauled back and clocked him in the jaw. "Muthafucka, wake up! I want to know what the fuck happened at NV tonight."

Not that he waited for an answer. He immediately launched into ripping everyone a second asshole, starting with Keef, who probably never realized how lucky he was to be in jail. As Jen had guessed, the man he attacked from the stage was Shane Daniels, his rival from prison. Keef capped him twice, once each in his shoulder and stomach. The entire 8MM Posse was arrested, but only Keef's charges stuck. His celebrity expedited his arraignment, but because Keef had been charged with attempted murder and had a record of assault, the judge denied bail.

G swiftly moved in on Primo, who was still reeling from St. Ides and the sucker punch. "And why the fuck you weren't there when all this shit went down, Primo?"

Cryciss answered in a singsong, " 'Cause he stormed off like a little beeyatch."

"You abandoned your crew over a goddamn song?"

"This ain't about crew, G," Primo slurred. "This is about business."

"Nigga, at Explicit Content crew is business!" G hollered. Except for Jen, every female in that room cringed with fear that he would hit Primo again. She nodded her head in agreement at G's every word. "At this label, crew is business, business is crew. And if you don't know that by now, take your bitch-ass over to Roc-A-Fella muthafucka!"

"A'ight," Cryciss said.

G whirled toward him. "Ayo, shut the fuck up, Jason. You and Earl knew that Keef's been fixin' to wild out ever since he heard Shane got sprung, and you let the crazy muthafucka stroll out this crib packin'. You call that lookin' out?"

He tore into Cryciss and Third Eye for another five minutes before he turned on Leila, Monica, and me. "And ain't it just like some bitches to jump in the ride and take off?"

I knew Leila and Monica would just eat it, but I'm Genevieve Rivers's daughter. I asked, "So what were we supposed to do, G?"

"Stay behind and gather some fuckin' intelligence . . ."

"Intelligence?"

". . . 'cause when shit like that goes down, po ain't gonna be checkin' for bitches. You should've hung back to help Keef get the fuck outta there. . . ."

"Word," mumbled Earl.

"You could've found out what the fuck was goin' on or made yourselves useful. Either followed the posse to the precinct, or even stayed behind at NV so when Jack and I got there you could fill us in rather than our having to—"

I jumped to my feet. "Son of a bitch, when you got there? Muthafucka, were you ever headed there?" I marched over to him. "You were never headed to NV. That's how you beat us back here. That's why you had to turn the fuck around and head all the way back into the City. Crew is business, business is crew, but where the fuck were you, nigga? Why the fuck weren't you at NV tonight?"

Primo said, "Keef's on lockdown, and she gonna whine about G not going to her little show."

I spun around and smacked his drunk-ass upside the head. "Fuck you!" I snatched my bag off the love seat. "Fuck the lot of you. Every so-called bitch affiliated with this bullshit label does everything expected of her whether she wants to or not. But you sick bastards get high, drunk, act the fuckin' fool, everything but what you signed on the bottom line to do. Then, when you get yourself into some shit, I'm supposed to jeopardize everything I've worked for to have your back? The only sorry-ass bitches at Explicit Content got dicks between their legs."

"And their ears," Monica said under her breath.

"Fuck alla you, I'm out!" I pushed G out of my way and headed out the parlor.

"Cassandra, get back here."

Leila stood. "Cassie, don't . . ."

I ignored them both, huffing past Patrick, who had just arrived for work and walked through the door.

"I mean it, Cassie. Get the fuck back here."

I walked out of the front door and continued down the driveway. Before I knew it, G raced behind me and tackled me to the ground. I crashed to the oily asphalt and a jolt of pain shot up my forearm. I felt a manly hand grab at my crown and yank backward. I screamed and tried to roll over. I looked up at G, who straddled over me with a cocked Beretta of his own in his hand, his eyes blazing with rage. "When I tell you to do something, you fuckin' do it." He backslapped me, and I heard Leila scream my name. "And you don't do a goddamn thing unless I tell you to do it. Do you understand me?"

My face burned with both the sting and humiliation of his slap. From where I lay on the driveway, I could see Leila crying and thrashing to run to me while Cryciss held her back. All of them were there, including the millworkers and Patrick, standing on the lawn and staring at me like a freak show. After a scene like this, if I had even the slimmest chance of continuing to come and go at will, I had to convince him that I wasn't fazed by his violent outbursts. G Double D had to believe that this was exactly as down and dirty as I always wanted to be. I had to be that angel with the dirty face he wanted.

I fought back tears and caught my breath. "All I wanted to do, G, was go back to our place and get some sleep. We're all talking shit because we've had a long night of drama. Just let everybody go to sleep, and we'll regroup later. All of us."

G hauled himself off of me and even offered his hand. I took it and he lifted me to his feet, sending another shot of agony through my forearm. I had a flashback to that night at 205 when I met G Double D for the first time, when Freight had twisted this same arm behind my back. This time it hurt a thousand times worse, beyond the physical level.

I cradled my arm in my opposite hand, and G finally noticed I was in pain. He peeled off his jacket and put it on me. Placing his arm around my shoulder, he steered me toward the guest house. He looked over his shoulder and waved the others back into the mansion. Cryciss dragged Leila inside while Jen shepherded the others like cattle into a barn.

When G and I entered the guest house, it flashed into my mind that he might beat me. I quickly walked into the kitchen where Lynn was dusting the window blinds and stood by the knife drawer.

"Good morning, Cassandra," she said as she gave me a curious stare.

I didn't answer. G soon entered the kitchen. "Lynn, we've all had a tough night and may need some special attention. Go to the mansion and give Patrick a hand with the others." Eager to finally spend a day with her secret love, Lynn zipped out the door, taking her fleeting concern for me with her.

G waited until he heard the door slam behind her. He reached for me and I gripped the handle on the knife drawer. "Cassie, you want me to take you to our doctor? He's just the next town over. Say the word, and I'll page him right now."

I assumed Dr. Next Town Over was probably on the Explicit Content payroll. G probably kept him on retainer should anyone OD on the smack, get overwhelmed by the fumes of processing it, or just if the 8MM Posse were their usual stupid selves and started busting off shots at someone else or each other. "Later," I said. "I just want to sleep now."

G held out his hand and waited for me to take it. He led me into the bedroom. I sat on the bed and he knelt on the floor before me and removed my boots and socks. The next thing I knew, G buried his head into my lap and started to cry. Understanding that his every gesture constituted some test of loyalty, whether conscious and subconscious, I willed myself to stroke his hair.

"I heard you ripped it tonight," he said. He looked up at me and

gave a little laugh. "And you know who told me? Keef. They finally let me see him, and I asked him what the fuck happened. I
meant like the fight, the shootout, and shit, but fuckin' Keef goes,
'First, Cassie and 'em did their thing. Aw, man, G, you shoulda
seen them. You woulda been mad proud. *I* was proud. Cassie was
like' . . ." G imitated Keef imitating me, with my head thrown
back yelling into the mic over my head. " *'We don't do subtle, so
are y'all ready to get explicit?* Yeah, G, Cassie, Leila, and that trick
Monica, they was super sick, yo.'

"And that's how I found out about Primo, 'cause I was like,
'Monica? What the fuck was she doing there?' Keef had me all
caught up, totally forgettin' why I'm talking to him in the jump in
the first place." He snickered and wiped his running nose, and I
forced myself to laugh along with him. "For real though, Cassie.
I'm sorry I wasn't there for your big night."

The only person I hated more than him at that moment was
myself, because as he shed tears over my thighs, I wondered for a
moment if he was sorry only because his presence might have prevented what happened to Keef and just apologized to tell me what
he thought I wanted to hear. I hated myself for thinking that. I
hated myself for caring after what I learned. After what he had
done to me.

And yet I had to go through all the motions so G wouldn't
question me. So when he began to nuzzle my neck and rub my
thigh, I couldn't resist him. He peeled off my clothes and pushed
me back onto the bed. I pulled my wounded forearm over my head
and bit down on my bottom lip every time G's thrust slammed it
against the headboard.

He finally came, rolled onto his side, and quickly fell asleep.
Even though I felt like I hadn't slept in three days, I couldn't crash
because of the flood of nightmares. Leila screaming for me as
Cryciss held her back. The mill girls clawing at my clothes. G
straddled over me with the Beretta in his hand as he pulled back
the other to hit me. Keef leaping into the air and landing on the

shadow of Shane Daniels. Monica sobbing in the backseat of the limousine. All these images were accompanied by only one sound, the same sound, and it wasn't Leila's screams, the police car sirens, or even the shotgun blasts. Only Keef yelling "NIGGA!" rang over and over again in my head, no matter the image. The first decision I made—no, more like a vow—when I finally rose from bed almost twelve hours later was to never utter that filthy word again.

And then I concluded that I either had to get down or be gone. I decided to be gone and to take Leila with me, if no one else. Since it took a series of ploys to get us into Explicit Content, I knew it would take a helluva ruse to get us out.

I played cool over the next few months or so, going into the studio to lay down tracks, participating in publicity jaunts, and so on. When I would return to Glen Ridge, I headed to the mansion and front like I was down with it all. I kicked back with the fellas— drinking forties and smoking blunts, watching thug-glam flicks and debating which rappers were perpetratin' hard-core and who was true gangsta. I even asked the occasional question about the underground enterprises, deep enough to fake interest yet shallow enough to avoid suspicion.

Since we didn't run the night of Keef's incident, the fellas eased up on Leila and me. We were allowed to be alone together for longer spells, although none of the guys ever strayed from us too far or too long. Those interludes lasted long enough for me to learn things like why Leila kept her nails so short now (one morning Primo tried to crawl into her bed and she scratched the shit out of him thinking he was Cryciss trying to get at her before the roofie wore off) and what happened to Vance and Junior (she broke up with Vance as soon as she signed with Explicit Content and Freight pistol-whipped Junior when he tried to approach her after a show). She told me that after Bokim took over that first recording session for "But Can You Feel Me?," Hi-Jack and Primo jumped him in the parking lot, stuck a gun in his mouth, and warned him to never forget his place in the studio again. Of course, Bokim never went to the cops, but he also vowed to never work for Explicit Content again. How the wanna-be models who were loyal to Explicit Content helped keep Monica and others like her in check. That Primo lured the starstruck Yolanda out of F.I.T. and into the mill by promising her designing jobs for the record label and the talent agency. We never had time, however, to discuss the critical issues like why she betrayed me in the first place and how we could shake loose from this nightmare.

But as that article once said about Leila, we both fronted like Bonnies to their Clydes and gradually earned more slack. They stopped tampering with Leila's food, and she regained that Rican appetite, putting on both pounds and hope. Her brighter outlook smoothed things between Primo and her, and she faked wide-eyed adulation for him as I did with G Double D. I convinced G to put Leila back into the studio and take charge of her album, and I did it so well he thought the idea was his.

G did come up with the idea of recording a duet between Primo and Leila, though, and promoting their personal relationship as if they were the Latino Beyoncé and Jay-Z although Leila rhymed while Primo did what he called singing. G used the track to get a deal creating the soundtrack for Queen Latifah's Christmas movie. Leila and Primo performed it live for the first time at the Explicit Content holiday party and toy drive G Double D threw at the Flat. The song had enough juice to make the soundtrack the season's bestseller, knocking Mya's Christmas album out of the top spot.

In fact, G was doing some of the best production work of his career. For the first time in a long time in hip-hop music, the critical acclaim and the record sales were in sync. The trades raved about the new singles, saying that G finally matured as an artist and with him at the helm of my and Leila's upcoming albums, critics looked forward to hearing them. One cat even wrote, "It seems that

Downs has a way with women. Perhaps they inspire him to reach for new heights of creativity never found on any other Explicit Content product." They speculated that the incident at NV temporarily freed him of Keef—and by extension the 8MM Posse, who collectively were the biggest source of Explicit Content's legal problems and financial leaks—and G took the opportunity to artistically turn over a new leaf.

G did floss less and work much harder. That included on the drug operation and prostitution ring, however, as much as in the studio. With Keef on lockdown, he began to work on Earl's solo album and had Cryciss assist Jen with Explicit Talent. I knew better than to blow up my own spot and try to hint he abandon the illegal enterprises altogether. Even though Explicit Content broke out of its financial slump, G still felt he didn't have enough money to really soar as a mogul or kingpin. He said to me during one of our Jacuzzi sessions, "Baby girl, my ventures on the DL is what's gonna finance the promotion your joint deserves, which is way above and beyond what Random's gonna do. And when your shit pops, that money's gonna help me expand, buy them chain of garages. The profit from that? That goes into your girl's album, which then generates investment into Explicit Talent. . . ." I snickered, and he splashed water at me, thinking I was teasing him for dreaming when I was actually disgusted with how closely G followed commercial hip-hop's shift from gangsta to pimp rap. If I had pointed that out to him, he might have mistaken it for encouragement. A rare occasion in hip-hop music when the critical acclaim and the record sales were in sync only to be wasted at a label that gave underground a new, sinister meaning. The irony made me sick, but I continued to play the role.

My spirits only worsened when Aunt Treece and her family visited for Christmas. Being around my family with such ugly secrets just robbed the joy of their visit. I had a few cool moments that made me forget about Explicit Content. Little things like having my aunt speak in Trinidadian Creole because it made me laugh and hearing Genevieve complain under her breath, "The woman was born and raised in the South Bronx." Watching my uncle Marques lose his mind over a botched pass in a football game.

Listening to Ivy talk about the trials and tribulations of being fifteen and remembering my own high-school years was the best. After a few questions about Explicit Content—the kind you might ask any relative about her job during a holiday visit—Ivy treated me as the cousin she always had. When I claimed the second drumstick at dinner after Uncle Marques grabbed the first, she even said, "Your mother earned that drumstick by cooking. Don't be showing out 'cause you have a record deal, Cassie."

"What you gonna do?" I said. "Stick me in the dryer?" And everyone laughed.

It felt great to make Ivy feel understood and yet also sad to wonder what might occur later to prove the meaninglessness of some of her current dramas.

Dealing with Kerwyn was the worst. The boy was all caught up in the bling-bling and bang-bang. He asked me endless questions about Explicit Content. What was everybody really like? What other celebrities had I met? Can I introduce him to G Double D before he went back to LA? Would I give him the tape Kerwyn and his friends had made?

He even pulled me into my mother's bedroom and handed me his Walkman so I could listen to it. "I don't want my moms to hear it 'cause she . . . you know . . ."

I put on the headphones and listened for less than a minute. Bitch this, nigga that, fuck every other thing. A blunt here, a ho there, everywhere a gat. He probably had two hairs on his balls, bragging about pimping tricks. I ripped the phones off my ears and handed him the Walkman.

"Cassie, you barely listened to it."

"I don't want to listen to that today. I hear that shit every day. You think I want to hear my thirteen-year-old cousin saying that on Christmas?"

"So you're saying I'm not original." If only that were the problem. It devastated me to come down on Kerwyn like that, especially when I rarely saw him and he seemed so proud of me. Within minutes he bounced back from it, saying, "I hear you Cassie. I gotta develop my own style, not sound so much like Hi-Jack. Can I, like, send you tapes, and when you have time, you can listen to them and give me feedback so I can get better?" I blew him off, telling him we'd talk about it later, that I really didn't want to talk about business while with the family. It got to the point where I actually couldn't wait for them to go back to LA, and I felt terrible about it.

After the holidays, I started going into the basement to kick it with the mill girls. None of them had a place to go, which is why most of them eventually accepted their situation and made the best of it. But even the few like Yolanda who didn't accept it had little choice because Jen convinced them they would end up doing hard time, if not worse. So these women built solidarity from despair, which meant they didn't trust each other at all. They would compete to befriend me in the hopes that I would put them on a track or in a video. With the exception of Yolanda, who replaced Andi on photo shoots, I resisted my urges to do so because I had made a decision. Not just to leave Explicit Content but to bring down the entire label.

In order to liberate so many, however, I couldn't allow sympathy to make me gamble with the temporary rescue of a few. If while on a legitimate assignment, a mill girl made a break for it and succeeded, Leila and I would go down with Explicit Content. If she attempted and failed, I would be held responsible and could forget about getting any of us out some way other than death or prison. And with the Segui sisters, I couldn't risk telling Yeribel that her sister was safe any more than I could assure Yolanda that her sister believed she ran away off with a seedy rap star. So when a desperate mill girl asked if she could work on my next track, I had to front as the benevolent yet powerless queen and say, "We'll see," knowing all along that only one of the men could set her free even if only for a day.

The fraud started to take its toll on me. One day after a forty too many, I even asked Jen how they prepared the heroin for sale on the street. She actually took me into the basement and showed me, weighing the mannitol, cutting it up with her playing cards, and mixing it with the dope like a Ginsu chef. "You try it," she said. I stood over the toxic mix not even a minute before I passed out. I came to on the sofa in the parlor room, everyone hovering over me like a family in the emergency unit. February chills came at me from all directions as they had opened every window in an effort to revive me. When they saw I was fine, they broke into relieved laughter. Leila shooed them away so I could rest, and on the way out, Hi-Jack brushed my sweaty bangs away from my forehead and said, "You scared us, Punchanella. Don't do that shit no more."

"Yeah, Cassie," said Cryciss. "Sometimes you're so smart, you stupid."

When they left me alone with Leila, I said, "Fuck them."

"*Maldita morena.*" Leila smiled as she handed me a cup of soup. "But in a way, he's right, you know. Curiosity killed the cat and all that." Then Jen walked back into the room, and Leila sighed. "*Maldita morena.*"

And that's when I knew the Explicit Content clan was sucking me into their fold. Leila had been trapped for months and still had not succumbed to their ways. But if I didn't get out soon, I'd start to accept their warped love as something normal and desirable. Something worthy of protection.

CHAPTER 24

INTEREST FROM MEGALOS

The idea came to me on Valentine's Day. G took me to a celebrity-studded party at Cheetah's. As we sat at a table overseeing the dance floor, G leaned over to whisper in my ear, "This time next year, you and me are gonna be hip-hop royalty, and all those muthafuckas down there nothing but our minions." I thought how just a year earlier, Leila and I had rocked SOB's and he had come and ruined everything. As he nibbled on my neck, I noticed how many people were exchanging business cards and beaming information across PDAs and hollering into cell phones. They came to this party supposedly to celebrate or even find love, and all they did was conduct business as usual. And then I got inspired and began to plan.

When I was ready to move, I called Genevieve and asked her to meet me for lunch for the first time in my life. To my surprise, she readily agreed without asking why. Before I hung up, she said, "I'm glad you finally called me." I waited for the rant about how I was a grown woman and as such I should find the time to call my mother on a weekly basis. However, Genevieve paused for an unusual silence, then said, "Meet me at the Houston's on the corner of Twenty-seventh and Park Avenue South next Wednesday at one o'clock."

"OK."

We hung on in silence. Genevieve then said, "Cassandra, I'm going to ask you something, and I don't want you to get angry."

"Why would I get angry?"

"I know you think I don't understand anything about this hip-hop industry you're in, and that you're always telling me that there's the culture and there's the commerce, and that sometimes . . . Well, whatever . . . My question is, Were you in anyway involved with the shoot-out at that club in November?"

Although I had nothing to do with Keef's wilding out, I still felt culpable. But that feeling could not compare to the hurt when I realized that if Genevieve could ask that question, the details of that gig never found its way from her notepad to her PDA the day I signed with Explicit Content. And because of the drama I had entangled myself in, I was not entitled to question her about it.

"We'll talk Wednesday, Mom," I said. Before she could protest, I hung up.

I managed to arrive at Houston's fifteen minutes early, as I'd planned. I asked the waiter to bring me a mojito. I could not let my mother see me drinking, but I needed something to quell my nerves. The glass had barely hit the table before the alcohol crashed down my throat. The wretchedness of my actions registered hard. Before Explicit Content, I'd had no problems with virgin margaritas and Shirley Temples even if people teased me. But in time I wouldn't be able to get through the day without a forty or two, just like the chronically depressed men on the label.

When I spotted my mother coming up the street, I flagged the waiter to get rid of my glass and told him not to bring another. As Genevieve walked through the door in her Bill Blass pantsuit, I

stood up to give her a kiss on her cheek. She took in my conservative attire with surprised approval. "I've been looking for pants
like those. Where'd you get them?"

Knowing that Genevieve has no problems finding whatever she
wants, I played along. "Burlington Coat Factory," I said, hoping
to impress her with not only how responsible I looked but how
sensible I sounded for not paying top dollar for my name brands.
It would make the outrageous thing I needed her to do all the more
plausible.

Genevieve looked at my shabby attempt at a French twist, and
said, "Nice to see you in something besides your little rapper attire. Now, if you'd only see my hairdresser."

Of course, that did it, no matter how much I swore to myself I
would not let her get to me. I hated the fact that even as a grown
woman, my mother could reduce me to a quivering mess. Leila always told me not to take it so personally. "Mothers are good for
that," she always said. "Thank God you have one and that she
cares enough to try to get under your skin. You don't think I wish
I had a mother to get on my case about my gear every time I head
out the door?" But Genevieve knew how to do this to everyone,
and when she wasn't tweaking my insecurities in some warped
quest to motivate me into becoming her idea of a better person, I
secretly hoped I would inherit her knack for tipping people off
center. If I had, it hadn't matured yet, and that was the reason why
I buried my pride and decided to endure her harping to ask for her
help.

She knew I had asked her to meet me for lunch because I needed
something from her and she was going to milk my neediness for
whatever she could. So I sat there trying to find a way to break it
down to her without breaking down all together, and Genevieve
read my silence as obedient acquiescence. So she rambled on about
my hairstyling preferences with the slight concessions she occasionally made to prove she was not unreasonable.

"Now I'm not saying the Dominicans aren't wonderful stylists, but for the life of me, I don't understand why they can't make appointments like everyone else. I'll tell you why. Because most of their clientele don't have normal jobs, if any. They have time to sit in a beauty salon, waiting, for hours. I don't. What's to stop them from taking both appointments and walk-ins?" said Genevieve. "By all means, if someone doesn't keep her appointment, take a walk-in. But the kind of customers who can't afford to sit around all day waiting to get their hair done are the kind of clientele they'd like to cultivate. Don't you think?"

"I hear you." She reminded me of my first conversation with G Double D in the bathtub at the guest house. "I guess if you're only going to have one salon, you might as well go upscale to get customers with money. But a lot of those neighborhood stylists tend to own more than one place so . . ." I sank into my seat.

"Cassandra, what's wrong?"

My chest caved inward from all I had been holding in for the past few months.

"Cassie, you're scaring me!" The last time my mother called me Cassie was when I graduated high school. The principal had just handed me my diploma. My mother had run up to me with a disposable camera, yelling, "Smile, Cassie. Smile," her inflection so heavy with a pride so rare, I cried like a baby.

And so I finally broke down at the table. It took some time for Genevieve to calm me down long enough to tell her what had happened. Before I did, she called her office. To whoever answered, she said, "Tell Ed I'm going to be late from lunch. . . . I don't know when I'll be back. My daughter needs me, and she comes first. I'll call when I'm on my way."

Then she gave me her full attention as I broke down the entire story from Leila's back stabbing to Darnell's double-dealing to G's empire building. Not once did she interrupt me, even when I told her that, yes, I had been at NV that fateful night and described Keef's murderous scuffle as the least of the worst. That the consolation of reconciling with Leila and benefiting from G's kept word regarding my album hinged on this shared affiliation with this twisted label turned syndicate called Explicit Content. That thinking myself some gracious starlet, I unknowingly pimped Yolanda right into the disaster. That I'd suspected trouble all along and stopped asking questions because I was so desperate to be put on.

When I finished fifteen minutes later, "Oh, my God," was all Genevieve could say. Even though my mother is a rare drinker who would never think of going back to the office with liquor on her breath, she called the waiter over and asked for a glass of brandy. When he asked me if I'd like anything to drink, before I could answer, she said, "No, she doesn't." And instead of getting angry with her, I grinned with a hope I hadn't felt in weeks. My mother intended to help me.

"I think I have a way out, but I need your help." I described my half-baked plan for liberating Leila and myself from Explicit Content and then blowing the whistle on the entire sham. "I know it's not perfect, but if you help me think it through some more and do what I ask, I think we can pull it off."

She resisted only one element of my plan. "Getting you out is enough of a gamble. Including Leila only heightens the risk. This whole thing started when the girl betrayed you, so how do you know she won't deceive you again to save her own fast hide? Let's just worry about you now, and once the authorities are involved, you can vouch for her, if you must."

Genevieve's reluctance to include Leila didn't surprise me at all. What did surprise me was how succinctly I answered her question. To anyone else it'd take volumes to explain how important Leila was to me and why. But as far as Genevieve was concerned, only the restatement of a simple fact was necessary. "Because when you put me out on the street just for trying to be who I really was, Leila took me in for the very same reason."

I didn't have to say anything more. Genevieve finished her brandy and called the office to say she would need the rest of the afternoon off. Then mother and daughter put our heads together to refine my escape plan.

About two weeks later, G admitted to receiving the calls. We were in bed, and I had just reached for the lights when he stopped me. "Cassie, I need to talk to you about something." I instantly knew that this was the moment, so I nestled myself under the crook of his arm not so much to cozy up to him but to hide my face.

"This A and R exec at Megalos named Johnetta Lawrence," he said. "She keeps calling me, saying she wants to buy out your contract."

"Can she do that?"

"She doesn't want just you, though. She also wants Leila. Said her peoples have been following you both from the start. When y'all used to perform together underground, when y'all did your thing separately at 205. And when they saw y'all together again at NV, that you were off the chain." I fought the temptation to say, *We were, but you wouldn't know that.* "They want to buy out both your contracts and put you back together as a duo."

"And what'd you tell them?"

He hesitated, and I knew if I played it right, we would have him. "I told the bitch hell no, I wasn't interested. She keeps calling though."

I looked up at him and forced myself to smile. "So how much am I worth on the open market?"

"A mil." I waited. As I started to speak, he continued. "For both of you." His need to fill the silence broke my heart. It proved to me that despite everything, I remained to him first and foremost a commodity to be sold whether to the public or the highest bidder. If he really cared about me, or even if my album had been a genuine calling, he would have been able to sit with the silence because there never would've been that unspoken question. "Five hundred Gs for each contract."

The risky moment arrived, and I prayed that he truly lived by the words he told me over our first dinner together. *No matter what goes down between family members, all aspects of business are top priority. You want to prove your loyalty to me? Always put the bottom line first.* I turned to look at him over my shoulder. "Ask for two."

G sat up. Then he laughed and eased back against the pillow. "You funny."

I slowly sat up and swung my legs over the side of the bed. With my back to him, I said, "I know you need the money, G. If you're ever going to be in a position to make ten times more than you do now pushing weight instead of CDs, you need the money." I crawled back onto the bed and kneeled next to him. "I mean, you'd have your money, I'd have my album, and we'd still be together, wouldn't we?"

"No doubt, baby girl. No doubt," he said.

"And I could stay here, right?" Genevieve always said that women had a much greater tendency than men to end their sentences with questions because they were unsure of themselves. That even when they stated an obvious fact, they added *Right?* or *You know?* or something like that because they expected people to question their credibility simply because they were female. She taught me this as I prepared for college interviews, and I always made a conscious effort to avoid it when talking to a man who could give me what I wanted, but now it had to be part of the role in order to hook G. "You could, like, negotiate to continue producing our albums. Folks collaborate across labels all the time, right?"

"Sure, but the question is, Do you want to go back to being part of a duo and sharing the spotlight with Leila?" G asked. "Don't you want to stay a solo artist?"

I can't front. My instinctual response was, *Hell yeah,* and for a moment I understood what Leila might have felt when G approached her for the first time. So I knew if I lied, he'd see right through me. "Of course I do, but if it's gonna help you do your thing . . . Maybe we can convince her to accept most of the material we've already done and to stick to a one-album deal. That way the album'll be finished soon, and I'll be free to resign again with Explicit Content. You'd resign me, wouldn't you?"

"No doubt," G said. He sat up to stroke my cheek, sending goose bumps down my back. I prayed that if he felt the shivers he would read them as the insecurities of a lover making a sacrifice that she hoped would not be in vain and not the fear of a liar fixing to cross a dangerous man. "You sure you want do this?"

"No," I said, surprising myself with that truth. "All I'm saying for now is that we talk to the woman. That's it."

G pulled me to him and kissed me. I truly wondered if I had made a mistake. Just because, despite all the terrible things he had done, he still asked me what I wanted.

G convened the roster and key staff in the parlor to inform them of the latest developments. The grand jury indicted Keef on attempted murder while Shane Daniels continued to fight for his life. So G started the meeting by saying Keef's defense was going to be mad expensive, yet he felt obligated to foot the bill. Through our pillow talk, G revealed that he had to cultivate the others' loyalty to him by showing loyalty to Keef.

"If that ain't bad enough, Om and his partners are about to take their business elsewhere," he said. When Jen became the object of dirty looks, he added, "Ayo, don't put this on Jenny. You put this shit on Keef. He shoulda been channeling all that shit into the studio. Jenny's pops hung in here this long because of her."

Jen gave the fellas a smug look when Hi-Jack said, "We can't do it, G. We can't move weight, make records, and defend Keef. Something's gotta give."

"And it ain't gonna be Keef," said Cryciss.

Hi-Jack shot back, "Nigga, how you figure? The weight's our cheddar, the music's our cover. They's inseparable. And like G said, Keef fuckin' did that shit to hisself and is about to take us down with him."

Cryciss and Hi-Jack started arguing, and G hollered to shut them up. "This is why we're gonna try to move the ladies to Megalos."

Now Jen got pissed. "Hold up, G. I've put in too much time and energy setting up Explicit Talent for you to be talking about moving it elsewhere. Do you know how hard it was to break them to the point where now they're actually down with the program?"

"Yo, G, how'd you get Megalos interested?" Primo asked. "I mean, where you heard they got down like that?"

"I'm not talking about Explicit Talent," G said. "I'm talking about Cassie and Leila."

"What?" Leila immediately looked to me to see if I were just as surprised as she. I didn't bother to try and fake it, and I could see she didn't know what to make of my silence. It killed me to not tell her about the setup, but I needed her genuine confusion when she found out to lend me credibility.

G explained the Megalos offer and the reasons why it was worth looking into. Now Hi-Jack and Cryciss exchanged scripts. While Cryciss was eager to be rid of us, Hi-Jack questioned the move.

"That bitch don't fool me," Jack said as he glared at Leila. "She fiendin' to be out of Explicit Content."

"So let her go, then, take Punchanella with her," said Cryciss, cackling. He and Third Eye exchanged a pound.

Hi-Jack stood up and yelled. "You niggas are so simple!" He punched a hand into his fist at every word for emphasis. "You too simple to know just know how simple you are. Fuckin' Tweedle Dum and Tweedle Stupid." He abandoned reasoning with them and turned to G. "Cassie, I understand 'cause she rolls with you, G. But Leila? Naw, I'm not feelin' that."

Primo said, "Muthafucka, what you tryin' to say?"

"I ain't *tryin'* to say shit. What I'm *straight out* sayin' is you don't got it like that. You been blazin' that shit all this time, and your bitch still looking for the exit, that's what I'm sayin'. Cassie got stake in this right here all around. Look at how she handled with that Chinese bitch when she bum rushed her on the video set. She ain't gonna catch a case of loose lip if she goes to another label. But Leila—"

"Sit down, Jack, and shut the fuck up," G cut him off. "Ain't nobody ever gonna catch a case of loose lip nowhere because they understand the consequences of that." Then he went down the line, starting with Leila. "Right, Leila?"

"Yes, G."

"Right, Jen?"

"Yeah."

"Hi-Jack?"

"A'ight."

"Primo?"

"Right."

"Cryciss."

"Word."

"Earl?"

"Uh-huh."

"Baby girl?"

"Whatever you say, G."

I knew better than to think he would spare me, but it terrified me that he had saved me for last.

Anyone who believes that men don't gossip as much as women is a fool. Like Leila once told me, "Sistas may lie about doing it, but at least we're honest enough to call it gossip. Men gotta add the stink to the shit by calling it networking." I guessed through networking with Hi-Jack as he helped him piece together the 8MM Posse's next album from material recorded before Keef got locked up, Darnell heard that G, Leila, and I had a lunch meeting at Justin's with Johnetta Lawrence from Megalos Records at the end of the week.

He must've waited a long time in the wings to get me alone. G gave me a break while he and the engineer mulled over a problem with the latest track. I had ducked out of the studio and was headed to the ladies' room when Darnell cornered me.

"Hey, Cassie, long time no see." He peeked over my shoulder to check for G Double D bringing up the rear.

"Yeah, that's how I know this isn't a chance meeting."

"I had to hear it from you. Is it true that G might sell your contract to Megalos?"

"Why? You worried about how it's gonna affect your deal with Explicit Content?" I tried to step aside him to enter the ladies' room, but Darnell blocked my way. "Don't be. It has nothing to do with you. You're in good now no matter where I go." Which wasn't totally true, but this was Darnell and I couldn't have cared less. I couldn't afford to care.

"It's got everything to do with me, Cassie, because I'm worried about you."

"Ni—" I caught myself. "Please."

Darnell grabbed my arm. "I don't blame you for feeling that way about me. But what I want to know is, Why don't you feel the same way about G? 'Cause he got a lotta money. Phat rides? A mansion? Why aren't you worried that he's going to play you like he's played all of us?" I had to smile. His perception meant my ruse was going well. The boys were discussing it, and no one suspected a setup. "You think this is funny? You think I'm just saying that to get a rise out of you? You getting off on my jealousy?"

"What if he is, D? How are you going to protect me when you're the one who delivered me to him in the first place?"

Then it was Darnell's turn to grin. "Cut the bullshit, Cassie. You were gonna get next to G whether you found me out or not. Remember you spent the night with him before you figured out the attack on my studio was fixed."

I didn't know how he found out I knew, but I didn't dare ask. And I was past caring to defend myself. Instead I tried to flip the script. "So how do we make it right between us, D? Let me guess. We sign a management contract right here and now so you can represent me at our meeting, and you and I can run away together to Megalos and live happily ever after."

Darnell looked as if I'd stung him. He dropped his head, then quietly said, "I did what I did, and I'm sorry. I really am, because I fell for you and lost you over it. But you gotta admit, Cassie. Even though I came into this going for mine, I still looked out for you."

"Only because you tied your ends to mine," I said. I turned around to leave and he grabbed my arm one more time.

"Cassie, I didn't come here to ask you to leave Explicit Content or sign with Megalos, not leave, not sign. I'm not here on industry shit. I came here to ask you to come back to me. It'll be sticky at first, but we can figure it out. G's first and last concern is money, and you and I together can make a lot for him. But even if he gets pissed off and cuts us loose, it's all good 'cause then we'll be free of him. We can go to Megalos, create our own label, or whatever you want."

And I seriously considered it. But then I remembered who was saying it. He believed the Megalos opportunity was real, and so I wondered if he would even be there if not for that. Besides, I had to follow through with my plan for the sake of the one person who had redeemed herself as far as I was concerned.

"There ain't a damn thing you can do for me, Darnell, save leave me the hell alone," I said. As I broke from him and headed to the ladies' room, I had no idea if he believed what I had just said. All I knew was that I wished I didn't believe it myself.

CHAPTER 25

A DEAL GONE AWRY

Three days before the deal went down, Genevieve almost bailed.

During a recording session, she called me in a panic on the cell. I waved Darnell to stop as I calmed her down. "G, I have to cut this short tonight," I said. "My moms needs me."

He wasted no time calling the driver to have him get me. As I grabbed and put on my jacket, G joked, "Ayo, Cassie, when you gonna introduce a brother to Ma Dukes?"

Darnell scoffed. "I never even got to meet her moms."

"Nigga, you ain't me."

"I told you not to say that around me," I said. Then to front nice, I kissed G on the cheek. "You'll meet my moms soon." Then I ran out the door.

When I got to Genevieve's crib, I saw what triggered her anxiety. G had followed my suggestion and called back Johnetta Lawrence to ask for two million. She countered with one point five, and he accepted. All over the floor around Genevieve's computer sat crumpled attempts to print a fake check that looked real.

"I can't do this, Cassie. This is too much. We're not that kind of people. This is going to backfire, and you're going to get hurt."

"Mom, we're supposed to have lunch with the man on Friday. If you bail now, G'll get mad, then suspicious. Then I'm really gonna be in trouble. You gotta help me get out of there the way we planned."

"Cassandra, I know lawyers," said Genevieve. "I have access to—"

"Who do you think we're dealing with here?"

"You don't have to yell at me. . . ."

"Mom, the kind of lawyers you know cannot help me with this."

"We can go to the authorities. . . ."

I had to get raw with Genevieve. "I sleep with the man, Mom. How long are they going to expect me to wear a wire until they're satisfied they have enough to put them all away so I can have my life back? What if one night he busts me, and the authorities don't come in time? And then what happens to Leila, Yolanda, and all the other girls who are there against their will? We have to do this my way."

Genevieve grabbed a crumpled sheet off the floor and thrust it in my face. "Your way is going to land us all in prison if not killed!"

"Mom, this shit runs deeper than some contract dispute with an ordinary record label," I said. "We gotta fight gully with gully." My own words sparked an idea. "If I can get cash, will you make one more call to G before Friday? He might still be with Darnell at the studio."

Before long Genevieve and I had rehearsed the conversation several times. If not for the circumstances, I might have enjoyed directing my mother for the performance of both our lives. My mother really was a great actress, and I felt sad that her talent did not take her were she wanted to be. But then again, look where I allowed mine take me.

After doing a breathing exercise from her acting days to relax herself, Genevieve picked up the telephone and called the studio. "This is Johnetta Lawrence calling for Mr. Downs. His assistant told me he still might be there. . . ." I figured Darnell must have answered the telephone. "Gregory, how are you? . . . Oh, I've had better days. . . . Yeah, I'm calling with some bad news. . . . Mega-los reneged. . . ." Genevieve held the phone away from her ear as G yelled and cursed. "I understand how you feel. I quit over this. . . ."

Then Genevieve chuckled. "I appreciate the offer, but actually I have a proposition for you. . . . I've been wanting for years to strike out on my own, and this might be my chance. If I can deliver cash, will you still release Cassandra and Leila so that I can sign them to my own label? . . ." She gave another coy laugh. "Do I really have to tell you about the kind of connections you can make in the entertainment industry? . . . OK, so let's meet as planned on Friday, and we'll work it out." And then in a brilliant act of im-provisation, Genevieve added, "Gregory, I cannot thank you enough for this. You're doing a lot more than closing a business deal here. You're turning a life around. Thank you."

"Thanks, Mom. You worked that lovely. Now promise me that you won't make that last telephone call until you leave for Justin's on Friday."

She hesitated, then said, "I promise."

Now I had to pray that I could get one and a half million dollars in two days, and I only had one possible source.

I pretended to make an appointment at Goldman, Sachs in search of financial advice. The driver dropped me off in front of their Broad Street building. I entered through the front, slipped out through the side, and rushed down the block to their competitor.

I raced into the office and told the receptionist, "I need to see Diego Mirabal right now. It's a life or death emergency."

"Are you a client?"

"Tell him Leila needs him now!"

She called him on the intercom, and Diego came racing out of his office. At the sight of me, he huffed in disappointment. I pushed past him into his office, and he followed.

"Cassandra, if you think that anytime you need some extra cash, you're going to barge into my life and extort me . . ."

"I couldn't give a fuck about you," I said. "I'm here for Leila."

The sound of her name made his eyes dance. "How is she?" he asked.

And I told him. The man broke down in tears, but I made no attempt to console him. His tears did me no good. I needed his money.

"It's just a scam," I said. "You'll get it all back."

"I don't care about that," said Diego, and I believed him. "Come back tomorrow around noon. I should have it for you then."

"I can't do that." I scribbled my mother's address on a notepad on his desk. "You have to see that it gets here."

"OK." As I turned to leave, Diego called my name. "Please find some way to tell Leila that I miss her."

"You'd better hope that this works so you can tell her yourself," I said.

And I hoped that when he did, Leila would haul back and slap Diego across his pathetic grill.

Before heading to Justin's that Friday, G, Leila, and I stopped at the Explicit Content offices to pick up the contracts, sign other paperwork, and the like. While I paced Jen's office, Leila chatted up Jen, who said, "You know, I'm really sad to see you gals go. I don't have to tell you that there's way too much testosterone in this goddamn place. Promise me you'll come back?"

"No doubt," said Leila. "Hey, do me a favor, Jen? I never kept any of my press kits, 'cause, you know, I don't have anyone to give 'em to. But now that I'm leaving, I'd like to have 'em if you have any left."

"Sure, hon. We probably have some extras in the basement. Just come with me." Then Jen turned to me, "Cassie, would you like yours, too?"

"Nah, I've gotten all I need from y'all. Thanks."

As I waited, I took one last look at the tear sheets of Explicit Content publicity spread across the table in the reception area. Only then did I learn that Cryciss had been expelled from a state college for allegedly running a prostitution ring out of his dormitory and did eighteen months before he signed with Explicit Content. The prosecutor slapped his wrist because Cryciss insisted that the five female classmates involved consented to his pimping. They claimed Cryciss drugged them, but he insisted they drugged themselves to deal with their decision to have sex for money. "They were tired of the broke student thing," he said in one interview. "They wanted mad, fast money, so they got down with me. But you know how women be, wanting it but fronting like they don't." It hurt the prosecution that four of the women would deposit and eventually spend the money they found on their desks after recovering from their blackouts. After the first and last time, the fifth woman took the money to the resident assistant who heard her story and then called the campus police. Fucking Cryciss went to college just to hunt for prey. I knew it.

My cell rang. G had called from downstairs. "Cassie, what you still doing up there? We're all out here waiting for you." When I left the building, he, Leila, Freight, and two more guards were already piled into the running car.

When we arrived at Justin's, Genevieve stood in the doorway already in character. Although the restaurant does not open until five, Jen had made a call to the manager. He opened the place and the kitchen just for us to hold our meeting with complete privacy.

Leila didn't recognize her at first. But when she did, Genevieve cut her off by thrusting her hand forward for a handshake. "It's such a pleasure to finally meet you in person, Leila. I'm Johnetta Lawrence."

Leila rolled with it as I knew she would. "Yes, I know. I've read all about you." Switching to that girlish charm, she turned to G and whispered in his ear, "G, she's the same rep who signed—"

"Yeah, yeah, I know," G said, cutting her off with a stern look. Of course, he had to front. We all introduced ourselves, and he motioned for all of us to sit down. I took the seat next to Genevieve.

Freight sat at a separate table close by, facing the door.

"Mr. Downs," Genevieve started.

"Please call me G."

"G." And she said it as if it were an honor to do so. I sipped my water, hoping to hide my shock. She wasn't Genevieve Rivers, who would have continued to call him Mr. Downs or Gregory because such informality with strangers made her uncomfortable. She truly was Johnetta Lawrence, former A and R executive for Megalos Records with questionable connections. The waiter came by to place bread and water on our table, and I couldn't help but think how fitting it was. "Thank you so much for indulging me by allowing Cassandra and Leila to sit in on this meeting. I know you would've preferred to meet with me alone."

"She wanted to see for herself that y'all had truly squashed any beef you might've had before negotiating this transfer," G explained to Leila and me. I worried what Genevieve might do if he continued to discuss me as if I were a piece of real estate.

But my moms stayed true to the game, turning to Leila and me and asking, "And have you?"

"Yes," Leila, said, smiling and nodding. At first I thought she was just getting into it for the sake of the scheme. But she looked me in the eye and said, "Cassie and me, we've been too close for too long. No matter what happens, we're always gonna be friends. We just gotta be. I realize that now."

"Yeah, and even though we're both hot in our own right, we're much better as a team," I said. "Together we'll go farther and last longer."

Genevieve reached for a suitcase by her feet and placed it on the table. "So we agreed on one and a half million in cash." "But first the contracts." Nice touch, I thought. Her hesitancy to hand over the money before having the contracts in hand gave the whole affair the sound of legitimacy.

G called Freight over to the table. Freight reached into the inside pocket of his blazer, pulled out our contracts, and handed them to G. He smoothed them out on the table, one next to the other. Genevieve spun the suitcase around, and then Leila gasped.

"Nothing," she said. "I'm just getting a little emotional." It was no lie, because when I followed Leila's intense gaze, I discovered that she had spotted the monogram on the suitcase and recognized the initials: D.E.M.

Before G noticed them, asked questions, and found us out before time, I tipped over my glass of water. The four of us leaped to our feet, grabbing everything within our reach. G saved the contracts while I lunged for my glass. Genevieve slammed the suitcase shut and held it over her head. The server came to assist us in cleaning the mess. While this commotion occurred, I caught my mom's attention and gestured toward the monogram. Genevieve got my hint so when we sat down again, she laid the suitcase back on the table with the monogram facing her.

"OK, let's get this over with." G Double D picked up Leila's contract and tore it in half.

Genevieve opened the suitcase again, pulled out a blue-backed document and handed it to Leila. "Once you sign this, I can say . . . well, I haven't thought of a name for my label yet. This all happened so quickly."

Sometimes Leila can be brilliant. She twisted her face at G and said, "Wait, I thought we were signing with Megalos."

She truly worried G. "C'mon, Leila, you know how it is. Folks jump from label to label. Companies merge and consolidate and shit." He picked up my contract and cradled it in his hands.

"But she just said her label doesn't even have a name."

"Leila, sign the damned thing."

"Well, I want to have a lawyer look at it first." Just like a chick who done learned her lesson.

Genevieve used Leila's improvisation to sharpen her character. "Leila, with so much money involved, I can't promise to keep this offer on the table." She stuttered, then said, "How about if I offer you a signing bonus?"

"Talk to me," said Leila. She got off on going tête-à-tête with my moms, who'd barely acknowledged her all these years except to trash her behind her back. And for a second I saw that my mother recognized the flame in Leila that had drawn me to her long ago.

"What did you get with Explicit Content?"

"I ain't get shit with them," Leila answered as she glared at G. "No advance, no signing bonus, not even a freakin' cell phone. Explicit Content gave me nothing but—"

"I can't do it," G said as he stared at my contract. "I can't let you have Cassie. I promised her an album, and she's gonna get it. She belongs to Explicit Content."

My back froze and I looked to Genevieve for help. "G, the deal is for the both of them. I want Cassandra and Leila as a duo."

"Fuck it, then." G summoned Freight. "We're out. Tell 'em to unlock the door." Freight rose from the table and headed to the back of the restaurant.

I could not believe it. A thousand things ran through my head, but only one thing came out of my mouth. "G, you just fucked over Leila. She's got no contract with Explicit Content, and without me she's not getting one with her."

"Look, I know Leila's your girl, so we'll look out for her," G said. "She can always work for us at the label."

"Hold up," Leila said, her voice tight with genuine confusion.

"She doesn't want that," I yelled. "She never wanted that. That's why you dogged her in the first place."

My moms tried to intervene, "Is it money, G? If you just let me make a telephone call, I might be able to . . ." If he gave her that opportunity, Genevieve would call the police. Hopefully, they were already at the SoHo office and the Glen Ridge mansion as we spoke.

"Ayo, this ain't about money, Johnetta, so just back the fuck off," G said.

Then Johnetta Lawrence became a mother. "Don't you dare speak to me that way. You not only double-crossed me, you deceived these poor young girls who trusted you with their aspirations and—"

Freight returned as the server shadowed his massive frame. "G, you OK?"

"This trick's buggin', but I'm a'ight. Just unlock the door so Cassie and I can bounce." He turned to Leila and said, "You do what you want to do."

And as if shit had not already gone far off course, when the server unlocked the door, Darnell rushed into the restaurant to blow us off the map. Freight dodged him, yoking Darnell around the neck.

"Darnell, what the fuck you doing here?" said G.

"Question is what the fuck you think you doing, 'cause that bitch right there ain't Johnetta Lawrence," said Darnell.

My heart raced as quickly as Leila's eyes blinked. "What the hell you talking about, Darnell?"

"I don't know what G's up to, Cassie, but that woman ain't no A and R exec. You know I know who's who and what's what in this muthafuckin' game, and when that bitch called the studio that night looking for G and her name ain't register, I knew something was up, man. I checked her out, Cassie. The trick ain't who she says she is. Johnetta Lawrence ain't no A and R executive at Megalos Records. She's just an assistant in their legal department. And she's a white chick in their Atlanta office."

Relieved that Darnell had no idea that I knew that, I had to play the card he dealt me. "G, is that true?"

Genevieve pushed the scene forward. "No, Cassandra, it isn't." Then she looked to G. "Who is this man?"

"Muthafucka, did it ever occur to you that I got took in this shit, too?" said G as he finally rose to his feet. I never saw him that furious since he tackled me on the driveway when I could no longer pretend to not know just how shady Explicit Content was. After all he had done *to* me, he still became outraged at the thought of my walking away after whatever he done *for* me. And now he yelled at Darnell from that same warped sense of loyalty. "Who are you bustin' in here accusing me of running some kind of game on Cassie like you some hero on a white horse? Same muthafucka who played her in the first place, that's who. Always tryin' to emulate me, but you can't even maintain at your little level, let alone try to stomp with a dawg like me. Ayo, Freight, just take this muthafucka out to the ride and keep him there until I get to the bottom of this."

Freight tightened his grip on Darnell and dragged him, kicking toward the door. "Get the fuck off me, man!"

"You sure you gonna be all right?" Freight asked.

G looked around into the face of the frightened Justin's staff. Then he faced Leila, moms, and me. He smirked just like a man who had seen *Scarface* too many times and turned back to Freight. "I'ma be lovely." Even though he had no idea which way was up, he was confident that none of us posed any real threat to him.

No sooner did the server lock the door behind Freight and Darnell did Leila yank a gun out of her waistband and point it at G's forehead. The staff screamed and dove, but the chaos didn't make her flinch. G stood there with the gun in his grill and his hands in the air.

"Ms. Rivers, take Cassie's contract and tear it up," Leila said. Genevieve did as she asked and stuffed the scraps into the suitcase.

"Now, Cassie, you and your moms take Diego's money and get out of here."

"Ms. Rivers?" G said. "Hold up. This is Ma Dukes?"

"Shut up," Leila said as she pressed the barrel against his head.

"Leila, where did hell did you get that gun?"

"Let's just say I borrowed it from Jen this afternoon."

"Cassandra, let's go."

"I'm not leaving without Leila," I told my moms. I said to Leila, "You wouldn't leave without me, and I ain't going without you."

Tears of rage streamed down Leila's face as she aimed at G Double D. "I'ma be fine now, so just go!"

"You ain't gonna be fine," said G. "Too late for you to ever be fine."

"I said shut up, G!"

" 'Cause Freight's gonna come back in here, and one of us is gonna catch ya. And if by any chance we don't now, we will later. No matter how it goes down, Leila, you're just gonna be yet another promising but dead rapper."

"If it's like that . . ." Then Leila cocked the gun.

And I truly believe she would have shot him had the police not busted into the restaurant through the back door. They told Leila to drop the gun, and she did. Then they put cuffs on her and hauled her away.

Genevieve and I left Justin's in time to see paramedics carry a bloody Darnell into an ambulance. I begged the cops to let me go with him, that I would answer all their questions at the hospital. They granted permission, and I hopped into the back of the ambulance before it sped away.

Over the next three days, Darnell slipped in out and of consciousness while he lay handcuffed in his hospital bed. In the alley next to Justin's, Freight gave him such a severe beating that even though the police had everyone in custody, they still posted a uniformed guard at Darnell's door. I stayed by him throughout his bouts of consciousness, and Darnell confessed to me.

He had idolized G Double D and always wanted to be down with Explicit Content. It didn't matter at all whether the label was dirty or clean, because from the time he stole that Roland W-30 keyboard, he was a man who could go either way.

"When I met G, I wanted so much to impress him," he said, "I told him that I'd followed the cat who bought the keyboard home from the store, watched him through the window as he wrapped it, and then broke into the basement to steal it. And none of that shit was true. I wasn't that fucked up then. But remember when you teased me about poisoning the DJ at the wedding to put myself on? You were right. I did."

I was done not asking questions, no matter how much I might not like the answer. "Was it your idea to drug Leila?" If he had said yes, I would've never found out the rest of the story, because I would've walked out on him forever.

"No, never. I swear."

Whether they were moving CDs or heroin, Darnell felt he could be an asset to G Double D, especially when so many of his clients were hustlers who wanted to rhyme. But the ability of these neighborhood dealers to spit on the mic were confined to their fantasies of large bills and screaming women. Then he met Leila and me and discovered a way into Explicit Content.

But largely because of me, Leila and I refused to sign a formal agreement with him of any kind. Still Darnell approached G Double D, pretending he had one, and he finally convinced G to attend Da Corridor at SOB's. They had agreed that if G wanted to sign us, he would break off Darnell with a production contract. Perhaps heeding his male artists' complaints about signing women to the label, G probably always intended to split us apart. When he saw Leila—a sexy Latina who talked hard and dirty—G decided that she would be the right choice. Then he sidestepped Darnell by signing Leila as a solo artist. Darnell never knew until I showed up on his doorstep that day in early March.

And that started the drama between Darnell and G Double D that Leila and I were too hungry in our own ways to stay clear.

Through his connections, Darnell learned about Leila's problems at the label and her upcoming surprise appearance at the 205 Club. Knowing that G Double D would be present, Darnell convinced me to enter. He wanted to rub in G's face that he had the true talent behind Sabrina Steelo and Fatal Beauty. But after placing on genuine merit and rushing his table, I peaked G's interest in a new way. When he wondered if he had signed the wrong bitch, he meant that perhaps I actually had all those qualities he thought Leila did when he signed her.

The freestyle fiasco at Leila's birthday party actually was G's test of my mettle not my skill. Only after I signed, did G admit to Darnell that he had ordered Hi-Jack to pen Leila's lyrics. Darnell never brought me there to be humiliated. Rather, G told him that he wanted to discuss bringing both of us to Explicit Content. And D believed him, doubting that G would invite him to an industry party at his home if he were not sincere. (Leila told me she only agreed to cheat in the hopes of chasing me away from the label when she learned that G's priorities were with crime and not music.) G liked the way I handled myself in that situation, showing a cool head in a stressful situation instead of wilding out the way Cryciss or Keef might have. He hoped that I would be so desperate to redeem myself that I would jump to sign with Explicit Content. But by that time, Darnell had started to hear rumors about Explicit Content's shady dealings with its talent, and he wanted to avoid getting crossed by G again.

So G Double D propositioned Darnell. If he convinced me to sign with the label, he would reward him with positions in its music and later its crime ventures. Darnell agreed, but he had to hedge his bets. Fearful that he would lose another artist to G without anything to show for it, Darnell began to romance me, hoping to deepen my allegiance to him before I signed with Explicit Content.

The last thing either of them expected was that I would refuse to even meet with G Double D. Even though our relationship had gotten personal, Darnell's words alone would not convince me to sign with Explicit Content. If anything, a sudden hard sell would raise my suspicions, so Darnell took a gamble that if I had a bona fide recording contract that enabled me to get back at Leila, I might not be principled enough to continue walking away from G's offer.

So they orchestrated the attack to scare me into meeting with G. Darnell warned him I would never sign an agreement like Leila or any of the others had. So G enticed me with a legitimate deal and concessions to some of my unusual requests. From there the plan was to allow me to believe that bringing Darnell to the label was my idea.

"We said that one day the three of us would be sipping Krug in a penthouse suite on Grammy night, laughing about it all," said Darnell. "That as long as you were making your music and getting paid, you wouldn't care what else we did. You wouldn't stay mad at us."

Then G Double D saw something in me that made him confident that if he eased me into his way of life, I eventually would come to not only enjoy it but to assume a major role in it. And that made him cross the line that turned a business agreement into a personal conflict. "And then the smart chick that everyone tried to play took down Explicit Content," Darnell said with a painful smile.

He asked me to forgive him. Although I made no similar confessions, I asked him for the same. And then Darnell slipped away one last time.

The morning of the day we met Genevieve, she tipped off the police. I had given her detailed information so that they would take her seriously and organize their raids at the most opportune times. While Leila, G Double D, and I met with her at Justin's, they raided the Glen Ridge mansion and the SoHo loft and arrested virtually everyone. As for the office staff and independent contractors like Andi, even when the government could prove they knew about the crime rings, they couldn't always link them to the actual operations. The majority of the folks they could connect copped pleas or turned state's evidence.

Yeribel bailed out Yolanda and forbade her to contact me. Eventually, we did meet at my attorney's office because he wanted to depose her for the upcoming trials. Yeribel accompanied Yolanda and heard her corroborate my version of events, at least what she knew. When the meeting ended, Yolanda walked around the table to hug me before she left. "Maybe when all this is over . . ." she said. I knew that it would take years for all this to end, but I just nodded my head and thanked her. Yeribel then led her sister out of the room. She gave me a last look filled with pity, and I found myself being grateful it wasn't a look of hate. Satisfied that Yolanda was a victim, the prosecutor dropped the few charges he had filed against her. In fact, as the multitude of trials unfolded, it came to light who were the women who eventually participated willingly and who were the women who were imprisoned against their will.

G Double D never stood trial. He posted bail and immediately disappeared. Some say he actually ran from the shady characters that gave him the money to start up Explicit Content. Others say they got to him already. The last thing he said to me as he walked out of the courtroom after posting bail was "Angel with the dirty face."

With G gone and much of his resources at his disposal, Hi-Jack hired Johnnie Cochran and beat the raps, the only one to so far. Jack vows to keep Explicit Content alive and even told reporters that in the end I would be sorry I turned my back on the label. When asked if he were threatening my life, he said, "Of course not. I'm talking about her career. How many time you bitches need to be told that trash talkin's all part of the game?" But right now he's too busy defending Explicit Content against a multimillion-dollar civil suit filed by Sean "P. Diddy" Combs over the impact of what happened at Justin's. It's the only funny thing to come out of this mess.

Cryciss and Third Eye went back to prison for violating their paroles. On account of the shooting back at NV, Keef was already there. Even though their lawyers—public defenders all—moved to have their cases tried separately, all three have it in for Hi-Jack, who they believed hung them out to dry on some Puff–Shyne drama. Because of their threats against him, the state correction's department shipped each of them to separate facilities.

Jen got caught out there with her hands in everything, and Papa Om's loot couldn't save either of them. Their involvement breathed life into the gangsta rap controversy as it lay on its deathbed from media overexposure, exhaustion by the intellectuals, and the resignation of hip-hop activists. All of us had come to accept that hip-hop's seamy alter ego had become the dominant personality. Then Jen's role in the Explicit Content scandal came to light and, for better or worse, heads began to care. Thrilled to be tossed such an exotic bone, the mainstream media exaggerated her role in the operations and painted her as the Dragon Lady of Explicit Content. As they damned well should have, Asian-American leaders lashed out at the stereotype. And even though Jen had done a lot she had to pay for, I actually was glad to see some women's groups protest that she had been hit with such hard time while Hi-Jack walked. The one who surprised and touched me most was Shelby J. Lee who wrote an open letter to the hip-hop community that spread over the Internet like a virus, calling on Asian and Black hip-hop heads to come together, own up to their prejudices toward each other, *and put a stop to the cross-cultural coonin' that keeps us all down.* I hear that. Especially after being embarrassed on the stand during Jack's trial when I testified to seeing Jen with the surgical mask and *emery board* and admitted resorting to the Korean manicurist stereotype.

Without the money to make bail, Primo got sent up, too, while he awaits trial. He sent word through the prison grapevine to Leila that when they're both out, he'd like to meet with her and maybe patch things up. When she responded less enthusiastically than he would have liked, he complained that he had tried to protect her as best as he could and for that he was entitled to a chance to make it right. I knew Leila had grown a lot from all she'd been through because she had her lawyer tell Primo's that if that were true, he would have convinced the others to let her go. "I told him, 'You tell him that the only way to make amends to me now is to leave me the fuck alone.' "

And she told Diego the same thing, too. In the beginning, he visited her every chance he had—not so much to support her as to alleviate his guilt—and she saw right through him. She told me he'd spend his entire visit crying apologies over what happened and his role in it, especially how after G's thugs demanded he quit Leila and put her out, he never questioned that she might be in danger. That he probably thought she had whatever was coming to her because she insisted on being a rapper. "I let him for a while," she said of his remorseful visits. "Just because I needed someone to apologize for what happened to me." And when she was convinced that Diego meant it, she finally told him, "I love you, Diego, and I forgive you, but I never want see or hear from you again." And knowing Leila like I do, she meant every word of it.

To his credit, Diego still helps her while she's on lockdown. She thinks it's just because his wife finally left him. Diana stuck by him even when his company fired him when his link to the scandal hit the papers even though he hadn't done anything illegal and had used his own money. She appeared in courtroom for both days of Diego's testimony during Hi-Jack's trial. But paying Leila's legal fees and stacking her commissary was too much for Diana and she finally bounced. I'm still not crazy about the man, and I'm glad Leila's done with him, but I did feel a little bad for him. In the end the guy came through, and that had to count for something. But all Leila could say was, "Well, I'm glad I cut him loose before he lost everything. Now he can't say I was with him for his money. Let that be his consolation."

Leila had broken up with Vance at the same time she told him about signing with Explicit Content. After going over the top with his congratulations, he got bent out of shape when Leila warned him that she might not be seeing him as much. Unlike Diego, who took Leila's hip-hop ambitions seriously even if he didn't approve, Vance always treated it like a hobby she'd outgrow, especially under his unsolicited guidance. So for Leila to tell him that record- ing her album might take time away from him offended Vance on don't-you-know-you're-lucky-to-have-me shit. So once again, Leila was like fuck that *güero* and as usual I was right there with her. She never heard from him again, even when she was all over the news, but Leila's more than cool with that, as am I. But I bet Vance is somewhere getting in good with some 'hood rats with his I-used-to-fuck-Fatal-Beauty stories.

On the contrary, the drama reunited Leila and Junior, at least as friends for now. Just like Diego, she had no intention of cutting him off, but she never got the opportunity to tell him about her deal. She had made a date with him, and as usual he'd flaked. Next thing she knew, G had forced her to move to Glen Ridge, and she never spoke to Junior again. At first, he thought Leila just wasn't speaking to him for standing her up as per their pattern. But then he called the apartment and got Diego's new mistress. Thinking she was Leila, he started in on his dirty apology mack, and only when she threatened in Spanglish to call the police did he realize something was up. Not until he saw Leila on a video did he realize she had signed with Explicit Content. When he showed up at a club and tried to approach her after she performed, Freight dragged him outside and pistol-whipped him in a dark alley. Ju- nior had enough balls to do more than Diego did, though. He went to the cops, but the label convinced them that Freight was doing his job and keeping stalker fans away from its artists. Thinking that Leila could have called him if and whenever she wanted to, Junior figured she was down with it and let it go.

Then the truth broke, and he has been in Leila's corner ever since. Leila copped a plea for having the gun and assaulting Jen in the basement to steal it, so she didn't have to prove herself by at- tending a trial, but he went upstate every time he said he would, and he wrote her in between visits. Leila's taking it slow with him though, because she wants to be sure his interest is not about her celebrity or notoriety. I think that's smart of her and hope Junior comes through, but that remains to be seen. So far so good.

With Junior came Kurt. He's called a couple of times and even stopped by my mother's to check in on me, and I can't say I haven't appreciated it. Even after I got a real deal with Megalos, he never once brought up my putting him on even though I waited for him to. He did drop a bombshell, though, when he told me he had a son with the girl he cheated on me with, although he claims they're no longer together. No matter, since I'm not planning on hooking up with him like that. He's got a friend so long as he continues to be one to me, but that's it. And one of the most important of the many things I learned during my time with Explicit Content, to have a true friend is to have a lot.

CHAPTER 27

THE COVEN

I thought the Explicit Content scandal would make me untouchable, but a few major labels actually rushed to sign me once I was cleared of all wrongdoing. I had no illusions that their interest in me had anything to do with my skills. Disgusted by the frenzy, I left Genevieve to field the offers.

The tabloids got it twisted when I eventually signed with Megalos, reveling in the irony, especially when Sony offered me much more money and Arista wanted more albums. Maybe Megalos did it because they themselves wanted to exploit the fact that my mother pretended to represent them in our attempts to free me from Explicit Content. The true reason I signed with Megalos was because it was the only company that offered me my own label.

See, I have no intentions of staying with Megalos. I signed with them so I could access all the resources they had to establish and grow the label. But I didn't kid myself for a second that the label was ever truly mine. My plan from jump was to learn the ropes and mind my ends and then eventually go independent by buying the label from Megalos. Maybe all the artists I sign will own it with me.

I call my new label the Coven because I intend to sign only female artists who are trying to do their thing on their own terms even if folks hate on them for it. Freaks, molls, and tricks need not apply. If your idea of sexual liberation is being willing to do whatever a man wants, save your postage. If you can match the best of the men without resorting to the dirt boys do, holla. I'ma find me a white girl who's *not* the female Eminem. I'ma sign a fierce dyke who is *out* of the closet. And if I happen to find the rare brother who's man enough to be down with all this on and off track, I just might put him on, too.

But of course, this is after I finish Leila's debut. She wrote a lot while on lockdown and has really blossomed as a writer. Her lyrics are still a bit choppy in places, but nothing I can't help her smooth out in the studio. If you ask her, Leila'll tell you she's better just because she had little else to do but write on some practice-makes-perfect shit. But that's only a little part of it, in my opinion. I think Leila's a better writer because being on lockdown forced her to write what's real. Instead of rhyming about how fly she dressed or how good she could fuck or anything she thought other people might want to hear, she wrote verse after verse from the heart.

Oddly enough, none of Leila's rhymes are about Explicit Content. At first, it bothered me. I worried that she might be in denial about what happened, and that it'd be much better for her to let go of all that pain and anger, if only on paper. But then I considered that perhaps nothing as ugly as Explicit Content could ever sully Leila in that place where she truly lives. The experience might have taken its toll on her mind and body, but it never touched her soul.

Some of her best rhymes are actually about me, and I have to tell you, not all of them are brimming with love and forgiveness. One in particular had me in tears and not once did it call me a name or prey on my insecurities. All it did was call me out on my many hypocrisies.

In my cell
With this gel
I find I must tell
The truth about us
Even if it's hell.

Yang to ying?
Respect or bling?
That's the thing.
We both wanted
All the same things.

But just in Bri
Could you see
Divinity.
But you never saw
The divine in me.

On me you blamed
"She just wants fame."
But when chance came
Without a blink
You rolled the same.

Riches, yes,
I did expect
But why never suspect
What I craved most
Was your respect?

All those times
You wrote rhymes
But I paid dimes
So you blew up
'Cause I buffed your shine.

I chose foul
Threw in the towel
Went on the prowl
Said let her hang
From her own dowel.

But I did wrong
And I paid long
When I got conned
When I lost sight
You were my word, my bond.

Yet as much as you talked
You, too, got mad caught
Not much made you balk.
Bri's fame and bank grew,
She betrayed her high thoughts.

But don't ever deny
Before me you shy
On my spirit you fly.
And when drama comes huntin'
Behind me you hide.

Fatal's turned a bend
And wants the hurt to end
Rebuild with Bri again.
We erred, we lost, we lived to tell
What it means to be a friend.

I went to visit her upstate after she mailed me that rhyme, and we talked liked we hadn't in a very long time.

Without a doubt, the drama pushed the sales of my first album to the top of the Billboard charts with over four hundred thousand units sold. With the mainstream media all over the Explicit Content trials, I knew that my joint would sell regardless of what I recorded. Still, the first week's figures surprised me because I knew so many fellas were hating on me for bringing down Explicit Content. The response gave me a boost, and I got a real boost from a photo I saw in the *New York Daily News* of three young girls standing in front of a record store, each holding up my CD *A Unique Steelo*. I avoided reading my album reviews for days though, expecting the critics to crucify me on some just-because shit. I learned my lesson about that after surfing the Internet and learning that some thought me a sellout biting the hand that fed me.

But then one day Genevieve called me into the kitchen and sat me down. She handed me a scrapbook I had never seen before. I thought maybe she was finally showing me the scrapbook from her acting days and had transferred it into a new cover. But when I opened it, I realized that my mother had been collecting all my positive album reviews. Unlike that slam book I had read in the Explicit Content waiting room last year, these clippings had nothing but encouraging words about me as an artist. My favorite reviews cautioned listeners to not confuse my joint with the usual Explicit Content fare or to sleep on my skills out of a righteous disgust with the label in particular and the thinning line between gansta rap and wanna-be-gangsta reality overall. *On every track of this poignant debut, Steelo displays a heart nurtured under the wing of true hip-hop only to be wounded in the shadows of its underbelly,* one reviewer wrote. *She should be given the opportunity to heal and grow. Then maybe together we can usher the overdue renaissance in hip-hop music that we've been longing for.*

I made a crack about my father appearing now that I had all this publicity around me. "Maybe he will, maybe he won't, Cassandra," she said. "But I want you to understand that his not being a part of your life is as much my doing as it is his." Then she patted my hand and said, "Anyway, you're a grown woman now and I know you'll do the right thing whatever that may be." Then she told me who he was.

He's neither a big Hollywood player or a nameless face in the mail room. He's one of those actors you always recognize in minor roles but never remember his name. Even I didn't know who he was until she ran down a list of bit parts he had in big movies until one clicked my memory.

When I asked my moms why she decided to tell me this after all this time, she said she hadn't wanted me to pursue him with any illusions that he might help me achieve my ambitions. Whether Genevieve thought he could or would, she admits she really didn't know. But she didn't want me seeking him out for that reason. Now that I had achieved success on my own accord, she felt I was ready to know. But I think Leila was kinda right about something. Mom knows now that whether I go after my father or not, she's not going to lose me.

Leila tried to convince me to seek him out when I went to LA to promote my album. Instead, I bailed out of that luxury hotel Megalos booked for me and stayed with my aunt Treece and her family. Kerwyn shocked me when he dropped his cool pose to run to me and throw his arms around me. "He's been so worried about you," Uncle Marques explained. That made me feel much better. I can't say I'll never look for my father or turn him away cold should he come looking for me. I'm just saying that for now I've got enough meaningful relationships to rebuild without checking for him.

As for my career, so far the highlight has been going to my old job for an album signing and realizing that I had produced an album that sisters stormed Tower Records on release day to buy. That and knowing that in less than in a month, I'd be back in the studio helping Leila do the same thing.

EXPLICIT CONTENT

BLACK ARTEMIS

A CONVERSATION WITH BLACK ARTEMIS

Q. Where did you get the pen name Black Artemis and why do you use it?

A. It's the norm in hip-hop subculture for artists to adopt personas so I thought I should too. Everyone does it—rappers, DJs, graffiti artists, and even dancers, so why not writers? There are other reasons as well, but *Explicit Content* is not based on anything I have personally experienced in the music industry. I did not adopt a pen name because this is a semi-autobiographical tale and I needed to protect myself or anyone else. In fact, I have never had a job in the music industry! I am not a rapper nor did I ever aspire to be one. I just did what a good writer should, and that's conduct extensive research so my fictional world would ring true.

As for the specific name I chose, I have always been a fan of mythology, and the figure that spoke to me the most was the Greek goddess Artemis. Artemis fascinated me because she was both a warrior and a virgin. Mind you, being a virgin in Greek mythology means something deeper than not having experienced sexual intercourse; a virgin actually was a woman that no man owned. So Artemis is known particularly for having an independence considered unusual for women. Of all the goddesses I read about, Artemis was the one I related to the most.

So why Black Artemis? While I'm not African-American, I do identify as a Black woman. Ethnically and culturally, I am Puerto Rican and Dominican, and my people have a rich African heritage that is often overlooked in favor of our European and indigenous history and culture. I wanted to adopt the name of an African goddess, but I did not find one whose mythology compelled me as much as Artemis' story. So I took on the pseudonym Black Artemis to both embrace the iconic power of Artemis and hold fast to the Black identity of which I am so proud.

Q. So if you're not African-American, why did you choose an African-American character as the protagonist of Explicit Content?

A. The most important reason is simply that *Explicit Content* just *is* Cassandra's story. Her voice came to me the most clearly and forcefully; she would have it no other way. I could have made this Leila's story, and at one point I even considered going back and forth between Cassandra's and Leila's points of view. But when I tried to do that, I became blocked. Sometimes as an artist, you feel drawn to certain choices. You don't know why. You only know that when you resist it, the creative process stops or the final work fails. *Explicit Content* was meant to be Cassandra's story, and Cassandra happened to be a young African-American woman. This is how she came to me.

Although this book is for all hip-hop heads, I wanted the story to speak specifically to African-American and Latina young women who love hip-hop even though they are often disrespected by it. For them to know "This story is especially for you," they had to be represented in the story. The story had to be about them. And being a Latina in hip-hop myself, it would have been both inauthentic and unsatisfying to make both characters African-American.

But most importantly, I wanted to bare witness to the deep, sisterly bonds that can and do exist between African-American and Latina women, especially when they're young women who grow up together and have much in common. Besides the multifaceted aspects of hip-hop, *Explicit Content* is very much about sisterhood, specifically the kind that emerges when women choose to develop emotional bonds with women to whom they are *not* related. Many women and girls including myself are like Cassandra in that we have known the blessings that come when you thumb your nose at people who say, "Why are you friends with *her*?" Such friendships can be acts of resistance in a society that thrives on division, and friendships between women that cross certain boundaries are particularly threatening. Cassandra and Leila navigate multiple obstacles to their friendship, from the disapproval of authority figures to the insecurity of men who want them to compete for their validation. Those are major obstacles, but I hope *Explicit Content* shows both what women gain if they overcome them and what is lost when we capitulate to external pressures and remain divided.

And right now as popular as hip-hop is in audiovisual media—as a thriving subculture, a form of expression, and even a vehicle for personal and social change—it remains almost invisible in literature. I wrote *Explicit Content* both to up the quotient of hip-hop proper in fiction, and to give voice to women in hip-hop. I think there eventually will be a vast array of works we can call hip-hop fiction, and I did not want that movement to be a decade old before we see female protagonists! I wanted women in hip-hop fiction represented from the start of this literary movement.

Q. How would you define "hip-hop fiction"?

A. Hip-hop fiction is truly about hip-hop, and defining it has only become tricky because we have forgotten what hip-hop is and is not. Take film. What makes a movie a hip-hop movie? A rapper in the lead role? A soundtrack with rap music? No, a hip-hop movie is a movie where hip-hop subculture is integral to the story which also means that it may or may not be a movie about the music industry. By that definition, there have been very few hip-hop movies.

There have been almost no works of hip-hop fiction. *Explicit Content* is hip-hop fiction not because it is set in the music industry. I could have written a story about two hip-hop artists who never leave their neighborhood or never interact with the music industry and it can still be a work of hip-hop fiction. It's hip-hop fiction because it is about hip-hop as a subculture, as something that gives people voice and their lives meaning. What *Explicit Content* shows is that meaning can be positive or negative and that voice can say something progressive or negative. Hip-hop is a form of cultural power and whether that power is a force for progress or destruction depends on how people use it, whether you use it on the street or in the studio, for fun or for profit, to build or destroy.

Q. So what is not hip-hop fiction?

A. I think most of what is being called hip-hop fiction today is not about hip-hop at all, and the implications unsettle me.

Often the term hip-hop is used as code for "Black and urban." Not all things that are Black and urban are hip-hop, and vice versa. Many novels that are referred to as hip-hop fiction have nothing to do with hip-hop, they're just stories with Black characters in urban settings.

I think novels about street life should be referred to as street life fiction, period, and that the term "hip-hop fiction" should be reserved for novels that are about hip-hop. Eventually, there'll be some works that can be referred to as both, but something that has nothing to do with hip-hop subculture should not be referred to as hip-hop fiction, especially if it perpetuates the myth that hip-hop is all about violence, drugs, misogyny, etc. These phenomena are not the sum total of hip-hop, and hip-hop is not the only subculture in which those elements exist so it is wrong to treat them as if they are one and the same.

Q. There is great debate over the continued use of the n-word especially by hip-hop artists. You use the word in the story and yet you have Cassandra undergo an experience that makes her pledge to never use the word again. So where do you stand on the issue?

A. In all honesty, I remain very conflicted about the use of this word, and I think *Explicit Content* overtly reflects my ambivalence. My activist side says, "When you know the vile history of this word, there's no excuse to perpetuate its use." I personally do not use it no matter how it's spelled, and I have a hard time buying that any people has the "right" to use it. But the world I am creating in my story is peopled with characters who do. Such people exist and their reasons for doing so run the gamut. So my artistic side says, "As ugly as it is, people do use it whether because of ignorance, apathy, or a desire to reappropriate the term. Just like the hip-hop slang, the Ebonics, and the Spanglish, this is a linguistic element that will make the world ring true to the reader." I strived to not overdo it and asked several friends—amazing artists and socially conscious people in their own right—to read it and honestly tell me if I did. None thought I went too far, and I hope the majority of readers will agree.

If *Explicit Content* can open dialogue or even deepen ongoing conversations about this or any other social issue it touches upon, I'm all for it. Even if those discussions are sparked by my shortcomings or contradictions as a writer or person, so be it. I never court controversy for its own sake, and the appearance of the n-word in *Explicit Content* is the least of the issues and themes it raises, I think. I hope people will focus on other aspects of the story, but if I moved them one way or the other even if not on the issues I would have chosen, I have succeeded as a storyteller.

Q. Are you working on another novel?

A. My next novel is called *Picture Me Rollin'* and focuses on a young Tupac fanatic who returns home from a stint in prison and struggles to rebuild her life in a positive direction. We see this story often in film, and my goal is to explore it in depth as a novel and take the prison genre formula into a fresh direction. However, I don't want to stop just at making the protagonist a young Latina; in films it is often an African-American man. The story deals with the themes of self-love, contradictions, and the power of ideas. The heroine, Esperanza—which means "hope" in Spanish—struggles to love herself so she can transcend her contradictions. She sees so much of herself in 'Pac that she needs to cling to the possibility that she can escape the same fate that he did. This is why she's fascinated with Tupac and indulges in fantasies that he's still alive. Esperanza discovers people and ideas which inspire her, but the question remains whether she can internalize their promising messages, if she is not too dependent on the affirmations of the wrong people to turn her life around before she finds herself imprisoned again or even dead. Writing *Picture Me Rollin'* has been both challenging and exciting, and I can't wait to get it into the hands of readers.

QUESTIONS FOR DISCUSSION

1. Cassandra and Leila are both young women who grew up without fathers. How do you think the absence of a male parental figure in their lives influenced the way Cassandra and Leila relate to men?

2. Although set in the present day, *Explicit Content* refers often to hip-hop history. What role does this history play in the story? How does knowledge of this history enable characters to achieve their goals?

3. Cassandra expresses strong convictions that sometimes she compromises. What causes her to compromise her values? What other characters stray from their expressed convictions and under what circumstances do they? Do you think it means that they actually never held the values they claim? Why or why not?

4. Cassandra and Leila are very different, but what are the similarities they share and how do they sustain their friendship throughout the story? Were their differences also valuable in keeping their friendship alive?

5. In what ways do the characters experience fates similar to the role models in hip-hop that each has chosen?

6. Cassandra's fear leads her to a variety of places. By what criteria does she determine when her fear is something she should heed or when it signals something she should explore? How do you decide whether it is better to obey or ignore your fear?

7. Both Cassandra and Leila feel comfortable around each other's racial/ethnic/cultural communities. Besides their friendship, what other things contribute to that comfort? What makes you comfortable around people who may differ from you ethnically or culturally?

8. How is power defined in *Explicit Content*? Who has power in the story? How is power gained or lost?

9. The novel explores hip-hop as both a subculture and an industry. What are the differences between the two?

10. Yolanda endears herself to Cassandra because she refers to hip-hop as *la hip-hop*. In this story, is hip-hop female or male? Does hip-hop's gender change throughout the story? Do you think it matters?

11. The theme of family appears regularly throughout the novel. What are each of the character's expectations of what family offers and how have those expectations been fulfilled or disappointed? How does the fulfillment or frustrations of these expectations shape the choices they make?

12. Before she signs with Explicit Content, Cassandra is wary of the record industry and wants to produce her music independently. When she chooses to sign with the label, she does her best to protect herself from corporate maneuverings only to find that the label is involved in enterprises she never considered. How common or rare do you think the line between legal and illegal enterprise is crossed in our society? Is this, as Cassandra once suggests, the American way?

13. Take the author's seat. How do you think *Explicit Content* might have unfolded if Cassandra had chosen to keep her job at Tower and independently produced her own album as a solo artist instead of signing with Explicit Content?

14. Project into the future. Do you think Cassandra will stay with Megalos until she is able to start an independent label in the future? Why or why not? Given all she has gone through in the story, what kind of future do you see for Leila once she leaves prison?

15. What message do you take away from *Explicit Content*? Do you agree or disagree with this message? Why or why not?